Duskbound

ESPRITHEAN TRILOGY BOOK TWO

Bree Grenwich & Parker Lennox

ONYX PUBLISHING

Copyright © 2025 by Bree Grenwich & Parker Lennox
All rights reserved.

No part of this book may be reproduced in any form or by any electronic or mechanical means, including information storage and retrieval systems, without written permission from the author, except for the use of brief quotations in a book review.

This is a work of fiction. Names, characters, businesses, places, events, locales, and incidents are either the products of the author's imagination or used in a fictitious manner. Any resemblance to actual persons, living or dead, or actual events is purely coincidental.

Edited by **Kristin McTiernan**
Synopsis by **Kristin McTiernan**
Cover art and Map by **Parker Lennox**
Character Art by **Karina Giada**

CONTENT WARNING

Duskbound is a dark fantasy set in a world of shadow magic and political intrigue, where two realms wage a desperate war for survival. It includes elements depicting war, graphic violence, torture, blood rituals, self-harm (blood oaths & magic), hand-to-hand combat, severe injuries, death of loved ones, genocide, starvation, mind control, psychological manipulation, trauma, imprisonment, child soldiers, alcohol consumption, drug use, nationalism, xenophobia, emotional abuse, graphic language, and sexual activities that are shown on the page. Readers who may be sensitive to these elements, please be aware.

PREVIOUSLY IN RIFTBORNE

In a world where magical essence flows from the realm itself, manifesting in individuals as unique magical abilities called *focuses*, Fia Riftborne has learned to live in shadows. Born to a persecuted people marked by brands on their left hands—descendants of rebels of Riftdremar who fought against the Sídhe kingdom during the uprising twenty years ago—she found solace only in her work at Ma's Apothecary and her friendship with fellow orphan Osta. Raised in the House of Unity orphanage, Fia has spent her life being taught that Riftbornes are inferior, dangerous, and deserving of their oppression. To make matters worse, she also experiences haunting dreamscapes that seem to come out of nowhere when she sleeps.

But Fia harbors a dangerous secret: a rare and terrifying focus that allows her to manipulate minds. When this power erupts in a near-fatal encounter with noble sisters Bekha and Jordaan Fairbanks, she draws the attention of General Laryk Ashford. He is a military prodigy whose own mysterious focus allows him to read and predict anyone's actions—except Fia's. Intrigued by her powers, he offers a stark choice: join his elite faction of the Base Guard called Venom or face execution for her crime.

Despite her hatred for the same Guard that destroyed her homeland, Fia accepts, desperate to master her lethal abilities. Laryk orchestrates a shocking confrontation by bringing in a guard who killed her friends. This triggers Fia's powers, helping her discover that her focus originates in her spine, manifesting as a translucent web of energy that she must learn to harness. She spares the man's life; Laryk does not.

As Fia navigates complex relationships within the Guard and forms bonds with team V, she faces hostility from Lieutenant Narissa, whose romantic feelings for Laryk fuel her prejudice against Riftbornes. A grave threat emerges when shadow creatures called Wraiths begin attacking the western borders of Sídhe. These shadow creatures that emerge from tears between worlds can suffocate their victims by stealing the air from their lungs, seemingly driven to obtain Sídhe's stores of arcanite, a powerful magical crystal.

Her world grows more complex through strained relationships with Ma, whose twin brother was changed by the Guard, and conversations about orphaned pasts with childhood friends Eron and Jacquelina. During an unauthorized gathering, a confrontation with Baelor Soleil reveals that Fia can not only attack minds but control them—an ability that draws both awe and suspicion, forcing General Ashford to help cover up the incident. While Osta takes a job at the Soleil estate and they no longer live together, the girls maintain their close friendship, with Osta continuing to support Fia's Guard duties and Fia remaining protective of Osta.

PREVIOUSLY IN RIFTBORNE

After surviving a harrowing simulation of a Wraith attack, Fia and her fellow recruits complete their training and take their final blood oaths. But when news arrives of a devastating Wraith attack in Stormshire that claimed sixty lives, Fia makes the risky decision to break her blood oath to warn Ma—who reveals she created "breathing tonics" to help combat the Wraiths' suffocating attacks.

Accompanying Laryk to the Western fortress city of Emeraal, their journey reveals growing tension and attraction, culminating in an intimate encounter after a heated confrontation at a party. Fia's powers continue to evolve as she discovers she can enter others' dreams, accidentally witnessing an intimate dream of Laryk's, and experiencing prophetic visions of an impending Wraith attack that are initially dismissed.

During a formal ball at Emeraal, as Wraiths launch their prophesied attack, Fia manifests unprecedented powers over darkness and shadow—abilities previously associated only with the enemy. Captured by the Wraiths, who identify themselves as Umbra, Fia is taken to Ravenfell in the realm of Umbrathia, traveling on winged horse-like creatures through the sky. There, a golden-eyed warrior named Aether reveals a shocking truth: everything she knows about her history is a lie. The Wraiths are not mindless monsters but warriors fighting against the Sídhe kingdom's exploitation of their world. But that's not all, she recognizes those golden eyes from the nightmares she's suffered over the last year.

Imprisoned in Ravenfell, Fia attempts to use her mind-manipulation abilities against Aether but finds her powers ineffective. She experiences an inexplicable, energetic connection that suggests a deeper bond between them. As shadows appear within her irises, Fia must confront the possibility that she is an Umbra—a shadow wielder—and question everything she believed about herself, her world, and the war she never truly understood.

Listen along to our Duskbound
inspired Spotify playlist.

Most are for the lyrics, some are for the vibes, and others might
just predict the future.

...athia

...pped

...e drought

The Void

FORT OCHRE

THE BURN

Eastern Rip

Vardruun

FORT XENTHE

Simbolt Pass

VILLIAGE OF YANDRE

Leidvra Region

PRONUNCIATION GUIDE

AETHER (AY-ther)
AINTHE (Ah-N-yuh)
ARCANITE (AR-kan-ite)
AOSSÍ (EE-shee)

CONLETH (Kohn-luth)
CROYG (KROY-g)

DAMPHYRE (DAM-feer)
DRAUG (DROG)
DRAXON (DRAX-on)
DUSKBOUND (DUSK-bound)

EASKATH (EE-as-kath)
EFFIE (EF-ee)
EIBHLIN (Eve-lin)
ESPRITHE (Esp-rith)

FIA RIFTBORNE (FEE-ah RIFT-born)

PRONUNCIATION GUIDE

FIRINNE (Fehr-EN-yeh)

GENERAL KARIS (KAIR-is)
GENERAL TALON (TAL-on)
GENERAL TALIORA (tal-ee-OR-ah)
GENERAL URKIN (UR-kin)

HOUSE ALFARSON (AL-far-son)
HOUSE BALDURSON (BAHL-dur-son)
HOUSE BREIDFJORD (BRAID-fyord)
HOUSE EIRFALK (AIR-falk)
HOUSE ELDGARDR (ELD-gard-r)
HOUSE GALDRYNNE (GAHL-drin)
HOUSE SKALDVINDR (SKALD-vin-dr)
HOUSE SVEINSON (SVAIN-son)
HOUSE VALLGRYM (VAHL-grim)

ILSTHYRE (ILS-thire)

KALFAR (KAHL-far)
KRAYKEN VINDSKALD (KRAY-ken VIND-skald)

LAEL (LAY-el)
LARYK ASHFORD (LAHR-ick ASH-ford)
LORD SOLIEL (so-LAY)

MALADEA THISTON (mal-AY-de-ah THIS-ton)
MIRA (MEER-ah)

NIAMH (Neev)
NIHR (NEER)

OSTA RIFTBORNE (OS-tah RIFT-born)

PRONUNCIATION GUIDE

RASKR (RAS-ker)
RAVEN (RAY-ven)
RAVENFELL (RAY-ven-fell)
RETHLYN (RETH-lin)
RIFTBORNE (RIFT-born)
RIFTDREMAR (RIFT-dreh-mar)

SIBYL (Sib-uhl)
SÍDHE (SHEE)
STRAVENE (stra-VEEN)
STRYKKA, THE (STRIE-kah)
SYRNDORE (SER-en-dor)

THERON (THAIR-on)
TRYGGAR (TRIE-gahr)

UMBRATHIA (um-BRAY-thee-ah)

VALKAN (vahl-KAHN)
VALTÝR (VAHL-teer)
VARDRUUN (var-DROON)
VEXA (VEX-ah)
VORDR (VOR-dr)

For those who learned that darkness doesn't devour.

It forges.

PROLOGUE

I had always felt safest in the shadows.

Before the Guard, I clung to them, hiding within their veiled embrace. It hadn't occurred to me much at the time, but the price of such a life is a stifled sort of existence, like a flower delicately pressed between the pages of a book. Preserved but stagnant. Reduced to the whims of those brave enough to steal a peek inside.

You never really know what you're missing until it becomes clear, either by chance or fate. In my case, it was by force.

Laryk had all but yanked me from the depths, throwing my flattened petals into water, but not the still pond that simply revived. No, he flung me into a tumbling maelstrom, the type of current meant to transform. The type that stripped away the layers of old, eroding familiar contours and shaping something anew.

Something that could exist in the light.

Yet, to my surprise, it wasn't the annihilation I'd always feared.

It was a revelation.

Being seen, truly seen, wasn't death. It was a spark of life I had never known. A love I had never wanted. It filled me with a power that, from the darkness, had always seemed so much like a curse. Beneath the waves, I'd learned to face it.

So as change typically goes, I abandoned what I once clung to. Darkness became a relic, and I turned my back on shadows in favor of the light.

Never once did I think they'd return to claim me.

CHAPTER ONE

Someone was knocking.

I didn't budge from my place at the window, head resting on the cool iron bars that kept me trapped amongst the clouds. An eerie nothingness sank into my gut, mirroring the fog that encapsulated the tower I now found myself in.

Tiny curving streets were a blur from this height, obscured even more by the mist that hung heavy in the air. A mist that never seemed to dissipate. Only muted rays of an eclipsed sun broke through, casting a dim light into the room—my prison of obsidian-carved walls.

My eyes blurred, adjusting their focus until my reflection stared back at me from the glass. Black ink curled in the corners of my eyes, reaching out towards the onyx of my pupils but never quite connecting. Avoiding the mirror had become my top priority. I couldn't face it. I couldn't face myself. I only dared an occasional peak in the semi-reflective glass of the window. But even then, I couldn't take in the sight for very long.

Shadow wielder.

The words never left my mind. Not for a single moment since the golden-eyed soldier had spewed them in my direction. That was days ago.

Four, five maybe?

I'd lost count.

The time of day hadn't seemed to change from the moment I'd arrived.

"I have your meal." The exasperated voice of a woman sounded from the hallway, muffled by the heavy door.

"I hope you're decent! I'm coming in!" she said before the grating of a rusted lock echoed through the room. "Aether's busy—of course, he is—so I thought, why not me?" The door creaked open.

I tensed, grabbing my dagger from the windowsill, quickly sheathing it against my thigh before turning towards my new visitor. Recognition bloomed as I noticed the lithe frame of the woman from the ball at Emeraal. Her soft voice did not match the previous image I had of her with the mysterious aura and crow attached to her shoulder. The perfect complexion from the evening had been wiped away and swapped for a color palette that accentuated the shadows around her eyes rather than mask them, and her dark hair was now pinned back with multiple bobbles that clinked together with each step. She wore a similar uniform to the one Aether had worn, but different whimsical patterns were pressed into the leather.

Her eyes lit up when she spotted me, as if she had just stumbled upon an old friend. "Oh, you're awake! That's good. I brought you some food!" She lifted the tray slightly, as if it were a trophy, and deposited it on the bed with a flourish. "It's just rice. Not very exciting, I know."

I said nothing, watching her closely, assessing her demeanor.

She didn't seem particularly threatening, but her casual approach grated on my nerves. My gut churned as I calculated my options.

She, oblivious to my silence, clasped her hands together. "You must be so confused! I mean, I'd be confused too—waking up in a strange place, unfamiliar people—but I promise, we're not here to hurt you." She smiled brightly. "I'm Effie, by the way. And you... well, what's your name?"

I schooled my expression into neutrality. "What am I doing here?" I asked, my voice tight.

Effie tilted her head, clearly debating her response. "How are you feeling?" she asked instead, her tone oddly earnest. Her gaze roved over me with fascination, as if I were some rare artifact she'd just acquired.

I clenched my jaw. "If you're not the enemy, then why am I being held hostage?"

"Oh, you're not a hostage!" she said quickly, though her cheerful tone faltered. "I mean, technically, you're locked in here, but it's not, like, forever. It's just that... well, Aether thought it might be best until we sort everything out..." Her voice dropped conspiratorially. "He's rather infuriating most of the time. Lucky he's so dreadfully gorgeous, because the dark and brooding bit gets exhausting after a while." She gave a light laugh, as if we were sharing some inside joke.

I crossed my arms, unimpressed. "I see."

Effie tapped a finger to her lips, apparently deciding to pivot. "My apologies about the rice. It's one of the only things that keeps these days..." She nodded sagely before trailing off.

Frustration prickled at me. "Tell me what a shadow wielder is," I demanded.

Effie shifted uncomfortably, glancing over her shoulder at the door.

"One that can harness nothingness and command it," she

responded, arching a perfectly preened brow as if it were the most obvious thing in the world.

"And you think I can do that?"

"We watched you do that." She didn't hide the exasperation in her tone.

A spark of anger tinged the back of my skull. "So your plan is to force me into your unit. To use me against the people I care about." Disgust laced my words.

Her expression shifted into something like horror. "Force you? Goodness, no! That would be—" She hesitated, her nose wrinkling. "Well, I suppose it would be efficient, but no, we couldn't." She gave a weak laugh, but her gaze darted nervously to the door again.

"Oh, but couldn't you?" The earlier experiment with my focus had been sharply shut down by the captor known as Aether. If my gifts were somehow linked to these people, then they could harness the ability to control my mind just as I had others. "Why not just push into my mind and demand it of me?"

Effie scrunched up her face in confusion. "I'm not sure what you mean."

My heart skipped a beat—a small kernel of hope forming, blurring my vision as I looked inward, seeking out the pulse of minds in the surrounding area. I could see Effie clearly in front of me, and others smaller, seemingly on the floor beneath us. They looked no different than the minds of the Aossí. It was only his mind that glowed in an unfamiliar golden hue. And as Effie so kindly mentioned in her arrival… he was currently occupied.

"So mind-control is not an ability of shadow-wielding?" I asked, trying to keep my voice level, layered with a bit of disinterest for good measure.

"Not that I'm aware." Her blue eyes narrowed. "But I'm no true shadow wielder. I'm simply a vessel." Her breath slowed as her eyes moved to inspect the door. A sigh of relief slipped out once she realized we were still alone.

I stopped the smile that threatened my lips.

"Perhaps I'm speaking too candidly. I have a tendency to do so, at least that's what Vexa always tells me, read the room." Her eyes relaxed again before rolling in a playful manner.

I kept my face calm, even as my focus roared to life. "Effie, I'm going to need your help." This time it didn't hesitate, just as eager to find a target that might be susceptible. The iridescent strands fluttered around her, caressing her mind before taking their hold. I almost sighed in relief when I wasn't met with resistance. My focus thrummed, sending tingles across my back.

"You will escort me out of here, taking the safest route back to the Isle."

Effie's confusion faded, muscles relaxing until she looked almost peaceful. Eyes staring at me unseeing, ready for my command.

This has to work.

Without a word, she turned towards the door and started walking. I kept my concentration on the link to Effie's mind as I followed, the thundering of my heartbeat my only distraction.

I thanked the Esprithe as the door swung open, revealing a hallway mercifully empty. The minds just beyond us beckoned—so close, so tempting—but I couldn't risk it. My teeth ground together as I fought the urge. I'd have to make my way through the building blindly. I'd ruin my chance of escape if I lost connection to my only guide. Even worse if she screamed for help.

I took in my surroundings as we crept down the hallway. The walls were made of a cold uneven stone and heavy wooden doors with locks lined the circular room. A stairwell arched across the wall showing there were floors even higher up. The smell of a burning hearth was somewhere near and I could only hope others would be preoccupied enough to not notice a guard and a prisoner of war casually walking by.

"Move faster," I commanded through the bond, nerves taking over.

Effie upped her pace, keeping to the outer edges of the stairwell as we began to make the descent in a dizzying loop. With each floor we passed my urgency grew, trying to move quickly enough to remain unseen.

I almost stumbled into her when the floor eventually evened out. It was an empty circular space that left us completely exposed with two open arched doorways on either side housing great halls that were empty, and a wooden door stationed directly in the middle. I couldn't hear over my thundering pulse and hyper focused on the middle door, knowing it was our way out.

A few more moments, and I'd be free of this Esprithe-forsaken tower. I refused to let myself think about what awaited beyond the walls—one step at a time.

Move, move, move.

Effie lifted her hand to push open the door. Just as her fingers wrapped around the handle, footsteps thundered from behind me. The air shifted, sharp and fast, before a force slammed into my back. My breath whooshed out, and I lurched forward, only to have the ground disappear beneath me.

It felt as if my gut had collided with a solid iron bar. I keeled over, gasping, and before I could get my bearings, I was yanked up over someone's shoulder. The connection to Effie snapped and frayed into nothing.

"Oh, no you don't." The husky voice vibrated through me. The man didn't even seem winded as he tossed me onto his shoulder like I was no more than a sack of grain.

Fuck.

"I admire your ambition," he said, his tone annoyingly calm, "isolation it is."

I slammed my fists into his back, thrashing like a wild thing. His body was a wall of stone, unyielding and utterly unmoved by my struggles.

"Let. Me. Go," I screamed, my voice muffled by his leather-clad back.

"No can do, Princess."

I felt the tilt of his jaw against my hip and nearly snapped. "And stop fucking calling me that."

His grip on my legs tightened. "Stop acting like one."

His words hit me like a whip, and I could feel the heat of anger crawling across my skin. That was it.

I slammed my hand against my thigh, tearing my hidden dagger from its sheath. The golden dusted emerald gave me away, reflecting the single flicker of light coming from a torch on the wall. Aether went rigid as I brought my hand down towards his leg at a maddening speed.

But it stopped. My hand froze just as a bead of crimson formed on the surface of his leathers. I tried and tried to plunge it deeper into his flesh, but an invisible force kept my fist in place, trembling.

"Pathetic," he said in a low tone, just as my fingers uncurled against my will, the dagger falling to the floor with a clang.

Without thinking, I snapped, sinking my teeth into his side.

He shifted, his body only mildly twitching at the attack, and let out a low hiss.

"Not helping your case."

My teeth ground together. "I swear I'm going to—"

"Bite me again?" His voice had a soft, satisfied edge. "You might just be the weakest Duskbound in the history of this realm."

I hissed in frustration, trying to kick him, but he was rock solid, barely even acknowledging my efforts.

A gasp echoed from the doorway just as Aether turned to begin the trek up to the holding cell and my eyes locked onto a very confused Effie, realization slowly dawning and flushing her cheeks.

"What–how did I get down here? What's going on?" She stumbled over her words, following after us.

"Effie, next time, do as you're told and wait." Was his only reply.

I felt ridiculous being jostled with each step as Effie's expression shifted to anger directed solely at me.

"You bitch!" she shrieked, her eyes pulsing. "I was so nice to you!"

And suddenly, her form disappeared, only to materialize a mere breath from my face.

"I brought you rice—" she began just as Aether cut her off.

"Don't waste it, Effie," he growled as he continued his climb, putting distance between me and the woman. She let out a hiss of exasperation and crossed her arms before spinning around.

I let my head slump as my eyes met the stone floor.

I did not feel apologetic in the slightest.

We ascended and my body went limp as heaviness settled into my bones.

Failure struck me.

When we reached the chamber, he didn't set me down immediately. Instead, his grip tightened, fingers digging into my flesh as he carried me to the window.

"Look," he commanded, his voice deadly quiet. "Look at what you're trying to escape to."

Beyond the glass, the mist had dispersed, and my eyes fell upon a gray landscape that stretched endlessly, broken only by twisted trees and crumbling ruins. The eternal twilight cast everything in shades of ash and shadow.

"This is what your people did," he growled, his breath hot against my ear. "This is what Sídhe stole from us."

He finally set me down, but before I could move, he had me

pinned against the wall. His golden eyes burned with an intensity that made my heart race—not with desire, but with fear.

"So tell me, Princess," the title dripped with venom, "did they teach you how to steal essence too? Or just how to control minds?"

"I don't know what you're talking about," I spat, but my voice trembled.

His laugh was cruel as he leaned closer, close enough that I could see flecks of amber in his irises. "No? Then why don't you explain how you absorbed our shadows that night? How you wielded them like you were born to it?"

"I didn't—"

"Don't lie to me." His fingers gripped my jaw, forcing me to meet his gaze. "I watched you. I saw what you are."

"And what exactly am I?" The words came out as a whisper.

Something dark flickered across his features. "That's what I intend to find out." He released me, and my back slid against the wall.

"The night we took you, you were dressed in that ridiculous gown." He began circling me. "But you fought like a soldier. So either you're someone of importance, or you're a part of the Guard."

"I was serving drinks," I spat.

His laugh was cold. "In that dress? With that dagger?" He pulled my blade from his belt—the one with golden-dusted emeralds, the colors of Sídhe. "Try again."

When I remained silent, he pressed closer. "Who are you to them?" His eyes narrowed. "Where are you from?"

"You know exactly where I'm from," I hissed, climbing to my feet.

"That's not an answer." His hand shot towards me, fingers curling around my neck. "We were going to do this the nice way, but since you clearly intend on making things more difficult than they need be, we'll do it my way." His face was dangerously close, and I could feel the heat radiating off of him. "How did you get to wind up in Sídhe? Did they take you, or did you enter their realm on your own accord?"

"I'm. From. *Sídhe*," I said through gritted teeth.

He studied me, narrowed eyes raking over my face as if unable to process my words. "And what is your station?" he asked. "In the Guard?"

"I told you—"

"The truth," he growled. "Or I'll have to assume you're an immediate threat to this realm. And I deal with threats accordingly."

The menace in his voice sent ice through my veins. But beneath the fear, anger sparked.

"You want the truth?" I snarled. "I don't know why I can wield shadows. I don't know why your darkness called to me that night. But I do know that threatening me won't get you the answers you want."

Something shifted in his expression—surprise, maybe, at my defiance. Or perhaps at the honesty he heard in my voice. His grip on my throat loosened.

"How are they doing it?" His voice was low. "How are they filling the towers?"

"Your questions make no sense to me," I seethed, "I have no answers for you."

He stepped back, something calculating replacing the rage in his expression. His golden eyes studied me with a new kind of coldness—not the burning fury from before, but something more methodical.

"I'll give you one last chance," he said, his voice dropping to a rumble. "Tell me the truth about who you are—how they're draining us, and I'll ensure you're treated with dignity."

I met his gaze, letting him see the defiance there. "I've spent my entire life being treated without dignity. What makes you think your threats mean anything to me?"

"Very well," he said, drawing closer, voice smooth but sharp as a blade. "Isolation it is." His eyes fixed on me one last beat before he dropped his arm and turned away, boots echoing through the chamber walls.

The door slammed behind him with finality, the lock sliding into place with a sound like fate sealing shut. A cry escaped my lips as I sank to my knees, the weight of failure crushing me.

My heart, rattling with hope only moments ago, stilled into a quiet rhythm. Silence spread through the space, encroaching on me like an invisible weight. I sank to my knees as the tears began, letting my face slide against the cold stone floor.

I stayed like that for days as the realizations tumbled in—how I would never get a chance to tell Raine goodbye, that I would never have a chance to tell her how much she really meant to me, as my friend. Osta's final expression haunted me, along with Laryk's hesitation, and Ma's heartbreak when she learned her worst fear had materialized… It all paralyzed me with a type of panic I'd never truly known until that moment.

Not until I realized I'd never see any of them again.

CHAPTER TWO

SIX WEEKS LATER

There had been no more attempts to visit me, no more interactions. Only the occasional slip of food under the door, the sound of keys turning in locks, and the oppressive quiet that settled in and never left. Six weeks of being locked in this cramped room with nothing but stale air, occasional meals that tasted like sand, and the constant faded light trickling in from the window.

It had become clear that I'd never have another chance at escape while Aether was around. And he was. Always and insufferably. Around. That golden mind pulsed through the air like an invisible weight, and I couldn't escape it—couldn't escape the man who loomed like my own personal sentinel, onyx hair catching the light, falling into that unnervingly perfect face—sharp angles and full lips that rested in a brutal kind of neutrality. Looking at him felt like stepping too close to the sun.

There was only time—too much time to think about things that were so painful they threatened to tear me into pieces. People and places that were so far out of reach, I had begun to question whether they had ever been real in the first place: Laryk's piercing emerald eyes, Ma's hibiscus-stained hands, Osta's innate optimism that I had always taken for granted.

I'd had dreams—in the beginning. Flickers of things, scenes set in the place I used to call home. Flashes of faces, sudden glimmers of the people I'd left behind. People who probably thought I was dead. It was hard to know, hard to discern whether those were anything more than my own consciousness tormenting me with past glances, sights I had once witnessed myself, or if they were more than that—tangible things happening in real time, glances in mirrors, maybe even memories from strangers. My focus pulled them to me with desperation, injecting them into my mind. I'd given up trying to figure them out. It hurt too much. And as my hope for escape, for rescue, dwindled, so did the dreams. My mind had gone as gray as the landscape surrounding this tower.

Three roaring knocks shot through the room then, icing my veins in an instant. I hadn't seen another soul in so long. When the Umbra brought food or new clothing to my room, it was always pushed under the door, or set inside while I was sleeping.

No one ever knocked.

I pushed myself closer to the wall, leaving the light of the window and pressing my back against the cool stone surface, heart slamming through my chest, forcing a gasp into my lungs. I couldn't remember the last time I'd been aware of its beating at all.

A woman stepped through first, her stride measured but unhurried. Aether followed, lingering at the threshold, his golden eyes flicking toward me for only a moment before he turned his attention to the hallway beyond.

The woman stopped, scanning the room briefly before her gaze landed on me. She tilted her head, a lock of jet-black hair shifting against her jawline. Leather armor hugged her frame, her silhouette studded with steel. A dozen daggers glinted against her torso, the blades reflecting the dim light. The handles were carved with unfamiliar symbols. Some looked worn, others ornate, and one appeared to be made of bone, its pale sheen sending a chill down my spine.

"I'm Vexa," she said simply, her tone light but steady. She stepped farther into the room, her boots barely making a sound against the floor. "And you are?"

I opened my mouth and then closed it, so shocked by the sudden intrusion that I didn't know how to respond. Unsure of whether I should even respond at all. Guilt tugged at my spine at the thought.

"Does she speak?" Vexa asked, throwing a glance over her shoulder at Aether. He didn't turn.

"Look, I know you probably don't particularly love being locked in this tower, but I think you're smart enough to understand we won't be making any changes to this situation—" She motioned around the room with wide eyes. "Without some kind of conversation. You don't have to talk about anything you don't want to, but for the love of—"

"Give her more time." Aether sighed with frustration, cutting Vexa off. "She'll crack, eventually."

"Aether. No one asked for your input," she hissed back, sarcasm drenching her words as her attention returned to me. "What can we call you?"

For some unfathomable reason, I gave in. I gave in to the small sliver of distraction she was offering. I gave in to the desperation gnawing at my tongue.

"Fia," I said, the word tasting unfamiliar.

Her violet eyes, swirling with dark tendrils not unlike my own, sparked with surprise.

I couldn't quite put my finger on why, exactly, I wasn't rushing at her, begging for answers of my own. Perhaps it was because I wouldn't believe her either way. Or perhaps it was because I had once again made peace with an old friend: avoidance. I didn't let myself think too hard about it. I didn't let myself think too hard about anything now.

"Fia. What an odd name," she murmured, turning onto her side, a victorious smirk etched into her lips. "You hear that, Aether? I win. Now we do this my way." She let out an amused chuckle as a vein in Aether's arm pulsed, his muscular frame still taking up the entirety of the doorway.

"He's a sore loser." She shrugged. "I guess he was just going to leave you up in this tower until you fell apart. Which was *clearly* going well."

My eyes shot to Aether as a spark of anger licked through me, nearly making me stumble from my place at the window. The last six weeks had been a monotonous string of numbness, where nearly all of my emotions had dwindled into nothingness. As I glared at him, I let that anger take its hold. It felt warm. I wanted to latch onto it and never let go.

Vexa followed my expression. "But perhaps you should wait outside. I don't believe she likes you very much," she said, eyes darting between us.

"Do you want him to leave?" she asked me, some kind of amused curiosity lacing her words.

I simply nodded.

"Alright Aether, wait outside. Your presence isn't exactly helping the situation."

"You remember what happened with Effie?" Aether said calmly, but the bitterness in his tone was not hidden very well.

"Well that insinuation is insulting." Vexa breathed. "If she decides to hijack my mind, I'm sure you'll catch her again," she stated, clearly losing patience with the back and forth. "Now go."

He hesitated before turning. "As you wish." And I heard the

metal door screech closed, the rusty lock sliding right back into place.

"Esprithe he's suffocating." She rolled her eyes, sitting up on the bed. "Better?"

I simply stared at her.

"Don't go all quiet on me. I have something to offer you." She smirked, chin falling into her hand. "I'm sure you're dying to get out of this room."

I felt my heart flutter involuntarily at the thought. I had started to believe it might never happen. That they'd just keep me trapped up here with my thoughts and the everlasting twilight.

"I can leave?" I asked.

"Don't get ahead of yourself." She raised an eyebrow. "We'll still be on the property... but I could take you for a walk. If you're interested."

Another pang of the heart. Outside? My skin longed to feel the wind, to feel something other than the stale air of this tower.

"Yes." It was the only thing I could muster.

"I can arrange it. But first, I have to ask you a few questions. Do we have a deal?"

I opened my mouth, nearly answering without thinking about the weight of my response. Another jolt ran through me. These were probably questions I didn't want to answer. She must have noticed my internal battle because she was quick to interrupt it.

"Why don't we just talk, and then you can decide."

"I'm not going to tell you anything without an answer in return." The words tumbled out, tinged with a fire I hadn't felt in a long time.

"Now we're talking." She grinned, something mischievous pooling in her eyes. "I'll go first. You wield shadows. Quite well, I might add. But you have no void burns. How do you do it?" She tilted her head, as if appraising me.

I hesitated, consumed by the ache that came when I remembered the last time I was interrogated about my powers. Who the interrogator was.

"I found out about the shadows the same moment you did. I know nothing about it. I know nothing of these void burns."

Vexa's brow peaked. "I'm sure that was quite the revelation." She let out a laugh and shook her head. "A Duskbound living across the rip. I would have never imagined it possible."

"A Duskbound?" I asked, pulling my hands into my lap and sliding my right palm over my Riftborne branding. I wasn't sure why I wanted to hide it, but something about Aether's previous reaction to the mark had me cautious.

"Yes, a Duskbound. A true shadow wielder," she said simply.

"So all of you wield shadows?" I asked, eyes hesitantly fixated on the door.

"Not exactly."

I paused, waiting for her to continue, but she simply shrugged. I guessed that was a topic she didn't want to discuss yet. Perhaps she wasn't allowed to. What had Effie called herself?

"Are you a… vessel?"

Vexa's eyes shot to the back of her head as she leaned back and sighed in exasperation. "Effie. I adore the girl, but Esprithe she's going to be the death of me." She reached up, sliding her gloved hand over her inky hair. "I don't know what all she told you. But as you can imagine, there are certain topics… we don't quite feel comfortable discussing with you yet. I also don't want to overwhelm you."

"Overwhelm me? You've captured me and *locked* me in a tower!" I couldn't control the rage that now drenched my words. This was ridiculous. They were clearly not concerned about my comfort, no need to pretend otherwise.

"Look, I can't tell you what I can't tell you. It's as simple as that. I'm open to answering other questions you may have, but there will always be a line—a *too far*. At least for now. Until we know what your intentions are," she said coolly.

I leaned back against the wall, our eyes locked in a stalemate.

"How much do you know about what is happening between this realm and the one you came from?" she asked.

"I know you've killed friends of mine—killed hundreds of my fellow soldiers."

Vexa's eyes went sharp with recognition as we continued to stare at each other, and I immediately regretted the admission—confirming that I had been a part of the Guard at all. She didn't speak for a long while, and neither did I.

"How exactly are we supposed to react to the lifeforce being sucked from our lands? Ask nicely for them to stop? To stop killing us?" she seethed.

"How do you know that's even actually happening?" I shot back.

She glared at me, dumbfounded.

"What exactly do you think those towers of arcanite are for? You think they just grew up out of the ground like that? In those locations? Do any of you even know where it came from—"

"Vexa." The growl came from the hallway, just beyond the door. Both our eyes shot in the direction, sending a slice through the tension that had begun building in the room.

Both of us froze, the word hanging between us like a blade. My eyes snapped toward her again. Vexa's lips twitched, a flash of annoyance passing across her face as she turned away.

"That's enough questions for today, I think."

I watched, rooted in place, as she stood, stretched her arms above her head in a lazy motion, like she had nowhere urgent to be. But I felt the space between us contract, the distance of this room closing in on me all over again.

She's leaving.

Something in my chest clenched tight. I'd grown accustomed to the silence, to the stillness of the tower. But with Vexa about to walk out, it felt more like abandonment. Like she was taking the last shred of interaction with her.

I swallowed, the lump in my throat growing as I tried to push away the cold emptiness that suddenly seemed so much more suffocating.

Alone. Again.

Just as she reached the door, she turned around and rested against it, crossing her arms and studying me before slipping a dagger from the sheath across her chest.

I froze.

But her body remained still, relaxed as she balanced the blade across a single finger, testing the weight and eyeing the construction. After a few seconds, she leaned her head back and sighed.

"Rest up. I'll take you to the stables tomorrow."

CHAPTER THREE

"These should work," Vexa said as she handed me a stack of black fabric and dropped a pair of boots at my feet.

"Erm, thanks." I managed to get out before she turned and climbed up onto the bars at my window and took a seat.

"No mind games? You promise? Don't make me look like an idiot in front of Aether. I'll never live it down." She arched an eyebrow, her lips twisting into something like a smirk.

"No mind games," I repeated, slipping out of my sleeping garments.

Her expression deepened, not quite friendly, but not entirely mocking either. I couldn't tell if it was humor or a warning.

"The Vördr," she said as her boots thudded lightly on the floor. "They may seem domesticated, but they're wild at heart. They only let us pretend we're in control. Never forget that."

I turned to face the mirror behind the bed, avoiding the reflection of my eyes. My gaze slid over the leathers. They were thicker than the ones I'd worn in Sídhe, etched with intricate patterns and burn marks that seemed to writhe and twist around my body like liquid smoke.

"Well," Vexa remarked, eyeing me up and down. "Seems like everything fits. Although you could fill it out a bit more." She huffed, then narrowed her eyes at my food tray, still half full, stale polenta clinging dryly to the plate.

"I'm still... getting used to everything here." I looked down, my fingers curling uncomfortably into my pockets. The food was bland, like the ghost of something once edible. Even its color seemed muted.

"The food is different."

"I'm sure it's much better where you're from." She clicked her teeth but she stopped herself from saying anything more.

The silence that followed was thick, uncomfortable. Vexa's eyes lingered on me for a moment longer, some kind of pain brewing in their depths before she turned around, her gaze sweeping the room. I let out a slow breath, my chest tightening. I was about to leave this tower for the first time, the last thing I wanted to do was piss her off and make her change her mind.

"What did you call them–the beasts, I mean," I said, forcing a softer tone.

"Vördr." She hummed, inspecting invisible lint on her left forearm before dusting it away. "And don't get any ideas. I know it might seem tempting to fly off on one of them, but they wouldn't let you mount them even if you tried."

"I'm not going to do that," I assured her, keeping my gaze on the floor as she turned away from me.

"Ready?" she asked, no sign of ice left in her voice.

I followed slowly, the scent of soot wafting off her, lingering beneath the sharp tang of iron. As if she had just come from a forge.

"Alright, let us out."

The metal screeched as the lock lifted. Aether's form filled the doorway like a shadow. I hated how he could make even the smallest gesture feel like a weight pressing down on me. He didn't even look in my direction. Not a glance, just a heavy silence that seemed to stretch on. I watched as his structured jaw ticked, framed by the raven-colored hair that barely brushed his shoulders. The simple movement caused his metal piercings to refract the light, and I caught a glance of those shimmering golden eyes. The ones that had haunted my dreams for the last year.

"Thirty minutes," his hoarse voice managed. My insides tightened at the sound, curling into a ball of resentment. If it wasn't for him, I'd be back home now. If it wasn't for him, I'd never have been captured in the first place.

"Understood?" he asked, irritation lacing his tone.

Vexa rolled her eyes, leaning against the doorframe and pushing her hand against his chest to allow her out. "I heard you the first twenty times you said it." She sighed, "I'm sure you'll be trailing behind us like our own personal guardian either way." She brushed past him and motioned for me to follow.

I took one step toward the door and froze. Not by choice. My body simply stopped responding, like every muscle had turned to stone. Vexa disappeared from view around the curve of the stairs.

Aether stepped into my line of sight, and the amusement written across his face made my blood boil. His gaze raked over me dangerously, taking in my futile attempts to move. Panic flooded me as I remembered that moment in the tower weeks ago —how my fingers had uncurled from the dagger against my will, how my hand had frozen mid-strike.

Fuck.

His breath ghosted across my ear as he leaned in. "You can try to mess with my mind all you want," he whispered, voice deadly soft, "but if you try your luck with any of *them*, I will make you wish you were dead."

"Is this really necessary?" I managed through gritted teeth, hating how close he was, hating even more how my body refused to move away.

"Just making sure we understand each other." The warmth of him was maddening as he lingered there, too near, his voice low enough that only I could hear.

"Fia?" Vexa's voice echoed up from below. "Do I have to drag you down the stairs myself?"

The pressure holding me vanished so suddenly I stumbled forward. Aether's hand shot out to steady me, and the brief contact sent electricity through my skin. When I met his eyes again, that dangerous edge had been replaced by that unreadable calm.

"After you," he said, gesturing toward the stairs.

I shoved past him, trying to ignore how my heart raced.

He waited for me to step down onto the first landing before trudging down the stairs after us, Vexa now pulling at my arm with calloused fingers as we began our spiraling descent.

When the door finally opened, I shielded my eyes in reflex, expecting the light of a blinding sun, like the small windowless descent through the tower had somehow robbed my mind of what I knew to be true. I had become all too accustomed to the night-less, muted days. Like this realm was stuck in time, the sun never peaking beyond the gray mountains, the moon never leaving its position in front. The day was gray, just like everything in its reach.

I followed Vexa out onto the lawn, stale grass crunching under my feet, as if it had been burned, or dead long enough to dry out on its own, leaving its frayed skeleton behind. Through glimpses of fog and the cramped towers we walked between, I could see the intimidating architecture of Ravenfell piercing the muted sky.

Stone creatures from nightmares were encroaching from their peaked windows and rooftops, adorning all of the spires as far as my eyes could see. We were nestled in what seemed to be a corner of the city, the right side backed up to some barren lands in the distance. To the left, sharp stone encapsulated the perimeter and beyond those walls looked to be the remains of a forest, the trees twisted and dried.

Eventually we stepped onto a path, and rocky bits of broken stone ground beneath my boots with each step. I gave myself a brief moment to savor the feeling of the wind on my skin before the smell of wet hay and manure invaded my nose.

I followed Vexa into a covered stable. The stalls were spacious with high walls made of sturdy wood, leaving open entrances without gates, allowing the inhabitants to wander in and out at will.

I wasn't sure what I was expecting to see, but it certainly wasn't the creature before me.

My mouth went dry as the beast huffed towards Vexa, its movements graceful, yet ominous. Its eyes gleaming with an intelligence that transcended the animal.

The Vördr's head retained the noble features of a horse, though much, much larger. Its long muscular neck led to a strong, regal face. The mane was thick, flowing, and dark as night, cascading down its back. However, where the ears would be, instead, there were subtle ridges and slight bony protrusions, akin to horns.

The most striking feature overall was the Vördr's wings. They were massive, with a span that stretched far wider than the horse's body. They were batlike as I remembered, with coarse dark hair covering their bodies, each movement causing their deep hues to shimmer like oil on water.

"Isn't she magnificent?" Vexa breathed in awe, reaching out her hand for the beast to sniff. It gave her a few uninterested blinks before tapping Vexa's hand with her snout in acknowledgment. Wings brushed the ground as it turned, exposing the ridged spines that curved down its back, becoming more prominent near the hindquarters.

Vexa walked to an elevated dock and climbed the steps before motioning over the Vördr. It followed her calls and she began unfastening the saddle that was crafted along its back.

"You're actually lucky Raskr is here today. We have stables across Ravenfell and these beauties only stop by of their own volition. It seems like her last rider had to run off before taking all of this off of her." Vexa made quick work of the buckles and patted Raskr lovingly on the back.

"So they just come and go as they please?" I asked, looking around at the gateless stalls.

"We would never try to hold a Vördr unwillingly. That would be a death sentence. Gentle beasts as long as they have their freedom." Vexa laughed as she carefully made her way down the steep stairs of the dock, carrying the saddle that rivaled her in size.

"But they often stay close to their riders," Vexa added.

"Is this one yours?"

"I'd never forget to remove Draug's saddle. Not that he would let me." She chuckled.

"So do you just choose which one you ride?"

Vexa eyed me curiously. "It's a rite of passage here, to be chosen by a Vördr. The highest of honors. The decision is all theirs. They know when they've found their Kalfar."

A sliver of annoyance licked through me at, yet, another word I had no context for. It was irritating how they spoke to me like I already shared their vocabulary, with no explanation for anything, always forcing me to inquire.

"Kalfar?" I attempted to keep the irritation out of my tone.

"We're all Kalfar." She shrugged, motioning to the tower behind us.

"I thought you were Umbra."

"Umbra is our title as soldiers in the realm's forces. Kalfar is what I am. What we all are, what *you* are," she corrected me.

"I'm Aossí," I said quietly, turning back towards the beast.

The Vördr's long tail whipped, brushing the ground as she

turned to make her way to the small field on the opposite side of the stables.

"Whatever you say," Vexa half-joked.

Looking around, I only now realized how empty this area was. Apart from Vexa and I, along with Aether leaning against the door we had come through, there wasn't a soul in sight. Preventative measures, I was sure.

"Do you remember flying here on them?" Vexa's voice whistled past me on the wind.

Of course I remembered. How could one possibly forget flying amongst the clouds? Waking to find the wind whipping past so quickly, it nearly robbed me of breath. The feeling of falling once we made our decline towards the bladed skyline of Ravenfell. How unconsciousness was thrust upon me unnaturally.

"Despite Rethlyn's efforts," I retorted, eyes returning to the Vördr.

"That was really more for your benefit than ours," she said, a laugh escaping her lips.

I pondered the answer for a few quiet seconds as her amusement dissipated. They probably thought kidnapping was more pleasant if unconscious. In theory, perhaps. But it also made it impossible for me to fight back, to attempt an escape. I'm sure that was just an added bonus. I eyed Aether, who lay against the darkened stone with his eyes closed, an unreadable expression on his structured face.

Maybe I wouldn't have been able to escape that night anyway. Not with *him* around.

"His mind looks different from the rest of you," I said, tilting my head towards Aether.

Vexa returned to my side, giving me a confused look. "Looks different?" she asked.

"The rest of your minds glow silver, his glows golden." I wondered for a second why I was revealing any of this to her. It didn't seem like anything they could use against me, against Sídhe, but it still felt odd to be divulging it.

"So you can see our minds?" Her voice was low now but still edged with curiosity.

"If I try." I looked towards the tower, eyes scanning the many levels as white orbs began to glow from the inside. Her attention followed mine.

"Ten minds in that room." I pointed. "Six descending the fourth-floor stairs," I murmured. Aether's eyes shot to me.

"Vexa," he said, starting towards us, but she whipped her hand out, halting him.

"Under control," she shouted, eyes tearing into me now. "You can see them, within the walls?" she said, a breathless kind of rustle to her voice.

It felt like we were entering dangerous territory, and I had no idea how they would twist this information to their advantage. So I turned, looking across the landscape once again, crossing my arms, staying silent.

"I've never heard of anything like that," she said, noticing my sudden apprehension. "You're far more than a Duskbound," she whispered, as if to keep the revelation to herself.

Her words sent a wave through me. In truth, I had never really known what I was. Who I was. At this moment, it seemed like more of a mystery than ever.

I watched as the Vördr paused at the edge of a platform that laid across the walled barrier, starting in the gray grass before inclining in elevation towards the sky. It scratched its hooves against the surface, the sound sharp against the stillness. Then, with a powerful neigh, it surged forward, its wings snapping open and carrying it up the incline. Without realizing it, my feet began to move, drawn toward the creature, eager for a closer view.

"Watch your step," Vexa called from behind me, her voice a warning just as the Vördr launched into flight. Its wings unfurled fully, cutting through the air with effortless grace. Only then did I notice the shapes in the distant sky—dark, bird-like silhouettes drifting on the wind.

As my gaze sharpened, I counted at least five other Vördr, their massive forms racing toward the fortress. Each was a study in shades of gray, from onyx as dark as night, to reflective silver, their coats streaked with patterns—swirls of smoke and ink that seemed to shift with every movement. Some had legs dusted in white, as if snow had clung to the tops of their hooves, while others sported long, braided manes in shades of ivory and charcoal, the intricate plaits winding down their necks.

The creatures descended in an arc, their wings brushing the stone of the nearest tower before they ascended once more, vanishing into the sky.

I stood rooted, breathless. They were unlike anything I had ever seen. The legends of any beasts had been little more than whispered stories back in Sídhe, told to children as fantastical tales, often dismissed as fabrications—or forgotten myths from a time long past. I had never imagined seeing something like this. Never imagined something like this even existed.

The crunching of footsteps broke me from my trance, and reality settled in around me, tugging the numbness back into my bones, its presence more clear than it had been before. Perhaps in contrast to the exhilaration of seeing the Vördr, free and magnificent, unrestrained.

Now I remembered where I was. How I had come to be here. The sadness pulsed, hitting me like a wave. Part of me wanted to push it away, to try and climb out from its depths, but it was too heavy. I had fallen far past the numbness, into a pain too great to bear. My core ached to go home. To be able to take to the sky, fly out of here and back to where I belonged. Back to Sídhe. To Laryk. I nearly crumpled to the ground at the weight of it—the weight of emotions I had been avoiding during my isolation. Ignoring them had felt like my only form of survival.

But now, they had returned in full force, blurring my vision with tears that fell just as soon as they welled. My breaths became hoarse and frantic as my heart jolted once more, stumbling forward as I hit the ground, everything around me sinking into darkness.

CHAPTER FOUR

The brush *of grass caressed my legs and my eyes adjusted to the crimson rays of a setting sun. A path was clearly stomped out through the overgrown blades before me and the cry of children's laughter had me moving towards the sound. I noticed them first, two young girls holding hands, looking to be five or six at most. They had dark hair braided down their backs and matching lace dresses. They ran ahead of a man and woman in fine clothing, fit for nobles. I was unable to see their faces but the similar midnight hair and clothing led me to believe they were a family. The woman looked tense as she leaned in, speaking in hushed tones to the man at her side. I noticed the stern shift of his shoulders in response.*

"Wait for me!" *one of the children cried. That was when I saw the wall of darkness. The two young girls were silhouetted by a mass of nothingness that seemed to leach in all the light around it, desaturating this entire corner of the realm. One girl stood in complete fascination, unmoving, while the other kept looking back towards her parents impatiently. Inky tendrils curled along the ground, moving closer to their small figures.*

"It's too early, they are too young!" *the woman called out desperately when the man broke away from her and began to walk towards his daughters, taking the hands of both.*

"Please can't we wait?" Her pleading was lost on the wind and he never turned back to acknowledge her. "Mommy? Don't cry, Mommy. I won't go!" The restless of the two girls turned, making an attempt to run back towards her mother, pulling against her father's grip.

Without pause, he scooped them into his arms and disappeared into the darkness.

THE DREAM CLUNG to me like a distant memory for days after that. I couldn't make sense of it. It occupied my mind more than anything else during the times I was left alone in the tower. Vexa had returned every day, taking me back to the stables, letting me breathe in the fresh air until Aether deemed the excursion had met its end.

Vexa had attempted light conversation, keeping a closer eye on me as I walked the grounds of the small field on the edge of the city, probably trying to anticipate another sudden fainting spell. I assumed she thought my panic-stricken attack was due to the nature of our previous conversation, and I didn't correct her. The longer I could go without more questions from her, while still getting to experience a fleeting moment of fresh air, the better.

I climbed from my place on the floor, near the window, anticipating her at any moment. Time was difficult to discern with the motionless and unchanging sky, but I had gotten better at deciphering how the passing of it felt, paying attention to the slight differences in behavior—the patterns of noises or minds that I saw in other levels of the tower.

I strode over to the chest at the end of my bed, opening it to find the leathers I'd worn the day before. I began undressing, and pulled the thick fabric across my skin before slipping into the boots she had provided. I glanced up, briefly seeing my reflection in the mirror behind the bed, and quickly looked away before my face came into focus.

But curiosity tugged at me. Slowly, I returned my eyes to the silver mirror, and let my gaze climb to the ends of my long hair, unruly and weightless as it had ever been, dancing around my head in a halo of white. I edged my view over to my face, body stiff with the urge to recoil as I finally settled on my eyes. But they looked normal. Well, not normal. But they looked as they always had, opalescent and beaming.

There was no sign of the dark tendrils that had danced in them weeks before, when I first arrived in Umbrathia. I ran to the mirror, desperate for closer inspection as I confirmed it to be true.

The shadows were gone.

Confusion enveloped me. Could they have been wrong about what they saw? Perhaps I wasn't a shadow wielder afterall. Perhaps even I had hallucinated them as well. What I expected to be relief was tinged with conflict, with panic, and I wasn't quite sure why. I should be ecstatic that I had returned to normal. That I was as I had always been.

But something clawed at me.

Perhaps I was worried that if my usefulness to the Umbra was gone, my life would be short to follow. Perhaps it was more than that, but I didn't let the thoughts get much further. I bit my lip as footsteps echoed from the other side of the door, and Vexa's voice became clear, speaking in hushed tones to Aether.

"They're here," she hissed. I used my focus to zone in on their minds as Aether's golden orb shot up, moving quickly toward the silver of Vexa's.

"What do you mean?" he responded in a low growl. "Urken told them not to breach the city limits until we sent word."

"He's not happy about it either. But they've become more and more insistent. We can't exactly enforce punishments. Not when things are so fragile." I heard a sigh, muffled by the wall between us.

"They've become uncontrollable," Aether spat.

"If you'd let me try my hand with her earlier, perhaps we wouldn't be in this current situation," Vexa retorted. I crept closer, attempting to better hear their conversation when I saw the golden mind shift, taking a few steps back.

"We'll discuss it later. In a more appropriate setting," Aether said at full volume.

It wasn't long before the lock slid open and Vexa appeared in the doorway. She seemed tired, less enthusiastic than our previous encounters.

"Well you seem quite eager today." She half-smiled, leaning against the stone wall, noting my closeness to the door.

"It's not like I have anything else to do." I sighed, sinking onto my hip.

"Well, in that case, I won't keep you waiting." She motioned for me to follow as we made our descent down the tower's chambers.

Two of the Vördr were on the lawn once we made it outside. The black one from the first day, wearing the saddle once again. The other was dark charcoal, with silver speckles up the legs. They were in the stables, chewing on discolored hay that covered the ground.

I took a seat on one of the benches, watching as they ate. Vexa sat down next to me, shooting a hopeful glance in my direction without focusing on me for too long. She leaned back, adjusting her leathers as an awkward sigh escaped her lips. I'd become accustomed to that over the last week–her not knowing what to say, not wanting to send me into another fit.

"The darkness, it's gone. From my eyes," I finally murmured, after a few awkward moments slipped past. She had to have noticed by now. The lack of contrast was obvious.

"It's been gone for a while," she responded, pulling her boot up onto the bench and gazing out at the expanse beyond the fortress walls.

"Why?"

"You haven't created any shadows to replace it. When you absorbed ours back in Sídhe, some of them stayed," she said simply, as if I would immediately understand the context.

"I don't understand how any of this works," I said quietly. I wanted to inquire more, but I didn't want to seem eager, didn't want to seem like I was interested in anything this realm had to offer.

"Duskbound can wield shadows naturally. They can create them," she said, finally attempting a look in my direction.

"If that's true, then why can't I feel that within me?" I asked, the words slipping out before I could stop them.

A knowing smile touched her lips. "It's in there. You just don't know how to access it yet. There's a process..." She paused, choosing her words carefully. "Where it will become clear to you."

"And a vessel... what is that?" I asked, assuming she would probably change the subject once again. "All of this language is new to me."

She looked at me for a long time, chewing on her lip before shifting her body to face me, arm lounging on the backrest of the bench.

"Technically, any Kalfar *can* become a vessel," she said as she removed her glove and began rolling up the sleeve of her top. Intricate designs covered her skin—abstract and vague like smoke.

"These are void burns," she said, pointing to the wisps of inky blackness that swirled across her hands. As if to demonstrate, she pulled shadows through her fingers like water, watching as they drifted through the air like black mist. They seemed to gravitate towards the markings on her arms, eventually seeping into the black shapes and disappearing completely. "They allow us to absorb the darkness, and use it. But we cannot create it on our own." She said, turning her hand over, where inky tendrils pooled in her palm. "These did not originate in me. They were given."

I went silent, watching as the last wisps of darkness disappeared into her burns.

"Once a Duskbound learns to forge them..." Her voice trailed off as her eyes met the ground, almost looking as if she was wrestling with something. "They can share their shadows with others."

A lump formed in my throat at her openness.

Esprithe, is that what they want with me?

Suddenly, the metal door swung open, and a tall, slender man with tawny, muted skin began his way toward the dark Vördr, clad in leathers similar to ours.

"Rethlyn," Aether's voice boomed, trailing close behind him on the gravel path. "What are you doing? This area is closed right now." It was only then that the man—Rethlyn—halted, shooting his eyes across the lawn until they fell on me and went wide with horror. The shadows beneath his eyes were deep, tapering into sharp points that cut across his cheeks. A thin bar pierced the center of his nose. The Kalfar seemed to have a penchant for such jewelry, not just lining their pointed ears but also embellishing their features.

"Oh, fuck. I didn't realize—" he began before Aether slammed a hand down on his shoulder, pulling him back a few feet. "I forgot to remove the saddle from Raskr before the conference. I just came out to—"

"Rethlyn, Esprithe sake, pull your head out of your ass. I had to take it off her just a few days ago," Vexa cut in, irritation lacing her tone.

"Sorry, I was running late," Rethlyn responded, pulling free from Aether's grasp.

"He's just asking to get trampled." Vexa sighed.

"Make it quick," Aether commanded, urging Rethlyn to continue.

"How's it going with…" Rethlyn's eyes cut towards me again, flaring up once they locked with mine. He chewed his lip.

"Later," Aether hissed, grabbing his shoulder once more and ushering him down the path to the stables.

"Imbecile." Vexa shook her head, letting out a breath that sounded half irritated, half amused.

"So that's the one who kept me under on the journey here," I spoke, then added, "Rethlyn."

Vexa's gaze flicked toward me, her brow furrowing just slightly in concern.

"No one's supposed to be here right now. Rethlyn knows that—if only he paid attention." She blinked away a thought, almost dismissively.

I hesitated before asking, "Is his focus—affecting consciousness?"

A strained grin tugged at the corner of her mouth. I instantly regretted asking, but I needed to understand. To figure out how things worked here, what we were dealing with. The more information I gathered on the Umbra, the better.

"Focus," she repeated, almost with a laugh. "Strange way to frame it. Like it's something to be manipulated or forged. Like it's not inherent. Not born into our blood the moment we exist."

I mulled over her words. I'd never questioned the name given to our powers—the way essence manifested within us, shaping the realm.

"What do you call them?" I asked, genuine curiosity slipping past my walls.

"Tethers," she murmured softly, her gaze drifting toward the ashen landscape beyond the fortress. "Our gifts bind us to the land. To the essence that flows through it."

I sensed a shift in her—a quiet heaviness in the way she held herself. But I couldn't quite place it.

Our two realms seemed more alike than different. Vexa was clearly the enemy, but she didn't seem like a monster. She didn't seem like the Wraiths I'd learned about at the Compound. I thought back to when they had been simply shadows wreaking havoc on the West—beings of darkness spilling from another world, hungry for power.

"Our tethers define us in every way. They are what make us Kalfar." Vexa's voice broke the silence, raw with emotion. "And it's disappearing."

I opened my mouth, but was unnerved to silence by her expression. Just as soon as I let my fear get the best of me, pretending to be focused on something on the lawn, Rethlyn's voice broke through the tension.

"We'll be at the keep for the rest of the night, *lucky us*," he said to Aether, their footsteps crunching against the broken ground. "Valkan and his men have overrun the place, insisting they need urgent Council." He shook his head, irritated. "He wants to change the date—to do it sooner—" Rethlyn continued, but Aether muffled his words with a hush.

"Not here," he scolded, and suddenly his gaze shot to me, melting into a liquid bronze as we locked eyes.

"Vexa. You've been summoned," Aether called out, turning quickly on his heel, pulling Rethlyn in the opposite direction as their voices quieted, lowering into something indiscernible. I watched as Rethlyn pulled open a gate leading into the city street, waiting. Vexa let out a loud sigh before standing.

"Guess you're stuck with Aether. I'll see you tomorrow," she groaned, and sauntered off towards the Umbra men. As the two disappeared beyond the wall, Aether appeared once more, trudging back towards me with a creased brow.

"Time's up for the day," he stated, reaching the edge of the bench and turning away from me.

I didn't budge. Irritation churned in my gut. I could tell it had been only half the time I was allowed out on the lawn the day before. I dreaded the thought of going back to that room.

"Let's go," he repeated, staleness drenching his words as his posture shifted into something more controlled, something that seemed lethal.

I knew it better to follow his orders, to allow him to escort me back up into that tower, but I couldn't force myself to move. Finally, he turned in my direction, but I didn't dare look at him, keeping my eyes focused on the landscape beyond, noting the few Vördr gliding on the wind in the distance. But the irritation radiating off of him was palpable.

"I'll drag you up there if I have to," he said flatly, and I saw him cross his arms in my periphery.

"Just a few more moments," I whispered, sucking in a breath, expecting the sudden jolt of being thrown over his shoulder again, as he had done before all those weeks ago.

To my complete shock, he merely let out a sigh and lowered himself onto the bench beside me, its wooden beams croaking under his weight.

We sat in silence, and I closed my eyes, trying to soak in the last few moments of faux freedom before being whisked back to my tower. I breathed in the air, tinged with the scent of wet mud and a fire burning somewhere in the distance.

After what seemed like an eternity, I let my lashes flutter open, still surprised by the silence that had slipped by undisturbed. I dared a peek in his direction, feeling myself cower as I took in his intimidating frame, noticing as wisps of his hair flew in the gentle breeze. His eyes were closed, breathing in the stillness as we sat together.

I thought back to that moment in the tower, my first inklings of consciousness after my capture. How the intensity of our encounter had left me in shambles, how something had sparked between us in the darkest and most confusing of ways. I wondered if he remembered. If he ever thought about that. What *that* was.

And suddenly, I was brave.

"How do you do it?" I asked, fixing my gaze on him. Every nerve inside me was begging for me to look away, to recoil, but I resisted. I stared. "How are you immune to my... tether?" I asked. That use of the word had his golden eyes shooting towards me, flying open. They rested on me for a moment, his leathered chest inclining as he breathed in deeply. I don't know why I even asked. Why I expected him to answer.

"I don't know," he muttered in a low tone, and I waited for him to say something else, anything else, but he never did.

Slowly, he stood. "It's time."

And then something inside me snapped.

"I know you all captured me for a reason. It's not because you cared about my safety and it's not because you don't leave Umbra behind." I shot to my feet, backing away from him. "You want something from me. And I demand to know what it is!" My voice boomed through the lawn, but I couldn't bring myself to care. He was going to drag me back to that Esprithe-forsaken tower either way.

"You want all of the answers, but you know as well as I that you won't believe a word out of my mouth. I can't convince you of anything. You'll see for yourself soon enough," he said, taking a measured step in my direction.

"Why would I believe you? What possible reason would I have to trust any of you in the slightest? You claim I'm a shadow wielder, you call me names like Duskbound, but none of you show me what that actually means," I hissed, curling my arms out as if to show him I wouldn't be taken against my will. Not again. Not back up to that obsidian prison cell.

Inky tendrils began to pulse from his eyes as he took in my defensive position, jaw clenched, his chin low.

"You want me to show you?" he growled.

I stood breathless, eyes locking onto his once more as I stood my ground. I couldn't take it anymore. The temptation in his expression riled something in me, something I hadn't felt in a long time. Something dangerous, something dark.

"Yes." My voice was barely a breath, unsure of what I was asking for, but I couldn't back down now.

He moved so fast, too fast. Before I could react, he was on me, grabbing my face with crushing force, his eyes now darker than the abyss. A scream tried to tear itself from my throat, but I held it back, frozen by the weight of him. Darkness erupted from his every pore, obscuring my vision from all directions.

"You wanted to see. Now let me show you," he muttered, his fingers sliding down to brush my chin, his grip unyielding. I thrashed, but he pulled me closer, his other arm encircling my waist, trapping me against him.

The shadows surged around me, crawling across my skin, burning, chilling, like some dark, familiar touch. My body tensed with the pressure of it, hairs standing on end as something in me began to break.

"Stop resisting," his voice was rough, low. "You have to invite them in." The words stirred something in me. I could feel it, the pull of it. It was too much, too overwhelming. But he was right. I stopped struggling, my breath shallow, as I inhaled the bitter smoke rising from his touch. It filled me, tore through me, and in an instant, my mind shattered.

I felt the shadows descend my inner walls, the barrier completely breached. And then they flooded me. There was no fighting back as they sent pulses of power through my blood, deep enough until they sank into my bones. I felt my body go limp in his arms, felt as the darkness took me over, how it spread through me like a drug.

I hated how it felt. Hated that it felt like some long lost piece of me had been nudged into place. Hated how it felt good.

And just when I thought the oblivion would suck me into its depths, leave me in a place of utter delicious night, they began to fray and snap like strings of ink thrashing in water.

Feeling only came back to my physical form once I felt the heaving chest of the man before me, my body pressed against him tightly. As realization hit me, and I remembered where I was, who the chest belonged to, I slammed my fists against it.

In an instant, he released me, and I shot out of range of his grasp, doubling over to catch my breath.

"Don't ever touch me again!" I screamed, the words raw in my throat as I leaned against the bench for support.

His eyes shot to mine, confusion creasing his brow.

"You wanted to see. And now you have. I believe a thank you is the more appropriate response," he said, readjusting his leathers.

"You showed me nothing," I hissed, but I didn't even believe my words. The second the power slithered into me, I knew it was right. It had found a home in me. But still, I resisted. I didn't want it to be true. It couldn't be true.

"You can lie to me all day, but you can't lie to yourself. Not truly. I watched you absorb our shadows, on that lawn across the rip, and just now, right in front of me. The longer you fight it, the more difficult it will become for you," he said.

"I'll never be what you want me to be. As long as I have a say in the matter," I seethed, inching backwards, running a hand through my unkempt hair.

"You couldn't fathom the weight of your decisions here."

"This isn't my home. None of this is my responsibility," I hissed.

"You're a Duskbound. Whether you like it or not. And you were right, we do need something from you. Something we can't take against your will. Believe me, if we could, I would have found a way to do it already. Because I'm no gentleman. Because we're running out of time. This realm is dying, and you're the single fucking thing that has the ability to save it."

He stepped towards me, darkness still sparking across the surface of his leathers, like they were bleeding smoke into the ether. Panic surged through me as he advanced in my direction once again. But something from above had his eyes shooting to the sky.

The sound of powerful wings beating tore through the lawn, sending bursts of wind through our hair, through the desolate grass and everything surrounding us, blowing out the remaining tendrils of his shadows. Aether retreated, creating a distance between us just as the frame of a silver Vördr slammed into the muddy earth in front of me, throwing chunks of dirt into the air. It lowered its head and sent threatening hisses of air through its nose, stomping the ground with a hoof, its full and utter attention on Aether.

Both icy and onyx designs danced along its fur, shifting in the muted light as its muscles tensed.

My heart skipped in my chest as its tail flicked dangerously close, the sheer size of it overwhelming. The air seemed to grow heavier as it stomped the ground with a force that shook the earth beneath us.

Aether stepped back again, and I thought I saw a flicker of amusement in his eyes, as if he half-enjoyed the occurrence. He clicked his tongue, the sound dripping with annoyance, before letting out a slow sigh.

"And if the shadows weren't enough to convince you, perhaps this will."

As I stood there, frozen, I felt its gaze shift toward me. Every muscle in my body screamed to run, but my legs wouldn't obey.

The creature's massive form loomed, becoming uncomfortably still.

It was then that the Vördr turned on its hindquarters and faced me, stepping close enough—so close I was certain it could smell my fear. Breaths came in shallow gasps, heart hammering in my chest, as the creature's gaze locked onto mine. It was impossible to look away.

Slowly, it bowed its head before me, its enormous form lowering to acknowledge me in some way I couldn't begin to comprehend.

"Tryggar has just claimed you."

CHAPTER FIVE

"You're going to have to get more momentum than that if you want to sling your leg over properly," Vexa said, crouching beside me on the platform inside the stables. The scent of hay and leather filled my nostrils, mingling with the distinct ashen smell that seemed to permeate everything in this realm. Tryggar stood just ahead, an ill-fitted saddle strapped to his back, his silver coat catching what little light filtered through the stable's weathered beams. Tiny motes of dust danced in the air between us, stirred by his occasional wing movements.

Finally, I had managed to stay out of that tower for more than my daily allotted time, but as much as I wished I could say it was intentional, that I was pretending to be absolutely miserable at learning to ride the Vördr, I couldn't claim credit. I was just, indeed, miserable at it.

Vexa had been trying to explain the mounting maneuver to me before we tried the real thing, and apparently, I couldn't get the movement right.

"Their backs are sensitive, and until we can have a proper saddle made to accommodate you both, you'll have to be extremely careful. I don't want any injuries. If you fall off one of these, it's very hard to get back on the next time. Trust me," Vexa said, demonstrating the maneuver on one of the saddles atop the docking platform.

I nodded, turning back to the saddle of my own, and lunged, jumping to sling my leg over it. I slid as I hit the smooth leather, but managed to grab the horn quickly enough to halt myself.

"Well that was, perhaps, too much momentum." Vexa chuckled, eyeing my sitting stance as she pursed her lips.

"We've been at this for hours. Maybe this just isn't for me." I eyed the silver Vördr behind me, who simply snorted and dug his hoof into the hay, tossing his tail to the side.

"Just take a break, I'll be right back," she called out as she edged off the platform, hitting the dusty ground with a thud. "Gonna go tell Aether we need more time."

My gaze followed her as she trudged towards him. We hadn't spoken a word to each other since our argument days before—when he had engulfed me with shadows. When I had brought them into myself.

My memories of the lawn, of the night in Emeraal when I was taken, had been a jumble of events I could never quite tie together. I had remembered Osta, Laryk, the entirety of the Guard staring at me with widened eyes as the shadows lifted my body.

However, the events that transpired before that had been nothing but a blur. Some empty corner of my mind that wasn't exactly missing, but couldn't be pieced together either.

When I let the shadows in, that night had come back in roaring force, and even more so in the days that followed. The feeling of them running through my veins had been immediately familiar, like something that happened once in a dream. But as I racked my mind for whatever part of me they had unlocked, I remembered it all.

The nothingness, whispers of a void. The darkness that overwhelmed me until I nearly lost myself.

I knew I couldn't run from the truth any longer, but I still didn't know what I wanted to do with this newfound acceptance. Perhaps Vexa was right about everything, perhaps this was where I belonged, but I was a stranger to this world. To those who lived here. In Sídhe, I had finally started figuring out who I was, what I stood for, and what I wanted to do with it. Was I ready to challenge all of that again?

Despite everything I was attempting to explain, to justify, I couldn't help that speck in the back of my mind that had begun a dark chain of questioning. It clawed at me from the tiniest of places, like a sliver of wood embedded in the skin.

If what Vexa said was true, if this realm was being drained of its power, if the ashen landscape and the stale food were truly ramifications of this drought… I didn't know what I would do with that truth. If Sídhe was behind it, there had to be a reason. Didn't there? There had to be a *catalyst*. Something.

Sídhe had attacked Riftdremar after the uprising. I knew the Isle was capable of great tragedies—I had never forgotten that. But it had maintained such an idyllic era of peace since the war, at least for the majority of those who lived there. Why would they want to disturb that?

Could I even take Vexa and Aether's word for it? They would certainly have a reason to lie to me. To manipulate me enough so that I joined their cause. They wanted me as a weapon, I felt it in my bones. And I would never be their weapon. Not for an army I didn't know. A realm I was a stranger to.

I needed proof. If people were truly suffering, I would need to see it with my own eyes.

A gentle brush against my hand snapped me back to reality, back to the dimly-lit stables. I scratched under Tryggar's chin, and he nudged me once again, sending a soft hiss of air through his nose. I gave him a few more scratches, chuckling under my breath.

"You really never stop, do you?" I muttered, feeling his soft press again. His dark eyes gleamed, and I couldn't help but think he looked pleased with himself.

I sighed, giving in to his demand and running my hand along his neck. He nudged me again, this time flicking his gaze toward a nearby basket. It was full of twisted, brittle pieces—dark and rough to the touch. Dried meat that looked like bark. The smell hit me before I even got close. Rusty and sour, like something that had been left out far too long.

He nudged me again, more urgently this time, his eyes fixed on the basket.

I raised an eyebrow. "You want that?"

Tryggar stomped a hoof, narrowing his eyes at the basket, then back at me.

I hesitated. There was something unsettling about it, but I reached for one of the pieces anyway. It felt cold and rough in my hand, like it had once been alive but now only a husk. I handed it to him, unsure of what else to do.

Tryggar snapped it from my hand faster than I could blink. He chewed it with a viciousness that almost startled me, tearing through it with a speed that made my stomach tighten. His jaw worked, muscles tensing as he swallowed in quick, unsettling gulps. The sound of it wasn't right—like bones breaking too loudly.

"Well, that's only mildly terrifying," I muttered, but Tryggar didn't seem to care. If anything, he looked pleased with himself, nudging me for more attention.

Suddenly, he stretched his wings out, sending a gust of air that knocked over a few baskets and sent hay scattering across the ground. I jumped back, watching as his wings unfurled, stretching wide. They were massive—silver and smoky in the dim light.

He looked at me, and I couldn't help but smile. "You're pretty, you know that?"

Tryggar lifted his head, spreading his wings wider, almost like he was showing off. The playful glint in his eyes was unmistakable, like he knew exactly what I'd said.

I laughed. "You're a real show-off, huh?"

Tryggar seemed content, healthy. Although his diet was questionable by most standards, maybe that made sense. The beast looked like he could devour a whole chicken, though I doubted he'd eat it fresh.

A flash of black caught my attention near the stable opening. Tryggar reacted instantly, spinning around so his back was to me, tail going still. He lowered his head as Raskr tried to enter. Tryggar hissed loudly through his nostrils and stomped, scraping his hoof against the dirt.

"It's just Raskr," I called, but Tryggar let out a low growl.

Raskr backed off, eyes falling on me almost fearfully before stomping back off into the lawn.

"Are you the only Vördr allowed in here?" I laughed.

Tryggar turned back to me, settling his nose into my palm once more, his eyes soft, falling onto the gates along the stone wall.

"Have you ever been out there?" I asked, nodding toward the city. "Beyond the walls? In the streets?" I paused, thinking about what Aether and Vexa had implied about the living conditions. "Is it really as bad as they say?"

Tryggar didn't respond, but he met my gaze with an almost knowing look. The bony protrusions on his head flicked, and he gave a small snort, like he could sense my unease. His nostrils flared, and then he stomped his hoof. He let out a long, drawn-out neigh before nudging my boot.

I sighed, giving him one last pat on the head before making my way over to the two Umbra. They seemed to be in some kind of hushed argument.

"It's only a matter of time before she'll be taking to the skies—"

"That's exactly why we need to speed things up." Vexa's voice cut through the air as she spun around at the sound of my boots crunching against the grass.

"Fia, I was just about to come back over there. How's it going?" She nearly sang in a tone uncommon for her.

"What is it like out there? Beyond the walls?" I asked, crossing my arms.

Vexa opened her mouth, and then closed it, pursing her lips. She looked to Aether, some silent conversation shooting between them, exchanging narrowed looks before Aether simply nodded. And just as Vexa turned her attention back to me, Aether pushed past us, his arm brushing against mine. I ignored the flare of irritation that sparked within me.

He glanced back in our direction, his eyes deliberately avoiding mine, before speaking with an edge I couldn't quite place.

"Perhaps it's time we showed you."

THE BLACK STONE wall that circled the fortress loomed closer as we made our way towards one of the outer gates that led to the city. I glanced over my shoulder taking in the monstrous castle that was situated behind the towers we came from.

The farther we moved away, the more it grew. What had seemed like a small city of its own was actually just a tiny courtyard in comparison. It was as breathtaking as it was intimidating.

Who ruled over this land? Who sat on the throne inside this monstrosity?

"You'll trip if you don't start looking where you're going," Aether spoke, breaking my concentration. I had been so distracted I hadn't noticed he'd moved to my right, only a pace behind. Vexa was ahead already waving down the Umbra stationed at the gates.

I blinked up at him, surprised he'd decided to speak to me at all.

"Careful, that sounds like something a gentleman might say."

"In that case, carry on." He didn't smile, but there was a flicker of light in his eyes. Probably glowing at the thought of me falling and busting my ass.

We caught up to Vexa just as the gates were opening. My heart rate increased as I moved into the unknown. I was sure this trip would be of no help in an escape plan, otherwise they wouldn't be bringing me along. That didn't mean I shouldn't take in every detail.

As if a sound barrier had been broken, the chaotic noise of a city flooded the lawn.

"Welcome to Ravenfell." Vexa's tone was somber.

What I saw before me was a mixture of beauty and tragedy. The cramped stone buildings of the city were just as intricate as that of the fortress, but the residents congested every street and alleyway. The conditions had me sucking in a long breath. Stalls were scattered down the street, devoid of the color of fresh fruits and instead offering grains and minimal jars of preserved items I couldn't quite make out. I watched as someone tried to deftly swipe a bag of rice from one of the merchants, which quickly resulted in a brawl that had the grain scattering across the uneven stone walkway. I had to swallow the bile in my throat when I watched as people immediately dropped to their knees scooping what they could of it into their palms, pebbles and all.

As I moved through the cracked streets, feeling the weight of eyes turning to me, I noticed that everyone in this vicinity had dark hair, cascading down their backs or tied in loose knots at the nape of their necks, black as the night sky—every single body. It was the same for the members of the Umbra I had encountered.

My gaze fell to the white curls that framed my face, and a lump tightened in my throat. I stood out like a sore thumb, the contrast stark and jarring. Vexa and Aether had made it seem like I belonged here, but I certainly didn't share this trait with the Kalfar. Despite the common characteristic, their skin tones ranged in muted shades of flesh from pale to onyx. All desaturated. All dull.

A group of children, looking to range in age between seven and ten stood near a well, their faces dirty. They were so thin—so uncharacteristically small that my stomach nearly lurched when I imagined what they went home to every day, if they had a home at all. They kicked a leather ball between them, one that seemed deflated and worn, the stitches fraying at the seams. I watched on as one of the boys smiled, and let out a laugh as he kicked the ball past the other two, celebrating his small victory. A part of me felt a spark of something warm at the exchange, but that sank into my gut once I realized how winded they were—how winded everyone seemed.

The air was thick with the smell of something burning in the distance, smoke lingering in the streets. It was a strange, sharp scent that stung the back of my nostrils. I hadn't prepared to see this. I placed a hand over my stomach, trying to quell the ache of seeing so many—so fucking many, with such dull pain in their eyes, still trying to live, to survive in this cramped place. How could they ever allow the city to become this overrun?

Before I could take a step away from the commotion, my path was blocked by a woman in a state of panic, her eyes already pleading with me. "Miss, my husband needs to see a medic, but the Queen only sends them every two weeks. Please, it's urgent. I beg of you."

I looked quickly at Vexa, whose face had softened with genuine pain. "When did they last come through?" she asked, her voice gentle.

"Ten days ago," the woman whispered, wringing her hands. "He's gotten so much worse since then."

Vexa shared a look with Aether, something unspoken passing between them. "They need time to recover enough essence to heal again. I wish—" She stopped herself, jaw clenching. "I'm sorry. We're sending them as often as they can manage without burning out completely."

The woman's shoulders slumped, but she nodded in understanding. This wasn't the first time she'd heard this explanation, I realized. Not the first time she'd had to accept that help wasn't coming soon enough.

"Which district?" Aether asked quietly.

"Eastern quarter, near the old well," she replied.

"I'll make sure they check there first next time," he said, and though his voice was steady, I could see the toll this took on him—having to walk away when people needed help.

More desperate faces were turning toward us now, drawn by the hope of aid. Aether's hand found my lower back, urging me forward. "Walk faster," he spoke in a low tone, pushing me forward into the crowd.

I hissed and smacked him away. "I told you not to touch me."

His hands flexed at his side before pushing them into his pockets.

"By all means, capture the attention of every beggar on the street. There's no shortage of them, as you can see." His tone was cruel, but I quickened my pace.

I felt desperate to turn back to the woman, but knew I would be of no help. I had nothing to offer.

"You don't have healers?" I asked aloud, the feeling of uselessness making me feel restless.

"They're called medics. But their tethers are weakened. It can take weeks for them to harness enough essence to be of help. Hence, the limited visits to the city." Vexa sounded exhausted.

I never could have imagined what a realm without essence would look like. It was so heavily relied upon in Sídhe but was so inherent it was barely given a second thought. Like breathing air for most. The loss of a focus would be a tragedy for many. It didn't compare to the loss of essence in the landscape. One could live without power, but not without food and water.

I couldn't help but compare it to Luminaria. The overwhelming abundance of plants and life. The community gardens lush with food for all—glittering canals brimming with fish. I tried and failed to recall the last time I'd seen someone with an illness.

As a Riftborne, life had never been easy, but it was certainly never like this.

"We get shipments of grain from the South but they're mostly rationed—and starting to come less and less as the land loses its nutrients. This part of the country is still livable but the Eastern side is a wasteland now," Vexa explained.

"We had a huge influx of people when Vardruun fell," Aether's tone was low, carrying an edge I knew was directed at me. "We lack the resources to house them all."

"I don't understand. When did all of this happen?" I asked, feeling a sense of desperation. I didn't try to hide the crack in my voice.

Vexa shot her eyes to Aether before responding.

"We don't know exactly when it began, but the Eastern border started drying up nearly a decade ago."

A decade?

"The effects weren't immediately noticeable. Especially the further you get from the rip."

We walked for a long while in silence. Bodies started to dwindle as we neared the end of the street and turned a corner. A small building with little foot traffic came into view.

"Should we stop in?" Vexa eyed Aether. "I'm sure they're inside practicing. You know how much they'd want to see you."

Aether simply nodded, shrugging casually.

"Don't let him fool you, Fia. He might be a complete drag when it comes to social interactions, but children really bring it out of him," Vexa teased, nudging his shoulder.

"And Vexa is a drag for all, including children, I'm afraid."

He cut his eyes at her, the hint of a grin playing at his lips as Vexa snorted. Then he stepped past me and continued through the open door. He must have known I wouldn't run off because he was no longer worried about guarding me from behind. I guess the city itself was its own deterrent.

"Who will be here?" I asked Vexa, matching her pace to follow her around the curved entrance that opened into a circular arena once inside.

"Just Carden, Lael, and Uma. Lael is finally old enough to enter the Strykka. Those three are inseparable. Carden and Uma will be training right alongside him until they can enter themselves."

Another word I didn't know. I bit back my annoyance at the lack of clarification.

Vexa must have noticed but she didn't bother to explain.

The three mentioned were in the center of the arena. It looked like two of them were about to begin a sparring match before they noticed Aether's approach.

"No way!" A boy looking no older than thirteen ran towards him. The other boy, sixteen at most, looked just as excited at Aether's arrival but seemed to be playing it cool.

"Aether! Vexa!" the girl called out with a wave. She wore all black. The fabric was cotton but it was clear she was trying to mimic the garb of the Umbra with a few belts that held no purpose wrapped around her waist.

Aether was ruffling the hair of the younger boy that had collided into him. A semblance of a smile crossed his lips, causing a dimple to appear.

As much as I tried, I couldn't look away.

"Me and Lael have been practicing all day. You should see how good we've gotten." Carden grinned up at him with admiration.

"Is that so? Maybe you can show me before we head back." Aether looked towards Lael and nodded. The attention put a crack in his stoic facade, causing a boyish grin to appear.

"Do you think I will be able to work with you Aether?" He looked hopeful.

"I would rather you help around the fortress," Aether spoke with indifference but the intensity of his eyes told me he meant it.

"I'm not honing my skills to stay locked in the fortress," Uma chimed in, leaning into a fighting stance and narrowing her eyes.

"Our tethers are way too cool for that," Carden added.

"You're not using your tethers too much are you?" Vexa's voice chided.

"We're saving them, don't worry," Lael said. "As hard as that is."

I had to admit it was strange to see these two go into such parental roles.

"Who is she?" Carden pointed at me, still glued to Aether's side.

"Why does she look like that?" Uma mused.

Vexa snorted, but it was Aether who responded.

"Our new friend." The sarcasm in his words was not lost on me. I fought back a grimace.

Uma tugged on her hair while looking at mine in fascination. "You're pretty," she hummed.

"Thank you," I replied awkwardly. It seemed I would never be able to take a compliment well. Even from a child.

Aether clapped his hands, making a sharp echo through the vaulted room.

"How about you all show me what you've been practicing?" His dimples appeared again when he smiled at the three of them bouncing with energy.

It took Vexa grabbing my arm and pulling me towards the seats along the edge to break my trance.

"Who are these children?" I asked once we were far enough away.

Vexa threw a glance back over her shoulder, eyes going soft. "Orphans from across the realm," she said. "When cities were evacuated, the Umbra took them in and gave them places to stay within our lodging. Clothes. Food. Uma and Carden are siblings, but Lael —we found him alone."

We watched them spar, Aether instructing from the sidelines with his hands clasped loosely behind his back. He gave encouragement and pointers every few movements.

"So, the Strykka? Is this a way to join the Umbra?"

"It's one of them. A set of trials one must complete to enter the elite units," Vexa murmured vacantly, fully focused on the spar happening in front of us.

"Don't you think they are a little too young?" My stomach churned at the thought of these kids becoming ruthless killers. They seemed too innocent for what they would surely be trained to do.

"Of course they're too young. They're children. But we don't have much of a choice these days. At first, people joined the Umbra in hordes when the drought began, knowing it was the easiest source of regular meals and a place to live, but even that slowed down after a while. Kalfar don't see a purpose in it anymore. They'd rather die with their loved ones, not on a battlefield a world away. We're lucky to get a few recruits per year."

"It feels wrong," I whispered, almost to myself.

"Yes, it does, doesn't it?" she said, not really a question. "A land ravaged by war is always brutal. Difficult decisions have to be made… but this–this is different."

We sat in silence for a moment, watching on as Aether turned the younger boy up over his shoulder playfully.

"Their tethers, are they being trained to use them?"

"It takes too much essence. They ration their tethers until it's time to prove themselves. They will be depleted once the Strykka is finished."

I nodded. Moments slipped by.

"If it's really Sídhe draining the essence from the land..." I trailed off, taking a deep breath. "I don't understand it. It's perfect there, I don't see why they would jeopardize that type of peace."

"Have you ever wondered why it's so perfect there?" she asked, turning to look at me now.

Bile rose in my throat.

"Have you never wondered why poverty and hunger are scarcities in your realm? Why harvests had become more bountiful than ever before, why your life spans grow while ours lessen?"

In truth, I had wondered about all of it. It had never made sense why Sídhe had experienced such economic growth, such prosperity out of nowhere. No one ever seemed to question it, so I guess I stopped questioning it myself. But I'd never—never once—thought it would be something like this.

We had been thriving while another realm turned to dust.

CHAPTER SIX

My mind was spinning with everything I had seen. The questions and revelations came one after another, only to bring about more questions.

I walked back to the fortress between Vexa and Aether. The street leading back to the gates was still active but most of the residents seemed to be crowding into the buildings seeking warmth.

I couldn't shake the feeling of helplessness. I needed to do something.

Raine would have stopped for that woman today and demanded help, or done what she could herself. All of team V would have.

I thought of them in their tents in Stormshire. Unaware that they were risking their lives to help a realm that was lying to them.

Now more than ever, I needed to get back to Sídhe. If the Guard knew, if the people fighting this war knew what they were doing, what they were contributing to, they would be shocked, perhaps they would even rise up, refuse to be a part of it. They would, wouldn't they?

My thoughts drifted to Riftdremar, my birthplace, and I wondered what had truly happened to it—what had truly caused the war, and if everything I had been taught was a lie. If it was simply an uprising turned catastrophic, or if there was more to it. If the Aossí who destroyed it even knew what they were doing, if they knew it would result in complete destruction, in genocide.

The real question was, what could I do? The thought of escaping on the back of Tryggar crossed my mind. But I knew I'd never be left alone for long enough to make a great escape. I wouldn't even be able to mount him fast enough to try. Much less how to fly him or command him to take me anywhere. Where to go.

As soon as we made it through the gates, the sounds of Ravenfell vanished once again, leaving only the crunch of our boots as we made our way towards the tower. I felt the eyes of Vexa and Aether weighing on me. The silence grew like a steady pressure in my ears. They had shown me the truth and were now waiting for my reaction.

All the things I wanted to say refused to form on my lips.

"Thank you for showing me," I managed to get out. My breath heavy. "I need time to think."

Vexa stepped forward, her expression softening. "Of course you do—"

"Time?" Aether's voice cut through the air like ice. "You've had nothing but time. Weeks of it." He turned to face me, shadows beginning to curl around his fingers. "And after everything you've seen today, you still need more?"

"Aether—" Vexa warned, but he continued.

"The devastation, the suffering—none of that moves you?" His golden eyes burned with barely contained fury. "Or perhaps you simply don't care. Perhaps you're too comfortable in your ignorance, removed from it all."

"That's not fair," I shot back, though my voice trembled. "You can't expect me to just—"

"To just what?" He stepped closer, his height towering over me. "To acknowledge the truth when it's right in front of you? To face what your precious Sídhe has done?"

"I'm trying to understand—"

"No," he snarled. "You're stalling. Buying time while your friends continue to drain us dry." His shadows deepened, and I could feel the temperature drop around us. "If time is what you need, I'm happy to provide more. Shall we see how another month of isolation inspires you?"

"That's enough." Vexa moved between us, her violet eyes flashing. "This isn't helping anyone." She turned to me, her voice gentler. "What you saw today... it's a lot to take in."

Aether made a sound of disgust. "We don't have time for coddling—"

"And we don't have time for threats," Vexa urged. She faced him fully now. "You want her to trust us? To believe in our cause? This isn't the way."

They stared each other down for a long moment before Aether finally stepped back, though the darkness still rolled off him in waves.

"Fine," he bit out. "Take all the time you need. But remember this—while you sit in that tower contemplating, children are starving. Families are losing everything." His voice dropped lower, deadly quiet. "Their blood is on your hands now too."

He turned and stalked away, leaving Vexa and me in tense silence. She sighed, running a hand through her hair.

"He's being an ass," she said finally. "But he's right about one thing—time isn't a luxury we have much of anymore."

I nodded, unable to find words as the weight of everything pressed down on me.

"Come on," she said softly. "Let's get you back to the tower."

The walk back was silent, heavy with all that had been said and unsaid. But Aether's words echoed in my mind with each step, burning like brands against my conscience.

Their blood is on your hands now too.

I heard the dull thud of the closing door and lock behind me.

Alone, I crawled into the bed trying to find warmth in the sheets I pulled over my head. I relived the day over in my mind until sleep finally took me.

Darkness surrounded me, illuminated by bright, glittering stars. Reflective dust was scattered through the velvet abyss, creating shapes and twisting as it morphed from pale white to pearlescent pastels. The place, wherever I was, felt familiar, like I had been here before, perhaps more than once.

And then I recognized the orb, the one fluttering in the distance, making its way towards me with effortless grace. It looked like a mind, but different somehow—as if it radiated colors beyond the spectrum, yet in simple flashes, never encroaching fully on the silvery opalescent shape.

I goaded the web up my spine, tingling as it braided itself gently, caressing my skull in shifts of those same colors, and let it spill out of me, tendrils twisting through the air, thrumming towards the orb.

I had seen it before, but it was always out of reach... always just beyond what I could try and understand, often fleeing off into the darkness when I got too close. But this time, it pulsed brighter as my web surrounded it.

I was gentle, and slow. I didn't want to scare it this time. I longed to know what it was—why it was always here, what this dream was, where this dream was.

A single fiber of the web reached out and neared the surface of the orb, the light pulsing from both just beginning to intertwine when—

Decide, Fiandrial.

The words came out like a symphony of hisses from every direction just before I made contact, panic rushed through me, and everything went dark once more.

But not for long.

Suddenly, I felt myself drop into a chair, into a room I didn't recognize. I tried to look around, tried to move, but I was trapped in place, my eyes locked on a desk and window ahead of me, the sun basking brightly through the glass. I felt fingers that were not my own thrum against the armrest of the chair, and a voice that was not my own clear its throat—his throat.

And footsteps behind me.

"There's a reason they haven't returned." A velvety voice spoke from behind, something strained in the tone, and my heart felt as though it might shatter right there. The sensation of eyes misting caressed my mind, but no tears formed at the ones I saw through.

Laryk.

I wanted to whip my head around, I wanted to look at him, but I was frozen.

"I know it's been hard for you. I don't understand their sudden absence either, but I don't think the two are connected. You have to move on, you can't keep doing this to yourself."

I recognized the voice coming from my lips as Mercer's.

"They attack nearly on a schedule. For the last two years, they have never rested for more than two weeks," Laryk hissed, his voice growing closer as I heard footsteps round the desk, and suddenly, he was in front of me. I felt my heart stop in my chest, or what should have been my heart.

His eyes were bloodshot, hair unkempt in a way I had never seen before. His typically perfectly creased black shirt bore wrinkles in the sleeves, and there was something gaunt about his features. I wanted to reach out, to touch him, but Mercer's arm stayed maddeningly still.

"They took her," he spat, a spark of rage flying across his eyes.

"No one survives a horde of shadows like that."

"They leave. The bodies. Behind," Laryk seethed, each word a calculated tick.

Mercer hesitated momentarily, bringing a glass with amber liquid up to his lips and taking a sip, the taste of whiskey invading my senses, burning my throat.

"If what you're saying is true, then it opens up entirely new questions," Mercer said softly, as if trying to make his rough voice as gentle as possible.

"And what exactly are you implying?" Laryk growled.

"You know how it looked, Laryk. Even you hesitated."

"They weren't coming from her. It was a trick of the night." Laryk's voice was strong, but there was a subtle crack in his tone.

I had never seen him like this. He had always been so poised, so collected and unreadable. So unbearably, infuriatingly confident—wearing that mask that kept his feelings unknown to all. I barely recognized the man before me, the man who looked like he was on the edge of a cliff.

"But that's not why I hesitated. You know this. I've already told you," Laryk murmured.

"The figure." Mercer sighed, placing his glass on the desk ahead.

"I know what I saw. For a split second. It happened so quickly." Laryk shook his head, squinting.

"The form of a man. Darkness rippled off of him. I've thought it this whole time, that there was more to them. That the shadows were a disguise."

A haunting silence fell as Laryk's eyes darted from Mercer to the window and down to a crate of glass jars, something dark flashing across his features.

"So what do you want to do?" Mercer simply asked.

"Employ everyone. Every single member of this Guard. Bring them here. To Stormshire."

"Laryk, you're acting from emotion—"

"The King has given me full control of the Guard," he countered.

"When they come, and they will, there will be no holding back. And we will be ready. They will finally feel exactly what we're capable of," Laryk continued, shooting up from the desk, turning to grip the windowsill, eyes fixed on something in the distance.

"We will rain destruction down on them. They will return what's mine."

My eyes shot open as the obsidian room closed in around me, my heart hammering against my chest. I threw the covers back, planting my feet on the ground and running to the door before slamming my fists into it over and over.

The lock slid open, and Aether's golden eyes narrowed at me.

"How unexpected," he drawled, taking in my wild-eyed state. "Finally reached your breaking point?"

"I'm ready to talk," I said quietly, meeting his gaze.

He merely crossed his arms, leaning against the doorframe, forehead creased in contemplation. But his eyes seemed to shift, something soft flashing across them in an instant, vanishing just as quickly as it arrived.

"Let's see if you truly mean it."

CHAPTER SEVEN

THREE PAIRS of eyes pinned me in place from across a weathered table. We sat in what must have been a war room of sorts, though it felt more like a tomb. Dark walls stretched up into darkness, the ceiling lost in shadow despite the iron chandeliers that hung at intervals, their flames casting an unsteady light. The space was circular with curved benches built into the walls.

Rethlyn hovered near one of the arched windows, his focus not on me but somewhere just over my shoulder, his brows creased in thought. The gray light filtering through the clouded glass caught the shadows beneath his eyes, making them appear deeper, more stark against his skin. Vexa sprawled in her chair to my left, one leg draped casually over the ornate armrest, a dagger flipping lazily between her fingers. The blade caught the firelight with each turn, sending brief flashes across the ceiling.

Then there was Effie, whose crossed arms and grimace told me she hadn't forgotten our last encounter. Her gaze was sharp as she sat rigidly in her chair, like she was just waiting for me to make a wrong move. I refused to meet it.

Aether sat beside her, silent and stiff, his gaze fixed on the far wall where an enormous tapestry hung, its edges frayed and worn. But the second I glanced in his direction, those golden eyes locked onto mine with frustrating speed. I swallowed hard and looked away, but I could still feel the heat of his stare long after I'd severed the contact. The room felt too warm, too close, despite its size. The air was thick with the smell of old parchment and burning wax, and something else. Something metallic that seemed to coat the back of my throat.

"Well, this is sufficiently awkward," Vexa broke the silence, her dagger catching light as it spun. "So I suppose I'll take the opportunity to ask you, Rethlyn." Vexa's nose wrinkled as she turned to face him. "What in the Void were you doing in your quarters last night? The entire corridor smelled like something crawled into the walls and died."

Rethlyn glanced at her over his shoulder, his mouth twisting. "Wine making is a delicate process," he replied from his window.

"Delicate isn't the word," Effie grimaced. "The fumes were quite literally an assault on the senses."

"Sure you're not trying to poison us all?" Vexa asked. "Again."

"That was one time," Rethlyn sighed, "and the recipe specifically called for—"

"Recipe?" Vexa barked out a laugh. "Is that what we're calling your experiments now?"

"I don't have to share." He turned slightly, a hint of defensiveness in his tone.

"We'd rather you didn't," Effie added, and Vexa let out a cackle.

"Laugh all you want. But who spent three hours yesterday throwing daggers at her own shadow?"

"It's called training, Reth." Vexa rolled her eyes.

"That was boredom," Effie corrected. "And you still owe me a new mirror."

Aether simply shook his head, which had Vexa's eyes falling on him.

"And this one's stuck in a perpetual state of *brood* now that he has to play prison guard instead of lumberjack," she shot towards him.

"His cabin is quite nice, to be fair." Rethlyn shrugged, a gesture that had Aether's eyes landing on him. "Full cedar logs, and larger than most. Little glass embellishments hanging in the windows—"

"Excuse me?" Aether raised that pierced eyebrow.

Rethlyn sank down into one of the chairs at the table, face turning pink. "It's not like I followed you. I was foraging out in Skullwood before it fell," he said with a shrug. "You were outside skinning a deer. It looked like a massacre, by the way."

Aether's eyes darkened. "Bloody work. I can show you sometime if you'd like?"

Rethlyn let out a nervous laugh. "Thanks, but I don't think you'll be able to find any deer for a demonstration."

"I wasn't referring to the deer," Aether murmured, and I could have sworn the ghost of a smile played at his lips, which sent annoyance licking up my spine.

"What is the point of this?" I asked, my voice echoing slightly off the stone. "Why are you all stalling?"

"Talon's late, as usual." Vexa sighed. Without looking, she drove the dagger into the table with a dull thunk. The blade quivered in the wood as she stretched her arms above her head and let out an exaggerated yawn.

Something in Effie's expression softened for just a moment as she watched Vexa, but it vanished so quickly I might have imagined it. "Must you always destroy the furniture?" she muttered, though there was less bite in her tone than I'd expected.

"Are *you* not capable of answering my questions?" I raised an eyebrow, my attention returning to Aether. The others shifted uncomfortably at my challenge, even Vexa's casual posture stiffening slightly.

"It's better to start with him." Rethlyn breathed, eyes darting quickly to mine before refocusing just beyond me.

"You all think I'm this Duskbound. Why are they so important to you? Where are the others?" I didn't know where to start or what to ask, but this was the question that clawed at me the most. Aether had said I was the only one who could save the realm, but no one had told me *why* or *how* they expected me to do that.

Vexa blew out air through her mouth and shrugged in Aether's direction.

"Only a Duskbound can harness shadows…" she began, resting her arms on the table. "Only a Duskbound can share them with vessels. Without one, a shadow wielder cannot exist."

"So all of you are vessels?" I asked.

"Clearly," Rethlyn said, waving his hand in an exasperated gesture. "Why else would we tolerate these void burns?"

"They allow you to absorb the shadows… the ones a Duskbound shares with you?"

Vexa nodded.

"Where are all the others? There must be more. Someone is supplying you with shadows currently. Why do you need me?"

"Because she's weak. She won't be able to do it for much longer," Effie cut in. Vexa's face shot in her direction as her eyes narrowed.

"Careful, Effie," Vexa whispered sharply.

"No, I told you. I want to know *everything*. So tell me."

"There used to be more," Rethlyn murmured, only half paying attention. "But they dwindled over the years. The crusades *certainly* didn't help."

"Crusades? What happened to them?" It felt deliberate—the way they spoke, revealing just enough to hint at the truth while keeping the rest shrouded in secrecy. And that was *not* the agreement.

"They were seen as a threat to those in power," Vexa said, her tone sharp. "In Umbrathia, the throne has always been held by a Duskbound. To keep it that way, the ruling class decided to hunt down and eliminate any others. Easier to secure your position when no commoner can rise to challenge it." She rolled her eyes, the disdain in her expression unmistakable.

"But there have been others? Others born throughout the realm?"

"Not in over a century. Not outside that bloodline." Aether's voice was level but tinged with something dark.

"Not until you—" Vexa began, just as a sharp clicking sound echoed from the corner of the room. The door creaked open then, and a smaller man in black robes hurried into the space, several ancient-looking books clutched to his chest. The formal cut of his clothing was different from the Umbra's leathers, more scholarly than militant.

"What is so urgent?" his quivering voice demanded as he approached the table. "You know it's possibly the *worst* time for me to be away from the Citadel." He set his books down with careful movements.

He halted mid-step when his eyes fell on me, and his attention darted between the others before settling on Aether.

"Relax, Talon." Vexa smirked. "We simply require your services."

"Why is she not restrained?" Talon nearly shrieked.

"She's under my protection." Aether's voice was low and even, though there was an edge to it that warned against argument.

"Personally, I think we should really consider this whole *restraint* idea." Effie flipped her hair, turning her heated gaze onto Vexa and jerking her chin towards me, gesturing dramatically with wide eyes.

"She's harmless," Aether said simply.

Harmless? I briefly considered snatching Vexa's knife from the table and burying it in his hand.

"Wait until Urkin finds out! That doesn't give you the right to—"

"Are you his second in command?" Aether questioned, cocking his head slightly to the side. "No, I believe that's *me*."

"We need you to observe her," Vexa chimed in, ignoring both the glare from Effie and the tension so obviously brewing between the two men.

"For what possible reason?" the man asked.

"She's a Duskbound." Vexa's words cut through the air, followed by several seconds of complete silence.

"Impossible," Talon muttered, slouching into his robes. "*That's why you requested me? You all keep saying that, but it simply cannot be true.*"

"But," Vexa continued, "that's not all. She also has a *tether*."

"It can't be both, you know that as well as I. I have never come across such a thing. Not in any of the ancient texts," he said, crossing his arms. "You really dragged me all the way over here for these baseless assumptions?"

"You're already here. Just *observe* her. Or whatever it is you call it," Rethlyn cut in, sighing in exasperation as he sank into one of the chairs.

Talon looked at me, eyes shifting for a few seconds before he shook his head.

"Give me your arm, girl," he muttered as he made his way around the table.

I shot my eyes to Aether, then to Vexa, neither of them deigning a look in my direction as the man shuffled towards me, rolling up the sleeves of his robes. In an instant reaction, my body tensed, and I stood quickly, taking a few steps back.

"Fia, relax. He's not going to hurt you," Vexa murmured.

"And what a shame *that* is." Effie scowled down the table.

"Can someone explain what is going on here?" I seethed, lifting my arms in a warning. The man halted.

"He's going to observe your tether—your *focus*. Whatever you want to call it." Vexa stood, gesturing with her arms as if to calm me down. And in an instant, my body relaxed outside of my own control. I sat down in the chair, confusion rippling through me as my breathing became slow and measured, meditative almost.

"What's happening?" I asked.

"Just trying to help you relax." Rethlyn came to stand next to me. "I swear to the Esprithe themselves that no harm will come to you," he offered, and another wave of intense relief flooded me. "If that helps."

He gave me a short smile. "Now, give Talon your arm."

I didn't react when the man reached for me, but concern flickered across his features as he wrapped his hand around my wrist and took a deep breath.

"It won't take long." He nodded as he closed his eyes. The room stayed eerily silent, the attention of all focused directly on me, on the man's grip.

"How strange," he whispered, his brow creasing.

"What do you see?" Vexa asked.

He stayed silent for a few more moments, pressing his lips into a hard line before he finally released my hand. I looked around to Vexa, to Aether, confusion pulling at me.

Talon lowered himself into the chair next to me, eyes slowly crawling to Aether.

"Essence runs through her, but it's not a *tether*," he finally said. "There is nothing tying her to the land. The essence within her is... self-sustaining..." He trailed off, blinking as if to force understanding.

Vexa and Effie shot their eyes in my direction as Rethlyn took a step away from me.

My heart stuttered in my chest. Self-sustaining? I'd always known my focus was different—had spent years hiding just how different—but I'd assumed it was because I was broken in some way. Not because I was... what? Something else entirely?

"What does that mean?" I asked quietly.

"You seem to... generate your own essence." The man eyed me cautiously.

The implications crashed through me like waves. Every lesson I'd ever had about essence—about how it flowed through the land, how we were merely channels for its power—had been wrong. Or at least, wrong for me. What did that make me? Not quite Aossí, not quite Kalfar. Something in between? Or something else entirely?

I thought of all the times I'd pushed my focus down, tried to make it smaller, more normal. How many times had I sensed that difference and chosen to ignore it? How many signs had I missed because I was too afraid to look closer?

"That sounds like you, Aether..." Effie's voice quivered.

"No, I told you. I've never seen anything like it before. I don't know how Aether harbors the abilities he does. I can't read a single speck of essence—or anything else—residing inside him. Like his powers come from nothing at all." Talon's eyes dragged across the room.

"I've seen it in her too," Aether interrupted, his voice slicing through the room.

Then all attention was on him.

"Whenever she channels, I can see it braiding around her—wisps of energy radiating through her—out of her." His eyes met mine, and for once, I couldn't look away. There was something in his gaze that made my skin crawl—not recognition, but understanding. As if he knew what it was to be different, to be something other than what everyone expected.

"Dear, have your abilities lessened since your arrival in Umbrathia?" Talon asked.

I hesitated, reaching for the web, allowing it to caress my spine in a gentle flutter. It felt normal, it felt as it had ever since I learned to control it.

"No," I managed.

If I wasn't what I thought I was, then what did that mean for everything else? For my loyalty to Sídhe? For my place in the Guard? For every choice I'd made thinking I understood who and what I was?

But there was something else too, something I didn't want to acknowledge—a sense of relief. As if some part of me had always known I was different, had been waiting for someone to finally see it. To name it. To understand it.

Rethlyn stepped towards me again with questioning eyes.

"Don't you dare," I directed at him, my hand flying up in a warning. "Whatever you did before, don't even fucking think about trying *that* again."

"Hey now," Rethlyn responded, holding his arms up in submission. "I was just trying to help."

"It's my turn to ask questions." I eyed Vexa, my voice rigid.

She matched my stare and nodded.

"Alright Talon, you're dismissed," she said, gesturing for him to leave. "Run back to the Citadel."

The man simply looked at me, then at Vexa, but his eyes rested on Aether the longest as he stood, straightening his robes.

"If you really believe she could be a Duskbound, you know there's only one way he'll ever believe it." Talon gave Aether a knowing look and turned for the door.

"What is he talking about?" I asked, glancing around, but the room grew heavy. Everyone seemed to stiffen—everyone except Aether.

He sighed, leaning forward onto the table. "You have to meet the Void."

Some unknown dread coiled in my stomach at his tone. "What exactly *is* the Void?"

"The most dreadful place you could imagine," Effie muttered.

"Effie," Vexa warned, her sharp tone cutting through the air. Turning back to me, she explained, "An ancient thing—a mass of darkness that engulfs the Northernmost part of the realm."

I shifted my gaze to Rethlyn. He had risen from his seat, his eyes fixed on the wall. "It's the only darkness our eyes can't penetrate," he said quietly. "The Void isn't just a place, it's an absence—an emptiness that consumes not only matter but the very essence of being. To step into it is to be unmade." His voice faltered slightly, his gaze distant, as though recalling some long-buried memory.

Acid churned in my stomach, a cold sweat breaking over my skin.

Vexa's voice dropped to a near whisper, as if she spoke of something she shouldn't repeat. "When you enter the Void, there are three possibilities."

She glanced at Aether, her words slow and deliberate. "If you can resist the cold—the death it promises—If you manage to survive in the first place, you'll stumble out with void burns. You become a vessel." Vexa looked down to her arm as she rolled her sleeve, revealing the black markings that covered her skin.

"Or?" I asked.

Aether's eyes flicked to mine, shadows pooling in the corners of his golden irises. His voice dropped, ragged and thick. "Or, you come out unscathed—at least on the outside. But make no mistake, you've been marked. These shadows stitch themselves into your very soul, carving their instructions so deep, they become inherent. As easy as breathing." He paused, his gaze sharpening.

"You come out a true wielder. You emerge a Duskbound."

I let out a sigh. "And the third?"

"Death."

CHAPTER EIGHT

"Well, it's certainly clear why you didn't lead with that." The words came out sharp, but they didn't match the tremor in my hands, the hollowness spreading in my chest. An ancient thing that consumed everything it touched. Was that what called to me? Was that what lived inside me?

I shot up from my chair, needing to move, to escape the weight of what they were asking of me.

"Fia wait. I know how it sounds." Vexa's voice called from behind me. "What you must be feeling—"

"*You* don't know anything about what I'm feeling." I spun around, my voice steadier than I felt. "I remember what the shadows felt like in Emeraal. What they *did* to me." I pressed a hand to my chest, where the shadows Aether had injected me with still stirred beneath my skin. "I nearly lost myself."

The room went silent. Even Aether's perpetual stillness seemed to deepen.

"And it terrifies me," I admitted, the truth of it burning in my throat. "Because what if I walk into that Void and I don't come back out? What if I do, but I'm not myself anymore? What if—" I swallowed hard, voicing the fear that had been growing since the shadows first touched me.

Rethlyn shifted uncomfortably, but Vexa's eyes softened with something like understanding.

Effie just blinked, as if she couldn't quite grasp my insistence. "Well, of course you're something else. That's rather the point, isn't it?"

I turned back away, my mind trapped somewhere between anger and despair. Aether's voice cut through the air, sharp and cold.

"Running won't change what you are."

I pushed through the door into the hallway, needing to escape the weight of their expectations, their certainty, their casual acceptance of what they were asking. But as I walked away, I could feel it—that darkness inside me, shifting and stretching like it was finally waking up. Like it had been waiting all this time for me to acknowledge its presence.

And maybe that was what scared me most of all. Not that I might fail, but that I might succeed. That I might walk into the Void and find out that this was who I was meant to be all along.

The door opened with a hiss from behind me, and I quickened my pace.

"Where are you going?" Vexa called out.

"The stables."

"But you're going the wrong way," Rethlyn chimed.

I paused, and took a deep breath in, trying to control my building anger, slowly turning on my heel and shouldering past them.

But it was Aether who stepped out behind me then, his form looming over mine. His shadows curled in my periphery. I could nearly feel his eyes burning holes in my back, causing the hairs on my neck to stand on end. I wasn't getting slung over *anyone's* shoulder today.

"Well, this is quite the fit," he said, his tone dripping with some sick kind of humor. The words sent heat rushing to my face. Esprithe, I *hated* him. Always lurking around every corner like some deranged stalker. What did the others even see in him? *Second in command?* Judgment here in Umbrathia was clearly lacking. I just needed time to think—to fucking breathe. *Alone.* But his footsteps remained mere feet behind me, scratching across the stone floor—an utterly *obnoxious* sound. It was as if he thrived on agitating me, like he *enjoyed* pissing me off. It seemed to be the only time even a hint of amusement touched him.

And he could *see* my web? No wonder he always knew when to halt me. I couldn't think of a worse person to have such an ability. And *why* could he see it?

What is he?

If everyone didn't leave me the fuck alone, I was going to explode. Without even intending to, I felt my web slam into my vertebrae and begin climbing.

"*Leave us,*" Aether shot towards the rest of them in a predatory tone, and their footsteps halted. "I'll handle her."

Handle me?

I tore towards the door, swinging it open before crunching through the stale grass of the lawn, the peak of the stables roof in the distance. Raskr was trotting along the edge of the expanse, near the border wall. I was surprised to see Rethlyn had actually remembered to remove his saddle today.

I prayed that Tryggar would be in the stables—prayed that I would be able to mount him. Either way, I was going to try. It was the only way I could imagine getting a lick of time to myself, with none of the Umbra looming over me. They weren't idiots, it's not like I could escape in any real capacity. I had no idea where to go, where we even *were* in regards to the rip—to Sídhe. I didn't even want to fly. I just wanted to get away from this place for a single fucking moment. My eyes shot to the ashen landscape of the world beyond the wall. I wanted to go *there*.

"You walk up behind a Vördr like that and you're going to get kicked in the face," Aether spoke, somehow already directly behind me.

"Wonderful. A coma is just what I need to have a few blissful moments away from you." I didn't slow my stride.

"You're more likely to get killed by a Vördr kick than the Void," Aether remarked calmly, like it was a known statistic.

"Doesn't sound promising," I tossed back, looking through the stalls for Tryggar.

"So you're a coward then? Like the rest of your realm."

I nearly choked on the audacity. "We're the cowards? You hide behind *shadows*."

"Of course you're a coward. The truth is literally slapping you in the face and you still run from it—still try to deny it. What's *happening* here." His voice turned dark.

"I'm not running from anything except *you*. I need to think. I need to process all of this. You won't give me a single moment of space."

"I gave you six weeks of space," he offered. I could almost feel his shoulders shrug.

"Imprisonment is *not* space." I finally turned towards him, almost slamming into his broad frame. My voice turned into a low growl. "Leave me alone."

"I won't. Not until you agree to work with us."

"I know you're probably used to ordering everyone around, but it's not going to work with me. This will be *my* decision. I've had my choices taken away from me before. I will *not* do that again," I fired back as he arched his brow.

That seemed to stun him momentarily.

"Tryggar!" I cupped my hands around my mouth and called out into the sky. Vördr were flying across the horizon, but they were so far, I couldn't make out if Tryggar was among them. I didn't even know if he could hear me.

A chuckle sounded from behind.

"You can't even mount him." His words were laced with that dark amusement once again. I needed that silver Vördr to drop down. *Now.* Preferably on Aether's head.

"Watch me." I shot him a sickeningly sweet smile, followed by my two middle fingers.

Aether's chuckle deepened, his golden eyes narrowing with a predatory gleam. "Oh, this should be good." He crossed his arms and leaned casually against the stable door, as if settling in to witness a spectacle. "Don't let me stop you, then. Go ahead. Call your beast."

I bit back a retort, refusing to give him the satisfaction. Instead, I scanned the horizon again, my heart pounding in frustration. "Tryggar!" I shouted, louder this time. The sound of flapping wings answered faintly in the distance, and I squinted, catching a glimpse of silver cutting through the gray sky. Relief swept through me.

"Your negotiating skills aren't nearly as powerful as you imagine them," I said.

His lip twitched, but he didn't bite. Instead, he straightened, stepping closer. Too close. "This isn't about power," he said, his voice low. "It's about survival. You think you're running from me, but you're running from what you are. And Duskbound don't just absorb the Void, they command it. They keep it contained. If you could go five minutes without having a tantrum, perhaps someone could explain it to you properly."

I laughed, bitter and sharp. "Oh, please enlighten me, Aether, because so far, all I've heard is cryptic nonsense and demands. If I'm so crucial—if you're running out of time, then why the fuck did you keep me isolated in a tower for six weeks?"

He tilted his head, studying. "I wanted to break you," he said simply, his tone unnervingly calm. "You were so blinded by the lies from your realm. You needed to fall apart so we could even *attempt* the truth."

"Break me?" I snapped, taking a step closer. For a moment, we were almost nose to nose, his shadow spilling over me. "You disgust me."

His eyes darkened further, the corners pooling with inky droplets. "The truth is, you're already part of this. Whether you want to be or not. I don't care if I disgust you. I don't care if you want me dead. If you weren't the key to saving this realm, I would have already ended you. Entitled and selfish. Everything about you is revolting to me. So don't worry, Princess, we're on the same page there."

Before I could fire back, a loud screech broke the tension. Tryggar's massive form swept down, wings outstretched as he landed heavily on the ground, scattering dust and stale grass in his wake. His gleaming silver coat caught what little light the sky offered, and his dark eyes locked onto me.

"Finally," I muttered, taking a tentative step toward him.

Aether's chuckle returned, soft and maddening. "Go on, then. Show me."

I ignored him, focusing on Tryggar. The Vördr's gaze was sharp, as if he could feel the tension he had just sliced through. My hands shook, but I stretched one out cautiously. "Tryggar," I whispered.

The beast huffed, his breath warm and smelling faintly of ash. He leaned forward slightly, just enough for me to brush my fingertips against his snout.

Behind me, Aether's voice was like a dagger. "Careful now. He can smell fear."

I shot him a glare over my shoulder. "You're not helping."

"I'm not trying to," he said, eyes shining.

"Come on," I murmured to the beast, gesturing toward the opening. "In here."

Tryggar snorted, his massive hooves crunching against the ground as he hesitated. He didn't move toward me, but he didn't fly away, either. *Stubborn Vördr.*

I spotted a saddle resting on a nearby rack, plain and worn but serviceable, and hauled it down, staggering slightly under the weight. Dragging it toward the mounting platform, I climbed the stairs. "Tryggar!" I called again, my voice softer this time, more pleading. The Vördr's shadow filled the doorway as he peered inside

"You're going to spook him," Aether warned. He was closer now. "Or hurt yourself. Honestly, this is painful to watch."

"Then stop watching," I snapped, fumbling with the straps. Tryggar shifted uneasily, his tail lashing behind him, but he didn't pull away.

"That's an interesting technique."

"Shut up," I muttered through gritted teeth, yanking the strap tighter. Tryggar huffed, and I winced, bracing for him to take off into the lawn. But instead, he stilled, his dark eyes boring into mine. My hands were trembling as I stepped onto the mounting platform.

"Alright Tryggar, we're going to go for a ride," I said, giving him a simple nudge.

"This should be good," Aether said.

I ignored him, gathering every ounce of bravery I had. Our last interaction had gone so well, but that was on the ground. I didn't know how he would react to being mounted. I took a deep breath and tried to shake off the nerves.

Okay, you can do this.

Three... Two... One...

With a clumsy but determined leap, I threw my leg over Tryggar's back, settling into the saddle. It wasn't graceful—far from it. I nearly toppled over, and my foot caught awkwardly in the stirrup. But I stayed on.

Tryggar shifted under me, wings rustling, but he didn't throw me. I exhaled sharply, relief washing over me as I straightened.

"That's a good Vördr," I said, surprised. I reached down and gave him a pet along his cheek. "Now, take me away from this man."

Tryggar snorted, and it almost sounded like a laugh. He took one step forward and hesitated, as if adjusting to my weight. But then took another, and another until we were out of the stable.

"Look at her go," Aether said evenly.

Tryggar kept a steady trot further onto the lawn. It only then occurred to me that Vexa and I hadn't gotten this far in our Vördr riding lessons. How exactly… was I supposed to steer this giant animal?

"Alright. I'm impressed," Aether admitted, though his tone was maddeningly flat. "Now bring him back and practice the dismount."

"The field?" I asked the beast nicely, but his eyes were set on the stone wall. I heard Aether's footsteps crunching from behind.

"Going flying, are you?" Aether's tone sounded vaguely like a hiss. My stomach tightened as I followed Tryggar's gaze, realizing with growing horror that flying was exactly what the beast intended. *Oh, Esprithe.* A part of me wanted to cave and ask for help, for instructions, for *anything* to stop this.

"As I said before," Aether sighed. "Completely insufferable."

I was just about to turn my head, to beg him to intervene when something slammed into me. Hard. The force knocked the air from my lungs, and I staggered, nearly sliding off the saddle.

The sudden movement startled Tryggar. The Vördr reared up with a sharp hiss, and I latched onto the saddle's horn and held on for dear life as his hooves clawed at the air before slamming down. The ground shook beneath his weight, muscles rippling like waves.

"What did you do?" I hissed.

"You'd better hold on," Aether murmured, his breath brushing my ear.

I didn't think. I just reacted, driving my elbow into his side with as much force as I could muster. He merely grunted softly in response.

Before I could tell him off, Tryggar lunged forward, tearing across the lawn at top speed. Aether's arms wrapped around me, locking me firmly against his chest. The rough leather of his armor scraped against my back, and my hair whipped wildly in the wind, lashing against his face. *Good.* I hoped it stung.

"You're too close," I muttered through gritted teeth, trying not to gag at the proximity.

He didn't say a word, but I could feel the subtle rise and fall of his chest, like he was suppressing something bigger than a chuckle —a full, unrestrained laugh.

A scream caught in my throat as Tryggar bounded onto the inclining platform and launched himself skyward. The force of the leap sent my stomach into my boots. His wings unfurled in a thunderous snap, catching the wind.

The ground fell away beneath us in a rush, the world shrinking as Tryggar's wings sliced through the sky. The air hit me like a whip, dragging my breath in ragged bursts. I should have been terrified, my mind screaming for the safety of solid ground, but all I could hear was the thundering of my pulse in my ears. And for the first time in too long, I felt a tug at the corners of my lips.

I had been suffocating. Every moment of silence, every second spent locked away in that tower, had smothered something inside me, something I hadn't known I was losing until now.

This *felt* like freedom, even if it was just the illusion of it. The kind that made my chest ache. For a brief second, I felt a surge run through me, something like lightning coursing through my veins.

And then it became clear—I had forgotten how to feel at all. The air was different up here. I felt weightless—I felt *alive*.

My fingers tightened around Tryggar's saddle as he banked, soaring higher. The ground was a memory now. The city we were leaving in the dust, the walls I had once been trapped behind—they didn't exist anymore. Not up here.

It felt like the first time I had truly breathed in months.

CHAPTER NINE

I ALLOWED myself time to adjust to the sensation of being airborne, trying to ignore my unwanted passenger. So far, I had just allowed the Vördr to guide our way, soaring above the clouds for what must have been half an hour at least. I didn't exactly know what I was supposed to do—how I was supposed to steer him. There were no reins. I'd never even ridden a normal horse with no reins—*on the ground.*

"If you want him to turn, press with your leg on the opposite side of the direction you want to go," Aether's voice broke through. We had been riding in such silence that I almost forgot he was behind me.

I tested his advice, pressing my left leg against Tryggar's side, but the Vördr merely snorted, continuing his path straight ahead as if I hadn't done anything at all.

"He's not listening," I called back.

"Press harder. He needs to know you mean it."

I dug my heel in with more force, but Tryggar seemed to take that as a challenge, surging higher into the sky instead. The sudden acceleration had me clutching the saddle horn, my knuckles white. Aether's grip on me tightened.

"Clearly, your teaching methods need work," I muttered through gritted teeth.

We crested just above the clouds, the mist cool against my skin, before Tryggar finally decided to break through them of his own accord. The landscape below came into view, and my sharp intake of breath had nothing to do with the altitude.

The world below unfurled like a nightmare made real. As we descended, my throat closed around a cry I couldn't quite swallow. This wasn't just destruction—this was obliteration.

Dried riverbeds carved through the earth like open wounds, and what must have once been forest stood as nothing more than a graveyard of twisted limbs reaching toward an eternally twilit sky. Each detail that came into focus felt like a physical blow. I thought the conditions in the city had been terrible, but nothing compared to the gray world below. This was death itself, stretching as far as I could see.

And we had caused this. My people. My realm. The Guard I had sworn my life to.

Bile rose in my throat as I remembered our training lessons, learning to fight the Wraiths, pride swelling in my chest as Laryk told me I was the answer—that I was what he'd been looking for to finally annihilate the foreign threat. He couldn't have known about this, could he? He had made me feel like we were the righteous, fighting for our realm, fighting for our survival.

We hadn't been heroes. We had been executioners.

"It's all gone," I managed, the words tasting like ash. Behind me, Aether's silence felt heavy, accusatory.

"Yes, most of it."

I turned my head slightly, trying to catch a glimpse of his expression. But his face was as inscrutable as ever, shadowed by his dark hair.

"The drought has spread, and with it, death. Entire villages abandoned. Crops failed. Water sources turned to dust."

My stomach churned, a mixture of the altitude and the grim reality below. Seeing it made it all too real.

Tryggar's wings shifted, and the creature let out a low, guttural sound, almost as if he, too, mourned the state of the land. The Vördr's shadow stretched long over the ground, a fleeting specter passing over the remains of what once was.

My gaze fell to a cluster of ruins below. What might once have been a village square was now a tangle of collapsed roofs and shattered walls. I imagined the people who had lived there—children playing, traders haggling, elders sharing stories by the fire. Now, it was nothing but ghosts.

"Let's land. There's a clearing there just to the left." Aether's voice came from behind me.

"Land? How am I supposed to—"

"How did you expect us to get back on the ground?" His words were slick with that annoying calmness he always managed to maintain. Made even worse by his grip on my waist. Given how tightly he was holding me, I might as well have been attached to him with iron chains.

"Well—" I started, nearly huffing to myself when I realized I hadn't thought that far ahead. I mean, I hadn't thought I would be *flying* today at all.

"I figured Tryggar would eventually just take me back to the city and land on the lawn!" I shouted through the wind, my grip on the saddle tightening as we soared higher, the ground below a blur.

Aether's voice brushed my ear. "Well, you managed to attract the most stubborn Vördr of the herd. If you're waiting on him, you could end up across the realm."

I gritted my teeth. "Don't tempt me."

Tryggar gave a loud snort and banked right. The wind whipped by as his wings beat powerfully, and my stomach lurched with the sudden shift.

"Careful. It'd be so unfortunate if you fell."

I shot him a look over my shoulder. "How *could* I fall off? I'm practically glued to you."

I felt my panic rising, creeping up from my chest and tightening my throat. This was nothing like riding a horse. There were no reins. No straps to hold on to. I was at the mercy of a giant, stubborn beast.

"Tryggar!" I yelled, half panicked, half frustrated, trying to press my heels against his side, but the Vördr just kept flying as if it was his sole mission to get as high as possible, indifferent to my distress.

Aether's voice broke through my mounting frustration. "You need to control him, not just yell at him."

"I'm not yelling at him, I'm begging him!" I snapped back, the words coming out in a breathless hiss as Tryggar's wings flared wide. We tilted dangerously, diving too steeply toward the ground. I could see the ruined village below, the broken rooftops and cracked stone, and my heart skipped a beat. He was flying straight towards it.

"Esprithe, Aether, we're going to die!" I shouted, panic flooding my voice as the ground rushed up too fast.

"Are you screaming for the Esprithe or for me?" he asked simply, even as we fell in a jarring descent.

"What do I *do*?" I shouted.

Aether's voice stayed calm, his tone no longer amused but sharp, almost as if I were the one being unreasonable. "You need to slow him down. Press your heels, and tug back on the horn of the saddle—don't just hang on like you're about to fall off."

"I'm trying! It's like he doesn't even feel it—" I half-screamed, clenching my fists as the ground was getting closer. Tryggar's descent was too fast, too much.

"Press with your heels, Fia! He's not just going to stop because you ask him to!"

I gritted my teeth, digging my heels harder against the Vördr just as Aether shifted, and slammed his legs against mine, shoving them hard into the beast. If we weren't potentially falling to our doom, I would have killed him for the complete invasion of feeling him so—utterly—intensely *against* me. Heat ripped through me as his form tightened. His breath warmed my ear even as the wind whipped past us. Every part of me wanted to jab him in the ribs.

With one last final thrust from Aether—one that felt as if it could have shattered my legs—finally, Tryggar's wings shifted, slowing our descent. It was sudden, but it was enough. Just as I was about to squirm away from him, Aether loosened his grip and slid back in the saddle. We were still touching, but his body wasn't *surrounding* mine anymore.

I exhaled sharply, but I could still feel my heart pounding in my chest as the ground loomed closer. I forced myself to pull against the horn, trying to keep my hands steady as the wind pushed against us.

The ground was just ahead now. I could make out the dilapidated structures—splintered wood and broken stone. Tryggar tilted his wings slightly, not a moment too soon, and we landed with a jarring thud on the cracked earth below.

Tryggar snorted, stretching his neck as he pawed at the dirt, completely unfazed.

I, on the other hand, felt like I might collapse right there in the saddle. My hands were still gripping the saddle like my life depended on it, my chest heaving with the aftershock.

I swung off Tryggar with shaky legs, barely managing to keep my balance. I nearly stumbled after hitting the ground from such a height, my boots sending puffs of ash into the air.

Aether didn't even acknowledge my near meltdown. "Well, we survived."

I shot him a look over my shoulder, heart still racing. "No thanks to you."

I hunched over, hands perched on my knees, and caught my breath.

"You're a miserable instructor," I shot in Aether's direction, "and Tryggar, we're going to need to have a talk back at the stables."

The Vördr simply pranced off, throwing up dust in his wake as he approached some twisted, skeletal trees. "He's not going to leave us out here, right?" I asked.

"He'll stay close." Aether's voice had taken on a different tone. He was looking just past me, something like regret spreading across those sharp features, his dark hair sweeping off his forehead in the breeze. I stood and turned, only to find he was staring at what must have been a garden at some point, a long time ago.

The soil was cracked and dry, a gray-brown that barely resembled earth anymore. No weeds, no grass, not even the faintest hint of life could be seen. Where plants had once stood, there were only twisted, brittle remains—stalks and stems snapped or shriveled to nothing. Rusted trellises sagged at odd angles, their frames tangled with remnants of vines that had long since withered away. Rows that had once been filled with vegetables were now just empty furrows, the soil so barren it seemed hollow. No insects, no birds, no sign of anything thriving.

A quiet stillness rushed across the landscape as I took it in.

"Where are we?" I asked.

"This was the village of Croyg," he said, moving past me and into the garden, twigs snapping beneath his boots. "It was the biggest supplier of produce in the realm."

"When did it fall?"

"Two years ago." His words sent a shock through me.

"It looks as if it's been abandoned for decades," I whispered, taking in the complete devastation. How could it have gotten like this so quickly?

"We evacuated it, taking residents back to Ravenfell. Many refused, not wanting to leave their belongings—their land, behind. All who stayed either eventually sought refuge in Draxon or died here in these houses." Aether turned, but he didn't look at me. Instead, he focused his attention on the dirt. "Lael was one of the children we brought back to the city. Both his parents had already passed. Poisoned by the very vegetables they grew, like the land had corrupted them."

I stood there, not knowing what to say. Not even knowing how to feel.

"The last time I was here was the day the sky stood still. First the sun, and then the moon. Night and day became one in the same. The seasons all blurred into each other. We're stuck—stuck reliving the same day over and over while the realm dies."

"You're fighting for this?" The bitterness in my voice surprised even me, but I couldn't stop the words. "For a land that's already dead?"

Even as I said it, shame burned through me. How dare I question the worth of saving this place? I thought of the children in Ravenfell, kicking their worn ball in the streets. Of the woman begging for a medic. Of Lael, orphaned by the very earth that should have sustained his family.

This wasn't just about a dying land. It was about people—people who had done nothing to deserve this slow death. People who still found ways to live, to hope, even as their world crumbled around them.

But helping them meant turning against everything and everyone I had ever known. It meant accepting that Sídhe's prosperity—the peace I had fought so hard to protect—was built on this devastation. That my service in the Guard had contributed to *this*.

"Would you abandon them?" Aether's question cut through my thoughts like a blade.

"No," I whispered, and the word felt like both a truth and a betrayal. How could I turn my back on such suffering? But how could I fight against my own people?

The weight of the choice pressed against my chest until I could barely breathe. If I helped Umbrathia, I would be betraying Sídhe. If I refused, I would be condemning these people to a slow, brutal end. There was no right answer—no path that didn't end in betrayal of someone or something.

"And you're certain that I am the answer to all of this?" It seemed unbelievable.

"I've never been more sure in my whole life."

"I'll do it," I said finally, my voice stronger than I felt. "I'll meet the Void." The words tasted like surrender and defiance all at once. I felt him hum in contemplation.

"We'll take you to see Urkin tomorrow. First thing," he finally said.

"Should I be scared?"

Aether didn't answer.

After a few moments, Tryggar pranced back up to us, a husk of dried bark hanging from his jaw, and we re-mounted, Aether helping lift me onto the Vördr's back. I was too drained to flinch as he slid into the saddle behind me.

We flew on in silence after that, the wasteland stretching out beneath us. I forced myself to keep looking, to absorb the full weight of what we were up against. I'd grown up hearing tales of glorious victories and noble sacrifices. But there was no glory here. Only ashes and shadows.

Tryggar let out another low sound, his wings tilting as they began to climb again, heading toward the horizon. I adjusted my grip, leaning into the movement, and for the first time since we'd taken flight, I felt a flicker of determination. The land below might be a graveyard, but perhaps it could be something again, one day.

"What's beyond this?" I asked, breaking the silence.

Aether's voice came quietly, almost as if he were speaking to himself.

"Whatever's left."

CHAPTER TEN

THE CITADEL PIERCED the mist like a blade of obsidian, its towers twisting impossibly high into the perpetual twilight. Where the outer city suffocated under masses of desperate people, these streets stood eerily empty, as if the very air had been carved away. Our footsteps echoed off black stone walls that seemed to absorb what little light remained.

Aether led me through a series of checkpoints, each guard more heavily armed than the last. Their eyes followed my every move, hands never leaving their weapons. Even Rethlyn's levity had vanished, replaced by a sharp alertness as he walked beside me.

The air grew colder as we approached the Citadel proper, and I could have sworn the shadows deepened, becoming almost liquid in their movement. A group of men in charcoal uniforms stood beyond the final gate, their red insignias gleaming like fresh blood against their sleeves. Something about their stillness set my teeth on edge.

"Valkan's men," Vexa muttered, "they shouldn't be here."

Aether's hand moved to his weapon, a subtle gesture that sent ripples of tension through our group. "Keep moving," he ordered, his voice low and sharp. "Don't look at them."

I slowed my pace, straining to hear their hushed conversation. Their voices carried an odd resonance, like multiple tones layered together.

"The Council actually agreed to negotiations?" Effie whispered, disbelief etched into every word. "After everything?"

"You haven't spoken to your parents?" Vexa asked, shooting a concerned glance at the men in gray. "Things are changing. Quickly."

"Having her here now..." Rethlyn trailed off as one of Valkan's men turned, milky eyes locking onto our group. He shifted closer to me, almost protective. "Especially after what Talon said—"

"Enough," Aether cut in, his shoulders tight. "We're exposed out here."

The Citadel's entrance loomed before us, a massive arch of polished stone that seemed to swallow all sound. Each step deeper into the structure sent chills down my spine. The corridors twisted at sharp angles, lined with torches that cast more shadows than light.

The others moved with familiarity through the labyrinth. Guards stood at attention at every intersection, their armor reflecting the red hues of the torches. Each one's eyes found me, lingering too long before sliding away.

We turned down a final corridor that ended at a heavy wooden door reinforced with black metal. Two guards flanked it, their hands resting on weapons that seemed to drink in what little light reached this deep into the Citadel.

"The General is ready for you," one said, his voice carrying an edge of warning as his gaze settled on me.

Aether stepped forward, his presence suddenly filling the narrow space. "Then we shouldn't keep him waiting."

The room beyond felt impossibly vast after the cramped corridors, circular walls stretching up into darkness. A massive table sat in the center, its surface etched with what seemed to be a map.

Rethlyn immediately claimed a spot against the wall while Vexa began a slow circuit of the room, her fingers trailing along the table's edge.

"Now we wait," she said, though the tension in her shoulders betrayed her casual tone.

My heart hammered against my ribs as I took in the maps, the careful notation of troop movements, supply lines, and something else—dark areas spreading across Umbrathia like a disease. The drought's progression, I realized.

"Perfect time to clarify something," I said, planting my feet firmly on the stone floor. "I agreed to meet the Void. I did not agree to fight against Sídhe. Not until we've considered every other option."

The silence that followed was heavy enough to crush stone.

"Oh, isn't that precious?" Effie pushed away from the wall. "The non-violent approach. While *our* people starve."

"I chose to meet your Void. I chose to hear you out," I kept my voice steady despite the rage building in my chest. "But I won't blindly agree to—"

"To what?" Aether cut in, shadows deepening beneath his eyes. "To save an entire realm? To stop the slaughter of innocent people?" He slammed his hand onto the map, right over a region marked with countless small crosses. "Each mark is a village, Fia. Dead or abandoned. Have you already forgotten what you saw out there?"

"Of course not," I snapped. "But there has to be another way. If I could just get back, talk to—" I caught myself before mentioning Laryk. "The right people."

"Right. Because they'll definitely listen to the shadow wielder." Effie's laugh was sharp as broken glass. "Face it, you're one of us now. Whether you like it or not."

"I'm nothing like you."

"Clearly." Her eyes darkened. "We actually fight for what we believe in. We don't hide in towers pretending the world isn't dying around us."

Vexa moved between us, but before she could speak, the temperature in the room plummeted. The shadows in the corners seemed to recoil as the door swung open with enough force to rattle the walls.

A man who must have been General Urkin filled the doorway. He was older than I'd expected, his dark gray hair pulled back severely from a face that seemed carved from the same stone as the Citadel. His uniform was pristine despite the perpetual twilight outside, decorated only with a series of small pins on his collar that caught the light.

The others snapped to attention. Even Effie's smirk vanished.

"General," Vexa said, inclining her head.

Urkin's dark eyes swept the room before settling on me with the weight of an avalanche. When he spoke, his voice was rough as stone on steel. "So this is the prisoner from Sídhe." He moved into the room like a predator, never taking his eyes off me. "The one you claim is a Duskbound." The word *prisoner* hit like a physical blow, but I forced myself to hold his gaze. Every instinct screamed to look away from those dark eyes.

"She is," Vexa said firmly, though I noticed how her fingers tightened around her weapon belt.

"Interesting." Urkin circled me with measured steps, each footfall echoing in the sudden silence. "And why exactly should I believe that? Why should I believe anything about her?" His voice dropped lower, taking on a dangerous edge.

"Sir—" Vexa began, but Urkin's hand shot up, cutting her off.

"Do you know what I see?" He stopped directly in front of me, close enough that I could see the anger burning in his eyes. "I see a spy. A potential threat. Someone who could very well be playing all of you for fools while her realm continues to drain ours dry." His lip curled.

"With all due respect, sir," Aether's voice cut through the tension, deadly calm. "If she were a spy, she's the worst one I've ever seen."

Urkin's attention snapped to where Aether stood in the shadows. "And you've all grown quite attached, haven't you?" His words dripped with contempt. "Taking her to the stables, showing her the city. Did you forget what she is? Where she comes from?" He turned back to me, eyes boring into mine. "Tell me, girl, how many of my soldiers have you killed?"

The question knocked the air from my lungs.

"I was fighting for what I believed in," I managed, my voice steadier than I felt. "Just like your soldiers."

"And now?" His eyes narrowed to slits. "What do you believe in now?"

"I believe there's more to this war than I was told." The words felt inadequate, but they were true. "I've seen what's happening to your realm. But I also believe there might be a way to stop it without more bloodshed."

Urkin's laugh was like steel scraping bone. "Naive. Completely naive." He turned to Aether, disgust evident in every line of his face. "This is what you've brought me? A girl with idealistic dreams of peace?"

"I've brought you a Duskbound," Aether said, stepping forward. His voice carried an edge I'd never heard before, and shadows seemed to pulse around him. "The first one born in over a century outside of the royal line."

"So you keep saying." Urkin moved to the table, his hands bracing against its surface hard enough to make the metal markers rattle. "You know how delicate things are right now. I don't have time for this. The Council has been swayed—"

"Who on the Council would agree to his terms?" Effie interrupted, genuine fear breaking through her carefully maintained facade. "I know my parents wouldn't."

"It's divided," Urkin said, shooting her a warning look that made her step back. "As things worsen, people become more... open to extreme solutions."

"The Queen would never allow it," Rethlyn said quietly. "Not if she was in her right mind."

Something passed between them then, a current of unspoken meaning that made the air feel thick enough to choke on. I looked between their faces, trying to piece together what I was missing.

"We have an alternative," Aether stepped closer, his golden eyes fixed on Urkin. "I can sense it in her. The shadows respond to her in a way I've never seen before."

"And you want to take her to the void? Now?" Urkin's voice dripped with skepticism. "With everything else happening?"

"Now is exactly when we need to do this."

"You're asking me to trust the word of a foreign spy—"

"I'm asking you to trust mine." Aether's words cut through the air like steel, carrying enough weight to make even Urkin pause. The two men stared at each other, some silent battle of wills playing out between them.

Finally, Urkin straightened, his face settling into something cold and calculating. "Fine. You want to prove she's a Duskbound? Then let her prove herself to the realm as well." He turned back to me, and the look in his eyes made my blood run cold. "You'll enter the Void during the Strykka."

"The trials?" Vexa's eyebrows shot up, genuine shock breaking through her composure. "But sir—"

"If she survives all three trials." Urkin's lips curved into something that wasn't quite a smile. "Then perhaps I'll believe you." His eyes locked with mine, filled with challenge and something darker. "That is, if you're willing to risk everything for a realm you claim to suddenly care about."

CHAPTER ELEVEN

"Well that went better than expected," Vexa drawled, her shoulders visibly relaxing as we walked.

"Did it?" My eyebrow peaked, genuine surprise coloring my tone.

"I mean, considering he didn't demand torture and execution, I'd say yes." She adjusted her leather vest with practiced nonchalance.

"I wasn't aware that was a possibility," I shot back, a tinge of relief pinching me, my hands unconsciously clutching at my sides.

"He's being cautious," Aether muttered, "it's understandable."

As we walked the streets, I began noticing familiar architecture. The weathered stone buildings rose around us. I looked to see my tower in the distance, slicing holes in the misty clouds, its dark silhouette a looming reminder of my confinement. A shudder ran through me, dreading the thought of spending the rest of the day locked away in those cold walls.

"Can I go to the stables for a bit?" I asked, hope tinging my voice.

"No can do, Duskbound. Think we would let you miss the best

food we've had in months?" Rethlyn jumped in, rubbing his hands together and licking his lips, practically bouncing with anticipation.

"We're taking a right here, Fia." Vexa motioned ahead, taking us down a different path that wound between two imposing structures.

"Best food?" I asked, regretfully skeptical about the truth in that, but I didn't dare voice it.

"Hot buns," Rethlyn said with a grin that stretched from ear to ear. "It takes forever to save enough ingredients for the kitchen staff to make them. They taste like the old days." His eyes glazed over with nostalgia.

"They're... certainly better than rice," Effie added. She had been so quiet, I nearly forgot she was trailing behind us, her footsteps barely making a sound.

"Don't try and deny it, Effie. I watched you shove three into your mouth last quarter when you thought no one was looking." Vexa let out a cackle that echoed off the stone walls.

Effie simply nudged her, making a clicking noise with her tongue, a slight blush creeping up her neck. "They're edible, I suppose. A girl needs her sustenance."

Aether looked to be in his own world, his eyes unfocused as he watched several Vördr glide through the mist on the horizon, their dark forms cutting clean lines through the haze. His brow furrowed in concentration, deep in thought, as his fingers thrummed along his weapon belt.

"Who were those men outside the Citadel? The ones in gray uniforms?" I asked casually. They seemed intent on shrouding their presence in secrecy, but there was no shame in simply inquiring.

Aether's jaw clenched, finally waking from whatever trance had taken hold of him.

"No one you want to concern yourself with. And now's not the time," he muttered, but the subtle shift in his demeanor was unmistakable. Now I was even more curious.

"Valkan—it's his men? Who is that?" I continued.

"Not. Now. Fia." He let out a hiss, eyes sweeping over our surroundings.

I decided to let it go, for now.

We approached a large stone building which seemed to be closer to the heart of the fortress. The dark walls blended into the surrounding battlements. Vexa stepped forward to pull on the heavy doors, their hinges groaning in protest, allowing us inside. I took in the vast hall and the iron chandeliers that cast a flickering light around the room, shadows dancing across the walls. Its vaulted ceiling was held aloft by towering pillars etched with insignias similar to those pressed into their leathers. Long wooden tables stretched in neat rows, worn smooth by years of people passing through, their surface scratched and dented.

At the far end, a massive hearth blazed, the scent of freshly baked bread filling the air and making my mouth water involuntarily. Kitchen workers stood behind a simple serving counter, their faces flushed from the heat as they handed out loaves straight from the fire. The noise of the room was a steady hum of conversation, punctuated by the scrape of chairs and occasional laughter.

"Go pick out a table, I'll grab us a tray." Rethlyn nearly got out before he bounded towards the opposite side of the room, weaving between tables.

I slid into the cool surface of a wooden chair, blatantly aware of the eyes that had fallen on me from across the room. I tucked a white wisp of hair behind the points of my ears. There was something peculiar about exploring more of the estate, witnessing where my former adversary performed mundane tasks like dining and mingling. These aspects had never crossed my mind previously, and it cast them in an unexpectedly relatable light that caught me somewhat off guard.

No one had mentioned the Strykka since we left Urkin's office, and it hung in the air around us. Lael would be entering the trials this year—the sixteen-year-old boy I'd seen training in the city. The one Aether had saved from Croyg. So it couldn't be that dangerous, could it? The thought provided little comfort.

I had agreed to enter the Void, but the Strykka, well, I knew nothing about it. The weight of my ignorance pressed against me.

Rethyln arrived with the tray loaded with steaming loaves, one already sticking out of his mouth. All hands dove towards the tower of rolls, and I waited until everyone seemed content before grabbing my own.

"Tell me about the Strykka," I said, aimed in Aether's direction for some reason I couldn't quite place. Vexa, of course, answered in his stead.

"There are three rounds—well, two if you're not selected for the Spectre Unit." Her words carried a hint of pride.

Spectre Unit? More vocabulary I wasn't aware of.

"The Spectre Unit—*Aether's unit*, includes all of us, the vessels." Vexa motioned around the table. "It's a part of the combat forces, under Urkin," she continued, leaning forward slightly. "The first trial is basic combat, hand to hand. I wouldn't worry so much about that, we're in desperate need of soldiers, so our expectations have definitely… leveled out." She pursed her lips, a shadow of concern crossing her features. "Then there's the tether observation. You will show the Council your, well, for the rest of us, we show our tethers… you'll display… whatever it is that you can do."

"Lovely," Effie echoed, observing her nails with exaggerated disinterest.

"Effie, it wasn't personal. I was panicking. Trying to get back to my home," I said, eyes drilling into her. As if that wasn't inherently obvious.

She simply sat back in her chair and crossed her arms, twisting a curl of raven hair through her fingers.

"She'll get over it. Eventually." Vexa's eyes wandered over to Effie in a way that seemed intimate, like I should look away. I could have sworn Effie brought her knee against Vexa's under the table, the two now sharing a quick smirk.

"What's the third trial?" I asked, breaking through the moment.

"If you succeed in the combat trial, and are deemed to have a powerful tether, you are then tested for the ability to join the Spectres. You are taken to the Void. Whoever emerges becomes a part of our unit." Vexa's tone carried a finality that made my skin prickle.

"So I'm essentially joining the Umbra?" I asked, sharper than intended. Irritation seized me, burning hot beneath my skin. This was not what I had agreed to. It was one thing to help with the Void. It kept me a neutral party, at least, that's how I had justified it to myself. This would be vastly different. I didn't know if I was ready to commit myself to another realm. I'd been lied to before. Something still pulled at me, wondering if that could be happening again.

I believed what they had shown me of this realm, but I still didn't know if I could trust the Umbra. The Isle had been so convincing. Perhaps I was just naive. Even if I wasn't, I wouldn't be joining a cause that could potentially hurt the people in Sídhe that I cared about. Not only were they clueless to what was going on, but some wouldn't even be able to defend themselves.

Did the Umbra even know how deep the lies went? Did they know the entire Isle was being deceived? Most had no idea a war was even brewing on the Western border. The ones that did had no idea what we were doing. That we were the villains in this story.

I wouldn't fight against those who were unaware. People needed to know what was really happening here. What the price of our prosperity truly was. The thought of more innocent blood on my hands made my stomach turn.

At this point, I wasn't sure whether that would even matter to the Umbra.

They were past the point of desperation. I couldn't say I wouldn't feel the same way if I were in their position. I hated Sídhe once, too.

Vexa's sigh splintered through my thoughts. "I know it wasn't what you were expecting." Her eyes lowered, looking past me. None of them were looking at me.

"No, no it wasn't." I shifted my gaze to Aether, who was still scanning his eyes over the arched window beyond. I had a distinct feeling that he wasn't listening to a word I said.

"You never mentioned this would be part of the deal," I shot in his direction, a sliver of ice in my tone.

His jaw clenched before he turned his head in my direction. For a few seconds, he simply observed me. Irritation pricked my skull.

"He doesn't trust you. This will show him you're serious. Duskbound are always intertwined with the Umbra, it's not really all that different from what we originally had in mind." His voice was gruff, no sign of that amusement that had drenched his tone only days ago.

"Not that different? I will be pledging myself to the *enemy* of my people. That actually means something to me," I hissed. Vexa and Effie simply looked away, but Aether's stare intensified.

"You've told me your position, and I did not argue with you. Remember that," he said in a near growl.

"Oh, I will."

"Nothing has changed. No one can force you to do anything you don't want. As I've made perfectly clear." Those golden eyes bore into me, something like annoyance twitching his upper lip.

Suddenly, I felt Vexa's gaze on me, then they turned to Aether. She raised a brow but stayed silent.

"I'm telling you right now, if I compete in the Strykka, I will still answer to *no one*. I will not be commanded."

"Not that you could," Aether spat.

A part of me wanted to take that jab as a compliment, but the darkness in his tone proved it wasn't meant to be.

"I want to be a part of negotiations. I might have ideas—information that could be useful. I will share whatever is necessary with all of you, but I will not be forced to fight against Sídhe. There has to be another way, one that doesn't end in mutual destruction."

"The masses don't even know a war is in full swing on the Western border. And the Guard—we've all been lied to. They don't know what they're doing. They deserve a choice. They deserve to know exactly what they're fighting for. If they still choose to support Sídhe, well…" I trailed off, not entirely sure what I meant by that. *If what was happening here didn't matter to them...* I didn't let the thoughts continue. I had to believe it would. That they would care.

Aether studied me, eyes finally leaving mine and raking down me. Somehow that made me even more uncomfortable than our locked eyes. I shifted in my seat.

"That will be between you and Urkin. We just have to get you through the Strykka first," Vexa cut in.

"I want assurance that I will have support from you all. That you agree to back my stance when it comes to negotiations. I need to know who and what I'm committing my life to. I need to know the political climate—and your ruler. I've already committed myself to one realm only to find out it was a lie. I won't do it again. I want to know everything. *Everything.* Agree to these terms and only then will I participate in the Strykka."

Effie snorted.

Vexa remained silent, eyes flickering to Aether.

Rethlyn bit his lip. "I don't know if we can agree to—"

"Deal." Aether's rough growl vibrated down the table, sending all eyes flaring towards him.

"Aether, I—" Vexa began.

"If that's the only way she'll be persuaded, then so be it," he murmured, standing from the table, his broad leathered frame seeming to absorb the light from the area.

"If that's the case... maybe we can bring her to the Conference?" Rethlyn suggested.

"Absolutely not. We cannot let his men become aware of her." Aether immediately shot it down.

"You just agreed to tell me everything and already you're leaving me out of important conversations and decisions," I snapped. "They may be under your command, but I am not. I'm going." My hand hit the table, still unsure what I was agreeing to go to.

"It's not the worst idea, Aether. We already know Fia doesn't always trust what she hears. She needs to *see*," Vexa urged. "If she wants to know how things work here—those who govern us, this would be the event."

"I do not see the benefit of Valkan finding out about her existence." Aether's words were tense.

"I don't know who Valkan is, but if you want me to enter the Strykka, then I will be involved in everything going forward. It's up to you Aether." It was nice having a bargaining chip.

"And we wouldn't go around introducing her as a Duskbound *obviously*." Vexa rolled her eyes.

Aether simply tensed his jaw but said nothing else.

Vexa rubbed her hands together. "Alright Effie, this is your wheelhouse. How can we get Fia into the Conference?"

Effie pursed her lips looking pleased at the acknowledgement but not so much that it involved me. "I suppose I'll figure something out."

CHAPTER TWELVE

MY HANDS MOVED THROUGH LINENS, the silver moonlight spilling through tall arched windows of a dressing chamber. Tapestries lined the stone walls, their threads catching the glow of scattered candles. At the far end of the room, two girls sat at a grand vanity—one in a black gown with an elaborate updo, the other in a robe, dark waves cascading down her back.

They were so similar, their hair, their bodies, even their mannerisms. Twins, maybe.

"Tell me everything," the one in the robe said, legs tucked beneath her as she perched on a cushioned stool. "Who embarrassed themselves tonight?"

A laugh drifted through the chamber as the other girl removed delicate pins from her hair, letting the dark strands tumble free. "Well, Lord Sveinson's son tried to impress Lady Vallgrym by showing off his sword techniques."

"No..."

"Yes. Knocked over an entire table of refreshments." More pins clattered against the vanity's marble surface. "The look on his father's face—I thought he might expire right there in the middle of the ballroom."

"Did Lady Vallgrym at least pretend to be impressed?"

"She didn't have to. She was too busy trying not to laugh into her wine glass. Though that didn't stop Lord Sveinson from attempting to salvage the situation by suggesting his son give her private lessons."

"He didn't!"

"Oh, but he did. You should have seen how red she turned." She began wiping rouge from her cheeks with a cloth. "Though not nearly as red as Lady Baldurson when she realized her daughter had been sneaking off to the gardens with young Lord Breidfjord."

"Finally! You said she's been making eyes at him for months."

"Yes, well, their mothers certainly didn't share your enthusiasm. I thought they might come to blows right there between the dessert courses."

"Over a kiss in the garden?"

"Over the scandal of it all. You know how they are about maintaining appearances." A yawn escaped her lips as she reached for her brush.

"And the Skaldvindr heir?" The girl in the robe's voice shifted to something softer. "Was he there?"

"Of course. Looking as dashing as ever." The brush paused mid-stroke. "Though he did ask about you."

"What did he say?"

"He wondered why you never attend anymore. I didn't know what to tell him."

"What could you say? That father won't—" She stopped as footsteps echoed down the corridor.

A man appeared in the doorway, his formal attire still pristine despite the late hour. "Are you ready?"

"Father, I'm exhausted," the girl at the vanity said, setting down her brush. "Surely we could skip practice tonight?"

"The darkness is ideal for honing your gifts." His tone left no room for argument. "Come."

She stood, smoothing her gown before taking his offered hand. As they turned to leave, his eyes fell on the other girl. Something dark passed *between them as she lowered her gaze to the floor. The silence that followed their departure seemed to echo through the chamber.*

"Watch your step, please. Those are couture," Effie said with a sigh, gesturing towards an open chest nearly blocking the entrance to her quarters.

I glanced down as I sidestepped the pile of glitter and silks. The room itself was simple. What you'd expect of a soldier's quarters. But it was far from empty. Stacks of trunks and ornate boxes filled nearly every available inch of the floor, their gilded edges clashing with the bleak surroundings. Every surface was covered in glittering brooches and the hair bobbles Effie was so fond of. Hints of colorful silks peeking out of overstuffed boxes. It was odd seeing so much color at once. I'd begun to believe they didn't live outside of the grayscale.

"I haven't had the need for my alterationist in so long." Effie looked me up and down before shaking away a thought. "Pity it's for you and not me."

We'd had alterationists back in Sídhe. Those who could change the appearance of others, painting their hair in different shades, drawing a natural rouge on someone's cheeks—all with their focus. I'd even heard of some who could morph features, blurring them until the person was completely unrecognizable.

Effie plopped down on her bed and sent me a narrowed look.

"I know you've convinced the others that you're not this wicked mastermind, but I'm still not sure about you." She turned up her nose in provocation.

"Don't worry, Aether is right outside." I smiled sweetly.

"Perfect. Would you like to pick out your own gown?" she said, eyes trailing down me, an apologetic look crossing her face. "Perhaps I should choose for you? You're quite tall." She stood, skipping over to the open trunk on the floor, and began throwing its contents all over the room—across her settee, tangled in heaps upon her bed.

The sight of it stirred something in me, and I turned to look away, feeling the mist forming in my eyes. Esprithe. I wasn't going to lose it now. Not in front of Effie.

But then Osta's face drifted into my mind—her beaming smile in Emeraal, sitting on the floor, digging through a chest so similar to the one Effie knelt before.

My heart sank, feeling the pain I'd successfully trapped somewhere unreachable now seeping out like cracks in a dam. Between my dream from last night and this, it seemed as though the universe itself was torturing me with reminders of her.

I sucked in a slow breath, trying to fight the quiver of the sound, hoping it was drowned out by Effie's chaotic hunting.

"What's your color?" she asked, excitement tinging her voice.

I nearly broke right there.

"I—I don't know. Black," I said, trying to keep my voice steady. Even as my back was turned, I could feel the shift in the room, the weight of her eyes on me. This was the last thing I wanted. For her to see me like this—for any of them to see me as weak.

"Are you... crying?" she said, a hint of confused amusement in her voice. "I mean, if you really want to pick it out yourself, you can... I fear it could be tragic, and I do have to be next to you all night... But I could do it, if—"

"It's not about the dress. I'm fine, just choose one," I repeated, wiping my eyes on the sleeve of my shirt.

Awkwardness crept in as a few silent moments slipped past, neither of us saying anything. I heard her gently rustling with the fabrics again, but not with the same vigor as before.

"Are you... okay?" she asked, her voice neutral, but strained. As if neutrality didn't come easy.

"Yes. I said I was fine."

"You don't seem fine. You know, I cry sometimes. I've heard it's a splendid way to reduce stress and balance emotions." She spoke as if she were trying to fill the silence, not quite sure whether to direct the conversation. "It's healthy, I've heard."

"Sure." It was the only word I could get out. Even her bubbliness despite the strain in our acquaintanceship was like her… Osta.

"Okay, well… we do need to start preparing for the evening. It takes an hour to get to Stravene. We don't really have time for… I mean, we should be of haste."

I turned back towards her and nodded, hoping my face wasn't nearly as sad as I felt, and wasn't nearly as red as the feeling gripping me.

"Oh, you were like—*really*—crying," she breathed, rushing over to the vanity and procuring a handkerchief. I took it from her without question, if only to have something to hide behind if I needed it.

"I—" the words were hard to say. "You just remind me of someone. From home." I looked down, a soft smile somehow breaking through the tense moment.

"Oh, well, in that case, I'm sure she's fabulous," Effie said with a flourish. Something about her nonchalant response had me feeling lighter, like I wouldn't fall completely into the depths today.

"Oh, she is," I agreed.

Effie smoothed her hands over her dress, seemingly unsure what to do with them. Then, as if struck by sudden inspiration, she brightened. "Well, since you've managed to ruin the moment with all this… *emotion*, I suppose I should tell you more about what to expect tonight." She waved her hand dismissively, but there was something almost kind in the gesture. "Can't have you completely ruining my family's reputation, after all."

"Your family?"

"The Eirfalks," she said, as if this should have been obvious. "One of the oldest noble houses in Umbrathia. Though I suppose you wouldn't know that, being..." She trailed off, wrinkling her nose. "Well, you know."

I blinked, trying to process this new information. "You're nobility?"

"Obviously." She rolled her eyes. "Why else would I have all these lovely things?" She gestured to the trunks surrounding us. "The Umbra certainly doesn't pay this well."

"But you're *in* the Umbra," I said, still trying to make sense of it.

"Oh, please. My parents practically pushed me into it." She began refolding the scattered gowns with unexpected precision. "I suppose they thought my tether was better served in combat than ballroom classes. As if I had any say in the matter." Her tone was light, but there was something beneath it—a hint of old resentment, perhaps.

"And your tether is...?" I asked.

"Teleportation." She smiled. "It made for quite the grand entrance. Before everything, at least."

"Ah," I breathed, suddenly remembering how she'd disappeared and then reappeared mere inches from my face back in the tower, all those weeks ago.

"It's not as strong as it was, of course." She sighed, annoyance creasing her brow. "Before, I could have taken us halfway across the continent."

Before I could respond, she shook her head, as if clearing away unwanted thoughts. "Now, about tonight. You'll be posing as my cousin Millicent—Millie. The Breidfjords haven't attended a conference since..." she paused, considering her words. "Well, let's just say they've fallen out of favor with certain members. Which makes Millie the perfect choice, really. No one will expect to see her, and few would dare question an Eirfalk's word."

"If you say so."

"So you'll be at my side for a majority of the evening. I can navigate any conversations that might arise. Don't try speaking to anyone on your own. I could only imagine how fast you'd blow your own cover." She sighed dramatically.

"I don't plan on speaking at all, lucky for you. Simply observing."

Three sharp knocks at the door made me jump. Effie practically skipped across the room, her earlier tension momentarily forgotten.

"Matilda!" she exclaimed, swinging the door open to reveal an older woman carrying a worn leather case. "Thank the Esprithe you're here."

"Miss Effie." The woman curtsied slightly, her eyes immediately finding me. "This is our... project for today?"

"Yes, yes. Come in." Effie ushered her inside, closing the door quickly. "We don't have much time."

Matilda set her case on Effie's desk, her movements soft. She gestured for me to sit in front of the mirror she'd brought and smiled in expectation.

"I've never seen hair this color." The alterationist hummed, her fingers gently lifting a curl up to examine.

"I've noticed it's... *uncommon*," I offered with a half smile.

"I'm sure you have." She smiled back at me in the mirror Effie had set up on her desk.

"This is Matilda, my family's alterationist." Effie smiled fondly, giving Matilda a quick hug. "Oh, how I've missed seeing you."

"The manor has been quiet without you Miss Effie." Matilda laughed. "Now tell me what I can help you with today?"

"We need you to make Fia look like Millicent. Do you remember my cousin Millie?"

Matilda pondered for a moment before nodding.

"As you know, I'm not as I once was Miss Effie. You're lucky I've had no use for my tether in so long. I've had time to gather essence." Matilda's hands were fluttering around me, brushing back my hair and tilting my chin towards the light. "I can't promise how long it will last either."

"So what do you suggest?"

"Well, it takes most of my tether's strength to alter facial features. It may be best if we just focus on changing her hair and use pigment and shadow to disguise the rest."

Effie nodded, squinting her eyes to see the vision Matilda had painted. "It has been years since Millie has joined any of the conferences. I doubt anyone would be looking too close anyways. My uncle is not particularly popular with the Council right now."

"May I ask what this is? Is this some kind of ball?" I couldn't imagine they would be hosting a ball. There was nothing I could imagine they would be celebrating.

"No. Not a ball. We haven't had one of those in years." Effie sighed wistfully. "This is more of a fancy political meeting. All the biggest contenders—those with power, will be in attendance."

Matilda's fingers moved through my hair and suddenly I felt it —a strange tingling sensation that started at my scalp and traveled down each strand. It wasn't uncomfortable, but it was foreign, like tiny threads of electricity dancing across my skin. The air around us seemed to thicken with essence, making it harder to breathe. In the mirror, I watched as darkness began to seep into my white locks, spreading like ink through water, transforming each strand from root to tip. Effie hovered nearby, eyeing the transformation with a critical gaze.

"You know, I never imagined I'd be the one playing dress-up with you," she mused, a hint of amusement in her tone. "Usually it's me getting made up."

I shot her a sidelong glance in the mirror. "Careful, Effie. You're verging on compliments."

She rolled her eyes dramatically. "Don't get ahead of yourself. This is strictly a necessity, not some grand bonding exercise."

"The color is taking well, Miss Effie," Matilda murmured, her focus never wavering from her work.

"Good." Effie nodded, then turned back to me. "Which means you need to be on your absolute best behavior. No mind games, no attempts at escape. You're Millie tonight, understand?"

"I already told you I'm only here to observe."

"Yes, well, forgive me if I don't entirely trust your word on that," she huffed. "Just... try to blend in, would you?"

Matilda's fingers gave a final tug, and the last white portion slowly darkened, becoming a rich, inky black. "There, miss. All finished."

I ran my own fingers through the transformed tresses, marveling at how the simple change made me look almost unrecognizable. "It's... different."

Effie leaned in, her critical gaze sweeping over the results. "Hmm, not bad. Though you'll still need some cosmetic touches to fully match Millie." She reached for a small compact, deftly sweeping a hint of color across my cheeks. "There, that's better. Now, let's see about finding you a gown."

She began rummaging through the ornate trunks once more, tossing aside silks and velvets with practiced disregard. "You know," she said, her voice muffled as she dug deeper, "if you actually manage to pull this off, I might have to reconsider my opinion of you."

"Don't worry, I won't hold my breath."

As I slipped into the rich fabric, I couldn't help but glance back at the mirror. The person staring back was a stranger—dark hair, flushed cheeks, the weight of nobility draped across her shoulders. But what struck me hardest was how natural it looked, how easily I could pass for one of them. One of the Kalfar. The shadows around my eyes, my pale skin, the sharp angles of my face—everything I'd tried to hide or deny about myself suddenly seemed to make perfect sense. Something in my gut twisted, a mixture of recognition and revolt. Only my eyes remained unchanged, gleaming like opals.

"Should we change my eye color?" I asked hesitantly, "They're a bit distracting I've heard."

"That would be nice, but it's impossible. I used to ask Matilda to do it all the time," she sighed.

"Why would you want to change your eyes—they're blue."

"Cerulean," Effie corrected. "They're cerulean."

"I'm afraid eyes cannot be changed. Even the strongest alterationist cannot transform their appearance," Matilda said, still gathering her belongings. "It's the one thing that stays true—always."

I shifted in my dress, pulling at the ruffles. I guess I'd need to avoid eye contact for the entirety of the evening.

"Stop fidgeting," Effie chided, adjusting the fall of the fabric. "A lady never shows discomfort."

"Is that one of the pinnacles of being a lady?" I snorted.

"Among other things." She stepped back to assess the final result. "Well," she said, "I suppose you'll do."

Aether was waiting at the base of the lodging towers, and for a moment, I almost didn't recognize him. Gone were the intimidating leathers I'd grown accustomed to during my imprisonment. Instead, he wore what I assumed to be his Umbra uniform—black pants that barely contained his thighs, and a fitted black suit-jacket that emphasized the breadth of his shoulders. I'd never seen him like this, and something about it made him seem more real, more present than the shadowy figure who had haunted my tower. The sight wasn't terrible—which only made it worse. I remembered how his shadows had felt against my skin just days ago. I pushed the thought away.

Vexa stood beside him, dressed in similar fashion. She was twisting a dagger through her fingers when she noticed Effie's approach and bounded over to us. "Well aren't you a vision." She murmured in a low tone before sliding her arm around Effie's waist and pulling her in for a kiss.

Oh.

"You clean up well, Duskbound," she said, finally acknowledging my presence. "Nice hair."

"Well, that credit goes to me." Effie stepped forward, a satisfied smile gracing her lips. "Or, Matilda, rather."

Aether turned towards us, his eyes raking over me. Suddenly I felt awkward.

He walked over, paying close attention to my hair. Something strange crossed over his eyes, and he shrugged.

"Wait up!" Rethlyn called from behind us, falling into a sprint. He appeared disheveled, his dress shirt only half-tucked into his trousers.

"She'll ride with me on Nihr." Aether started towards the stables.

"Why can't I ride Tryggar?" I asked, catching up with him. But before I slowed down, he turned and I nearly slammed into him. He looked down at me with a questionable expression.

"Seriously?" It was all he said, eyes lingering on me for another beat before he turned back around.

Once we arrived at the stables, his whistle nearly knocked me over. And soon enough, the giant beast appeared above us, wings slamming against the wind, sending my midnight locks flying.

Nihr found a clearing on the ground, her black wings showing off the specks of silver that dotted them.

I began walking towards the mounting platform.

"Where are you going?" Aether called from behind me. Vexa and Effie skipped past me, arms interlocked as they called Draug over.

I turned to see Aether waiting, impatience splayed across his face.

"What?"

"Come here," he said, a hint of exasperation in his tone.

I trudged back over to him, trying not to look like a petulant child as he lifted me up. His hands were firm against my waist, the touch brief but burning even through the layers of fabric. As he placed me on Nihr's back, I caught a whiff of him—rain and ash, like a storm about to break.

The saddle was warm beneath me, and I had just enough time to adjust my skirts before I felt him mount behind me. His body was rigid, carefully maintaining a sliver of space between us, but it didn't matter. I could feel the heat radiating off him, could sense every slight movement as Nihr shifted beneath us. The formal jacket did little to disguise the strength coiled in his frame, and I found myself sitting unnaturally straight, trying to minimize any point of contact.

"Relax," he muttered, his breath stirring the hair near my ear. "You look like you're being led to execution."

"Aren't I?" I shot back, but my voice wasn't as steady as I'd have liked.

He made a sound that might have been a laugh—or might have been a warning—and Nihr spread her wings, preparing for flight. As we took to the air, the wind whipped my newly darkened hair back, and I felt rather than saw Aether lean away slightly. When he spoke again, his voice was almost too low to hear over the beating of Nihr's wings.

"It's better the other way."

I wasn't sure if he meant my hair, my posture, or something else entirely. I didn't ask.

CHAPTER THIRTEEN

A GRAND HALL opened before us, a cavernous space dominated by sweeping archways and massive iron chandeliers. Black candles dripped steadily onto the stone floor below, their flames dancing in drafts that seemed to come from nowhere. The effect was unsettling. Like the room itself was breathing.

Nobles gathered in clusters, their voices a low hum of quiet conversation. Despite their fine clothing and rigid postures, there was something predatory in the way they watched each other, in how their eyes darted between one another.

"Your parents are here?" I muttered back.

"Later," she hissed, pulling me along with the crowd. "Just remember to keep your head down and your mouth shut."

We followed the stream of nobles into what appeared to be some kind of chamber. Tiered seating surrounded a central floor, giving the space the feeling of an arena. The ceiling stretched up into darkness, lost beyond the reach of candlelight.

Aether and Vexa had disappeared into the crowd, but I could feel their presence somewhere in the shadows. Rethlyn positioned himself near one of the exits.

"The Conference is now in session," a hooded figure announced.

"Where is the Queen?" I whispered.

Effie hesitated briefly. "She doesn't attend anymore."

General Urkin stood first, his medals glinting in the candlelight. "Before we address new matters, we'll hear from General Taliora of the Medic's Unit."

A woman with sharp features and practical military dress rose. Despite her rigid posture, exhaustion lined her face. "The drought has reached the mid-Western townships. Our medics can barely maintain enough essence to treat the most critical cases. We've lost three more villages this month alone."

"Lost how?" interrupted a woman. "To starvation or to Draxon's *hospitality?*"

"Who are all these people?" I whispered to Effie.

"That's Lady Baldurson," Effie responded in a low tone, gesturing towards the woman speaking. The name sounded familiar. Is that what one of the girls had mentioned in my dream?

Murmurs rippled through the crowd. Several Council members exchanged dark looks.

Effie leaned closer, her eyes darting to an elderly man who'd just stood up. "That's Lord Sveinson—terribly traditional family, absolutely despises anything that threatens the old ways."

"My people are dying *now*," the man declared, his face reddening. "The grain shipments barely feed a quarter of—"

A woman with calculating eyes cut him off. "Perhaps if you hadn't been so quick to sever trade relations—"

"Lady Vallgrym," Effie supplied under her breath.

Yes. These were the same names from my dream. Anxiety coiled in me as I watched on.

"You dare suggest we trade with those who—" Lord Sveinson's anger seemed to fill the chamber.

"Enough!" Urkin's voice boomed through the space. "We cannot afford to be divided. Not now. Not with our enemy growing stronger by the day."

The mention of my realm sent another wave of whispers through the crowd. I felt Effie shift uncomfortably beside me.

A man with dark eyes that seemed to absorb the candlelight stood next. "Our scouts report increased activity near the rip. Their towers draw more essence each day, while we grow weaker. The Umbra's current strategy clearly isn't working."

"Lord Skaldvindr," Effie breathed, a hint of disgust in her tone. "He's the head of the most influential noble family. A majority of the families will vote as he does."

Skaldvindr... Another name I recognized. I wondered, for a brief moment, if I should tell her—or Vexa— about the dream from the night before. I still had no idea of its importance. Who the two girls even were. But now I knew, beyond a shadow of a doubt, that it had happened here. In Umbrathia. But when? Was it a memory, or something happening now? Was it the same two girls from my first dream?

But I didn't want to tell the Umbra about that ability yet. Because even an innocent conversation about the dreams would lead to revealing things I wasn't ready to. I wanted to trust them, but I still wasn't sure if I could. And I didn't want to give them any information that could turn me into an even bigger asset to them. Information they could use against Sídhe.

That's when the side doors opened. The effect was immediate —like all the air had been sucked from the chamber. A man entered, moving with fluid grace, his fine clothing a stark contrast to the darkened robes of the Council. Despite the realm's suffering, he looked vibrant, life and color flooding his skin in a way that seemed almost obscene among the muted pallor of the crowd. But his eyes... his eyes were wrong. Milky and faded, like clouds had settled over them, yet they missed nothing as they swept the chamber. His glossy black hair was cropped short, emphasizing the sharp angles of his face—his beauty stark and mesmerizing.

"Valkan," Effie whispered.

"My friends," Valkan began, his voice smooth as silk. "How long will we continue to debate while our realm dies around us?"

A murmur rippled through the crowd. I noticed several Council members shift uncomfortably in their seats. Urkin's jaw tightened, but he remained silent.

"The essence-drought spreads." Valkan's voice dropped lower, more intimate, as if he were speaking to each person individually. "Our children grow weaker. Our tethers fade. And yet we sit here, bound by antiquated views, while Draxon's fields still produce." His gaze settled briefly on our section, and I felt Effie stiffen beside me.

I thought back to the whispered conversations I'd overheard in the tower, the way Aether and the others had tensed at any mention of Valkan's name. The nobles spoke of trade with Draxon as if it were something unthinkable, yet their lands remained fertile while the rest of the realm withered. What could be so terrible about this man that they'd rather watch their people starve than accept his help?

"My Lord," a woman's voice cut through the tension. An elderly Council member stood, her silver hair gleaming in the candlelight. "Your terms are—"

"My terms ensure survival." The words carried a hint of sharpness beneath their silken surface. "Allow my men to serve in the Umbra forces. Let them enter the Strykka, prove their worth to the realm... to the Void. And we will re-open trade routes to Draxon."

"The Void is sacred," someone called out. "To allow them to—"

"Sacred?" Valkan's composure cracked for just a moment, revealing something darker underneath. The candles flickered violently, their shadows writhing on the walls. "What good are our sacred traditions if we're all dead? Sídhe grows stronger while we cling to old ways. They must be brought to their knees, and my men know how to do it."

A chill ran across my skin, my web nearly pulsing in the depths of my spine.

"These negotiations cannot be rushed," Urkin's voice cut through the growing chaos. "The Council needs time to—"

"Time?" Valkan laughed, the sound sharp as breaking glass. "Look around you, General. Time is the one luxury we no longer possess."

He gestured to his men in gray, and they moved forward as one, their movements too smooth to be natural. There was something wrong about them—something that made my skin crawl.

I leaned closer to Effie, keeping my voice barely above a breath. "What's wrong with them? His men—they're not..."

"Don't," Effie whispered sharply, "we will discuss after."

The implication hit me like a physical blow. These weren't just soldiers. They were something else. Something that made even the Umbra seem tame in comparison. And Valkan wanted them in the military, wanted them to enter the Void...

"The Council will deliberate," Urkin announced, but his voice wavered. "Until then—"

"Until then," Valkan cut in smoothly, "remember that Draxon's bounty could feed your starving people. Remember that my men could end this war. Remember that pride is a luxury the dying cannot afford. And to solidify that memory, enjoy the feast. Courtesy of Draxon's harvest."

As he turned to leave, his pale eyes swept the chamber once more, and this time, I was certain they lingered on me.

Bodies began to shift throughout the space, whispers and murmurs echoing through the chamber. The Kalfar filed out in waves, their dark forms blending together in the dim light.

"What's going on, Effie? What is he talking about?" I whispered, trying to mask the dread coiling in my stomach.

"Not here." Her voice was tight. "We need to find the others."

We joined the crowd flowing into the great hall. Ahead, Aether and Vexa stood near a massive fireplace, its flames casting dancing shadows across the stone walls. Something in Aether's posture made me pause—his jaw clenched, shoulders rigid, those golden eyes burning with an intensity I hadn't seen before. His gaze caught mine briefly before shifting to Effie. They exchanged a subtle nod.

Vexa turned down a corridor that branched away from the main hall, opposite from where the crowd was heading. The temperature dropped as we followed, our footsteps echoing off the cold stone.

"Can someone please explain to me—"

Aether's voice cut through the air. "Wait until we're alone."

"I had no idea the support had shifted so much since our last Conference," Vexa breathed, running a hand through her hair. "And now he's trying to buy everyone's loyalty with a feast, of all things. Deplorable."

"So... are we going to join the fea—"

"Effie. Really?" The edge in Vexa's voice could have cut glass.

"I mean, it's already here." Effie shrugged, her affected manner returning as she glanced over her shoulder toward the distant sound of voices. "Seems cruel to let it go to waste."

"She's seen enough." Aether's eyes fixed on some distant point, his voice low. "It's time to leave."

"It's more suspicious if we leave," Effie countered. "Urkin will wonder..."

"Let him."

"Who is he? Who is Valkan?" The words burst from me before I could stop them. "Answers. Now."

"He's the Lord of Draxon." Vexa pulled us deeper into the

corridor where it curved left, out of sight. "It's the city farthest from the rip. On the Southwestern edge of Umbrathia."

Bile rose in my throat. "You know what I'm asking. Why does he have fertile land while everyone else starves? Why does the Council look at him like he's some kind of monster? What aren't you telling me?"

"A difference of opinion when it comes to navigating war," Effie said quietly, all playfulness gone from her voice.

"I don't understand. You're all so desperate to stop Sídhe. What about him is so repulsive that you draw the line there? What am I missing?" The words came out in a hiss. They were doing it again—giving answers that only led to more questions.

Vexa's eyes darted to Aether, who stood like a statue, before turning back to me. When she spoke, her voice trembled with barely contained rage. "What he—what his people do to sustain life is... blasphemous. Outlawed across the entire realm. A disgusting rite that goes against everything we are as Kalfar. The defilement of essence is the biggest heresy one can commit, yet he's raised a sizable army of them."

"Of what?"

"Damphyre." The word fell from Aether's lips like a curse.

"They no longer require food," Vexa continued, her voice dropping lower. "They take their sustenance straight from the blood of others. They consume the essence of other Kalfar."

Horror crawled up my spine. "You mean they feed on people?"

Their silence was answer enough.

"But—I don't understand—how is that sustainable?"

Vexa drew a shaky breath. "They provide their... volunteers with a life of near luxury. You'd be surprised what people subject themselves to when everything is taken from them. Since the Damphyre have no use for food, there's more to go around for the Kalfar they drain from."

"So what does that do to their tethers?" I steadied myself against the wall, suddenly dizzy.

"It strengthens them. Makes them more powerful than before the drought."

The pit in my stomach grew deeper.

"And they want to join the Umbra..." The realization hit me like a physical blow. "To join the fight against Sídhe..."

"Plenty of bodies brimming with essence, and no restrictions on how many they can kill." Vexa's voice was bitter. "The void burns are just an added bonus. It makes Valkan look better when he tries to usurp the crown."

My body went still. *This is why they wanted me. This is why they were so desperate. I was the alternative to—*

"What do we have here?" The voice drifted down the corridor like silk. Valkan stood against the wall, watching us with those unsettling milky eyes, his perfect features arranged in an expression of curiosity.

Effie's sharp intake of breath made me look down. The black was fading from my hair, retreating like smoke being pulled into the air. White locks began to appear.

"Valkan." Aether's voice had dropped to something terrifying. He moved in front of me, his form suddenly seeming larger, more dangerous. "You have no business here. Leave."

Valkan's lips curled into something that wasn't quite a smile. "I'm simply curious about your new friend, Aether. Don't be rude —it's unbecoming of you."

He took a step forward, those dead eyes fixed on me with horrible interest. Aether moved with him, maintaining the barrier between us. "Perhaps I wasn't clear enough," he growled. "Leave, before I make you."

"No need for hostility." Valkan raised his hands in mock surrender, but his voice held something darker. "It's a dinner party, after all. Where are your manners?"

In a blur of movement, Valkan was against the wall, his feet dangling as if held by an invisible hand at his throat. But that terrible amusement never left his face. Aether stepped closer, tilting his head, arms folded carefully behind his back. "I guess we'll do this the hard way then."

"Oddly protective, Aether. Who is she to you?" Those dead eyes found me again. "You're lucky I'm in my best suit. Otherwise, I might have to retaliate against this vicious, unwarranted attack. How would your Urkin explain that one?" His smile widened, showing too many teeth.

"Vexa. Get her out of here. Effie, find Rethlyn and do the same."

"But Aether—"

"I won't repeat myself." The shadows around him seemed to writhe.

Vexa's hand closed around my arm like a vise, pulling me down the corridor. I could feel her pulse hammering where our skin met, matching the frantic rhythm of my own heart.

"Until next time, dear." Valkan's voice followed us as Vexa shoved through a heavy door into the gray air. We ran across the field where the Vördr waited, the sound of our boots on frozen grass nearly drowning out the thunder of my pulse.

Nearly.

CHAPTER FOURTEEN

The metallic tang of blood filled my mouth as my cheek slammed against the cold training mat. The impact rattled through my skull, vision blurring at the edges. The vast stone room spun for a moment before settling back into focus.

Aether had thrown me. Again.

I sucked in a sharp breath and pushed up onto my hands; the ache spreading through my arms as I glared at him. Last night's revelations churned in my gut. This wasn't about choosing sides anymore. This was about stopping something far worse than anything I'd imagined. If Valkan gained enough power, if his army of Damphyre grew strong enough to take control... both realms would suffer. The thought of those milky eyes turning towards Sídhe, towards civilians who didn't even know a war was coming, made my blood run cold.

And I was undoubtedly out of shape.

Aether stood above me, infuriatingly calm, with barely a drop of sweat on his brow. The dulled light filtering through the high windows caught on his piercings, making them gleam like tiny daggers.

"You're slow," he said, his voice low and even, like he wasn't just taunting me but delivering a fact. His shadow stretched across the mat between us.

I growled under my breath, shoving myself upright. "I'm not done."

"Good," he replied, his golden eyes sharp and assessing. He kept his hands folded behind his back, motioning for me to come at him with a nod. "Try again."

I didn't waste time. Lunging forward, I aimed a punch straight for his ribs, putting all my weight behind it. But Aether shifted, just slightly, and my fist grazed air. The momentum carried me forward, leaving me exposed. Before I could recover, he caught my wrist, twisting it sharply enough to send a jolt of pain up my arm. His foot hooked around my ankle, and suddenly, I was on the mat again, my back slamming into the ground this time.

I gasped, the breath knocked from my lungs. Fury burned in my chest as I rolled away, narrowly avoiding the follow-up strike he could have delivered but didn't. The smell of sweat and leather filled my nose, mingling with the metallic taste that still lingered in my mouth.

That had been my favorite move. The one Laryk had taught me, back when I thought I knew who the real monsters were. Now I wasn't so sure. The Umbra might be ruthless, but at least they didn't feed on their own people. At least they were trying to protect something beyond themselves.

"Sloppy," he muttered. Each word felt like another weight pressing down on me, reminding me how weak I'd become through the weeks of solitude.

I shot to my feet, ignoring the ache in my ribs. "Say that again," I spat, my fists tightening.

He tilted his head, a faint smirk tugging at the corner of his mouth. "Sloppy," he repeated, slow and deliberate.

This time, I didn't think. I lunged, feinting a punch before pivoting into a low kick. My shin connected with his calf, and he staggered—just for a moment—but it was enough to reignite my confidence.

I pressed the advantage, surging forward and locking his arm in a grapple. For half a second, I thought I had him. But then Aether shifted, his strength surging against mine.

In one fluid motion, he flipped me again. The mat rushed up to meet me, my shoulder hitting first this time. Pain flared, and I bit back a curse as he pinned me, one knee pressed firmly into my side and his forearm lightly braced against my throat.

"Better," he said, his voice calm, almost bored. "But not good enough."

I glared up at him, my chest heaving with frustration and exhaustion. "Get off me," I growled.

He arched a brow, the faintest glint of amusement in his eyes. "Not until you learn."

"I had months of training. It's not about learning, it's about regaining my strength."

His look dripped with skepticism.

I twisted under him, trying to break his hold, but he didn't budge. My muscles burned, and the sting of failure gnawed at me. The weight of him, the heat radiating from his body, made it hard to think clearly. The torchlight caught his eyes, turning them to liquid gold, and for a moment, I forgot to struggle.

"Again," I demanded hoarsely, blinking the thought away as sense managed to find its way back into my mind.

Aether leaned back, releasing me without protest. He stood and offered a hand, his expression unreadable in the shifting light from above.

I slapped it away, climbing to my feet on my own. My body screamed in protest, but I ignored it, resetting my stance. The silence of the training room pressed in around us, broken only by our breathing.

"Where was the Queen last night?" I asked, the question that had been nagging at me finally breaking free. "Shouldn't she have been at the conference?"

Aether's expression hardened, but he didn't answer immediately. Instead, he motioned for me to attack again. The shadows beneath his eyes seemed to deepen.

I stayed where I was. "The way everyone talked around her absence... is she ill?" The Council's careful avoidance of mentioning their ruler hadn't escaped my notice.

"The Queen's condition," Aether said, his voice low enough that I almost missed it. "It's... complicated. And if Valkan knew the full extent of it..." He trailed off, but his meaning was clear.

"What is her condition?"

Aether's eyes raked over me with irritation.

"I said I want to know everything," I reminded him with an arched brow.

"Her mind fragments more each day," he said, voice tight with something like grief. "She can't bear to be near others anymore—their energy, it overwhelms her. She becomes... unstable. The Council knows she's unwell, but they don't understand how far gone she truly is. And they can't. Not until—"

"Until you have a new Duskbound?"

The look in his eyes told me everything I needed to know.

"Come on," I said, shaking the thought from my mind. If I was going to be of any use to anyone—Duskbound or not—I had to get my performance back.

His lips quirked, not quite a smile, but close enough to make my blood boil. "Whenever you're ready."

My fists were up before Aether even finished his sentence, and I charged, determination burning through the exhaustion weighing down my limbs. I lunged for a left jab, then swung a right hook aimed squarely at his jaw.

He didn't flinch.

Aether ducked effortlessly, stepping into my space like it belonged to him. His hand shot out, gripping my shoulder like a steel vice, and before I could react, he twisted. My feet left the mat, and in an instant, I was on my back, the impact jolting through my spine.

I gasped for air, my chest heaving as I rolled to the side, scrambling to my knees.

"I thought you said you were good at sparring?" Aether said, his tone as unbothered as ever.

I glared up at him, brushing hair from my sweat-soaked face. "I just need more time."

"You don't have time," he said, motioning for me to get back on my feet. The words hit differently now. Time. It's what Valkan had weaponized at the conference, using the realm's suffering to push his agenda. How long before desperation tipped the scales? How many more would choose his hospitality over starvation? Rage burned through me. Time. And we had wasted so much of it.

"You want to talk about time? If you hadn't kept me locked away for six weeks trying to break me maybe we wouldn't be in this situation," I huffed, forcing myself upright. My arms felt like lead, and every muscle in my body screamed in protest.

"Well it worked didn't it?" Aether replied bluntly, crossing his arms. His golden eyes locked on mine, calm but unyielding. "You didn't have to let your body become so weak."

Something snapped inside me.

Fuck this.

I launched myself at him, throwing my entire body weight into his chest, my arms curling around his neck like a vice. The impact knocked him backwards, surprise flashing across his face as we crashed to the floor. The wooden boards creaked beneath us as we rolled, my elbow catching his ribs as he tried to gain control. A chair toppled over as we tumbled off the mat, my knee nearly connecting with his jaw before he managed to grab my leg.

In a single move, he flipped us over, using his full weight to slam me onto my back. His thighs straddled my hips as he caught both my wrists in one hand, pinning them above my head. His other hand gripped my waist, fingers digging into my flesh as he held me down. Every inch of him pressed against me, hard muscle and slick leather.

"Now that's more like it," he said, a dangerous smile playing at his lips.

"Get. Off. Me." I snarled, trying to buck my hips against his, but the movement only made him press down harder.

"Not until you stop acting like a child." His face was inches from mine, jaw tight with irritation. I could feel every breath he took, mocking how helpless I was beneath him.

"I'd rather act like a child than an arrogant, piece of shi—"

"Careful, princess." His grip tightened on my wrists. "You're in no position to be throwing insults around."

Heat flooded my face—from rage, I told myself, absolute fucking rage. But my skin blazed everywhere he touched me. The proximity was infuriating. I wanted to scream, to keep fighting, but my body had turned traitor, limp and breathless and entirely too warm.

A beat passed between the two of us, locked in this maddening position.

"Are you quite finished?" I lifted an eyebrow, refusing to show how affected I was.

Something in his eyes shifted as they dropped to my lips. "No," he said softly, "We still need to work on your tether observation."

Then he released me, rolling to the side and climbing to his feet in one fluid motion. He extended his hand to help me up, but I scoffed, scrambling up on my own, trying to ignore how my legs trembled slightly. My heart was still racing, though whether from the fight or something else, I refused to analyze.

"You haven't used it in a while," he said, running a hand through his tousled hair. "You need to practice."

I looked around, gesturing obviously towards the empty training room. "On what exactly? The architecture?"

"On me."

The word hit me like a slap to the face. "It doesn't work on you."

"No," he said, "I don't let it work on me. There's a difference."

My stomach dropped. He'd let me believe I was powerless against him.

"You're telling me all those times you blocked me out..."

"Were a choice, yes." The satisfaction in his voice made me want to throw something at him. Or at his mind. Both seemed equally appealing right now.

"Anything else you've been allowing me to believe?"

"Many things." His expression remained neutral, but something flickered in those golden eyes that made my pulse quicken.

He moved toward the seating area beyond the mats. I watched him walk, trying to reconcile this version of him—the one willing to let me into his mind—with the man who'd kept me locked in that tower, with the one who'd just slammed me to the ground. "What exactly is the range of your ability?" he asked.

The question stirred something I'd been avoiding, so I decided to ask one of my own. "You said you could see it. My web."

He paused, raising an eyebrow. "I see energy flow out of you, white and pearlescent. Like wisps and tendrils snaking through the air." His eyes tracked something invisible near my shoulder, and I suppressed a shiver. The idea that he'd been watching my power all this time, seeing it exactly as I did, felt strangely intimate. "At first, I thought everyone could see it."

"So, any other hidden talents you're not sharing?" I crossed my arms, using sarcasm to mask how unsettled I felt by his admission.

"Or do I have to serve another round of isolation for those revelations too?"

"You'll need to get over that soon." His eyes studied me with an unnerving focus. "Anger doesn't exactly suit you."

"I'm not angry." The lie tasted bitter. "I just find it interesting how selective you are with information."

"Says the woman clearly holding something back right now."

I opened my mouth to protest, but his raised eyebrow stopped me. The dreams pressed against my mind—memories of seeing through others' eyes, of watching Laryk through Mercer's. The thought of telling Aether made my stomach twist. He already had too much power over me. And something that could spy on either side of this war... I couldn't risk it falling into the wrong hands.

"Well," I said instead, "My abilities first manifested as something far more chaotic, and admittedly, horrifying. My friends back home call me mind-shredder."

His brow peaked at that. "Should I be concerned?"

"Probably." I smiled sweetly, enjoying the rare moment of having him off-balance. "It was described to me as grappling a mind so hard that it breaks."

"Charming." But I caught the ghost of amusement in his eyes. "Perhaps we save that demonstration for another day."

"Afraid?"

"Cautious." He leaned back, and I tried not to notice how the shadows played across his face. "Taking a mind is one thing. Breaking one..." He studied me with a new interest that made my skin prickle. "How does it work?"

I shifted under his gaze. "To take it? Simple really. My web latches onto the right area, like a key turning in a lock. Then I can send commands down the bond."

The shadows in the room deepened, and I couldn't tell if it was him or my imagination. "Show me."

"You're sure?" My heart thundered against my ribs. "No blocking me this time?"

"Unless you give me reason to." That dangerous edge crept back into his voice.

I took a deep breath, summoning the web. It braided up my spine with that familiar spark, spilling out from my skull into the air around us. His eyes definitely tracked its movement now, and the air between us grew electric as the tendrils moved towards him. But he didn't look afraid, he looked as he always did. That unreadable calm etched into his features.

I surrounded his mind gently, not making contact yet. The memory of his previous rejections made me wince—each one had felt like taking a hammer to the skull. But there was no resistance this time as I latched onto that golden orb. His mind felt different from any I'd encountered—brighter, more intense, like stepping into direct sunlight.

His eyes remained locked on mine, fully aware, chest rising and falling deeply. I tried to ignore how intimate this felt, having him let me in like this.

But I didn't hesitate.

Aether's palm cracked across his own face.

He blinked, then blinked again as I released him. A laugh bubbled up my throat before I could stop it. The sight of Aether slapping himself was something I'd treasure forever.

"Feeling better?" He rubbed his jaw, but I caught that slight curl of his lips. My chest felt lighter than it had in weeks.

"Much." I couldn't help my grin. "Though I'm sure you allowed that too."

"Don't get cocky. It's still the only hit you'll ever land."

"We'll see about that." The words slipped out with more challenge than I'd intended.

His expression sobered, but something sparked in his eyes.

"When you do that, do you enter the mind fully, or access it from the outside?"

The question doused my momentary triumph. "Are you asking if I can read thoughts?"

"Obviously."

"Not that I know of." I shifted, Laryk's dream flashing through my mind again. In that one, I did seem to have access to his thoughts, but none of it was intentional.

"Have you tried?"

"That would be quite an invasion of privacy," I murmured.

"Says the woman who just made me slap myself."

"Different kind of invasion." I cocked my head to the side, meeting his stare. "Why, offering to be my test subject?"

He shrugged. "Why not?"

I let out a deep breath, trying to ignore how the air seemed to crackle between us. With mind control, it was just a simple bond that could be manipulated—commanded. But this... this would mean actually entering his thoughts. My stomach flipped as I realized what I'd agreed to. I was about to attempt reading the mind of the most dangerous man I'd ever met—and he was going to let me.

"What number am I thinking about?"

Seconds later, the tendrils were fluttering back out of me, caressing his mind in pearlescent wisps. I searched for the access point, and when I found it, I hesitated. Instead of sending a command down the bond, I lingered there, letting the feeling settle in around me. I used the tendrils to search, oddly aware of their movements. It felt like there might be something in there, this space at the border of Aether's mind, but—and then I felt it. Another point, leading deeper into the golden abyss. The tendrils reached out, closing in on the lock, and in an instant, my vision went black.

A woman—one of the most beautiful women I had ever seen—with jet black hair and golden eyes, running towards me with anguish streaked across her face. The desperation in her movements made me want to reach out, but the pain was too great, too much. I was moving away from her—floating, or flying? She screamed something, but I couldn't hear her, as if my eardrums had gone numb. And then it was black again.

I snapped back to the training room, realizing I had nearly lost my balance in the chair. Aether's arm was gripping my shoulder, keeping me straight up. His eyes were narrowed on me, but his forehead seemed to be creased in concern.

"What happened?" he said in a low tone.

"You didn't see her? Who was that?" I asked, pulling out of his grip and blinking in the surroundings. It felt like I had been holding my breath.

"What do you mean? What her?" He stood, pacing towards the other side of the gym, hand dragging down his mouth and chin. I'd never seen him so... rattled.

"The woman, the one with black hair and golden eyes."

Aether went chillingly still as he turned back to look at me, something dark pulsing in his glare.

He stared at me for a long time as if trying to figure something out.

But then, he broke his gaze, and walked out of the room without another word.

The silence he left behind felt heavy, charged with questions I wasn't sure I wanted answered. The image of the woman's anguished face lingered in my mind, along with the echo of a scream I couldn't quite hear. Something told me I'd stumbled onto a memory Aether had buried deep—something he'd never intended to share.

CHAPTER FIFTEEN

My muscles burned as I rounded another corner of the fortress wall, boots crunching against the dried grass. Two weeks of running this route had strengthened my endurance, but the ache was still there, pushing me forward. The unchanging gray sky stretched overhead, the eclipsed sun casting muted shadows that never seemed to move. Time felt different here—stagnant, like the realm itself was holding its breath.

I'd found my rhythm though, counting my breaths instead of trying to track the unchanging light. Twenty laps had become thirty, then forty. The weakness from my isolation was slowly burning away, replaced by a familiar strength I'd thought lost. Even my combat skills were returning, though not as quickly as I'd hoped.

Aether was nowhere to be seen. Ever since that day—since I'd glimpsed that woman in his mind—he'd barely looked at me. No more tether practice, no more observations. Just combat training, delegated more and more to Vexa or Rethlyn.

The vision still haunted me. That beautiful woman with golden eyes like his, reaching out in desperation, her silent scream... I couldn't shake the feeling that I'd seen something I shouldn't have. Something private. Which is precisely why I'd been hesitant about trying it in the first place.

The fortress grounds were busy—I could see them through the gates of my section, Umbra soldiers moving with renewed purpose as they prepared for the upcoming Strykka trials. Only a week remained. My stomach tightened at the thought. Despite my progress, the prospect of facing them filled me with a cold dread. Especially the Void.

"Look who's already at it!" Vexa's voice cut through my thoughts. She leaned against the wall ahead, a knowing smirk on her face. "You know, most people actually wait until they're fully awake before torturing themselves."

I slowed to a stop, wiping sweat from my brow. "Bold of you to assume I sleep."

"Well, today you can take a break from running in circles." She pushed off the wall, her violet eyes gleaming. "It's time you learned to fly properly. Can't have you relying on Aether to chauffeur you around forever."

The launch platform stretched before us, Tryggar's wings rustling restlessly beneath me as we waited. Being up here felt different somehow—knowing I wouldn't have someone's arms locked around me, knowing it would just be me and this massive, temperamental beast. I adjusted my grip on the saddle horn, watching as Draug pawed at the weathered stone beside us.

"You know, he hasn't had a rider in nearly half a century," Vexa said, gesturing towards Tryggar.

"Truly?" I asked, eyeing the silver Vördr beneath me.

"Truly. He was probably just a bit rusty before."

At least this time, the saddle was well-fit–perfectly crafted to accommodate both Tryggar's back and my shape. The one Vexa had sent orders for had finally arrived, and even the Vördr seemed calmer, more confident.

"He's been flying these routes with me for years," Vexa added, patting Draug's neck. "Tryggar will follow his lead—they have a good rapport." She smirked.

I couldn't help but think of that first flight with Aether, how Tryggar had plummeted toward the ground at terrifying speeds. The memory should have made me more nervous about flying alone, but somehow it didn't. Maybe because this time I wouldn't have to worry about whatever strange tension always rested between Aether and me.

"The wind patterns shift constantly up there," Vexa continued, "but Draug knows how to read them. Just trust that Tryggar will follow, and try not to overthink it."

Try not to overthink it. If only she knew how impossible that request was for me. But before I could dwell on it further, Draug's wings snapped open, and we were airborne.

Tryggar surged after Draug without hesitation, his wings cutting through the mist. The sudden acceleration stole my breath, but I leaned into it, remembering to keep my weight centered. The fortress fell away beneath us, its dark spires piercing the clouds like obsidian blades. I watched as Draug banked left and felt Tryggar adjust beneath me to mirror the turn.

"See?" Vexa called over the wind. "He knows what he's doing. Now let's try something a bit more challenging."

She guided Draug higher, spiraling through a bank of clouds. The moisture clung to my skin, cold and refreshing, as Tryggar followed. When Draug descended, Tryggar matched his pace. When they leveled out, the two Vördr fell into an easy rhythm, wings beating in tandem.

"You're a natural," Vexa said as she guided Draug alongside us. "Though I shouldn't be surprised. You seem to have a way with difficult creatures." Her lips quirked. "Tryggar included."

"A way with difficult creatures," I echoed, thinking of Aether's sudden distance these past weeks. "Has he always been like that—Aether?"

"Like what?" Vexa asked, though something in her tone suggested she knew exactly what I meant.

"So..." I searched for the right word. "Closed off."

"Aether's complicated. The Umbra is pretty much his whole life—has been since before I joined." She shrugged. "He doesn't date. He has no family, no friends. Unless you count me, and I'm not sure he does most days."

Vexa was quiet for a moment, adjusting her position as Draug caught an updraft. "I mean, the man clearly has his demons, you can tell just by looking at him, but I think it's best to let him tell his story in his own time."

"How long have you known him?"

"Since he pulled me out of prison five years ago." A wry smile crossed her lips. "I thought he was there to execute me, actually. Instead, he offered me a place in the Umbra. Said my skills could be put to better use than arming assassins."

"You were in prison?"

"Oh yes. Got caught selling spelled weapons to an illegal guild." She laughed, but there was an edge to it. "Not my finest moment, but when you grow up alone in Eastern Umbrathia, you learn to take whatever opportunities you can get. And I was always drawn to sharp things."

Vexa guided Draug into a gentle turn, her eyes fixed on the horizon. "The thing about desperation is it makes you forget there might be other choices. I learned to forge weapons because I had to survive, and because my tether allows me to imbue them. The illegal dealings..." She shrugged. "They just seemed like the next logical step. Until they weren't."

I watched a group of Vördr glide in the distance. "What happened?"

"Got sloppy. Started drinking too much. Made deals with the

wrong people." Her voice held no self-pity, just a matter-of-fact acceptance. "Ended up in a cell wondering if execution might be better than rotting away. Then Aether showed up, offering redemption in the form of military service." She shot me a knowing look. "Sound familiar?"

My heart stuttered. "More than you know." I took a deep breath, the cold air filling my lungs. "I nearly killed two noble girls almost a year ago. I couldn't control my abilities—my focus, as we called it. One moment they were taunting me, the next..." I swallowed hard. "A General in the Guard found me. Said I had a choice–join them or face the consequences."

"Some choice," Vexa muttered.

"Yeah." I adjusted my grip on the saddle horn, remembering Laryk's face that day—how his emerald eyes had seemed so dark that night. But I couldn't tell Vexa that part. Couldn't explain how that initial coercion had transformed into something else entirely. "The Guard became everything after that. My purpose. My home." The words tasted bitter now.

Vexa tilted her head, considering my words. "You know, I used to think redemption meant erasing who you were before. Becoming someone new." She glanced toward Ravenfell, barely visible through the mist. "But sometimes it's about accepting all of it—the mistakes, the choices, even the parts that shame us."

The words hit closer than I expected. I thought of the shadows that had emerged in Emeraal, how I'd tried so hard to deny that part of myself. Even now, knowing what I was, accepting it felt like another matter entirely.

"When did you know?" I asked. "That the Umbra was actually where you wanted to be?"

A smile tugged at her lips. "Well, probably when a certain noble decided my charm was irresistible."

"Effie?" I couldn't help but smile. "That must be quite a story."

"Oh, it is. She was absolutely horrified by me at first. Called me uncouth, barbaric—" Vexa's eyes softened at the memory. "Now look at her, sneaking down to the forge just to watch me work, pretending she's not completely smitten."

A sharp cry from Draug cut through our conversation. The Vördr's head snapped toward the ground, wings going rigid. Beside me, Tryggar tensed, a low warning sound rumbling in his chest.

"What is it?" I whispered, but Vexa had already raised her hand for silence.

She guided Draug lower, careful to keep us within the cover of clouds. That's when I saw them—figures moving along a narrow road that wound through the wasteland. Even from such a distance, their movements were unnaturally graceful—uniform.

"Damphyre," Vexa breathed, her earlier warmth completely gone. "At least a dozen. Headed to Draxon."

"Why would they be out here?" I asked, noting how far we were from the main roads.

"That's what worries me." Vexa's eyes narrowed. "This route... it's old, barely used. The only reason to take it is if you're trying to avoid being seen from Ravenfell." She watched the group for a moment longer. "And it leads straight to the rip."

CHAPTER SIXTEEN

The ceremonial black leathers felt stiff against my skin, new and difficult to move in. Effie circled me like a predator, adjusting straps and smoothing nonexistent wrinkles.

"Stop fidgeting," she scolded, batting my hands away from the collar for the third time.

"You're the one shoving me around." I shifted again, just to watch her eyes twitch.

Vexa lounged on my bed, absently tracing the void burns that spiraled up her arm. "Let her be, Effie. We all fidgeted before our ceremony."

"*I* didn't fidget," Effie sniffed, but her hands went gentle as she adjusted my sleeve.

"No, you just threw up in the waiting chamber."

"I did not!" Effie spun to face her, color rising in her cheeks. "I was... momentarily overwhelmed."

"Right." Vexa's lips quirked. "Is that what we're calling it now?"

I watched their exchange, noting the undercurrent of tension beneath their banter. "What was it like?" I asked. "Your ceremonies?"

Vexa's smile faded slightly. She sat up. "Different. There were more candidates then. The drought hadn't spread so far, and people still believed..." She trailed off, shaking her head.

"Believed what?"

"That joining the Umbra meant glory," Effie said quietly. "Not just survival."

Silence settled over us, heavy with unspoken weight. Effie's hands stilled on my shoulder, and for a moment, I saw past her affected manner to something deeper.

"I sacrificed my family crest," she said finally. "Generations of Eirfalk nobility, condensed into a single medallion."

"But you don't regret it?" I asked, meeting her gaze in the mirror.

A soft smile played at her lips as she glanced at Vexa. "Never."

"My sacrifice was simpler," Vexa said, standing to join us. "My first forging hammer. Illegal work or not, it kept me alive when nothing else would." She shrugged, but I saw how her fingers tightened on her arm.

Three sharp knocks cut through the moment. The door opened before anyone could respond, revealing Aether's broad frame. He'd worn the sleeveless leathers today, the ones that showed his void burns in full glory, which seemed unusually dark against his skin, almost breathing in the dim light. In his hands, he held something that made my breath catch—my emerald dagger, the one I had been given when I joined the Guard.

Vexa straightened, her eyes fixed on the blade. "Pretty," she breathed, professional appreciation warring with something else in her voice.

"Your sacrifice," Aether said, his golden eyes meeting mine for the first time since that day in training. Since I'd seen the woman in his head.

The emeralds caught the light, their color a painful reminder of other eyes I tried not to think about. This dagger had marked my beginning in the Guard, my pledge to protect Sídhe.

Effie's hands fell away from my shoulders. "Well," she said, her voice artificially bright. "I suppose it's time."

"Are you ready?" Aether asked, his voice low and steady. His fingers lingered on mine for a beat too long as I took it from him, their warmth sending shivers up my arm. The dagger felt familiar in my hand, the weight a reminder of the day I'd received it at an entirely different ceremony.

"Well, don't just stand there looking tragic," Effie said, breaking through my thoughts. "We have a ceremony to attend." But there was something gentle in her tone, something almost like understanding.

Vexa moved to the door. "The Vördr will be waiting." She paused, looking back at me. "Remember what we said about the gates. Don't hesitate when you step through."

I nodded.

"Come," Aether said, his golden eyes unreadable in the dim light. "It's time."

I gripped the dagger tighter and followed him into the corridor, where the real weight of what I was about to do finally began to sink in.

The hall stretched ahead, lit by flickering torches that cast long shadows against the stone walls. I followed Aether in silence until we reached the outer doors.

"Shouldn't you be with Lael?" I asked, remembering how young he'd looked during training. "He must be nervous."

"I'm going to him." Aether didn't slow his pace. "After I drop you off."

The gray twilight enveloped us as we crossed to the stables. Nihr waited near the entrance, her dark form massive against the ashen sky. Aether lifted me onto her back, his touch brief and impersonal. And then he was behind me, keeping that careful distance between us.

"What if I'm not what they need?" The words slipped out before I could stop them. "This realm has suffered so much already. If I fail them—"

"You won't." His voice was quiet but certain.

"You can't know that."

"I've watched you since the moment you arrived." Though he kept his distance, something in his tone had shifted. "You could have chosen the easier path. Could have denied everything about who you are. But instead, you're here."

"Being here and being what they need are different things."

As Nihr took to the sky, the fortress fell away beneath us. The unchanging gray stretched in every direction, broken only by ancient stone structures emerging from the wasteland. In the distance, a massive hillside rose from the earth.

My fingers tightened around the dagger at my hip. The weight of it felt heavier now, like an anchor to a life I was choosing to leave behind.

"You think letting go of that means betraying them," Aether said, reading my thoughts with unsettling accuracy. "The people you care about there."

"Doesn't it?" I traced the emeralds with my thumb. "I'm pledging myself to a realm they see as the enemy."

"Caring for the fate of both realms isn't a betrayal." His hand moved slowly, deliberately, until it covered mine where it gripped the dagger. The touch was careful but firm. "You can fight for Umbrathia without turning against those you left behind. The two aren't mutually exclusive."

The warmth of his hand against mine seemed to carry more meaning than his words as we descended near an entrance cut directly into the rock. The sound of a gathering crowd drifted up from below, muffled but growing louder.

Before I knew it, we had landed, and he was pulling me off of Nihr, steadying me on the rock below my boots.

He motioned for me to follow him. The passage twisted downward, lit by torches that cast our shadows long against the rough stone walls. The sound of the gathering crowd echoed from somewhere ahead, but felt distant, separated by layers of rock.

Soon enough, the passage opened into a small antechamber. Two Umbra guards stood at attention beside an ornate door, beyond which I could hear the full weight of the crowd.

"This is where I leave you," Aether said, his voice neutral once more. "When they call your name, present your sacrifice."

"I got it. Go find Lael."

He met my eyes one last time, and for just a moment, I saw something crack in his carefully maintained features. But then it was gone.

"Try not to fall," he said, and turned away, leaving me alone.

The guards motioned for me to follow them, and led me to a small waiting chamber. Through the stone walls, I could hear the muffled sound of voices, but couldn't make out what they were saying.

The emerald dagger felt heavy in my hand as I paced the small space. No one had actually explained what I was supposed to do when I got out there. *Present the sacrifice.* It sounded a bit ridiculous and overly dramatic, but who was I to judge? At least they hadn't asked me for my blood.

Yet.

Time dragged until finally, a guard opened the door. "They're ready for you."

I followed him down a short corridor, my boots echoing against stone. Ahead, a voice boomed—Urkin's, I realized, but I couldn't make out the words.

The corridor opened into what looked like a massive underground cavern, carved entirely from black stone. The sudden space after the cramped passage made my head spin. But it was the silence that hit me first—a sudden, crushing quiet that fell over the crowd as I emerged.

Hundreds of faces stared down from tiered seating that rose into shadows. I felt their eyes rake over my white hair. Some leaned forward, whispering to their neighbors. Others simply stared, unmoving.

At the center of it all stood some kind of altar, where Urkin waited. To his right, a line of Kalfar stood at attention, their black uniforms stark against the stone—contestants, perhaps. The ones who had gone before me. His voice faltered for just a moment as he took in my appearance.

The silence stretched. I gripped the dagger tighter and moved forward, my boots echoing far too loudly against the stone floor. Not a single face looked away. That old instinct crept up my spine. The urge to duck my head, to blend into the background until I disappeared completely. I'd spent so many years perfecting that particular skill.

But this wasn't about hiding anymore. This wasn't about staying safe.

The emerald dagger felt heavy in my hand. Another army. Another pledge. The memory of Laryk's voice whispered in my head. *You're different.* He'd meant it as a gift, but now the words felt like chains. How many times would I let others decide what that difference meant?

I approached the altar, trying to focus on the simple task of walking without stumbling. I looked up at the other contestants, their faces now close enough to recognize. Most wore an unreadable mask, but then I saw Lael. He looked so much older than he should have. His dark hair was slicked back, and he wore the same leathers as the rest of us. We locked eyes for a moment, and I could have sworn his mouth cracked into a smile.

"You present yourself to face the Strykka?" Urkin's voice boomed through the room, dancing off the walls.

"Yes," I breathed, feeling the weight of the entire room.

"Present your sacrifice." His eyes fell on me, and I watched the subtle narrowing of his brows. He still didn't trust me.

I lifted the dagger, its familiar weight in my palm sending a wave of memories through me. I remembered how Laryk's emerald eyes had gleamed with satisfaction the day he saw it fastened to my chest. A blade forged in Sídhe's finest flames, beautiful and deadly—something that was entirely mine. It had been my first real possession as a member of the Guard—something that marked me as one of them, something that was entirely mine. A symbol that I belonged somewhere, that I was more than just a branded outsider. Now, laying it on this altar felt like severing another tie to my old life.

I laid the dagger on the altar, watching as the emeralds caught the dim light one last time, and I forced myself to pull my hand away.

Urkin turned to address the crowd, his voice carrying authority that seemed to fill every corner of the cavern. "Before us stand those who would give everything to serve Umbrathia. In times past, the Strykka was a path to glory, a way to prove one's worth." He paused, his eyes sweeping over the assembled nobles and military leaders. "But now, as our realm faces its greatest challenge, these brave souls offer themselves for something far darker—the survival of our realm."

The weight of his words settled over the chamber. Even the whispers had died away.

"Three trials await," he continued. "Combat, to test strength. Observation, to measure tethers. And finally, for those deemed worthy, the Void itself. If any candidate completes the first two rounds successfully, they will be given a choice. To enter the Void, or to be placed into the highest tier of the Unit they will best serve.

The Medics. The Archivists. The Scouting Regiment. Or the Sentinels." His voice grew sharp with pride. "To emerge from the Void marked by shadow is to become something greater. It is to ascend beyond what any Kalfar could dream. Our realm may be suffering, but our warriors—our Spectres—they are what hold us together. They are what give us hope."

That's when I heard it—movement from somewhere behind me, a shift in the crowd's energy. The silence took on a different quality, tense and electric. Even Urkin's eyes moved past me, fixing on something near the entrance I'd come through.

A murmur rippled through the crowd. I noticed several Council members shift uncomfortably in their seats. Urkin's jaw tightened, but he maintained his composure. Finally, I turned around. My blood ran cold.

Valkan. The Lord of Draxon himself stood there. A murmur rippled through the crowd as he approached. He flashed Urkin a wicked smile as he took his place in front of the altar, holding out what seemed to be a bloodied diamond, and letting it fall onto the surface.

"I present myself to the Strykka," he said in a voice that could command thousands. The room ran silent once more, and I could have sworn a vein in Urkin's throat snapped. His eyes shot up to one of the elevated seating boxes, a shocked expression creasing his features.

Valkan shrugged, and walked to the empty space next to me. Chills ran across my skin as I felt him lean in.

"You're even lovelier up close."

CHAPTER SEVENTEEN

AETHER'S HAND closed around my arm the moment we cleared the arena floor, pulling me into the dim corridor. My heart was still hammering from Valkan's entrance, from the weight of what had just happened. Before I could protest, he was yanking me through the twisting passages, his stride so quick my feet could barely keep up. We rounded a corner and there, in a shadowed alcove, Rethlyn, Vexa, and Effie were already waiting, their faces tight with tension.

"The Skaldvindrs," Effie spat, pacing the narrow space. "It had to be them. My parents said they were wavering, but I never thought—"

"They wouldn't dare," Vexa cut in, but uncertainty tinged her voice. "Not without assurances from the other houses."

"They would if they were desperate enough." Aether's voice was deadly calm, but his grip hadn't loosened from my arm. "The drought hit their lands hardest last month."

I looked between them, trying to piece together the implications. "How could one family's vote change everything?"

"Because the Skaldvindrs don't act alone," Effie said, "they have allies. Old alliances." She shot a meaningful look at Vexa. "And now

Valkan has exactly what he wanted—a chance to prove himself to the realm."

"We have to speak with Lord Skaldvindr," Effie said, already moving toward the corridor that led to the upper levels. "Before he leaves."

"And say what exactly?" Vexa's voice was sharp with frustration. "His lands are dying. His people are starving. Valkan's offering him salvation."

"Why don't you just kill him?" The words tumbled out before I could stop them. "Valkan. End this before it begins."

The silence that followed was deafening. Even Effie stopped pacing.

Aether's fingers finally loosened from my arm as he turned to face me. "You think we haven't considered it?" His voice was low, dangerous. "With Valkan's influence—"

"The entire realm would collapse," Vexa finished. "Half would blame the crown, the other half would blame each other. We'd have civil war within days."

"And Draxon's army would descend on Ravenfell before his body was cold," Effie added, a shudder running through her. "His followers... they're fanatics. They'd tear the realm apart."

"The Skaldvindrs might listen to reason," Aether said, though his tone suggested he didn't believe it. "If they saw proof of another way—"

"Proof?" Effie's eyes lit up suddenly. "We have proof. We have a Duskbound." She turned to me, something calculating in her gaze. "If Lord Skaldvindr saw what she could do—"

"It's too risky," Aether cut in, but Vexa was already nodding.

"No, she's right. The Skaldvindrs abandoned Valkan's cause once before when they thought the Queen's power could save us. If they knew we had another Duskbound..."

"Their box is in the upper tier," Effie said, already moving. "If we hurry—"

"This is a mistake," Aether growled, but he followed, keeping close to my side as we climbed the narrow stairs toward the noble houses' private viewing areas.

My chest tightened with each step down the hall, my vision blurring in the corners. They were talking about me like I was some kind of solution—*the* solution. But what if I failed? What if I couldn't be what they needed? What if both realms fell because of me?

The upper-level corridors were wider and lined with doors marked by family crests. Voices drifted through the walls, their tones urgent. I had never seen Effie look so concerned or walk so *fast.*

"Here," she whispered, stopping before a door marked with a crest of thorned vines wrapped around a crescent moon. "Lord Skaldvindr always leaves early to avoid—"

The door swung open. A tall man emerged—the one I had seen at the conference. The one wearing a black dress suit with silver embroidery—the same look he had on tonight. He paused at the sight of us, his eyes narrowing first at Effie, then settling on me with sudden, sharp interest.

"Lady Eirfalk," he said smoothly. "What an... unexpected pleasure."

"Lord Skaldvindr." Effie looked up at the man. "We need to speak with you."

"I'm afraid I have other obligations—"

"About your vote," Vexa cut in. His expression hardened instantly.

"I don't believe my family's political decisions are any concern of the Umbra." His gaze swept over our group with calculated dismissal. "Or of foreign prisoners."

Aether stepped forward, his body now rigid, taking up the entirety of the door as Skaldvindr stumbled a few paces back.

"She's a Duskbound," he growled in such a low register, I almost couldn't hear his words.

A flash of emotion crossed the noble's face—too quick to read. "Is she?" His voice dripped with skepticism. "How convenient. Just when Valkan forces our hand, you produce another *solution*."

"You've seen what his Damphyre do," Effie pressed. "What they are. Is that really the salvation you want for your people?"

Lord Skaldvindr's jaw tightened. For a moment, conflict flickered across his eyes. "What I want," he said carefully, "is to keep my people alive. Valkan's lands still produce crops. His people still have essence. While the rest of us..." He gestured sharply at the air around us, at the perpetual twilight beyond the windows. "We're dying. All of us. Would you have me ignore a solution simply because you find it distasteful?"

"We're offering you an alternative," Vexa said.

"You're offering me nothing but words. And as you might recall, I don't put much trust in the sanctity of traditions of this realm." His voice turned sharp. "Prove it. Show me this supposed Duskbound power. Show me she's worth more than Valkan's immediate aid." He looked directly at me then, and the weight of his gaze felt like drowning. "Show me you're more than just another Umbra deception."

My throat closed. The walls seemed to press in, the shadows deepening at the corners of my vision. Everything they'd said about Valkan, about the realm's desperation, about what would happen if he gained more power—it all crashed over me at once. And now this man was staring at me, waiting for me to prove I was worth choosing over the monster who could save his people.

"I—" The word caught in my throat. My chest felt too tight. My breath came in short gasps. The room started to spin.

"Fia?" Vexa's voice sounded distant.

"I need—" I stumbled back a step. "I can't—"

Skaldvindr gave Aether one last skeptical look before slamming the door closed.

"Aether!" Urkin's voice boomed from down the corridor, making me flinch.

"I need air," I choked out. "I have to go—"

"Take her," Aether ordered, his eyes meeting Rethlyn's. Something passed between them—some unspoken understanding. "We'll handle this."

Rethlyn's hand replaced Aether's on my arm, gentler but just as urgent as he guided me away from the nobles' boxes. The corridors blurred past, my vision swimming at the edges. I couldn't get enough air. Couldn't think past the roaring in my ears.

We burst through a side entrance, the gray twilight a shock after the dim corridors. My legs gave out and I slumped against the stone wall, sliding down until I hit the ground.

"Let me–" Rethlyn started, taking a step toward me.

"Don't," I gasped, throwing up a hand. "Don't use your tether. Don't try to calm me." My voice cracked.

But the panic wouldn't release its grip. My chest constricted until each breath was a battle, spots dancing across my vision. And then—something *shifted*. A sensation ripped through me, like my insides were being hollowed out.

"Fia?" Rethlyn's voice wavered.

Horror froze me as I felt it start. Shadows began pouring from his void burns, but not like Vexa's from before. This was violent. Hungry. They twisted through the air toward me like they were being yanked by invisible hooks.

"What's happening?" My voice came out strangled as the darkness flooded into me. I tried to move, to break whatever connection had formed, but my body wouldn't respond. "Make it stop—I can't—"

"Fia!" Rethlyn's cry sent terror shooting through me. He tried to scramble away but remained locked in place, shadows ripping from him faster now. I could feel his fear mixing with mine, could feel him weakening with each second.

Stop stop stop stop— My mind screamed but my body only pulled harder. The darkness was everywhere, flooding my lungs, drowning me. I couldn't see, couldn't breathe, couldn't tell where I ended and the shadows began.

My throat tore open in a scream just as golden light exploded through the darkness. Strong hands gripped my shoulders, and Rethlyn's voice cut through my terror:

"*Enough.*"

And then, in an instant, my heart stilled, and a haze began fluttering across my mind, seeping into the darkness. But the feeling fled just as quickly as it had arrived, and terror overtook me again, but I was in control. The shadows snapped back to Rethlyn with such force that we both cried out. I collapsed forward, retching, my whole body shaking. He'd used his tether, and I couldn't exactly blame him.

"Rethlyn?" My voice shook as I watched him struggle to sit up. "Why do you look—are you in pain?"

He managed to lift his head, and the exhaustion in his eyes made my stomach turn. "Sharing shadows is one thing," he said, sighing, "but you just ripped them from me. Tore them out like they were being shredded from my bones."

Fresh horror washed through me. I'd *felt* his pain, I realized. Those fragments of sensation that had mixed with the shadows—that had been him. I scrambled backward until my spine hit stone, trying to put as much distance between us as possible.

"I didn't know I could—" My voice broke. "I didn't mean to—"

"I know." He winced as he shifted. "Sometimes one reaches for them in desperation."

"I'm sorry." I murmured.

He took a step towards me but stopped, concern etched into his features. After a moment, he simply sat down beside me, close enough to reach but not touching. We sat in silence as I focused on my breathing, on the feeling of cold stone against my palms, on the distant sound of Vördr wings beating against the wind.

"You know," Rethlyn said finally, his voice softer than I'd ever heard it, "I saw you. Back in Sídhe."

I turned my head slightly, confused by the sudden shift.

"The way you handled those shadows—absorbing them, wielding them on such a large scale without any training?" He shook his head, something like awe in his expression. "Even a practiced wielder would struggle with that kind of raw power. But you? You just... adapted. Like they were always meant to be yours."

"I almost lost myself," I whispered, remembering the darkness that had threatened to consume me.

"But you didn't." He picked up a small stone, turning it over in his hands. "That's the thing about power—it's not about controlling it perfectly. It's about choosing to keep fighting even when it feels impossible."

I drew my knees to my chest, suddenly feeling very young. "Everything's different now. My life, for so long—I was just... hiding. From everyone. From myself." My voice caught. "I never wanted any of this. The expectations, the pressure. Being told I'm the key to ending a war I didn't even know existed. No one ever expected anything of me."

Rethlyn was quiet for a moment. "I have a sister," he said finally. "She's everything my parents ever wanted. Master medic, perfect tether, perfect life." A wry smile touched his lips. "Meanwhile, I couldn't figure out what my tether was even for. The black sheep who could make people feel things they didn't want to feel."

"What changed?"

"I stopped trying to be what they wanted. Found people who

saw me—really saw me." He glanced at the entrance where we'd come from. "The Umbra gave me purpose, but more than that, they gave me a home. Somewhere the numbness couldn't reach."

I knew what that was like. I had always had Osta, and then Ma came around. And I loved them both dearly. But the first person who ever truly saw me, truly saw that I could be something more —was Laryk. He believed I could be something extraordinary.

Rethlyn turned to look at me fully then. "It's not about proving them wrong, you know. It's about proving to yourself that you're worthy. That you always were."

The words hit something deep inside me. I thought about the tower, about the girl who had spent weeks staring out that window, numb to everything. But before that—before the Umbra —there had been years of hiding in Sídhe. Years of pushing my power down, making it smaller, more normal. Years of pretending to be something I wasn't, because the alternative was too frightening to face.

And then the shadows had found me. In that moment in Emeraal, when darkness had surged through my veins, it should have felt wrong. Foreign. Instead, it felt like waking up. Like some part of me that had been sleeping finally opened its eyes.

"I'm scared," I admitted.

"Good," Rethlyn said. "It means you understand what's at stake." He stood, brushing off his leathers before offering me a hand.

I took it, letting him pull me to my feet. My breathing had steadied, though my chest still felt tight. But something had shifted —some small kernel of certainty taking root beneath everything else.

As if he had anticipated my distress, Tryggar's wings emerged from around the mountain, beating against the wind furiously. Seconds later, he was landing on the platform and trotting over to me.

"Think you can handle him on your own?" Rethlyn asked.

"Am I allowed to?" I shot a hesitant look over my shoulder as Tryggar nudged me.

"I think we're past all of this prisoner business," he said, eyes lingering on me a beat longer before he slipped back inside.

CHAPTER EIGHTEEN

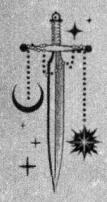

"Defense will always win out in the end," Vexa said, adjusting the straps of my leathers. We stood in a dimly lit preparation chamber, the sounds of the gathering crowd muffled by ancient stone walls. "Don't strike until you've tired them out. The Sentinels are trained to outlast their opponents—they'll be waiting for you to make the first mistake."

I nodded, trying to memorize every word. In a few minutes, I wouldn't have her counsel anymore. Or any of them.

"Remember," she continued, "the Generals aren't just looking for victories. They want to see control. Discipline." Her violet eyes met mine. "You've got the skill. Just don't let them see your fear."

"Or your tether," Effie added from where she leaned against the wall. "They're particularly strict about that."

"We have to go," Rethlyn's voice cut through the tension. He sat on a stone ridge that lined the wall of the chamber. "The trials are about to begin."

Something passed between him and Vexa—a look I couldn't quite interpret. Then Vexa squeezed my arm one last time. "Show them what you're made of."

Rethlyn lingered, hanging in through the doorway. The look on his face seemed apologetic.

"You're going to be fine," he said, giving me a soft smile

"Aether is with Lael, right?" I asked.

"Of course."

I sighed, something about that calmed my racing heart.

Rethlyn gave me one final glance before ducking out. Through the door, I could hear other voices now—the other candidates arriving.

We were back in the mountain, but the chamber from before had been transformed. Where the altar had stood now rose a fighting pit. An audience sat higher, looking down with eager expressions.

Above the main ring, four chairs had been positioned on a raised platform. The Generals of the Umbra sat—Urkin in the center, his face carved from stone, flanked by General Taliora of the Medic's Unit and Talon of the Archival Unit. In the fourth chair sat a man I didn't recognize, though I knew from Vexa's whispered advice the night before that this must be General Karis of the Scout's Regiment. She'd told me he could become a powerful ally if I managed to impress him today.

"We have time before they start," Lael said, settling beside me on one of the benches in the waiting area. "They always make us wait. Builds the tension, Uma says." He tried for a grin but it came out more like a grimace.

"How are Uma and Carden handling it?" I asked, grateful for the distraction. "Training without you?"

"Oh, Uma's convinced she could be here right now if they'd let her." His grin became more genuine. "Carden at least pretends to be patient about it." His expression softened. "Aether says they'll both be ready in a few years, though. Says Uma's got the makings of a real fighter, if she can learn to focus."

"Aether said that?" I bit back a grin, thinking of Uma's boundless energy.

"Yeah," Lael said, his voice dropping. "I mean, I know what people say about him. But they don't see him teaching Carden how to fall properly, or spending extra time helping Uma with her forms. No one else does that." He picked at a loose thread on his leathers. "After my parents... when he found me in Croyg... he didn't have to help. But he did."

"I'm Kenna," a voice cut in. A woman had drifted closer. "Sorry to interrupt, but standing alone was getting a bit..." She glanced toward one of the practice areas where Valkan was now executing combat forms with his personal guards. "Uncomfortable."

A tall man lingered at the edge of our group, his sharp eyes never settling in one place for long. "Theron," he offered in a clipped tone, though he made no move to come closer.

"Not exactly the social type?" Kenna asked him with a hint of amusement.

His only response was to shift his gaze to another corner of the room, as if cataloging every shadow.

A young man stepped forward then, speaking so softly I had to lean in to hear him. "Soren," he said, then nodded toward a girl who hadn't stopped moving since she'd entered the chamber. Her hair was pulled back so severely it seemed to strain against her scalp. "And that's Mira. We came together."

Mira's only acknowledgment was a slight pause in her pacing.

"Where did you train?" Kenna asked, brushing a loose strand of onyx hair behind her ear. Her question seemed casual, but something sharper lurked beneath it.

"Here and there," Soren replied vaguely. His hands were calloused but precise in their movements, like someone used to detailed work. "Lately, wherever we could find shelter."

Mira's pacing brought her closer to our group. Her boots were worn nearly through, the leather cracked and stained. "We didn't all have the luxury of proper training," she said, her voice rough.

I noticed Kenna's smile falter slightly. "No," she said after a moment. "I suppose we didn't."

Theron scoffed, the sound drawing my attention back to him. He'd positioned himself against the wall, one shoulder pressed to the stone as if ready to spring away at any moment. Despite his height, there was something almost delicate about his features.

"Proper training hardly matters now," he said. His eyes fixed on something beyond us, and we all turned to look.

A different man approached, looking to be in his mid-twenties. His dark hair was long on top but shaved on the sides. He cast a curious glance over the group of us before his eyes fell on me. "Raven." He nodded before sitting down.

In the practice ring, Valkan had stripped off his formal jacket. Even from here, I could see the unnatural pallor of his skin, the way his muscles moved too smoothly as he sparred with his guard. There was something wrong about it—something that made my stomach turn.

"They say his entire regiment fights like that," Kenna whispered, a shudder running through her. "Like they don't even feel pain."

"They don't." Mira's voice cut through the air like steel. She'd finally stopped pacing, her slight frame coiled with tension. "I've seen them."

A silence drifted over us for a few seconds.

"My sister..." Soren started, then stopped himself, running a hand through his dark curls. "She used to say there are worse things than dying." His voice had dropped so low I almost missed it.

"Used to?" Kenna asked.

But Soren just shook his head, his shoulders hunching slightly.

"Look," Lael broke in, clearly trying to change the subject. "The

Sentinels are starting their warm-ups." He nodded toward the other practice rings where black-clad figures moved through combat forms.

I studied their movements, trying to memorize each stance, each transition. These were the soldiers we'd have to face. Some bore visible scars, others moved with the telltale signs of old injuries. All of them carried themselves with the kind of confidence that should be intimidating, but for some reason, there was a touch of—something, maybe sadness—in their movements.

"They're slower than usual," Theron observed, his analytical tone betraying more than casual interest. "The drought affects them too."

"You seem to know a lot about their fighting style," Kenna said, arching a brow.

Something flickered across Theron's face—too quick to read. "I make it my business to know things."

Across the pit, Valkan's milky eyes shifted in our direction. Though he kept moving through his forms, there was something predatory in the way his attention settled on our group. His personal guards were a blur of movement around him, their skin sharing that same sheen.

"Stop staring," Raven muttered, "he enjoys it."

"And how would you know that?" Kenna asked, but her practiced smile had faded completely.

Before Raven could answer, the metallic sound of steel on stone rang through the chamber. One of the Sentinels had struck their weapon against the pit's edge. The room fell silent as the last of the nobles filtered into their seats above.

"Finally," Mira breathed, but I noticed her hands were trembling slightly.

I looked up at the platform where the Generals sat. Urkin's face was unreadable as he surveyed the candidates, but there was something calculating in General Karis's gaze as it swept over us. A man in Archivist robes approached, carrying a black cloth bag.

"Well," Kenna whispered, straightening her shoulders. "I suppose we're about to find out who's actually ready for this."

Lael's hand found mine and squeezed once before letting go. When I glanced at him, his face had settled into something determined. In that moment, he no longer looked like the boy Aether had rescued, but someone older.

The first number was about to be drawn.

Urkin stood, his voice carrying across the chamber. "Candidates, step forward."

We formed a line before the Generals' platform, our shadows stretching long behind us in the torchlight. The Archivist moved down the line with his black cloth bag. Kenna reached in first, her grace faltering slightly as she drew her lot. A small breath of relief escaped her when she eyed the stone.

The bag moved to Theron next. His stoic nature never wavered as he selected his stone, though I noticed his jaw tighten at whatever number he saw. Mira snatched hers quickly, like removing a bandage, while Soren's hand seemed to tremble as he reached in.

When it was my turn, the fabric felt rough against my fingers. I drew out a small black stone, its surface worn smooth by years of use. The number three was carved into its surface—my stomach lurched, but at least I wouldn't be first.

Lael was last before Valkan. His fingers closed around his stone with determination, but I saw the color drain from his face as he read the number.

One.

He was first.

Lael descended into the pit, each step echoing against the stone. The Sentinel circled slowly as if she was testing him—watching how he handled the pressure of her approach.

For a moment, neither moved. The silence stretched, broken

only by the soft scrape of boots on stone. Then the Sentinel struck—so fast I almost missed it. Her fist shot toward Lael's face, but he was already moving, ducking under the blow. He spun away, maintaining his distance, his feet never crossing as he moved.

The Sentinel's lips curved slightly.

She pressed forward, forcing Lael a few steps back with a series of quick jabs. He blocked each one, his movements precise but defensive. I could almost hear Vexa's voice: *Let them tire themselves out. Wait for the opening.*

A kick swept toward his legs. Lael jumped, using the momentum to create space between them. Smart. But the Sentinel had anticipated this. Her next strike caught him in the shoulder, sending him stumbling back. The crowd above murmured.

Lael recovered quickly, rolling with the impact. When he came up, his eyes were sharp with focus. The nervous boy from moments ago had vanished, replaced by something harder.

The Sentinel's next attack was a feint—a punch that transformed mid-motion into an elbow strike. But Lael saw it coming. He stepped inside her guard, a move that reminded me of Aether, and used her own momentum against her. The Sentinel hit the ground hard.

For a heartbeat, no one moved.

The Sentinel straightened slowly. For a moment, she simply studied him. Then she nodded—a sharp, respectful gesture—and stepped back.

"Enough," Urkin's voice rang out. "Well fought, both of you."

Lael's shoulders sagged with relief. As he climbed out of the pit, I could see his hands trembling. But he'd done it. He'd won.

"Candidate Theron," Urkin called. "You're next."

Theron fought with odd precision, like someone who had studied combat rather than lived it—like it was an academic pursuit. When he eventually won, there wasn't even a flicker of emotion on his face—just a slight nod, as if confirming something he already knew.

"Foreign-born," Urkin's voice echoed through the chamber. "Step forward."

With my heart hammering in my chest, I descended into the pit. The wall's domed ceiling seemed higher from down here, the nobles' faces blurring into shadow above. The Sentinel who stepped forward was different from the others—taller, broader, with scars that riddled his frame.

"Commander Darius leads our combat training," Urkin announced, a hint of something sharp in his tone. "He has graciously offered to test our... foreign candidate."

The silence that followed felt heavier than before. I caught Lael's worried glance from above, saw Kenna's lips press into a hard line. Even Valkan's milky eyes had settled on the pit with renewed interest.

Movement in the shadows of the upper level caught my eye. Vexa gripped Aether's arm, her face tight with concern as she whispered something urgent. Even from this distance, I could see the tension in his jaw, the way his golden eyes had turned sharp and dangerous. Effie's lips moved quickly, but whatever she was saying only made Aether's expression darken further.

I forced my breathing to stay even, remembering all of my training. But as Darius began to circle, silent and lethal, I realized no amount of training could have ever prepared me for this.

"Begin."

Darius struck like a viper, giving me no time to think. I barely managed to block his first blow, the impact sending shockwaves up my arm. He was testing me, but not like the other Sentinels had tested their opponents. This was different.

I spun away from his next strike, trying to create distance, but he followed ruthlessly. Each movement flowed into the next, leaving no room for error, no space to breathe. My arms burned from blocking hits that felt like they could shatter stone.

Darius's next combination drove me backward. I ducked under a strike that would have knocked me unconscious, the force of it whistling past my ear. His fist connected with the empty air where my head had been, and the sound of his knuckles cracking echoed through the chamber like breaking bones.

He was going to kill me, I realized. Or come as close as he could without actually crossing that line. This wasn't a test—this was a message.

I couldn't catch my breath. Every time I tried to create distance, he was there, his strikes coming faster, harder. My arms felt like lead, muscles screaming from the pain of deflecting his blows.

His next combination came too fast to track. A feint turned into an elbow strike that caught my temple. The world tilted sideways. I stumbled, trying to regain my footing, but he was already there. His knee drove into my ribs with crushing force. The impact knocked what little air remained from my lungs.

I felt my web curl around my spine, acting out of its own volition—braiding and twisting, desperate to protect me. But I couldn't let it loose. One slip, one moment of losing control, and I'd be disqualified. I used every last ounce of strength to force it down, to keep it contained. But that moment of distraction was all Darius needed.

I saw the final strike coming but couldn't move fast enough to avoid it. His fist connected with my jaw, and darkness exploded behind my eyes. The last thing I registered was the cold stone rushing up to meet me, and then nothing at all.

CHAPTER NINETEEN

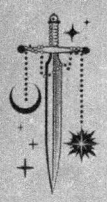

I FOUND myself on a stone bench in what looked like a courtyard garden. The space was enclosed by high walls covered in climbing vines. Gravel paths wound between neat beds of roses and herbs, all arranged around a central fountain. Stone archways connected different sections of the garden, their weathered surfaces smooth from years of rain. The late afternoon sun cast long shadows across the paths, and a cool breeze carried the scent of lavender blooms.

Someone sat beside me, though I couldn't quite turn my head to see who. Through the archway ahead, I recognized a woman immediately—the same girl from my previous dream, though older now—one of the twins. Her dark hair was elaborately styled, and she walked arm in arm with a handsome man in formal attire.

"The Northern trade routes have been quite profitable this season, Lord Skaldvindr," she said, her voice carrying that same tone I remembered from the night at her vanity. Her fingers tightened slightly on his arm as they passed our bench.

"Indeed." His response was polite but distant, his attention seeming to drift. As they rounded the rose bushes, his eyes flickered toward where I sat, and something in his expression softened—a small smile touching his lips before he returned his attention to his companion.

"Father says the silk merchants have been particularly generous in their offerings," she continued, though his gaze had already begun to wander again. I watched her try to maintain his interest.

They made another circle of the garden, their conversation a steady stream of trade agreements and political niceties. Each time they passed, I noticed the same pattern—his careful glances toward our bench, that subtle warming of his features. The person beside me shifted, and when I turned, I caught only a glimpse of a flushed neck as she bent her head, dark hair falling forward like a curtain. My heart skipped—it was the other sister, the one who had sat in her robe asking about balls she never attended.

"Perhaps we should discuss the upcoming harvest festival," the other sister said, her grip on Lord Skaldvindr's arm tightening as she steered him toward another path. But even as she led him away, his eyes found our bench one last time.

The sister beside me remained still, but I could see the rapid rise and fall of her breath, the way her hands trembled slightly where they rested in her lap. The tension between them was palpable now—this careful dance of stolen glances and unspoken words.

They disappeared around a corner, though the sister's voice still carried—eager and hopeful as she detailed plans for upcoming celebrations. The tension beside me seemed to ease slightly, but that flush remained, creeping down past the collar of her dress. I wanted to turn fully, to finally see her face clearly, but the dream held my gaze just out of reach. And then, the steady sound of voices began to pull me from sleep.

"None of this would be happening if you just took the position when they offered it to you." It was Vexa's voice, hissing with frustration.

DUSKBOUND

Consciousness came in waves, like being pulled through murky water. Everything hurt. The world existed only in fragments—the scratch of rough fabric against my skin, the dull throb at my temple, and the sound of whispers just beyond.

"I'm not discussing this again," Aether's response was low, almost a growl.

Their words faded in and out. I tried to open my eyes but my body wouldn't respond.

"But it was yours. You earned it." Vexa again.

"Irrelevant." Something in Aether's tone made me think this wasn't the first time they'd had this argument.

A groan escaped my lips before I could stop it. The voices ceased immediately, followed by the sound of quick footsteps.

This time when I tried, my eyes actually opened. The room swam into focus—stone walls, iron torches. Some kind of infirmary chamber carved into the mountain. The bed beneath me was narrow but solid.

"How are you feeling?" Vexa appeared at my side, concern etched into her features. Behind her, Aether leaned against the doorframe, his arms crossed. Even from here I could see the tension in his jaw, the way his golden eyes had turned sharp with something that looked like anger.

"I'm sorry," I managed, my voice rough. "I lost. I assume that's why I'm here."

"Don't apologize." The words snapped from Aether like a whip.

Vexa shot him a look before turning back to me, her expression conflicted. "It's not your fault. Urkin has never had any contestant fight Darius before. He knew exactly what he was doing."

The words hit like another blow. "So I'm finished then?"

"No," Vexa said quickly. "The combat trial and tether observation are cumulative. You showed skill today—lasting that long against Darius..." She shook her head. "Your score isn't as high as we'd hoped, but if you can make up for it tomorrow with your tether demonstration, you could still move on to Void considerations."

Aether shifted against the doorframe. "I'm going to check on Lael." His eyes met mine for a moment, intense enough to make my breath catch, before he turned and disappeared into the corridor.

Vexa settled onto the edge of the bed, her eyes scanning my face with a wince. "You look terrible."

"Thanks." I tried to smile but my split lip protested.

"No, really. When you hit the ground..." She shook her head. "I've never seen Aether move so fast. He was halfway over the railing before Effie and I could grab him."

I touched my temple gingerly, feeling the raised bump. "What happened after?"

"Chaos, honestly. The other contestants were horrified." She ran a hand through her hair. "We went straight to Urkin, demanded to know what he was thinking, putting you against Darius."

"I'm guessing that went well."

"Oh, perfectly." Her voice dripped with sarcasm. "He said since you're an outsider, you need to prove yourself more than the others. That the challenge was completely fair," she scoffed.

"How did the others do?"

"Kenna's quick—managed to hold her own. Mira too, though she took a nasty hit to the ribs. Soren..." She pursed her lips. "Let's just say the medics have been busy today."

I shifted, trying to find a position that didn't hurt. "And Valkan?"

Something dark flashed across Vexa's face. "He requested to spar with two Sentinels at once." Her fingers curled into fists. "And bested them both. With *flying colors*."

The silence stretched as I processed everything. My head

throbbed with each heartbeat, but something else nagged at me—the conversation I'd overheard.

"Aether was supposed to have Urkin's position?"

Her eyebrow arched. "You heard that?"

"Some of it. Before I fully woke up."

Vexa stood, keeping her back to me. "You should focus on tomorrow. The tether observation will be crucial if you want to continue—"

"Why didn't he take it?"

She turned, studying me for a long moment. "It's not important."

"None of this makes sense." I pushed myself straighter despite the pain. "The way everyone defers to him, even when Urkin's in charge."

"Fia..." There was a warning in her tone.

"The Council wanted him to lead instead of Urkin, didn't they?"

Vexa sighed, leaning against the stone wall. "Yes. All of us did. Even being second in command was more than he initially agreed to, but they convinced him to take that much at least."

"Why him?"

She hesitated, something cautious creeping into her expression. "Aether has always been... different. The Council saw that, especially as the drought worsened. While other Kalfar grew weaker, his abilities never faltered. They wanted to create a new position for him—Commander of the entire Umbra forces."

"What do you mean?"

"They wanted him to oversee everything—the Ground forces, Archivists, Scout Regiment, Medics. One leader to command them all, someone who could unite the different units." Her fingers traced one of her void burns absently. "It made sense. His experience, his strength... especially now, with the essence failing..."

I tried to process this. "But he refused?"

"Multiple times. Then two years ago, when General Doran

retired, they practically begged him to at least take control of the combat forces. It would have been a compromise—less responsibility than commanding everything, but still..." She shook her head. "He wouldn't do it. So Urkin stepped in."

"And now we're stuck with him," I muttered.

"Yes. Even though Aether has been serving this realm for thirty years." Her voice turned bitter. "Don't repeat this, but Urkin was never cut out for the job."

The words hung between us. Thirty years. The number kept repeating in my head, refusing to make sense. Aether couldn't be a day over thirty. And hadn't she mentioned how the drought affected...

"That's not possible," I said slowly. "Thirty years? You told me the drought has shortened Kalfar lifespans. And Aether... he can't be more than thirty himself."

Vexa's expression shifted, becoming guarded. "I shouldn't have mentioned the timeframe."

"But you did." I pushed myself up straighter, ignoring the throb in my temple. "How can he have served for thirty years when he looks barely that age himself?"

She moved to the doorway, checking the corridor before turning back. "Some things about Aether are... complicated."

"That's not an answer."

Vexa sighed, leaning against the stone wall. "No one knows where he came from, or how he came to be in the Void."

"What do you mean, *came to be* in the Void?"

She exhaled slowly, conflict clear on her face. "I'd rather Aether tell his own story, in his own time, but..." She met my eyes. "The Queen found him there, thirty-five years ago, looking exactly as he does now. With no memory of who he was or how he got there."

Thirty-five years. The man who'd spent weeks trying to break me, who seemed to have every answer about what I was supposed to become, didn't even know his own past. There was something unsettling about that—about how much of himself was just... missing.

The contestants' common room was little more than a circular chamber carved into the mountain, but at least it had windows. Gray light filtered through the narrow openings, catching dust motes that danced in the air. My body protested as I lowered myself onto one of the benches built into the wall. Everything ached, but my mind was worse—spinning with what Vexa had told me about Aether.

Thirty-five years. Found in the Void. How was that even possible?

"Here." Kenna's voice broke through my thoughts. She held out a cup of something steaming. "It's willow bark tea. Helps with the pain."

Her words hit me somewhere deep, and I nearly doubled over. *Ma.* That tea was her solution to nearly every form of suffering. Suddenly, memories were flashing through my mind, every time she'd made me a cup when I'd accidentally burned myself on the cauldron lighters.

What must she think now? That I was dead, like her brother. Another person she loved claimed by the Guard. The thought of her grief—of her facing that apothecary alone—made my chest ache with a pain no tea could touch.

I forced the room to come back into focus around me, noting the odd expression on Kenna's face as I reached out to take the tea. A bruise bloomed across her jaw. She'd fought after me, I remembered. Had held her own, according to Vexa.

"Thanks." The tea was bitter but warming. "How are the others?"

"Soren's still with the healers," Theron spoke from his place by the window, his gaze fixed on something outside. "Mira's refusing treatment. Says she's had worse."

As if summoned by her name, Mira emerged from the shadows of the far corner. She moved stiffly, one arm wrapped protectively around her ribs, but her eyes were sharp as ever. She settled against the wall, something haunted in her expression.

"Tomorrow will be different," Kenna said, clearly trying to lighten the mood. "The tether observation is more... structured."

"Will it?" Theron turned from the window. "After today?"

"The Council takes tether observation seriously," Lael said with surprising conviction. "It's tradition."

I watched their faces in the dim light, each marked by the day's trials in different ways. Kenna maintained her graceful composure despite her injuries. Theron's analytical distance seemed to have deepened. Mira's eyes never stopped moving, like she was tracking invisible threats.

"What exactly happens during the observation?" I asked, trying to keep my voice steady. "How do they judge it?"

"They'll want to see control," Theron said. "Precision. How well you can harness your abilities under pressure."

Under pressure. I thought of Aether then, how he'd survived thirty-five years in a realm where essence was failing. How he'd emerged from the Void itself with abilities that never weakened. Would I be able to prove myself worthy of the same path?

"We should all get some rest," Kenna said, standing. "Tomorrow will be... interesting."

As the others began to drift away, Lael lingered. He looked younger in the dim light, reminding me that he was only sixteen—far too young for any of this.

"You did well today," I said quietly as he settled onto the bench near me. "That move you used at the end—the way you turned their momentum against them. That was impressive."

A ghost of a smile crossed his face. "I almost ran. When they called my name first..." He picked at a loose thread on his leathers. "I thought my legs would give out right there."

"But they didn't."

"No." His smile grew a fraction. "Guess I'm too stubborn for my own good."

We sat in comfortable silence for a moment, watching the eternal twilight through the windows. There was something reassuring about his presence—no expectations, no hidden meanings, just quiet understanding.

"Are you nervous? About tomorrow?" I asked.

"A little." He said it so matter-of-factly, I bit back a grin. "But my mom always used to say that being scared just means you're about to do something really brave. Or really stupid." He shrugged. "Probably both in our case."

"Probably." I couldn't help but laugh.

His smile faded as he looked out the window, at the sun forever frozen in its partial eclipse. "I remember the day it stopped moving," he said quietly. "We were in the gardens—what was left of them." He drew in a shaky breath. "That was the day Aether found me in Croyg. The day everything changed."

I stayed quiet, letting him find his words.

"The gardens used to stretch for miles," he continued softly. "My mother used to say you could walk for days and never see the same plant twice. The air always smelled like earth and growing things. Like life." He took a deep breath. "But by then, everything was gray. Dead. The soil turned to dust between our fingers."

"Your parents..." I started, but wasn't sure how to finish.

"They wouldn't leave. A lot of others had left. Either to Draxon or Ravenfell." His voice had gone flat. "They kept saying the land would recover, that it always had before. They didn't understand that this was different." He picked at a loose thread on his leathers. "When the food ran out, they started eating the spoiled crops. Said we couldn't waste anything. That's what killed them in the end."

The weight of his words hung in the air.

"The worst part is..." He hesitated, wrapping his arms around himself. "Sometimes I worry I'm starting to forget things. Like what my mother's laugh sounded like, or exactly how tall the sunflowers grew. It feels like betraying them somehow."

"You're not betraying them by surviving," I said quietly. "By moving forward."

"Aren't I though?" His voice was barely a whisper. "Joining the Umbra, learning to fight... sometimes I wonder what they'd think of me now."

He stared at his hands, so young but already marked with calluses. "They were healers, you know? Well, not officially. But everyone in Croyg came to them when they were sick. My mother knew every medicinal plant in those gardens. Which leaves could bring down a fever, which roots could ease pain." A ghost of a smile touched his lips. "She used to say the land provides everything we need, if we just know where to look."

The smile faded. "But then the land started dying, and nothing she knew could fix it. I watched her try everything. Even when the plants came up twisted and wrong, she kept hoping the next batch would be different."

His voice cracked on the last word, and I fought the urge to reach out to him. I'd never truly been the best at comforting people, but something about his pain was too real—too familiar. I'd never known my parents–didn't have any memories to hold onto. And the thought of them was something I mostly avoided. But when I was younger, before I'd decided to compartmentalize so many things, tucking them away in places difficult to reach, I'd missed them. In a way of missing something you didn't know.

"Do you think it could be like that again?" he asked suddenly, cutting through my thoughts. "If we stop what's happening? If we fix things?"

The question hung heavy in the air. I wanted to tell him yes, to promise him that everything would go back to the way it was. But he deserved better than empty promises.

"I don't know," I said honestly. "But we're going to try."

Something in my heart tightened at the words—at how much I suddenly needed them to be true.

CHAPTER TWENTY

THE WAITING chamber felt smaller than yesterday, the stone walls pressing in as we gathered to draw lots. My muscles still ached from the combat trial, each bruise gnawing at me, reminding me how spectacularly I'd lost the day before.

Another Archival assistant stood before us, holding that same black cloth bag from yesterday. Urkin loomed behind him, betraying nothing as his eyes swept over our group. When his gaze reached me, it narrowed almost imperceptibly.

Soren's absence was notable. He was still too weak from yesterday's beating to compete in the trial today. The others tried not to look at his empty place in line, but Mira's hands were clenched at her side.

"The order of demonstration is final," Urkin's voice filled the chamber. "You will present your tether to the Council when called. Any use of abilities before your turn will result in immediate disqualification."

My stomach churned as the bag made its way down the line. I watched each contestant draw their stone, studying their reactions. Theron's face remained impassive as he read his number, but something like satisfaction flickered in his eyes. First, then.

"How fortunate," a smooth voice came from behind me, sending a chill down my spine. "It seems we'll have plenty of time to become acquainted."

I turned to find Valkan standing closer than I'd expected, his dead eyes fixed on me with unsettling intensity. Even in the dim light, his skin seemed to glow with an unnatural vitality that made my stomach turn.

"I must admit, I find myself... intrigued. A foreign contestant in the Strykka—that's never happened before."

My gaze drifted to the upper level where the Umbra gathered. Aether stood near one of the stone columns, his golden eyes fixed on our interaction, jaw clenched. Even from this distance, I could see the shadows writhing beneath his skin.

"And yet here we both are," Valkan continued, moving closer. "Breaking tradition." His smile revealed teeth that seemed too white. "Tell me, how are you enjoying your time in Umbrathia?"

Before I could respond, Urkin's voice cut through the tension, "Candidate Theron, take your position."

I moved away from Valkan, grateful for the excuse. But his voice followed me, soft enough that only I could hear: "Perhaps we'll continue this conversation later."

The arena had been transformed since yesterday. Where training dummies once stood, now elaborate targets had been erected. The tiered seating above was packed with nobles and military leaders, their faces expectant. *This* was what they had come to see.

Theron stepped into the center of the arena, looking just as confident as he had since meeting him yesterday. At Urkin's signal, Sentinels emerged from the shadows, surrounding him with weapons drawn.

The first Sentinel struck, blade arcing through the space, but

Theron was already moving. The air around him began to shimmer, like heat rising from stone. Suddenly, where there had been one Theron, there were dozens, each moving independently, each perfectly detailed. The Sentinels hesitated, weapons hovering as they tried to distinguish the real target from the illusions.

Theron's duplicates wove between the Sentinels. Each time a blade found one, it simply dissolved into mist, while three more appeared elsewhere. The Sentinels raged into a frenzy, striking at phantoms while the real Theron moved unseen among his creations. When the demonstration ended, he stood calmly at the center of the arena, not a scratch on him.

"Next," Urkin called.

Valkan strode into the arena, and conversations turned into murmurs. He surveyed the crowd before he smiled—a predator's smile. Fresh Sentinels took position around him, but they seemed more hesitant than before.

Valkan's form rippled like water, bones cracking and reforming as his body twisted. Where he had stood now prowled a massive panther, its coat as black as night. The transformation was flawless, disturbing in its perfection. The beast's eyes remained that same milky white as it launched itself at the nearest Sentinel.

The Sentinel's blade passed through air as the panther shifted mid-leap into a giant bird of prey, talons raking across armor before taking wing. The other Sentinels moved in formation, trying to corner him, but Valkan was never where their weapons struck. Each transformation flowed into the next—wolf, bear, serpent—each form more lethal than the last. Unlike the rest of the realm, there was no sign the drought affected him at all.

The display ended with Valkan back in his original form, standing among the Sentinels who had all been disarmed. Not a hair was out of place. He wasn't even breathing hard.

The silence that followed was deafening.

A girl I hadn't met yet was called next—Cassia—her movements graceful but hesitant as she approached the center. New Sentinels took their positions around her, and when the first one struck, she reached out with startling speed. At her touch, the soldier stumbled back—confused as to what she had done to him. It was only then that his armor began to decay, crack and burst... eventually crumbling to a pile of ash. The other Sentinels backed away, but she pursued them, her face carefully blank even as everything she touched disintegrated. A slight smile tugged at her lips when she saw the judge's faces.

Kenna followed. As the Sentinels closed in, whispers began to fill the arena—countless voices speaking at once, growing louder until they became overwhelming. The Sentinels clutched their heads, their formations breaking as the whispers seemed to pierce right through them. Some dropped their weapons, others stumbled back. Through it all, Kenna stood perfectly still, conducting the chaos like a maestro.

Lael was next. He moved to the edge of the arena where shadows pooled deeply and, to everyone's shock, grabbed hold of something massive in the darkness. With visible strain, he dragged the corpse of a giant wolf into the light. The beast's matted fur was dark with decay, its empty eye sockets somehow more terrifying than if they'd held eyes.

The crowd drew in a collective breath as Lael positioned the wolf's body in the center of the arena, his small frame dwarfed by the creature's massive form. The Sentinels circled cautiously, weapons raised, but their uncertainty was clear.

Lael began to lift his arms, and the wolf's limbs jerked, then smoothed into fluid motion as it rose to its feet. At his silent command, the beast launched itself at the nearest Sentinel, its movements unnaturally quick despite its decaying form. Rotting teeth attacked the steel armor as it drove the Sentinel to the ground.

The other Sentinels moved in, but the wolf was too fast, too strong. It fought with the abandoned savagery of something that couldn't feel pain, that had no fear of death. Within minutes, the Sentinels yielded, backing away from the creature that continued to prowl between them and Lael.

As Lael ascended the steps from the arena, a grin split his face despite his obvious exhaustion. His leathers were covered in dust and decay from dragging the wolf's corpse.

"Sorry," he said, dropping onto the bench beside me. "For the smell and all. I was hoping to find a fresher one."

Despite everything—I couldn't help but smile. The boy who'd seemed so nervous yesterday had just commanded a dead beast. Something like pride bloomed in my chest.

"You can control the dead?" I asked softly, still trying to process what I'd witnessed.

"Aether found me practicing on dead rats in Croyg," he admitted, picking at some dried mud on his sleeve. "Said I was wasting my talent on rodents." His eyes lit up. "You should see what I can do with a bear. Though those are harder to drag around."

I laughed, genuinely laughed, and the sound surprised me. When was the last time I'd done that? "Well, the wolf certainly made an impression."

"You think?" he beamed.

"Definitely. You should have seen the judges' faces. Just as impressed as they were horrified." I smiled.

Before he could respond, Urkin called the next contestant. But as Lael stood to make room, he squeezed my arm. "You're going to do great," he whispered. "Show them what you can really do."

Raven was next, his movements hesitant. As the Sentinels advanced, he pulled out what looked like shards of mirror from his pockets, placing them strategically around the arena. When the first Sentinel struck, his reflection appeared in one of the fragments, calling out a warning to himself from another angle. But the ability, while fascinating, proved impractical in combat. The

Sentinels quickly overwhelmed him, though the judges seemed impressed regardless. I noted how Talon whispered something to Urkin, who nodded.

Mira stepped into the arena next, her slight frame nearly lost in the vastness of the space. The Sentinels advanced, weapons raised, but something strange began to happen. Each time Mira's gaze locked onto a Sentinel, the air around them seemed to blur and distort. One by one, they staggered backward, their weapons clattering to the ground as they recoiled from something I couldn't see.

Their faces contorted in what looked like pure terror, though there was nothing visible causing it. Whatever Mira was showing them, it was enough to make even these trained soldiers retreat. Through it all, her own expression remained haunted, as if she could see whatever horrors she was inflicting on them.

All the contestants had gone, and I felt nerves race across my skin as Urkin stood once more, eyes locked on me. He hesitated for a moment, letting the intensity of his stare infect me further.

"Foreign-born." He couldn't quite hide the distaste in his tone. Murmurs ran through the crowd, no doubt people discussing my horrible performance the day before. I forced my breathing to calm as I entered the arena, my steps slower and less confident than I would have liked.

The Sentinels emerged from the shadows one by one, surrounding me in a tight circle. Their weapons caught what little light filtered down, steel gleaming with deadly promise. I could feel the weight of hundreds of eyes bearing down on me from above—nobles, military leaders, the other contestants. All of them expecting me to fail. Again.

My heart thundered so loud I was sure they could hear it. Yesterday's bruises seemed to throb in time with each beat. I had been planning this since last night, but now, standing here, doubt crept in. I'd never attempted anything like this before, never dared to use this much power at once. Not on purpose.

I closed my eyes, trying to steady my breathing. The web stirred along my spine, familiar but dangerous. Usually, I kept it carefully contained, only letting out what I absolutely needed. But today, I was using every last drop.

The first Sentinel moved. I could hear the whisper of steel through air, feel them beginning to close in. It was now or never.

I reached for the web, yanking on it with more force than I ever had before. For a terrifying moment, nothing happened. The power stayed locked inside, refusing to budge. Panic clawed at my throat. I pulled harder, desperately, feeling the strain all the way down to my bones.

Then something broke loose.

The web exploded up my spine with such force it nearly knocked me over. White light burst behind my closed eyes, snapping open as power flooded through me, raw and overwhelming. Too much—it was too much. I could feel myself losing grip on it, feel it trying to spiral out of control.

Through the chaos, I could see the Sentinels' minds glowing silver, so close now. But my tendrils wouldn't respond. They writhed and twisted, refusing to take shape. Sweat beaded on my forehead as I fought for control, fought to shape this wild surge of power into something I could use.

Just when I thought I would drown in it, something clicked into place. The web steadied, and I felt my feet leave the ground.

My vision snapped back to find myself suspended in the air, my hair whipping around me like a tempest. The arena had gone completely silent. The Sentinels had frozen, weapons half-raised as they stared up at me. My web flowed out in pearlescent tendrils, caressing all six minds simultaneously, wrapping around them like silk.

A smile tugged at my lips as my gaze drifted down to Urkin, still sitting while the other judges had risen in shock.

And I sent the command down the bond.

One by one, each Sentinel turned on their fellow soldiers and raised their weapons. A beat of silence rang past as they kept their arms up.

Attack.

Chaos ensued as the Sentinels surged toward each other, blades flying with untamed ferocity, steel against steel. The clamor echoed through the entire arena as audience members rose to their feet, gasping. Finally, Urkin stood and took a few agonizing steps towards me, gripping the railing until his knuckles turned white. His eyes pierced me like blades.

Perhaps I should have been scared—terrified about what consequences might follow this. But he had asked to see my tether, so I was going to show him in the truest way possible. Remind every single one of them what I was capable of. What I could do If I really desired it.

I had never felt the web at its full strength, but I had to admit, I *liked* it.

Through the destruction, my eyes found Aether, mind shimmering with that golden hue. He was the only one in the crowd still seated, leaning back in his chair, hands pressed together, his chin dangerously low. The strangest expression graced his face. One I had never seen him wear before.

Pride. But it was darker than that. A kind of dark satisfaction that made my hair stand on end, that made heat rush through my veins.

Just as one of the Sentinels cried out in pain, I halted them.

Armor clanged against the ground as each Sentinel fell to their knees in exhaustion, confusion blooming on their faces as they realized where they were—what had just happened.

The silence that followed was deafening. Not a single person moved, as if the entire arena was frozen in that moment. I could feel my heart thundering in my chest, but my hands were steady as I lowered them to my sides.

Through the quiet, a slow clap echoed off the stone walls. My eyes shot to its source, and I felt my blood run cold.

Valkan.

He stood at the edge of the arena, eyes fixed on me with an intensity that made my skin crawl. His lips curved as he continued his solitary applause.

"Magnificent," he breathed, just loud enough for his voice to carry. "Simply magnificent."

Just as I lowered myself, my feet touching the ground once more, the spell broke. Suddenly, the arena erupted in a symphony of voices—some cheering, others arguing in heated whispers.

Urkin's face had gone completely rigid, but there was something else in his expression now. Something that looked almost like fear. *Good.*

General Taliora was whispering urgently in his ear, while Talon scribbled furiously in his notebook, occasionally shooting glances in my direction. Karis simply studied me.

My attention snapped back to Valkan as he drifted closer, his movements unnervingly smooth. "I believe," he murmured, his voice slicing through the noise, "you might be the most extraordinary thing I've ever laid eyes on." His pale, lifeless gaze pinned me in place. Not with awe, but with something far darker. A hungry, twisted fascination.

"What a shame it will be, indeed, if you die in the depths of the Void."

CHAPTER TWENTY-ONE

The half-dead trees creaked in the wind, their brittle branches casting strange shadows in the firelight. We sat in a small clearing just beyond the mountain's entrance, where twisted roots broke through gray earth.

"You both understand this little excursion isn't something we can advertise to the other candidates," Effie said, smoothing invisible wrinkles from her uniform. "We're not exactly supposed to show favoritism during trials."

Rethlyn had all but dragged us out here, explaining that he had already set up a small celebration. A fire pit ringed with stones, weathered logs arranged in a circle, and promises of his rice wine —which he swore would "put hair on our chests."

"Or fraternize with potential recruits at all," Vexa added, pulling Effie closer against her side. "Though after that performance today, I'd say some celebration is warranted."

"Rules like that seem pretty stupid considering everything that's happening," Rethlyn said, producing a clay bottle from his leather bag. "Besides, I've been brewing this for months. Seems like the perfect occasion to finally try it."

"The last time you said that three Sentinels ended up in the medical wing." Vexa eyed the bottle suspiciously. "Didn't one of them temporarily lose their eyesight?"

"That was a different batch," Rethlyn said dismissively. "And they could still see shadows."

"Oh, well in that case," Effie rolled her eyes, "totally safe."

"I've perfected the recipe," Rethlyn insisted, already uncorking the bottle. A smell like burnt metal and overripe fruit filled the air. "Mostly perfected it."

"If I die from this," Vexa reached for the bottle anyway, "I'm coming back to haunt you."

"That's fair." Rethlyn grinned. "Though technically, you'd have to get in line behind the others."

I shifted on the log I shared with Lael, still unsure how to act in such a casual setting with people I'd considered enemies mere weeks ago. But Lael's presence helped ground me—his excitement about the day's events provided a welcome buffer.

"I still can't believe how you controlled that wolf," Vexa said to Lael. "Even Urkin looked impressed, and that's practically impossible."

"Not as impressive as making six Sentinels turn on each other." Lael grinned, nudging my arm. "I thought General Taliora was going to fall out of her chair."

The memory sent a thrill through me. Six minds—more than I'd ever imagined. I could still feel the echo of their consciousness against mine, the way they'd yielded to my will. The look on Urkin's face had been particularly satisfying. That scowl had cracked into something closer to shock when his Sentinels turned their weapons on each other. Even now, hours later, the memory of his barely contained outrage brought a smile to my lips. I only hoped it made a difference.

"Do you think it was enough?" I asked, voicing the worry that had been gnawing at me since the demonstration. "To make up for yesterday's combat trial?"

"Based on Karis' face alone?" Vexa leaned forward, firelight dancing across her piercings. "I'd say you more than made up for it."

"The only one who looked like he'd swallowed something sour was Urkin," Effie added, accepting the clay bottle from Vexa. "But he always looks like that, so I wouldn't worry."

Vexa turned toward the quietest member of our group. "What do you think, Aether? You've been awfully silent about the whole thing."

"She did well," he said simply, his voice carrying that familiar weight that made even simple praise feel significant.

I couldn't help but study him across the flames. It was fascinating how different he seemed here—calm, collected, almost peaceful—compared to the coiled intensity he carried when we were alone.

"What about the Void?" Lael asked suddenly, his voice pitched with curiosity. "I mean, if we make it through the trials, that's next."

The casual atmosphere shifted, something heavier settling over our group. Effie was the first to break the silence.

"I remember it being... intense," she said, "but the actual details are... fuzzy."

Rethlyn nodded, absently touching his void marks. "Same here. I know I went in, and I know I crawled out, but everything between is just..."

"Like trying to remember a nightmare," Vexa interrupted, her hand finding Effie's. "You know it happened, but the specifics slip away."

An awkward silence fell as everyone's eyes shifted to Aether. He didn't flinch under their gazes, just continued staring into the fire, the embers reflecting in his golden eyes.

"What was it like for you?" Lael asked Aether directly, either too naive or too brave to read the tension. "In the Void?"

The silence stretched, broken only by the crack and pop of burning wood. When Aether finally spoke, his voice was low and measured.

"The Void tests you in ways unimaginable," he said, his eyes never leaving the flames. "It shows you things—makes you see, feel, experience whatever it takes to break you. The key to surviving isn't strength or skill. It's endurance."

His words seemed to drop like stones into still water, rippling through our small gathering.

"What it really wants," he continued, "is for you to lose yourself. To become so twisted in its darkness that you never find your way out. You have to show it you won't succumb."

Lael had gone very still beside me, his earlier excitement replaced by something closer to dread. Aether finally looked up from the fire, his expression softening slightly as he met the boy's gaze.

"It's late," he said, rising smoothly to his feet. "You should rest. Tomorrow's journey won't wait for tired recruits."

"But—" Lael protested, looking around the group. "We just got here. And I wanted to try Rethlyn's rice wine—"

"Which you're too young for anyway," Aether cut in, his tone leaving no room for argument. He moved around the fire and placed a firm hand on Lael's shoulder. "Come on."

Lael shot me a pleading look, but I just shrugged sympathetically. Even I knew better than to argue with Aether when he used that tone. The boy finally stood with a dramatic sigh that reminded me of Effie.

"Fine," he grumbled, dragging his feet as Aether guided him toward the mountain entrance. I watched them disappear into the depths.

"Well," Effie broke the lingering tension, "that was cheerful. Speaking of more pleasant things—" She turned to me with renewed brightness. "What's it like where you're from? I mean, besides the obvious trying-to-kill-us part."

The question caught me off guard, though I should have expected it. These moments of almost-friendship made it easy to forget how things used to be.

"Esprithe, tell me about the food," Effie moaned, leaning forward and handing me the bottle of wine, which I reluctantly accepted. "I miss real food. Do you know how long it's been since I've smelled anything fresh? Like those spiced meat pastries from the street vendors?" She closed her eyes as if trying to conjure the memory. "The ones wrapped in those flaky shells that steam when you break them open? Or proper blackfruit preserves that actually taste sweet instead of..." she gestured vaguely at nothing, "whatever we're pretending to eat these days."

The rice wine burned in my throat as I swallowed. Every word from Effie felt sharp—not meant to hurt, but cutting all the same. How exactly was I supposed to talk to these people about Sídhe? The abundance there? Especially now knowing where it had come from, and what it had cost. It felt cruel.

"The market in Ravenfell used to smell amazing," Vexa added, her voice wistful. "Before the drought. Remember those roasted mushrooms, Reth? We used to stuff ourselves."

I caught Rethlyn watching me, his expression sympathetic. He must have sensed my discomfort—probably literally, given his abilities.

"What about your family?" he asked, clearly trying to change the subject. "Back in Sídhe?"

Relief washed over me at the shift in conversation, though it was quickly replaced by a different kind of ache. "I lost my parents when I was very young." I traced the rim of the bottle with my finger. "But I have someone—a friend I grew up with. She's basically my sister. She's the person I miss most."

"So," Effie piped up, her eyes sparkling with sudden interest, "no handsome suitor waiting for your return?"

The question hit like ice water, and I felt my face harden before I could stop it. The change didn't go unnoticed—Vexa's eyebrows shot up, and Rethlyn shifted uncomfortably.

"Well," Vexa drawled, "I guess we'll take that as a yes."

The group leaned in, their curiosity palpable in the firelight. I considered lying, or deflecting, but the rice wine had already loosened my tongue.

"There is someone," I said hesitantly. "It's not serious."

Laryk's face flashed in my mind—that crooked smirk, the rare occasion in which his emerald eyes would soften from the hardness he showed everyone else. I missed him with an intensity that scared me. Because I didn't know what we were.

"Your reaction certainly seemed to imply it was something serious," Effie pressed, cutting through my thoughts. I hadn't realized how hard I was staring into the flames.

"It's just complicated. He—we both had a lot going on." I gestured vaguely at our surroundings. "And we didn't have much time together before... well." The words hung heavy in the air, the unspoken *before you kidnapped me* making everyone shift uncomfortably.

The silence stretched until I felt compelled to fill it. "We aren't together. He doesn't do monogamy."

"Well that doesn't sound all that romantic." Effie turned up her nose, exchanging a look with Vexa.

"Everyone has their own way of doing things," Vexa said carefully, studying my face. "But the way you say that... it doesn't sound like it's what you want."

I stared into the bottle, watching the dark liquid ripple. Laryk's words echoed in my head: *You're different.* I clung to that phrase like a lifeline, even as I felt pathetic for doing so. What kind of fool builds hope on two vague words? Especially when I knew his reputation, knew exactly what I was getting into...

"Men are hopeless," Effie declared. "Always an excuse ready. They're seeing only you, but they can't make anything official. They need time, or space, or to focus on their—"

"I take personal offense to that generalization," Rethlyn protested, pressing a hand to his chest in mock outrage.

Then I noticed Vexa's gaze catch on my Riftborne branding as it reflected the flames from the fire. Her forehead wrinkled.

"I've been wanting to ask you what that means," she said, gesturing towards my left hand with her chin.

I looked down, anxiety blooming in my gut. "It's a branding—a Riftborne branding." Weeks had passed since I'd even thought about it. No one here knew what it meant, and it had been a nice change, in a way, not having to worry about the judgment that came when a stranger's eye fell upon it.

"Riftborne?" Effie asked.

"My parents were from Riftdremar... All of their children were branded after the Uprising," I said in a low tone, avoiding their eye contact.

Silence swept over the clearing and I swallowed the lump forming in my throat.

"Your parents were from Riftdremar?" Rethlyn leaned forward, shooting Vexa a confused expression.

"We weren't aware there were any survivors," Vexa nearly whispered.

"How do you know about Riftdremar?" I asked, a chill running over my skin. "Aether mentioned it once—when I first got here." How had I forgotten about that?

"We were taught about the conflict when we entered the

Umbra," Effie said, furrowing her brow. "When we learned about arcanite."

"Arcanite? What does that have to do with Riftdremar?" My voice was hoarse from the wood smoke.

The three of them exchanged confused glances.

"What are you not telling me?" I asked again, defensiveness creeping into my tone.

"What do you think the war was fought over?" Vexa narrowed her eyes—not in a cutting way, but as if some very obvious truth hung before me that I refused to grasp.

The uprising? Riftdremar had opposed Sídhe's influence... They wanted freedom after nearly a century of Sídhe's involvement in their culture. They wanted to retaliate against the hand that fed them, that invested in their advancement...

"Independence," I said, my eyes shifting between the three Kalfar.

"I suppose that's one way of looking at it," Rethlyn breathed, suppressing a sigh.

"Fia... Sídhe was ravaging the arcanite stores in Riftdremar for nearly a decade before they burned it down."

Something sharp ripped through me, and I felt as though the air evaporated from my lungs. I knew the uprising never made sense. At some point, I guess I had just started believing what Sídhe was selling me—selling all of us. How many more times could I handle this rug being ripped out from under me? How many times was I going to learn that everything I'd ever known had been a carefully constructed lie? I stood, pacing to lean my shoulder against a tree.

Breathe.

"How do you not know this?" Effie said quietly.

"How do *you* know this?" I shot back, whipping around. Dread coiled in my gut, threatening to pull me under.

"You think the only rip is in Sídhe?" Vexa asked. "We've known about the one in Riftdremar for far longer."

Her words shocked me to silence.

"You've been to Riftdremar?" the words came out a whisper.

"None of us, no. But before—before it was burned to the ground, some Umbra were there." Rethlyn's eyes held an intensity I couldn't quite place.

"What were they doing there?"

"Discussing an alliance." Vexa's words ran another blade through me.

An alliance? Against Sídhe?

Moments slipped by. I wasn't entirely sure how many, or for how long we stayed like this. The gray sky loomed above, the gnarled forest blurring as my vision shifted.

"They didn't tell you about any of this, I see." Rethlyn took another sip of his wine, and leaned back, a heavy expression on his face.

I shook my head.

"Easier to control the masses if you've fed them a story that paints them in a good light," Vexa mumbled.

"I don't understand. If you were branded, painted as a rebel to these people of Sídhe, how did you even end up in the Guard?" Effie asked, her voice verging on exasperation.

The words sank in. "I wasn't given a choice."

"They forced you to fight for them—after everything?" Vexa's tone was laced with disgust.

"That's how it started out—" I stumbled over my words. "It wasn't like that in the end. I thought I was doing what I was meant to. What was right."

"This man you spoke of earlier—he's also in the Guard?" Effie raised an eyebrow.

I nodded.

The silence that followed felt charged with their poorly

concealed judgment, even as they tried to maintain polite expressions.

"Well," Rethlyn said finally, swirling the wine around in the bottle, "I suppose I should give you the standard response of 'you deserve better than that.'"

"You don't understand," I finally said, my voice sharper than intended. "I know how it seems to all of you. But you didn't know me before. When he brought me into the Guard, everything changed."

"The General you told me about before?" Vexa asked, her expression connecting the dots.

I looked away, unable to meet their eyes.

"Well, that's a nightmare in power dynamics," Effie muttered.

"It wasn't like that," I insisted, heat rising in my cheeks.

"He forces you to join the Guard—the one who destroyed your home and branded you? And you *fell* for him?" Vexa's voice wasn't cruel, but it was pained. I wasn't sure which was worse.

I knew how all of it looked. How it must sound to all of them. Even hearing it all playing out in my head was making me nauseous. Their pity was suffocating. I could feel it rolling off them in waves.

"Well there was clearly a lot of manipulation going on," Rethlyn sighed, running a hand through his dark hair. "You're right Fia, none of us have the slightest clue what it was like to be in that situation." He shot Vexa a look.

The words tumbled out before I could stop them, driven by wine. "Laryk taught me so much about myself, how to wield my focus, how to fight. He was the only person who ever saw something useful in me."

"Sounds like he was creating a lovely new weapon in you." Vexa clicked her teeth.

I went still. "I don't know why I'm bothering to explain any of this to you," I said, my voice trembling. "I didn't have a life—a purpose—until Laryk found me. I don't care how it comes across to you. I *experienced* it firsthand. I was drowning, and he saved me from myself."

I could feel tears threatening to spill, and I refused to let them see me cry. I turned away from the fire.

"Fia, wait!" I heard Vexa's voice call from behind.

Their apologies followed me as I strode into the darkness, but I didn't slow down. I was so focused on holding back tears that I nearly collided with a solid form in the shadows.

Aether.

Of course it would be him. Of course he would see me like this, with tears streaming down my face despite my best efforts to contain them. I waited for the criticism.

"Don't," I said, when he fell into step beside me. "I just want to be alone. In the quiet."

But he didn't leave. He just walked silently beside me, his presence somehow steadier than before.

"Don't let them get to you," he said finally, his voice low. "I ignore them most of the time anyway."

The simplicity of his response, so devoid of judgment or pity, made something in my chest loosen just slightly as we walked back toward the mountain. But as I glanced up at it, I realized I didn't want to go back to it either. To the confinement.

I stopped.

Aether's eyes cut back to me, raising a pierced eyebrow.

"I'd rather—" I started, looking around desperately, "I don't want to go back there yet."

He turned fully then, crossing his arms, "and where do you want to go?"

I let out a gentle sigh as I realized I had no idea. But if he was willing to get me out of here—if that's what he was offering with his question, I was going to take it.

"Can we just walk?" I asked.

Instead of answering, he simply examined me for a moment, narrowing his eyes. Finally, he moved further into the brush, in the opposite direction of the mountain. Before I knew it, he was turning to me, walking backward through the gnarled branches.

"So are you coming, or not?" he asked, the ghost of a smile playing on his lips.

I brushed the remnants of salty tears from my eyes and followed.

The forest was quiet save for the crunch of leaves beneath our boots. I welcomed the silence after the chaos at the fire, though my thoughts kept drifting back to their questions about Laryk. How they seemed incapable of understanding.

Aether's arm suddenly shot out across my chest, pulling me to a stop. I followed his gaze to the ground where rotting wooden spikes protruded from a concealed pit.

"Old trap," he said, guiding me around it. "The forest's full of them."

"You seem to be in your natural habitat out here." I remembered Vexa calling him a lumberjack, Rethlyn's mentions of his cabin. "It's surprising. You don't seem the rural type."

His eyebrow arched. "And what type do I seem?"

"Well, I've never seen a hunter with that much metal in his face."

A rare laugh escaped him, deep and rich. "The piercings are tradition. You'll learn about that eventually." His golden eyes sparked with amusement. "I wasn't aware appearances dictated who could prefer forests to fortresses."

"So you admit you're a recluse?"

"I prefer the term selective socializer."

"Selective socializer," I echoed. "Is that what you call hiding in the woods?"

"Says the woman who's currently hiding in the woods with me."

"I'm not hiding, I'm..." I searched for the right word. "Strategically avoiding conversation. And responsibility."

"Clearly that's working well for you." A dimple appeared as he navigated around a fallen log.

A comfortable silence fell between us as we walked deeper into the forest. The tension from earlier had dissolved into something relatively peaceful, considering. I found myself studying him when he wasn't looking—the way he moved through the trees with such familiarity.

"Watch your step," he said, pointing out another trap. "These get harder to spot the deeper we go."

"How many times have you fallen in one?"

"None." A hint of pride touched his voice. "Though Vexa managed to find the deepest one last spring."

He shook his head, as if recalling a memory.

"She's convinced I set up elaborate traps just to spite her," he said, "as if I have nothing better to do."

I couldn't help but smile at the image of Vexa, covered in mud, hurling accusations at him. It was strange seeing this side of him— the subtle humor, the way his absurd brooding had mellowed into something almost companionable.

"So what do you actually do out here? Besides leading unsuspecting people into deadly pits?"

"Exist, mostly." He ducked under a low branch. "The forest's quieter than the fortress. Less politics."

A screech echoed overhead, and we both looked up to see a dark shape cutting through the gray sky. Nihr's wings stretched wide as she banked sharply.

"Does she always follow you like that?"

"She's a protective one." Aether's eyes tracked his mount's movement.

"They seem..." I hesitated. "Particular. For animals, at least."

"They are." That hint of pride returned to his voice. "Nihr found me shortly after I emerged from the Void. Wouldn't leave me alone for days. Eventually I stopped trying to chase her off."

"You tried to chase off a Vördr?"

"Not my finest moment." The corner of his mouth twitched. "Though in my defense, I wasn't exactly thinking clearly at the time."

I tried to imagine what that must have been like. Emerging from the Void with no memories, no sense of who you were or where you belonged, and then having this powerful creature decide you were worth following. Did he even know what a Vördr was then? Or was Nihr just another strange thing in a world that made no sense?

Nihr dove through the canopy, branches swaying in her wake. "And she just... decided to stay? Even after your hesitation?"

"Vördr choose their riders for life. Once they've decided, that's it. Stubborn beasts." He shrugged. "No point arguing with a creature that's lived for centuries."

"How old is she?"

"No one knows exactly. The records mention a black Vördr with silver-tipped wings during the first war, but..." He glanced up as Nihr circled overhead. "It's impossible to tell if it was her."

"So, I'm assuming that would make her ancient?"

"Hence why I stopped arguing." That slight smile appeared again.

"Fair point." I paused, curiosity getting the better of me. "What was the first war?"

His golden eyes darted towards me curiously. "The war that put the Valtýrs on the throne. Before them, the Syrndore bloodline ruled." He cracked his knuckles, the sound echoing through the dry wood. "But the Valtýrs were Duskbound. They claimed it was a divine right to rule."

"And that's why they won?"

"They united the other noble houses. The records say the

fighting lasted decades." His jaw tightened. "Nearly destroyed the realm before the Valtýrs claimed the throne."

I nodded as we fell into comfortable silence again.

"We should head back," Aether said, "you'll need your rest come tomorrow."

I followed him towards the mountain, avoiding twigs from the thick, dead brush, suddenly aware of how much lighter I felt.

CHAPTER TWENTY-TWO

The mountain arena felt different today. Colder somehow, as if the stone itself knew what was coming. We stood in the antechamber, the air thick with anticipation and something else—fear, maybe, though none of us would admit it.

Kenna paced in small circles, nerves radiating off of her. Even Theron's mask had slipped, his fingers drumming against his thigh in an uneven rhythm. Mira stood perfectly still, but her eyes never stopped moving throughout the space. The only one who seemed truly at ease was Valkan, lounging against a pillar with his personal guard, looking for all the world like this was merely a social gathering.

Vexa's boots echoed against stone as she approached our group, her leathers marking her as Spectre. "Those offered the choice will fly to the Void's location this evening," she said, her voice carrying an official weight that still felt strange coming from her. "If you accept, there's no turning back."

Her violet eyes swept over us, lingering on each face. "Those who decline, or aren't selected for the Void, may be offered positions in other units based on your abilities. The ground troops, scouts, or archival units all need capable soldiers." She paused, something flickering across her expression. "Each role serves the realm. Remember that when you make your choice."

I could feel her gaze on me, heavy with the weight of last night's conversation, but I kept my eyes fixed on the far wall. The awkwardness still hung between us, made worse by the formality of the moment.

"Fia," she said finally, gesturing to a quiet corner. "A word?"

I hesitated, remembering her sharp comments about Laryk, how I'd nearly cried my eyes out in front of them. The others pretended not to watch as I stayed rooted in place.

"I'll be quick," she added lightly. Something in her voice made me follow.

She led me to an alcove, away from curious ears. For a moment she just stood there, absently tracing the designs on her leathers.

"I was harsh last night," she said finally, meeting my eyes. "And that's the last thing I wanted to be. It's just... you've always seemed so sure of yourself. So strong. Like nothing could touch you."

I almost laughed at that. I had been their prisoner for a majority of my time here, and that didn't necessarily scream strength.

"Hearing about what happened in Sídhe," she continued, "how they treated you, how they..." She shook her head. "It caught me off guard. Made me angry. Not at you," she added quickly. "At them. At how they took someone with your power and tried to..." She gestured vaguely.

"Turn me into a weapon?" I supplied, unable to keep the edge from my voice.

"Into whatever they needed," she corrected softly. "With no regard to what they had taken from you. All while concealing the truth."

The words hit something deep inside me. I thought about that scared girl in Sídhe, the one who'd been so afraid of her own power. The one who'd hidden from everything until she had no choice but to fight. When had that changed? When had I become someone others saw as strong?

"I'm not—" I started, then stopped, unsure how to explain. "I wasn't always like this. Before everything, I literally just kept my head down—stuck to the shadows." A bitter laugh escaped me. "Ironic, considering."

"And now you command six Sentinels at once and make Urkin squirm in his chair." A hint of that smirk returned. "People change. Sometimes for the better, sometimes not. It sounds like your experience helped you grow. And that's never a bad thing."

I thought about that—about all the ways I'd changed since joining the Guard. Some changes had been forced upon me, others I'd chosen. But which was which? The line between them felt blurrier every day.

"I am sorry though," she added quietly. "About what I said. You didn't deserve that."

"Why does it matter to you?" I asked, the question slipping out before I could stop it. "A few weeks ago I was just your prisoner."

Something flashed across her face—pain, maybe, or recognition. "Because we're not so different." She shrugged.

Before I could respond, movement near the arena entrance caught my attention. Valkan stood with his personal guards, his milky eyes fixed on our conversation.

"He did well in the trials," I said, trying to redirect.

Vexa's mouth hardened into a line. "Too well. The drought doesn't seem to affect him at all. His abilities, his strength—none of it has diminished like the rest of us. I understand the Council's desperation, but I'd rather die than serve alongside that."

A horn sounded from above, cutting through our conversation. The sound reverberated through the stone, making several candidates jump. Through the archway, I could see nobles filing into their seats.

"Candidates," Urkin's voice boomed through the chamber. "Take your positions."

Vexa squeezed my arm once before moving away. "Whatever happens next," she whispered, "You've proved yourself already."

We filed into the arena proper, where the Generals sat in their elevated seats. The crowd seemed larger than before, the noble boxes packed with anxious faces. I couldn't help the pang in my gut at remembering that they chose Valkan. They allowed such a monster into this competition. Gave him even more power—more influence.

"Candidate Theron," Urkin's voice filled the chamber. "Step forward."

Theron moved with the same confident stride he'd shown in his trials, but I noticed a slight tremor in his hands. He stood before the Generals' platform, the torchlight reflecting off his dark hair.

"You have proven yourself worthy of the choice," Urkin stated, his voice carrying to every corner of the arena. "Your abilities show not just power, but control. Discipline." He paused, letting the words settle. "Do you choose to give yourself fully to Umbrathia? Do you choose to embrace the shadows? Will you meet the Void?"

"I will." Theron's voice carried clearly through the chamber, unwavering despite the weight of hundreds of eyes upon him. Applause erupted from the crowd as he was led away by two Spectres.

This was really happening. I swallowed the lump forming in my throat.

Kenna was next, appearing solemn as she accepted. When Cassia declined, whispers rippled through the crowd, but the Generals merely conferred briefly before offering her a position with the scouts. Her relief was palpable as she was escorted from the arena.

"Candidate Lael," Urkin called, and my heart clenched.

The boy who'd sat beside me at the bonfire seemed transformed as he approached the platform. His shoulders were set, his chin high. Aether's words from last night hung in the air. *The Void tests you in ways unimaginable.*

"I will," Lael said, his voice laced with determination. I felt a lick of pride flare at the smile that broke across his face.

The ceremony continued. Raven's abilities with mirror communication earned him a place in the Archival Unit. Mira accepted the choice.

Then Valkan stepped forward, and the very air seemed to still.

The Generals' faces had gone rigid, though they maintained their composure. Even Urkin's perpetual scowl deepened as Valkan approached, his movements like a predator.

"Lord Valkan," Urkin's voice carried a weight I hadn't heard before. "You have proven yourself worthy of the choice." The words seemed to cost him something. "Do you choose to give yourself fully to Umbrathia? Do you choose to embrace the shadows? Will you meet the Void?"

Valkan's smile was radiant and wrong. "My friends," he addressed the crowd directly, ignoring protocol entirely. "This is but the first step toward Umbrathia's salvation. Together, we will restore our realm to glory." His dead eyes found mine. "And we will do whatever it takes to achieve that end."

The nobles shifted in their seats, some leaning forward eagerly, others drawing back. Valkan continued speaking, but I barely heard the words. His gaze felt like oil on my skin, making my stomach turn. As he passed me on his way off the stage, he paused.

"Such raw power," he murmured, just loud enough for me to hear. "What a magnificent shadow you'll become."

Finally, only I remained. The silence stretched as the Generals conferred in hushed tones. I could feel the weight of the crowd's attention, the mixture of curiosity and suspicion that had followed me since my arrival in Umbrathia. Urkin's eyes bored into me, but I refused to look away, remembering how he'd watched me command his Sentinels. *Let him see that strength now.*

"Never before," he said finally, his voice filling the chamber, "has an outsider stood where you stand. Never before has one proven worthy of this choice." His jaw tightened. "But after much deliberation, we have decided you have earned the right to further prove yourself to our realm." He straightened in his chair. "Foreign-born, do you choose to give yourself fully to Umbrathia? Do you choose to embrace the shadows? Will you meet the Void?"

Relief flooded me.

I thought of everything that had led me here—the lies I'd been told in Sídhe, the truth I'd discovered in this dying realm. I thought of Vexa's words about choice. The Void might break me, might show me horrors beyond imagination, but at least this time, the choice was mine.

This time, I knew what I was fighting for. And I knew what I was fighting against. I stepped forward, eyes sweeping the panel of Generals. Each one nodded as my gaze met theirs.

"I will."

THE CLOUDS PRESSED in around us, thick and gray. Nihr's wings cut through them with ease, sending wisps of mist dancing across my skin. I shifted in the saddle, trying to ignore how close Aether sat behind me, how his shadows seemed calmer now than they had in days.

The other candidates were somewhere ahead of us, each paired with their own Spectre escort. Tradition, they'd called it, though I suspected it had more to do with making sure none of us lost our nerve at the last moment. Not that turning back was an option now—even if I wanted to.

The silence stretched between us, broken only by the steady beat of Nihr's wings. I thought of all the questions I still had, all the things I still didn't understand about what was coming. But asking felt like admitting fear, and I'd already shown enough weakness these past few days.

A sudden gust of wind rocked us, and I gripped the saddle horn tighter. The temperature had been dropping steadily as we flew North, the air growing thinner. Even the light seemed different here. Darker, maybe, or deeper. Ice began to form along Nihr's harness, crystallizing in delicate patterns.

My teeth chattered despite my best efforts to stop them. The cold had begun seeping through my leathers, burrowing into my bones. Behind me, Aether radiated heat. Before I could stop, I found myself leaning back slightly, drawn to that warmth.

I felt him stiffen for just a moment before relaxing. Neither of us spoke, but he didn't pull away.

"The cold gets worse," he said, his voice close to my ear, his breath warm against my skin. "The closer we get."

I fought back a shiver that had nothing to do with the temperature. "How much further?"

"Not far." There was something in his tone—not quite concern, but something adjacent to it. "You can feel it, can't you?"

I knew what he was asking. Something had been tugging at my consciousness since we'd crossed into the Northern territory. Like a whisper just below hearing, or a shadow seen from the corner of my eye. It felt similar to how the darkness had called to me in Emeraal.

"Is that normal?" I asked, hating how small my voice sounded against the wind.

He paused, and I felt him shift slightly behind me. "No. But I thought it might call to you."

Another gust of wind hit us, this one carrying a bite that cut straight through me. Nihr's wings beat harder against it, sending us into a slight tilt that pressed me further against Aether's chest. The heat of him was maddening—a stark contrast to the ice forming in my hair, on my eyelashes. I should have pulled away, maintained some semblance of distance, but the cold had become too brutal to fight.

"The others," I started, then hesitated, trying to focus on anything except his proximity. "They don't remember their time in the Void."

"They remember parts of it," he said after a long moment, his voice a low rumble I could feel through my back. "The mind protects itself from the worst of it. Buries what it can't handle." His voice dropped lower. "But some things leave marks that can't be forgotten."

The clouds ahead had begun to thin, revealing glimpses of the landscape below. Or what should have been landscape. Instead, there was... nothing. An absence so complete it hurt to look at, like trying to see into a hole in the world itself.

"There," Aether said, though he didn't need to. I could feel it now—a vast, hunger that seemed to pull at something deep inside me. "The Void."

Nihr banked slightly, and the clouds parted fully. I forgot how to breathe.

It stretched as far as I could see, a mass of writhing shadows that consumed everything in its path. No light escaped it, no sound emerged from it. Even the dimmed light seemed to bend away from its edges, as if the very air feared being devoured.

This was what had changed Aether. What had marked all of them. And in a few hours, I would have to walk into its depths.

And suddenly, I recognized it. From my dream with the girls—the father dragging them into the darkness, their mother sobbing in the wake of it all.

"Remember," Aether's voice was barely a whisper now. "It's not about surviving. It's about choosing to keep fighting—*resisting*—even when everything inside you wants to give in."

I thought I felt his hand brush my arm—just for a moment, but when I turned to look at him, his eyes were fixed ahead, his expression unreadable as we soared towards the unending darkness of the Void.

CHAPTER TWENTY-THREE

The five of us stood before the wall of nothingness, its mass of darkness stretching endlessly in every direction. Even the perpetual twilight seemed to bend away from it, as if the very light feared being consumed. Five Spectres I didn't recognize stood behind us, their void burns dark against their skin, while Aether addressed us from the front.

"The nobles and Council members will arrive by the time you emerge," he said, his voice carrying across the emptiness that separated us from the darkness. "They come to witness either your triumph or your failure."

"But it's nearly a day's ride from Ravenfell," Kenna said, her composure cracking slightly. "How long will we be in there?"

"As long as it takes." The finality in Aether's tone left no room for further questions.

The Void's pull had grown stronger since we'd landed, like something alive reaching for me. That whisper that had started during our flight was now a constant thrum under my skin, making it hard to stand still.

"You're free to enter now," Aether said. "I hope to see you on the other side."

No one moved. The words hung in the air between us and that wall of darkness. Kenna's hands trembled as she took a half-step forward, then stopped. Theron seemed frozen in place, his eyes darting between the Void and the Spectres as if searching for some hidden clue. Even Valkan's confidence appeared to waver, if only for a moment.

But the pull was too strong now. It sang in my blood, a symphony of shadows that promised answers.

I didn't look back at Aether. Didn't check to see if the others were watching. I simply walked forward, each step more certain than the last, until the darkness reached out with eager fingers and pulled me in.

It consumed me instantly. Tendrils of shadow slid across my arms, my legs, my torso—their touch both burning and freezing at once. My vision went black, and then my sense of gravity disappeared entirely. Up became down, or maybe there was no up or down anymore. Just endless, suffocating nothing.

The shadows weren't content to just surround me. They seeped through my skin, clawing their way beneath the surface, burying themselves in every muscle, every tendon, every bone until I couldn't tell where I ended and the darkness began. It flooded my lungs, and no matter how hard I tried, I couldn't breathe.

My web latched onto my spine in desperation, braiding itself upward as I writhed against the invasion. But even that familiar power felt wrong here—weak and foreign in this place of absolute nothingness. I felt it begin to fray, to dissolve, as consciousness slipped further away. The shadows pulled me deeper, deeper, until there was nothing left of me at all.

And then—

I sucked in a giant, clean breath.

My vision snapped back into focus. Music pulsed through my

body, and above me, an enormous flower orbited slowly, its petals casting shifting patterns of light across the crowd. The Enclave. I was at the Enclave. In Luminaria.

The familiar hum of liquid euphoria coursed through my veins. Through the shifting lights, I saw them—Osta, Raine, and Briar, dancing and laughing as they twirled through the crowd. A smile tugged at my lips. They looked so alive, so real. I felt myself let go, melting into the dancing figures around me. The melodies thrummed through me as minds began to glow around us, pulsing in rhythm with the beat.

Then something shifted.

One by one, faces turned toward me. The smiles remained, but their eyes... their eyes went white, empty. Hollow. Each person I looked at contorted in agony, their features twisting into masks of pain as blood began to pour from their nose, then their eyes, then their ears, soaking their collars with crimson streaks.

I screamed, but the sound was lost in the music. Bodies dropped by the hundreds. Osta. Raine. Briar. All of them, because of me. Because I looked at them.

I slammed my eyes shut, pressed my palms against them until colors burst behind my lids. *It's not real. It's not real. It's not—*

When I opened them again, I was somewhere else entirely. Sunlight streamed through arched windows, illuminating a lobby I'd never seen before. But I knew these people—Eron and Jacquelina, the people I had grown up with in the group home— The House of Unity. The first Riftborne couple to bear a child in Luminaria. They sat rigid in their chairs. Between them sat a small girl with curious eyes. Leila, their daughter.

A woman approached, hand extended toward Leila. She went willingly, her innocent smile never faltering. Jacquelina collapsed into Eron as tears streaked down her face.

No. I knew what came next. I didn't want to see this, didn't want to—

But the scene shifted anyway. Leila sat in the center of a room, a man standing before her. The branding iron emerged from strange-colored flames, and her smile finally broke.

"Stop!" I screamed. "Please, stop!"

The world tilted, twisted, and suddenly I was looking through Leila's eyes. Those small fingers—my fingers—reached out as the brand descended. The pain tore through me as the hot metal met my skin, my flesh melting against the burn. I screamed. Writhed. The pain was unimaginable until consciousness drifted out of reach.

The apothecary materialized around me, familiar wooden shelves laden with dried herbs and tinctures. I was at my desk, the one where I'd spent countless hours grinding herbs and copying Ma's recipes. The air felt thick, heavy with an unfamiliar stench.

"Those unruly herbs giving you trouble again?" Ma's voice carried from behind me, warm and familiar. I turned to find her organizing bottles, hibiscus stains marking her hands like always. Her silver-threaded chestnut hair was coming loose from its bun, just as I remembered.

"Something smells awful today," I said, falling into our usual banter despite the wrongness creeping at the edges of my mind.

"Worse than the time you let those mushrooms rot?" She shot me that knowing look, the one that always made me feel like a child again.

Movement flickered in my peripheral vision. My eyes shot to the back shelves, and my heart stopped.

They stood there—Bekha and Jordaan—their eyes hollow and white, skin gray and peeling. The stench of decay rolled off them in waves. *No. No, they're not dead. I didn't kill them. I didn't—*

Ma's eyes were wide with horror as her gaze fell upon their bodies, hands flying up over her mouth as they pointed at me.

"Did you do this, Fia?" Ma's voice cracked as she stumbled

backward. The fear in her eyes cut deeper than any blade. "What are you?"

"They're not dead," I whispered, the words tumbling out faster and faster. "They're not dead. No. No. No—"

I stepped toward her, reaching out, but she recoiled.

"Stay away from me!" the scream tore from her throat, ripping through my chest.

Something shattered inside me. Tears welled up, blurring the horror before me. When they finally spilled over, the scene dissolved, reforming into—

Silk sheets beneath me. A familiar weight above me. Burnt amber and vetiver filled my lungs as Laryk's breath ghosted across my neck, his fingers tangled in my hair. My heart swelled at his closeness.

"Perfect," he murmured against my throat. His emerald eyes locked with mine, softening in that rare way they did only for me, before darkening as he moved. A moan escaped my lips and his grip tightened.

"You're different," he breathed. "Unique. The most incredible thing I've ever laid eyes on." Each word sent warmth blooming through my chest, erasing the hollow ache that had lived there for so long. This was everything I'd wanted, everything I'd missed.

My fingers traced the planes of his back as pleasure built between us. His mouth found mine, and I lost myself in the kiss, in the perfect rightness of this moment.

And then he was at my throat, teeth gliding across my skin before he kissed, pulling more of me into him. But the next time he spoke, his voice was different. "My favorite weapon," he groaned against my collarbone.

"What?" The word caught in my throat.

His hand fisted in my hair, yanking my head to the side. "Look how stunning you are," he commanded, forcing my gaze toward the mirror on the wall.

Narissa's face glared back at me, her red hair spilling across the silk sheets like fresh blood.

Bile rose in my throat as her eyes met mine in the mirror, her lips curving into a knowing smile. I lurched to the side of the bed, my body convulsing as I retched. The silk sheets twisted around me as the world tilted—

And suddenly I was on my back, dead grass crackling beneath me. The bed was gone. Laryk was gone. Only darkness stretched above me, absolute and endless. Reality slammed back into focus with brutal clarity—the Void. I was in the Void.

My chest heaved as I gasped for air, the shadows pressing in around me like a physical weight. The grass beneath my fingers felt wrong, each blade sharp enough to draw blood. Had I imagined everything? Osta's blood-filled eyes, Ma's terror, Laryk's—

No. *Don't think about it.* Don't—

But the darkness was already reaching for me again, its tendrils wrapping around my thoughts, pulling me under. I tried to fight it, tried to hold onto this moment of lucidity, but the shadows were stronger. They dragged me down, down, until consciousness fractured once more.

CHAPTER TWENTY-FOUR

Darkness stretched in every direction, but this time it was different. Not the suffocating nothingness of before, but something alive. Shadows writhed and twisted around me, their whispers growing louder, more insistent. They spoke of power lying just beyond, waiting to be claimed.

In the distance, two images shimmered like mirages. On one side, I saw Ravenfell, its people wasting away as the essence drained from their land. Vexa cradling a lifeless Effie. Lael collapsed in the street. Even Aether's golden eyes had gone dull, his shadows fading as the drought consumed everything.

On the other side, Sídhe blazed with stolen vitality. The Guard gathered at the border, Laryk at their head, preparing for war. They didn't understand what they were doing—that their prosperity came at the cost of an entire realm. That they were destroying everything.

The shadows coiled around my ankles, sliding up my legs with seductive grace. *We can give you the power to stop this*, they seemed to whisper. *To save them all.*

I could feel it—that impossible strength hovering just out of reach. All I had to do was let go. Stop fighting. Let the darkness consume everything I was, everything I'd built myself to be. My web, my memories, my will—all of it would dissolve into shadow.

We can show you how, the shadows purred, wrapping around my waist now, my ribs, my throat. *You've only touched the surface of what you could become.*

The images shifted. I saw myself wielding shadows like they were extensions of my body, tearing holes between realms, commanding armies of darkness. I could force peace through sheer power. I could make them all stop fighting, stop killing each other. No more lies, no more theft of essence, no more death.

But something deeper than my bones knew the cost. I would lose everything—not just memories, but the very essence of who I was, transformed into something unrecognizable. I would become like the Void itself. Endless. Hungry. Absolute.

The shadow-version of myself turned to look at me with eyes like the endless dark. Not cruel, not kind—simply rid of everything that made me *me*. No trace of the girl who'd grown up in Ma's apothecary. No remnant of the fighter Laryk had seen potential in. Nothing left of the person who'd found something worth fighting for in this dying realm.

You've always been meant for this, the shadows whispered. *Why else would we call to you so strongly?*

They were right. I'd felt it from the beginning—that pull, that sense of recognition. The shadows had never felt foreign, never felt wrong. They felt like coming home.

Just let go.

I closed my eyes, feeling the darkness press against my skin, seeping into my pores, trying to merge with my essence. One simple choice. Sacrifice everything I was to become something powerful enough to save everyone.

The power sang through my blood, promising everything I'd

ever wanted. An end to the war. An end to suffering. An end to having to choose sides.

All I had to do was stop being Fia.

The shadows pressed closer, wrapping around my throat like a lover's caress. It would be so easy. Just one moment of surrender and all of this—the pain, the choices, the weight of two realms—would dissolve into pure power.

The visions shifted again. I saw myself standing between armies, my mere presence enough to make them lower their weapons. I saw essence flowing freely through Umbrathia once more, saw children playing in gardens that had sprung back to life. I saw Sídhe's people learning to live without stolen power, adapting, growing stronger on their own.

You could end it all, the shadows promised. *Right now.*

My web gave one last desperate pulse against my spine as the darkness began to seep into it, beginning to transform its pearlescent strands into something darker. The pain was exquisite—like being unmade and remade all at once.

I felt myself starting to fade, my memories becoming liquid, slipping through my fingers like water. Ma's smile. Laryk's emerald eyes. Aether's golden gaze in the firelight. They began to blur, to lose meaning.

Let go, the shadows sang. *Let go let go let go—*

"It's not about surviving."

The words cut through the darkness like a blade, sharp and familiar. Aether's voice.

"It's about choosing to keep fighting even when everything inside you wants to give in."

The shadows hissed, tightening their grip, but the words had already taken root. Fighting. Not surrendering. Not letting go. *Fighting.*

The shadows writhed, their whispers turning sharp, desperate.

You're making a mistake. Think of what you could become. Think of what you could save.

The visions flickered faster now—Ravenfell restored, Sídhe at peace, both realms thriving under my absolute power. But beneath those promises, something darker pulsed. A hunger that would never be satisfied. An emptiness that would consume everything, even after there was nothing left of me to give.

You cannot fight what you are meant to be, they hissed. *You cannot deny your true nature.*

But Aether's words echoed through me again. Fighting. Fighting against the temptation to take the easy path. Against losing myself to power that promised everything but would cost more. Because it was a lie. *This* was the test. The Void wasn't offering me power, it was trying to consume me.

The shadows pressed harder, trying to force their way deeper into my essence. My web sparked against my spine, no longer yielding to their invasion. Each tendril of darkness that tried to corrupt it was met with fierce resistance.

You're weak, the shadows snarled. *You could be infinite.*

"I'd rather be myself," I whispered, and felt the truth of it burn through my veins.

The darkness recoiled, but only for a moment. It surged back stronger, determined to break me. But now I understood—this was the real test. Not whether I could survive the Void, but whether I could survive it without losing myself.

I held onto that truth as the shadows raged around me, as they tried to tear me apart, as they showed me every horror that would come from my refusal. I held on, and I fought.

I slammed into the dead grass, every muscle screaming in agony. The ground felt wrong beneath my fingers—brittle and sharp as I clawed my way forward through the darkness. My arms trembled as I pushed myself up, willing my legs to work, to run, to get away from the shadows still reaching for me.

I ran. For hours, maybe days—time had no meaning here. My throat was raw from screaming, though no sound emerged. Just endless silence and darkness stretching in every direction. My legs burned, my lungs ached, but I kept moving. Had to keep moving.

Something solid caught my foot and I pitched forward, landing hard. My hands found fabric, then flesh—a body. Ice shot through my veins as I tried to make out who it was in the darkness. A wet, gurgling cough broke the silence.

"Lael?" My voice came out strangled. "Lael!"

He coughed again, the sound thick and wrong. Something in me snapped. I grabbed him under his arms, trying to drag him with me, but my strength was gone. Tears streamed down my face as I pulled harder, desperate to get him away from here.

"If you take him, you'll owe me a debt, dear child."

The voice thundered through the nothingness. Deep, guttural, and terrifying. It wasn't like the whispers from before. This was something else entirely.

"Everything has its price," the voice boomed louder, making the very darkness tremble.

"I felt you the moment you stepped into my realm." The voice seemed to press against my skin, making my ears ring. "You're not like them, you know. Not like the others. Not like him."

It felt like something yanked Lael from the darkness, but I held on tighter, my fingers digging into his arms.

"I passed your test!" I finally screamed, my voice breaking through the suffocating silence. The words tore from my throat, raw and desperate.

"Test?" The voice held something like amusement, though the sound made my skin crawl. "That was merely an introduction, dear child. The real question is—what would you sacrifice for him?"

My heart stopped.

I clutched Lael tighter as invisible forces tried to tear him away. I had just avoided the pull of the darkness—just escaped its grip on me, despite their temptations. I looked down at Lael, feeling the rise and fall of his chest—shallow, labored. He was a child, fighting in a war that had taken everything for him. I thought of his parents. Thought of how he longed to see life return to the realm.

I couldn't let him wither into nothing in this place, consumed by darkness.

"Anything," I choked out.

"Dangerous words." The darkness seemed to pulse around us. "To offer such things to forces you don't understand."

"I don't care what it costs me." My voice cracked. "Just let me save him."

"And there it is." The voice grew heavier, pressing in from all sides. "The truth of you. So willing to bargain with darkness to save someone you barely know. It will suit you well for what's coming."

"Who? Suit me—what's coming?"

"Accept my bargain, dear child. Owe me a debt to be collected when I choose. And you may keep your precious charge."

My arms ached from holding onto Lael. Everything in me screamed that this was wrong—that making deals with ancient, unknowable things could only end in tragedy. But I couldn't let him go. Couldn't leave him here in this endless dark.

"I accept," I whispered.

"One last scene for you, dear. I think this is one you've been waiting to see, perhaps, for your entire life."

The darkness rippled, and suddenly Lael's weight vanished from my arms. My vision blurred, and I found myself under a starlit sky, flames roaring all around me. Through the inferno, I saw them—a couple locked in an embrace. The woman's hair was almost like mine. Unruly, and long, but darker, more blonde than white. The man who held her had skin nearly as gray as the smoke surrounding them, long black hair falling in intricate braids down his back. And shadows. Shadows around his eyes.

Their arms tightened around each other, golden bracelets hanging on both of their arms, reflecting the raging fire surrounding them. One last look—one last glance of understanding. A look I'd never shared with another person.

They clung to each other as the flames descended, consuming them.

And then they were erased from existence.

Reality snapped back to darkness, and I choked on phantom smoke, my lungs burning. Lael's weight returned to my arms.

"What was that?" I gasped. "Who were they?"

Silence answered.

"It's not like them to intervene. They must truly fear what awaits."

"Who?" I demanded. "What are you talking about?"

"I believe these belong to you now."

The words hit like a physical force. Darkness whipped around me, through me, into me—but this time it didn't try to consume. Power surged through my veins as I clutched Lael to my chest. Intoxicated. I was intoxicated—just as I had been on the lawn in Emeraal. Just as I had been when Aether touched me. But I fought through the sensation. I needed to get Lael *the fuck* out of here.

I shot upward through the nothingness, my feet leaving the bladed grass behind, Lael hanging in my arms. I wasn't quite sure how I knew where I was going, but I did. Not in any conscious way, but it was more of a feeling, a magnetism from the shadows pulling me. The darkness melted around us like liquid night. And finally, I was there. I could see the hint of a gray sky beyond the dark mist. I slammed into it.

Breaching the barrier between Void and reality felt like flying through weighted water, the pressure pulling my frame, slowing me down. Finally, we burst into dulled air. And every murmur muted to nothing. The shadows didn't dissipate but rather coiled around me like a living cloak, dancing with my hair as it whipped wild and white against the gray sky.

My eyes scanned the crowd below, searching. Nobles in their finery, Council members, citizens of Ravenfell—all of them blurred together until I found what I was looking for. Aether. His golden eyes locked onto mine, then dropped to Lael's limp form. He was moving before I even landed, shouldering past nobles, cutting through the crowd.

Lael's breathing grew more labored, each shallow gasp tearing at something inside me. The shadows carried me down, my feet slamming into the earth. The crowd parted before me as I rushed forward.

"He needs help," I said as Aether reached me, my voice hoarse. The void burns on Lael's skin crawled up his neck in the twilight, spreading across him like smoke. My arms that wrapped around him were untouched by such markings.

"Please."

Aether moved without hesitation. That hard edge that normally permeated his entire presence seemed to crack as he helped support Lael's weight. I saw it then—the fear in his eyes as he looked at the boy he'd saved from Croyg.

"Get the medics." Aether's voice carried a desperation I'd never heard before. "Now!"

The shadows still curled around us, but I barely noticed them, barely registered the whispers from the crowd. All that mattered was the labored rise and fall of Lael's chest, and the way Aether's hands trembled slightly as he checked the boy's pulse.

As the medics rushed forward, I caught Aether's eye once more. The mask had fallen completely now, replaced by something raw.

"Behold," Karis's voice boomed from behind me, his feet crunching through the dead grass. "A Duskbound has emerged from the Void."

CHAPTER TWENTY-FIVE

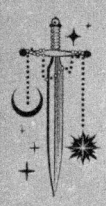

The Void stretched before us. Whispers from the crowd drifted across the empty space behind, but I kept my eyes forward, searching for any sign of movement. Vexa stood beside me, uncharacteristically silent.

"How long was I in there?" I finally asked, my voice still raw.

"Twelve hours." She shifted her weight, crossing her arms. "Theron emerged first, then Mira. You came out with Lael about an hour ago."

I nodded, processing this. The medics had taken Lael immediately, working quickly to stabilize him. He was unconscious but alive—that's what mattered. Time had felt impossible to track in there, stretching and compressing without logic or reason.

"Twelve hours," I repeated. "It felt like weeks. And also like minutes."

"That's normal." Vexa's lips quirked, but the smile didn't reach her eyes. "Though emerging with another person? That's... rare." She glanced at me. "Want to talk about what happened in there?"

"Not really."

"Fair enough." She went quiet for a moment. "Kenna's still in. And Valkan."

Something in her tone made me look over. "You're worried about Kenna."

"Wouldn't you be? That *thing* is in there with her." She didn't need to specify who she meant.

I wanted to tell her Kenna would be fine, but the memory of that darkness was too fresh to offer empty comfort. Instead, I watched the Void, silently willing it to give us Kenna next. And hoping that Valkan would never come out at all.

The other candidates had gathered near one of the stone outcrops. Theron sat with his back against the rock, eyes fixed on some distant point, while Mira paced in tight circles nearby. Their void burns looked raw, fresh—painful in a way that made my own skin itch in sympathy.

"Did you see anything in there?" Mira's whisper caught me off guard. She'd stopped pacing, lingering just a few feet away. "Besides the darkness, I mean."

I opened my mouth, but before I could respond, nobles began arriving in clusters, their fine clothing stark against the gray landscape. Lord Skaldvindr led one group, while Lord Sveinson guided another. Their quiet conversations carried an edge of tension.

"They're all here for the same reason." Rethlyn appeared beside me, his playful demeanor replaced by something harder. "To see what comes out of that darkness next."

"You mean who," I corrected.

"No." His eyes tracked the noble houses as they positioned themselves strategically around the area. "They don't care about Kenna. They're here for him. Valkan's emergence could shift everything."

"The Council's already divided," Vexa added in a low voice. "If he makes it out of there…"

She didn't need to finish. I'd seen how quickly the noble houses had changed their allegiances since the conference. How desperate they were for any solution to their dying realm.

A figure began to materialize in the shadows.

Valkan emerged from the darkness with the same fluid grace he'd shown during the trials. As he stepped into the gray light, he wiped something dark from his lips. Blood. My stomach turned. Was that his?

His eyes swept over the crowd before falling to his bare arms. A smile spread across his face.

No void burns marked his skin.

"How is that possible?" I whispered to Vexa, but she looked just as confused as I felt.

The word *Duskbound* rippled through the crowd as Valkan raised his arms, commanding their attention. "My friends," his voice carried across the space, smooth as silk. "The Void has chosen me. It required no trial, no demand, no sacrifice. I simply had to find my way back to you."

I caught Theron and Mira exchanging looks of disbelief. Their void burns seemed to darken in contrast to Valkan's unmarked skin.

His milky eyes found mine, and his smile widened into something predatory. He crossed the space between us with measured steps, close enough that I could smell the blood on his breath.

"I knew you were special," he whispered. Before I could react, he grabbed my hand, raising it with his own. "Look!" he called to the crowd. "Two Duskbound emerge to lead Umbrathia into a new era!"

I yanked my hand away, but instead of retreating, I held my ground. Something about his perfect smile, the way his eyes raked over me, made anger churn in my gut.

"Hello lovely," he murmured, stepping closer. "You look ravishing."

"Where's Kenna?"

A soft laugh escaped his lips. "So concerned for others. It's quite... endearing." He reached out as if to touch my face, but I jerked back. "We could be magnificent together, you know."

"You didn't answer my question."

"No," he agreed, his smile widening a fraction. "I suppose I didn't." He ran his tongue over his teeth.

"Did you find her in there?" I pressed, even as dread pooled in my stomach.

"The Void shows us what we truly are," he said simply, his voice dropping lower. "Some of us simply embrace our nature more... readily than others." His eyes flickered to my lips. "You will too, in time. Once you understand what we could accomplish together."

The realization hit me like ice water.

"You killed her."

His smile never wavered. "Quite an accusation, pet." He leaned closer, his breath cold against my ear. "There are better ways to use that pretty mouth."

Disgust fractured through me, churning my stomach. Before I could step back, Aether materialized at my side. His hand closed around my arm, yanking me behind him as he positioned himself between me and Valkan. Even through his leathers, I could see the tension coiled in his frame, ready to strike. For once, I didn't mind his interference.

Urkin stepped forward, the other Generals trailing behind him as they broke through the crowd. A heavy silence fell over the area, shattered only by the sound of their boot. Urkin's eyes went wide as they fixed on Valkan's untouched skin.

"It's not possible," he said, voice barely carrying.

"You experienced nothing?" Theron stood, his voice sharp with disbelief. "In there?"

"Just pure darkness." Valkan spread his arms wide, his smile never wavering. "Darkness that recognized its own."

"A Damphyre has never entered the Void before." Talon stepped forward, adjusting his archival robes as he studied Valkan. "We cannot know what effect it would have."

The crowd physically recoiled at the mention of *Damphyre*. I watched Valkan's smile falter for just a moment before smoothing back into place.

"There are no shadows in your eyes," Vexa spat. She moved to step forward but Effie caught her arm, pulling her back.

Valkan's personal guard materialized from the crowd, taking position around him, milky eyes narrowing. Their movements were too fluid, so graceful that it sent a chill over my skin.

"The foreign-born emerged swathed in shadows," General Karis said, his calculating gaze moving between Valkan and me. "You, however, have come out exactly as you entered."

Something dark flashed across Valkan's face, cracking that carefully maintained charm.

"Do you see my skin marked by void burns?" Valkan's voice rose, carrying across the crowd with practiced authority. "Only three outcomes exist when one enters the Void. Clearly, my emergence speaks for itself."

"Prove it." Mira's voice cut through the tension as she shot to her feet.

"A simple demonstration would settle this." Rethlyn shrugged, moving to stand beside Vexa and Effie. The casualness of his stance didn't match the edge in his voice.

Valkan's eyes narrowed, though his smile remained fixed in place. "No other Kalfar has ever emerged from the Void unmarked without claiming the title of Duskbound. I will not be forced to prove myself. I remain the Lord of Draxon. It would suit you to remember that."

Lord Skaldvindr emerged from the crowd then, flanked by members of other noble houses. His dark eyes swept over the scene with careful calculation. "Lord Valkan, we request that you show us. It would put all doubts to rest immediately."

Valkan strode to Skaldvindr, closing the distance until mere inches separated them. He leaned in, whispering something I couldn't hear. Whatever it was made Skaldvindr's face drain of color before anger replaced his shock.

"My friends..." Valkan turned back to address the crowd, his voice carrying that practiced charm once more. "Have I not proven myself time and again? While other lands wither, Draxon's people thrive. While others starve, my people feast. And now you would question my worth, after I've passed your trials with unprecedented success?"

His words carried a different weight now, an underlying threat beneath the charm. I watched several Council members shift uncomfortably.

"If you are unable to prove yourself," Aether's voice cut through Valkan's rhetoric, "then crawl back to Draxon."

Valkan spun toward him, and for just a moment, that mask slipped completely. Pure hatred flashed in those milky eyes. Then his gaze found mine, and something worse replaced the hatred—a promise. A hunger that made my blood run cold.

Before anyone could react, his form rippled and twisted. Where he had stood, a massive black bird now towered, its wings blocking out what little light remained. With one powerful beat of those wings, he took to the sky.

The crowd erupted into chaos as Valkan disappeared into the clouds. Lord Sveinson immediately turned to his allies, face flushed with rage as he gestured toward where Valkan had stood. Other noble houses began shifting alliances before my eyes—those who had supported Valkan at the conference now desperately trying to distance themselves, while others seized the opportunity to denounce him openly.

Lord Skaldvindr broke away from the other nobles, approaching our group with calculated steps. His dark eyes swept over me, lingering on the shadows that still clung to my skin.

"You've done well," he said, though his tone carried more assessment than praise. "The realm will remember this day."

I met his gaze. "Which part? The part where a Damphyre claimed to be chosen by the Void? Or the part where everyone just let him leave?"

Something flickered across his face—anger or fear, I couldn't tell which. But his diplomatic expression never slipped. "And what exactly were any of us supposed to do? He's a free man. What would we hold him for?"

Behind him, I watched the Skaldvindr family guards subtly repositioning themselves, creating a barrier between their Lord and Valkan's remaining supporters.

Effie pushed through the crowd then, her face tight with worry as she reached for Vexa. "I can't believe he even made it out of there." She looked toward the Void, then back to our group. "And Kenna—has anyone seen—"

"She's not coming out." The words felt like ash in my mouth. I watched realization creep into their faces. The silence that followed was deafening. Lord Skaldvindr's carefully neutral expression cracked, just for a moment, revealing something like genuine horror beneath.

"Valkan made sure of that."

CHAPTER TWENTY-SIX

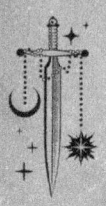

THE LEATHERS FELT heavy in my hands as I hung them in the wardrobe of my new quarters. Black and sleek, marked with patterns that identified me as Spectre. As Umbra. I ran my fingers over the material. The sound of footsteps down the hall had my eyes creeping towards the door. At least this time, I had a lock on my side instead of theirs.

I sank onto the edge of the bed, exhaustion seeping into my bones. The others had said the memories of the Void would fade—that the mind protected itself by burying the worst of what it showed you. But right now, every vision felt razor-sharp.

The Enclave. Leila's branding. Ma's horror. Laryk's... Each scene designed to break me, to make me surrender to the darkness. But it was the last vision that haunted me most. It felt different from the others. Real in a way the rest hadn't been.

I closed my eyes and replayed it in my mind. The woman—her long, unruly hair. The man who held her, his skin pale and devoid of color, shadows around his eyes. Their arms had tightened around each other, golden bracelets hanging on both of their arms, reflecting the raging fire surrounding them. The look that passed between them pulled at something inside me.

The Void had said it was the vision I'd been most waiting for, though I hadn't known I was waiting for anything at all. But something about it felt significant, even if I couldn't figure out why. The way they'd chosen to face the flames together... My eyes fell on my reflection in the small mirror above the washbasin.

Vexa's words echoed in my mind. *You're far more than a Duskbound.*

I traced the shadows beneath my eyes, so similar to the ones the man in my vision had worn. A Kalfar, clearly. But the woman...

I shook the thought away. The Void had shown me exactly what it knew would hurt most—my deepest fears, my hidden shames. Why should this vision be any different?

You're not like them. The Void had said.

I resumed my pacing, the stone floor cold beneath my feet. Even Aether had noticed something was different about me. He could see my web—something that should have been impossible.

I sank back onto the bed, my legs suddenly unable to hold me. The Umbra had been in Riftdremar trying to forge an alliance. I'd learned that much from Vexa and the others. They'd been there before the war, before the Soleils burned it all to ash. There would have been contact, negotiations. The timing would align with...

With what? I wasn't even sure what I was trying to piece together.

The woman's face flashed in my mind again. There had been something so achingly familiar about her features. About the way her hair had moved in the heat of the flames, wild and uncontrolled, like...

My hand flew to my own hair, fingers tangling in the white strands.

A Kalfar and an... Aossí? The thought felt dangerous even in my own mind. Were those Soleil flames surrounding them?

My fingers found my Riftborne branding, tracing the familiar mark. I'd carried it my whole life, a symbol of my parents' supposed treachery. But there was so much more to the story. So much I still didn't know.

My blood turned to ice. The golden bracelets. Like the one I had come to Sídhe with as a child—my only possession tying me to Riftdremar. To my family.

Was it even possible?

Half Kalfar, half Aossí. The possibility felt like a blade against my throat. It would explain so much—why I'd never felt at home in either realm, why my abilities had always been different. Why my web worked unlike anything they'd seen before. Why I looked like both, but neither at the same time.

But if it were true...

A knock at my door cut through my spiraling thoughts. I quickly wiped my face, not even realizing tears had fallen. When I opened the door, Aether stood there.

"Lael's awake," he said. "Eating everything in sight, actually."

Relief flooded through me, but confusion quickly followed. There was something different about the way he was looking at me. His eyes didn't hold that normal scowl.

"How are you feeling?"

The question caught me off guard. "Are you actually interested, or just making small talk?"

"I can go," he said, his eyes flickering to my face. "I've clearly caught you in the middle of something."

Heat rushed to my cheeks as I realized he could probably tell I'd been crying. But he motioned toward the piles of leather uniforms scattered across my bed, offering me an out.

"For a dying realm, you all sure have a lot of leather," I said, grateful for the deflection.

A smile almost quirked at his lips. "Well, we don't skin a cow every time someone enters the Umbra, if that's what you're implying." He paused, looking me up and down before his gaze fell on the window. "We do have reserves of it from across the realm." The words came out awkward, like he wasn't quite sure why he was explaining this.

"So, what can I do for you?" I raised an eyebrow.

"Must we stand in the doorway?"

I angled my head at him, suspicion creeping in, but stepped aside to let him enter. His presence immediately made the room feel smaller, more confined. He moved to the window, and I found myself studying the way the dim light caught on his piercings, how the shadows beneath his skin seemed at peace.

A silence stretched between us, punctuated by strange, almost awkward glances. I kept waiting for his request, his task, whatever reason had brought him here. But he just stood there, like he had all the time in the world.

"Playing nice now that you got what you wanted?" I finally asked.

"Just coming to gloat, really." His eyes met mine, that hint of a smile returning.

"To gloat? That's unbecoming," I shot back.

"You're the one who came flying out of the Void like you were putting on a performance." His tone was dry, but there was something almost like amusement in his eyes.

"Well, someone had to make you look good." I couldn't help but match his sarcasm. "Your reputation was at stake after all."

"My reputation?" One eyebrow arched. "And here I thought you were convinced I was just a glorified jailer."

"Weren't you?"

That almost-smile twitched at his lips again. "You know, most people would show more gratitude to someone who just came to check on them."

"Gratitude?" I pressed a hand to my chest in mock offense.

"Should I thank you for all those times you threw me into the training mat too?"

"You're welcome."

I shot him a narrowed look before returning to the bed, slipping the sleeve of a black uniform through a hanger. If he was just going to stand there and look pleased with himself, I might as well continue with my organizing.

"In all seriousness, I did actually come here to thank *you*," he said from behind me.

Something in his tone made me pause, my hands stilling on the leather. When I turned to face him, the amusement had faded from his eyes, replaced by something more intense.

"For Lael," he continued, his voice lower now. "You didn't have to do that. To risk yourself like that." He hesitated, and I could see him wrestling with something. "How did you even find him in there?"

I thought back to that endless darkness, to the feeling of Lael's body beneath my hands. "I just... did. I couldn't leave him there." The memory of that terrifying voice echoed in my mind, of the bargain I'd struck. But I pushed it away. It didn't seem like the time to discuss it. I wasn't sure if I ever would.

"Only one other person has ever done that," he said quietly. "The Queen. When she found me."

The admission hung in the air between us. I studied his face, noting how the shadows beneath his eyes seemed to deepen at the mention of it. For once, I decided to push.

"How much do you remember? From before she found you?"

His jaw tightened, but he didn't immediately shut me down like he usually did. "Nothing." He moved to the window, his fingers absently tracing one of his void burns. "It's like my life began in that darkness."

"But thirty-five years..." I hesitated, then pressed on. "You don't look—"

"Older?" That ghost of a smile returned, but it held no humor. "Another mystery, I'm afraid."

"Do you ever wonder who you were? Before?"

He was quiet for so long I thought he wouldn't answer. When he finally turned back to me, something had shifted in his golden eyes. "One memory seemed to slip past the Void. But it doesn't tell me much."

Realization washed over me.

"I saw her," I said quietly. "That day in training, when I tried to read your mind. She was there."

The shadows around him pulsed, but he didn't retreat like he had that day. Instead, he studied me with an intensity that made my skin prickle.

"I know," he said finally. "That's why I left. No one else has ever..." He trailed off, running a hand through his dark hair. "The Queen tried for years to help me remember. The best healers in the realm attempted to unlock whatever the Void took from me."

The weight of what that meant settled between us. I thought of my own vision in the Void, of the two people facing the flames together. Of all the questions still burning inside me.

"Do you think she was family?" I asked, unable to keep my own uncertainties from coloring the question.

"I don't know."

"She looked like you," I said quietly, returning to the wardrobe.

The silence seemed to stretch on, and I couldn't help myself from filling it.

"The Void showed me something. I can't stop thinking about it," I finally said.

The sound of shifting fabrics echoed from behind me. I turned to find Aether pulling out the chair at my desk. "Do you want to talk about it?" he asked.

Clearly.

His stillness had cracked, replaced by something almost...

uncertain. He had never been much of a talker—outside of verbal assault, of course. Yet here he was, actually attempting conversation. Voluntarily. In my quarters.

"I just don't know what to make of it, really," I continued, breaking away from his curious gaze.

"The Void tends to have that effect on people," he said.

"I know." I shot another narrowed glance over my shoulder. "But this felt different. The voice implied it was the vision I'd been waiting for."

"The voice?" Aether readjusted in his chair.

"Yes—the voice. The overwhelming, booming monstrous voice. The Void, I guess."

"I've never heard of the Void speaking to people." He suppressed a laugh, and the look on his face had irritation racing across my skin.

"Forget I said anything." I rolled my eyes.

"My apologies. The voice said it was the vision you'd been waiting for..." He bit back a smile, gesturing for me to continue.

"I saw two people," I said, keeping my voice steady. "In Riftdremar, I think. During the burning." I watched his expression carefully. "A Kalfar man and... someone else. A woman who wasn't Kalfar."

"The Void often shows us—"

"You were here then, weren't you?" I cut him off. "When the Umbra were in Riftdremar? Before everything happened?"

He nodded slowly. "I had just entered the Umbra. The Queen had sent representatives across the rip for negotiations."

"The timing..." I started, then stopped, gathering my courage. "The timing would align perfectly. The Umbra's presence in Riftdremar, the uprising, my birth." The words came faster now. "The woman in my vision—she looked like she could have been Aossí. And they both wore these golden bracelets, like one I had when I came to Sídhe."

Understanding dawned in his eyes. "You think they were your parents."

"Is it even possible?" I asked, the question burning in my throat. "A Kalfar and an Aossí?"

He was quiet for a moment, his golden eyes distant. "There were... interactions. More than most know. Men stationed there for months at a time. But this wasn't exactly public knowledge. We had just discovered a new realm, foreign to ours. Leadership didn't want to cause a mass disturbance." He looked at me directly.

I nodded, eyes falling on the stone floor.

"I can look into it. The archives might have records from that period, though many were destroyed."

My gaze shot back to him faster than I would have liked. "You would do that?"

"You saved Lael," he said simply. "Consider it a debt repaid."

CHAPTER TWENTY-SEVEN

Urkin's office felt smaller with all of us crowded inside. The other initiates and I stood before his obsidian desk while the rest of the Spectre unit lined the walls. Maps covered every surface, their edges curling from constant handling, while reports lay scattered across his desk, unreadable from where I stood.

"Three days," Urkin said, his voice tight with carefully controlled anger. "Three days since Valkan disappeared, and not a single noble house has heard from him." His fingers drummed against a letter bearing the Skaldvindr seal. "Though some have made their positions quite clear."

He turned his attention to me then, his expression shifting into something less hostile, though no warmer. "And we've managed to find a true Duskbound. The first in centuries to be born of common blood." The words seemed stilted. "And to a foreign-born, no less." I could almost catch the lingering disdain in his tone. He sighed, as if to calm himself. "Your emergence from the Void was... impressive."

The compliment felt strange coming from him, especially given our previous interactions. But before I could respond, he was already moving on.

"The Skaldvindrs withdrew their support the moment he fled," Effie offered. "The others followed within hours."

"Like rats abandoning a sinking ship," Vexa muttered from her place near the wall.

"And what of his men?" Urkin's eyes swept over our group. "Any sightings?"

"None," Aether said. "They vanished with him."

"Probably still crawling back to Draxon," Theron threw in.

"He's lost the support of the Council, but don't underestimate the will of his subjects. This is still a tense situation. And I would believe the events that happened outside the Void have only stoked his anger further."

The implications of that hung heavy in the air. My stomach turned at the memory of those milky eyes, that unnatural grace.

"What about Kenna?" Mira asked. "Will there be consequences for what he did to her?"

The room went deathly still. Urkin's face twisted with disgust, but when he spoke, his voice was measured.

"Without proof, there's nothing we can do."

"Nothing?" My voice came out like a blade. "He emerged from the Void with blood on his mouth, and Kenna never came out. What more proof do you need?"

"Careful," Urkin's tone dropped dangerously low. "You don't understand the delicacy of this situation."

"Then explain it to me."

Several of the Spectres shifted uncomfortably. But Urkin just stared at me, his jaw working as if physically restraining himself.

"We are trying," he finally ground out, "to prevent a civil war. Valkan's influence runs deeper than you know. His followers are fanatics. One accusation—one *hint* of persecution—and half the realm would rise up." He stood, palms flat against his desk. "Is that what you want? More death? More chaos? While Sídhe continues to drain what little essence we have left?"

The mention of Sídhe sparked something in his eyes. "Speaking of which," he straightened, switching topics with practiced efficiency, "it's been nearly two months since our last mission. The drought spreads while we sit here debating politics."

"Actually," I stepped forward, seizing the opening. "I've been thinking about that. What if I could speak with the leadership within the Guard? Try to make them understand—"

A harsh laugh cut me off. "Make them understand?" Urkin's voice dripped with mockery. "You think you can just walk up to the border and have a friendly chat about how they're draining us?"

"You don't understand. The masses in the Guard don't even know that you're people. They're told you're monsters filtering in from another world, bound and determined to destroy the arcanite stores and send the realm into a death age."

"*Poetic*," Vexa grumbled.

Urkin paced behind his desk. "That matters little to me. Our soldiers stay in their spectre-forms to protect themselves. Revealing what they truly are will only leave them vulnerable. More will die."

"You're just helping Sídhe's lies then," I said and I thought Urkin's eyes might explode from his head.

"I've served this realm for thirty years. Do not think, for one second, little girl, that you can come in here and command me. That you have any idea how to wage war."

"I went into this with the agreement that we would consider alternative solutions."

"*I* made no such agreement with you," he spat.

My eyes shot to Aether, then Vexa, silently pleading for backup. They had promised.

Vexa stepped forward, her voice tempered. "She has intimate

knowledge of their military structure, their leadership. That kind of insight could be invaluable."

"She has knowledge of their *Guard*," Aether added, his golden eyes fixed on Urkin. "And their decision-makers. A perspective we've never had access to before."

"She's no use to me if she's not supplying my troops with shadows," Urkin snapped.

"I've already told you," I fought to keep my voice steady, "I will not aid you in attacking Sídhe without considering other options first."

Urkin's laugh was cold. "You simple girl. Do you think that's all the shadows do? That we simply use them as weapons?" He sighed, exasperation clear in every line of his face. "They serve far greater purposes than that."

"The shadows allow us to gather intelligence," Rethlyn cut in, stepping away from the wall. "Most of our work involves collecting information without detection. Moving unseen through their territory."

"They've already increased the Guard on the Western border," I said, the words tumbling out before I could stop them. A heavy silence fell over the room.

"And how exactly would you know that?" Aether's voice carried an odd note of curiosity.

"Because that's what Laryk—" I caught myself. "What the Generals would do."

"But why would you think that?" Aether pressed. "We haven't crossed the rip in months."

"Because you took *me*."

"Are you really that self-important?" Urkin's tone dripped with disdain.

I felt Vexa's glare from across the desk. She mouthed a harsh *no*, and I realized too late the dangerous territory I'd wandered into. Not just nearly revealing my first-hand knowledge of Laryk's intentions I saw through Mercer's eyes, but also verging on admitting my rather intimate relationship with a Sídhe General.

"I'm providing you with valuable information," I redirected quickly. "Is that not what you want?"

Urkin pinched the bridge of his nose, a vein pulsing in his temple. "You want to prove your worth? Fine. But first, you will complete the void-letting. Today. These recruits need to begin their training, and they cannot do that without shadows." His eyes narrowed. "Complete the ceremony now, and I'll give you one week to present an alternative plan. After that, we proceed how I see fit."

The weight of his demand settled in my gut.

"The void-letting ceremony—" I started, but Urkin was already striding toward the door.

"Now," he barked over his shoulder. "All of you."

Vexa stepped forward first, exchanging glances with Aether. "Come on," she said, motioning for us to follow. "Let's just get it over with, Fia."

They led our group deeper into the Citadel, down winding passages of obsidian carved stone. The walls seemed to press closer here, the flames from torches warming my skin. Finally, we entered a circular chamber that made my steps falter.

In the center stood what looked like some kind of raised platform with jilted edges. Channels had been carved into the floor, leading to the contraption like veins to a heart.

"This," Effie gestured with a flourish that seemed at odds with the ominous machinery, "is where the magic happens."

"It looks more like some form of antiquated torture device," Mira muttered, her eyes tracing the sharp angles of black metal.

"Have you managed to conjure any shadows yet?" Effie asked me, ignoring Mira's comment. "Since emerging from the Void?"

The question caught me off guard. I hadn't even tried.

"So this is how you share the shadows?" Lael stepped closer, fascination clear on his young face.

"More or less," Rethlyn said. "The channels help direct the flow, make it more... controlled." He gestured to the intricate patterns carved into the floor. "Otherwise it can get a bit..."

Theron's gaze swept over the machinery, eyes narrowing. "And this works better than direct transfer? I've read they can be shared through skin contact."

"It can work in a pinch." Vexa smirked. "However, direct contact through the skin is not recommended."

Effie bit back a laugh.

I was just about to ask what joke we weren't clued in on before Mira spoke up.

"So how exactly does it work?" she asked, moving closer to examine one of the channels. Her usual haunted expression had given way to genuine curiosity.

"The shadows flow through these pathways," Effie explained, tracing the intricate patterns with her finger. "Each channel leads to a different point where a vessel can receive them. The runes help control the flow, make the connection stronger."

"I've been working on forging a portable version," Vexa added. "But for now, this is the most reliable method."

"You'll understand more once the process starts." Aether's voice came from the shadows near the wall. "Fia, take the center. The rest of you, position yourselves at the connection points."

My heart thundered as I stepped onto the platform.

"The void burns act like pathways," Vexa explained as the others moved into position. "They're marks from the Void itself—permanent channels that allow vessels to absorb and hold the shadows. Once they are absorbed, you will be able to wield them."

Metal restraints clicked softly as they locked into place around the recruits' wrists. Lael's eyes were wide with anticipation, while

Theron maintained his analytical calm. Mira's face had gone carefully blank.

"How many can you do at once?" Lael asked, his voice betraying his nerves.

"Six," Rethlyn answered. "Any more and the connection becomes unstable."

I eyed the contraption warily. The metal seemed to drink in what little light reached this deep into the Citadel, and something about those channels made my skin prickle. "What do I need to do?"

"Just stand in the center," Rethlyn said, gesturing to a circular platform. "And try calling the shadows. They should respond naturally."

"Should?" Theron asked, arching an eyebrow.

"The Void left its instructions." Aether's voice came from the shadows near the wall. "They're written into her now, whether she realizes it or not."

I stepped onto the platform, trying to ignore how everyone's attention was fixed on me. The metal felt cold beneath my boots.

"Just like that?" I asked. "Just... call them?"

"You'll know what to do," Vexa said softly. "Trust yourself."

I closed my eyes, expecting to have to search for the shadows like I did with my web. But the moment I opened myself to them, they surged forward eagerly, as if they'd been waiting all this time. Dark tendrils spilled from my skin, flowing like liquid night into the channels at my feet.

"Esprithe," Lael breathed.

My eyes shot down to find the entire contraption alive, the symbols seeming to pulse as the shadows touched them. They moved through the pathways with purpose, filling each groove until the floor looked like a maze of flowing darkness.

"Well..." Vexa grinned. "Looks like someone's a natural."

"Can you feel them?" Mira asked. "The shadows, I mean. Do they... respond to you?"

I nodded, unable to find the right words to explain how natural it felt. Like flexing a muscle I hadn't known I had.

"How long will they last?" Mira asked as the shadows began reaching for her burns.

"Depends on how much you use them," Vexa said. "Some can last weeks—months even. But only with this method. The runes allow for full absorption. A direct transfer might only last a day or two."

"The last time the Queen performed a letting, it was quite potent, so the ones we retain have lasted a while. Which is a blessing, truly. With her being in such a delicate position, I think it became clear she wouldn't be able to keep doing this," Rethlyn added in slowly, shooting me a grin. "And now she doesn't have to."

I watched as my shadows found each recruit in turn, seeping into their skin through the marks the Void had left. Theron's breath became heavy, fingers curling against the restraints. Mira's eyes widened as the darkness followed the patterns of her burns. When they reached Lael, he let out a small gasp.

"It feels..." he started, then stopped, unable to find the words.

"Familiar," Mira finished quietly.

The shadows continued flowing until all three had received their share. After a few moments, the dark river ceased, sitting now like a pool across the chamber floor. The restraints clicked open, allowing the recruits to stumble back, examining their arms where the burns seemed darker now, more alive.

"Well," Vexa said, stepping up to one of the remaining connection points. "Might as well top off while we're here." She settled into position, the metal restraints clicking softly around her wrists.

"Vexa," I chided.

"Relax, Fia. I'm not about to fly out to the rip and go on some murder spree." The darkness flowed into her burns as she spoke, and her head tilted back, eyes closing. "Wow... those are divine," she said, as if absorbing some form of magical narcotic.

I couldn't help but roll my eyes.

"And that's it?" Mira asked, leaning closer to examine Vexa's arms where the shadows had vanished.

"That's it." Vexa flexed her fingers as the restraints released. "Simple, really."

I stepped down from the platform, feeling oddly drained. Not physically—the shadows hadn't taken anything from me. But watching them flow into others, knowing they would use them for whatever came next... it felt heavier than I'd expected.

Lael was already experimenting, small wisps of darkness curling around his fingers. Theron studied his arms with analytical interest, while Mira stood very still, as if adjusting to the new sensation.

"When do we start Spectre training?" Lael asked, a gleam in his eye.

"Rethlyn will begin with you tomorrow, bright and early," Vexa said, "Well, not bright, I guess. But early."

Rethlyn nodded. "Lael, Mira, and Theron. We'll meet in the courtyard."

"What about me?" I asked.

"You won't benefit from this type of training, Duskbound. It'll come to you with time. As Aether said before, it left instructions within you," Vexa responded, eyes now fully consumed by black inky swirls.

One week. I had one week to figure out how to stop a war, or these shadows—my shadows—would be used for unimaginable destruction. The weight of that responsibility settled over me as I watched darkness dance across my fellow recruits' skin.

CHAPTER TWENTY-EIGHT

I FOUND myself seated at a small side table, quill poised over fresh parchment as five men settled into their chairs before an immense desk. The wood carved from mahogany, gilded up the legs, its surface gleaming in afternoon light that spilled through tall windows. Behind it, two emerald serpents coiled around a blade on the wall—the crest of Sidhe.

My eyes found Laryk immediately, his presence impossible to ignore. His fingers drummed against the arm of his chair, his other hand pressed against his mouth as he stared ahead, brow furrowed in thought. The other men shifted in their seats—one with his arms crossed tight over his chest, jaw clenched as if physically holding back words, another fidgeting with the hem of his formal jacket.

The door swung open, and the King of Sidhe swept into the chamber. Sydian. Despite the darkness beneath his violet eyes and the slight dishevelment of his peppered hair, he carried himself with the grace that came so naturally to royalty. The Generals rose as one in a bow, but the King barely seemed to notice as he sank into his chair. He rubbed his eyes, exhaustion evident in every movement.

My quill scratched against parchment, recording the time and date, the positions of those present.

"You requested this meeting." The King's eyes fixed on one of the men, the one whose arms remained crossed tight over his chest.

"Your Grace." The man straightened. "We've seen no activity at the border for over two months, yet I'm forced to keep my entire faction stationed in the West. My soldiers grow restless—they have families scattered across the Isle who need them. I can no longer justify keeping them all there."

The King's gaze flickered to Laryk before returning to the first General. I dipped my quill and began recording the exchange.

"I'm requesting permission to release half my forces back to their home stations."

Laryk muttered something under his breath that I couldn't catch, though my hand noted his interruption.

All eyes turned to him.

"I second this request." Another General stood—the head of the healers' faction, his voice less certain than the first General's. "Our best healers remain stationed at the border. We could better serve our people if—"

"I've put Laryk in charge of all Guard decisions and stationing." The King's voice cut through the chamber.

Another General rose then, his chair scraping against stone. "Sir, we don't believe that to be in the best interest of the Guard."

Laryk shot up, closing the distance between them in two strides. "I haven't even requested help from the base faction," he seethed, close enough that the other General took a step back. "So I fail to see why you feel qualified to speak on this matter."

"Sit down." The King leaned back, shadows deepening under his eyes. "All of you, sit down."

My quill raced across the parchment, capturing every word as the Generals found their seats.

"Ashford," the King continued, "explain to me why you need such excessive presence in the West when we've had so little activity at the tear."

Laryk sighed, collecting himself before speaking. "Because they're coming back. I don't know when, but I know we have to be ready. We have a new strategy, as you're aware." He leaned forward, bracing his elbows on the desk, and something in his eyes made me pause in my writing. "I saw something remarkable the night they descended on Emeraal. Something I had never before witnessed—something that seemed impossible."

The scratch of my quill was the only sound as he continued.

"I held this back while I tried to determine if what I saw was real. But after consideration, I'm certain." His voice dropped lower. "A man among the shadows, his form clear as day. These are no monsters from storybooks. These are intelligent, capable soldiers who can somehow cloak themselves. They are an even bigger threat than we could ever have known. Perhaps there's more to their attacks than we originally thought."

Several Generals scoffed, but the King's entire demeanor shifted, his attention suddenly razor-sharp.

"That's quite a claim, General Ashford."

Laryk held his gaze. "And they took her. Fia Riftborne. The one thing that could have potentially revealed what they were."

"The girl was killed, Ashford," one of the older Generals cut in. "You're behaving like a madman over a simple initiate."

Laryk's chair crashed backward as he rounded on the man. "They leave the bodies behind. There's a reason they took her. And there's a chance she's still alive."

The King stood then, slamming his hands against the desk hard enough to make my inkwell rattle. "Ashford, I realize you lost a great potential focus that night. I know how hard you had been working to prepare her. I understand your loss. But I must agree, the girl is most likely dead." He paused, and something in his tone made my hand still over the parchment. "Because if she is not, and she has spent two entire months with the enemy, if she has not found a way back to us... Well, according to our statutes, she would be considered a threat to the realm. And would require immediate questioning."

Laryk went completely still. "Respectfully, Your Grace, that statute is antiquated and completely lacking the nuance the situation requires. What if she is incapable of coming back to Sídhe? What if she's being held as a prisoner? What if—"

"I will hear no more." The King's voice cracked through the chamber like lightning. "Ashford, you may keep the factions in the Western strongholds, but I won't hear another word of this. I chose you for a reason, do not make me regret my decision."

Just as he turned to leave, a knock echoed through the silence.

"Enter," the King commanded, exhaustion heavy in his voice.

The door creaked open to reveal a soldier in a green uniform, his face drained of color.

"I'm sorry to interrupt, Your Grace, but there's been a situation." The man swallowed hard. "Every General is needed in Stormshire immediately."

My quill clattered against the desk as the dream began to fade, but not before I caught the look that passed between Laryk and the King.

I shot out of bed, eyes flaring as I recognized the room around me—my new quarters in the Umbra lodging.

I pressed my hand against my chest, feeling my heart racing beneath. The Generals. They were either unaware of what was truly happening across the rip, or they were incredible actors. The King, however... his reaction to what Laryk saw that night in Emeraal, his insinuation that I would need to be questioned if I ever returned. I couldn't think of a single reason he would be so avoidant unless he knew. Unless he knew exactly what he was doing, who he was stealing from. The secret he was keeping even from his higher-ups.

I touched my feet down onto the stone floor and ran a hand through my hair, trying to process all of the new information. Laryk was going to keep the Guard stationed in the West, that was nothing new. But he said something about a new strategy, and the thought of that made my blood run cold. If Urkin's ultimatum wasn't already sitting on me heavy enough as it was, this just added more pressure. I had to find something—anything.

And I knew what I needed to do.

The corridor outside my quarters felt strangely empty without Aether's looming presence. No dark figure against the wall, no golden eyes tracking my movements. I almost missed it—almost. At least when he'd been my jailer, I'd known exactly where to find him.

Gray light filtered in through the windows as it always did, but the fortress was still quiet, most of its residents still asleep. A woman emerged from the communal shower room, eyes falling on me before she hurriedly turned the corner.

I tugged at my own collar, still unused to the stiff fabric of the Umbra casual wear. The word *Spectre* felt heavy where it was printed across my chest pocket. It wasn't so different from my Guard uniform, not really, but the shape was more streamlined, more fitted and structured compared to Sídhe's grandeur. I felt a pang of guilt churn through me. The King wouldn't be totally off-base for wanting me questioned. With the decisions I'd made, I wouldn't even be a threat anymore. I'd be a traitor to the realm. I knew that's how it would look. I just hoped Laryk would believe I was trying to save us all.

My head ached from lack of sleep. I'd spent half the night hunched over my desk, trying to devise a plan that wouldn't end in more bloodshed. But every attempt had fallen flat, every strategy crumbling under the weight of what was really going on. The truth was, I didn't know enough—about Umbrathia, about its history, about Riftdremar or arcanite or any of the factors that had led us here. If I was going to stop this war, I needed to understand it first.

Which meant I needed the archives. Which meant I needed Aether.

Vexa had mentioned that higher-ranking members lived on the upper floors when she'd shown me to my quarters. "Hierarchy," she'd said with a roll of her eyes. If the Generals occupied level six, then logic suggested Aether would be on five. A part of me wondered if they would have erected another tower, had Aether accepted their offer to be commander of the entire Umbra forces. The other part of me wondered why he hadn't taken it. I shook the thoughts away as I climbed past shadowed corridors. It wasn't much to go on, but it beat wandering the fortress aimlessly or asking for directions.

Finally, I reached a door with a silver plaque that simply read *Aether*. The only one without a last name.

I knocked once, then again, pressing my ear against the wood when no response came. Of course he wasn't here. He was probably off somewhere being mysterious and brooding this early in the day.

"Can I help you?"

The deep voice came from behind me, and I turned to find Aether standing there with nothing but a towel slung low around his hips. Water dripped from his dark hair onto shoulders marked with void burns, trailing down his chest in a way that made my mouth go dry. I spun back around so fast I nearly lost my balance.

"Sorry," I managed, the word coming out embarrassingly weak.

"Interesting way to start the morning," he said, "though I suppose it's better than finding you trying to escape again."

He stepped past me to unlock his door, close enough that I could smell soap and rain. I jerked away, and he glanced at me with a raised eyebrow.

"Someone's jumpy."

"Someone's underdressed," I shot back, fixing my gaze firmly on the wall.

"It's my floor." The lock clicked open. "And you're the one lurking outside my door."

"I wasn't *lurking*. I was knocking."

"Ah yes, with your ear pressed against the wood. Very dignified."

I risked a glare in his direction, immediately regretting it as another droplet traced its way down his chest. "I was hoping you were going to the archives today."

"Calling in your favor so early?" He leaned against the doorframe, apparently unconcerned with his state of undress.

"You don't seem to have anything better to do, after stalking *my* door for weeks on end."

"Aren't you supposed to be devising a plan for Urkin?" He narrowed his brow.

"Yes. Precisely why I need to visit them," I shot back.

He disappeared into his quarters, leaving the door open. I stayed firmly in the hallway, studying the intricate stonework of the ceiling.

The silence stretched until I wanted to scream. Through the open door, I caught glimpses of his quarters—spartan but neat, with maps covering one wall and what looked like weapons displayed on another.

"So, should I take your silence as a yes?" I finally asked.

"If you'll allow me to change into something more presentable. I'd prefer not to scandalize the entire tower."

Another wave of heat washed over me. "I'll just wait out here."

"Probably wise." Was it my imagination, or did his voice carry a smile? "Though you might want to work on your poker face if you're planning to negotiate peace. You're still blushing."

"I am not—" I started, then caught myself. "Just hurry up."

The walk to the archives took us across the fortress grounds, past the training yards where a few early risers were already running drills. The archive building itself rose between the fortress and Citadel—all sweeping stone and towering windows, glass stained with what seemed to be tributes to the Esprithe.

Inside, peaked wooden archways stretched overhead, creating

shadowed corridors between the tall shelves. The scent of old parchment and leather bindings filled my lungs as we entered, and something about it reminded me of Ma's collection of medicinal texts. I pushed the memory away before it could take root.

Multiple levels rose above us, connected by wrought iron staircases that spiraled up. Brass oil lamps cast pools of warm light at intervals, their glow barely reaching the vaulted ceiling. Somehow, the archives had maintained a sort of timeless beauty that the drought hadn't managed to touch.

Movement caught my eye—Talon stood at a desk near the back, surrounded by a small group of Archivists. I recognized Raven among them, his attention fixed on whatever Talon was explaining about their sorting system. At our approach, Talon looked up, his expression shifting as he noted our presence.

"Take a break," he told the others, straightening his robes. "I'll return shortly."

He met us halfway down the main aisle, inclining his head slightly. "Can I help you find anything specific?"

"I know my way around," Aether said. "No need to interrupt your lesson."

"Nonsense." Talon's eyes fixed on me. "It would be awfully impolite not to be of aid to our new Duskbound."

Heat crept up my neck at the title, but I managed a nod. "Thank you."

"I'll be in the classified records section," Aether said, already moving toward one of the spiral staircases. "When you're finished here."

Talon led me through the maze of shelves, occasionally gesturing to different sections as we walked. His movements were delicate, reverent almost, as if each book and scroll was precious beyond measure. Given the state of their realm, perhaps they were.

"Most of our older texts are kept in temperature-controlled rooms," he explained, his voice carrying through the space.

I followed him, trying to memorize the layout as unease sank into my gut. I was going to need far longer than a week to sort through the sheer volume.

"Do you have any records about arcanite?" I asked. "Its properties, its uses?"

Something flickered across his face—interest, maybe, or wariness. "We do." He studied me for a moment. "What exactly are you looking to learn?"

"Everything," I said. "If I'm going to help stop this war, I need to understand what started it."

Talon glanced around the aisles before lowering his voice. "Umbrathia was never home to large deposits of the mineral. We depleted what stores we did have nearly a century ago. Some texts, I would have to assume, have also been lost to time..." He shook his head. "What remains is fragmentary at best."

"Just point me in the right direction, and I'll see what I can find."

I DROPPED the stack of books onto the table with a dull thud. Aether sat at the other end, legs propped up, deeply engrossed in whatever he was reading. His casual uniform hugged his frame in a way the combat leathers didn't, the fabric pulled tight across his thighs. His head was tilted back, square jaw tensed.

What caught me off guard, though, was the pair of wire-rimmed reading glasses perched on his nose, shadowing the contour of his cheekbones. Something about seeing him like this—the brutish warrior wearing scholarly spectacles—struck me as utterly absurd. I laughed out loud.

He looked up, one eyebrow raised over the frames. "Something amusing?"

"I didn't realize you wore glasses." I gestured vaguely at his face, still fighting a smile.

He sighed, turning his open book face-down on the table. I caught a glimpse of the text—impossibly small print that made my eyes hurt just looking at it.

"Ah," I said, moving back to my own stack. "Found anything of interest?"

"There's a lot to sort through." His eyes returned to his page, black hair falling down over his forehead. I found myself staring longer than I should have. "Most of it irrelevant."

I nodded, turning back to my stack of books.

"And how old are you?" Aether asked as I sat down.

"I was born twenty-three years ago, on the sixth day of Ainthe."

Aether tapped a quill against the table and I glanced over at him. He studied me with a curious expression.

"Your birthday was a few weeks ago. That would make you twenty-four now." He raised an eyebrow.

How had time passed so quickly? Twenty-four. My mind drifted to the year before—what I had done to celebrate. I was never big on birthdays, but Osta would usually drag me out of the apartment and buy me dinner. Last year, I'd been so out of control I hadn't even allowed that. She had picked up food on her way home from work and we played card games on the floor. I bit back a smile.

"Well, then twenty-four, I guess," I said after a few moments.

"That will help tremendously, thank you." He turned his attention back to his records.

I pulled out one of the books on arcanite, trying not to think too hard about what he might be searching for in those records. Did I even want him to find anything about my parents? I'd gone my whole life not knowing who they were. Learning the truth now felt dangerous—like it might shatter whatever fragile understanding I'd built of myself.

The leather binding creaked as I opened the book, its pages yellowed with age. The first few chapters covered various minerals and their properties. Some I recognized from Sídhe—precious stones used in crafting, metals that could enhance enchantments. Others seemed unique to Umbrathia, their uses foreign to me. I found myself getting lost in the descriptions.

Finally, I reached the section on arcanite:

Arcanite serves as a conductor for essence. Once found in abundance within the Northeastern mountain range of Freyheim, it was primarily used in weapon-making before being rapidly mined and distributed throughout the realm. The mineral possesses a unique quality unknown to any other substance in Umbrathia—the ability to both store and disperse essence. When enchanting weapons with arcanite, some wielders successfully transferred their tether into the stone, enhancing its capabilities.

I read the passage twice, then again. Something wasn't right. I scrunched my nose, flipping through the next few pages, searching for more information.

"This text is wrong," I said finally. "It says nothing about arcanite creating essence."

"Because that would be inaccurate," Aether said without looking up from his book.

"In the Guard, we learned that arcanite is where essence is made. That the realm would die without it." The words felt hollow even as I said them.

"And I'm telling you, that's incorrect." My eyes fell onto his lips as he brought his hand up, wetting his finger before flipping a page. "Umbrathia hasn't had arcanite deposits in over a century. Sometimes you might find an old family heirloom, a sword or weapon encrusted with the stone. But that's all that remains."

I sat with that for a moment, my fingers tracing the words on the page before me. The implications twisted in my gut.

"It can store essence," he added, his voice softer now, "but it's not the creator. That comes from the realm itself."

The realization settled over me slowly, then all at once. The Guard had lied—just as they had about everything else. A fear tactic, exactly what Ma had always accused them of. We'd been taught the Wraiths were after the arcanite, that losing it would plunge the realm into darkness. It had kept us from asking questions they didn't want to answer.

How far up did these lies go? I thought of Laryk, but quickly pushed the thought away. These deceptions had probably started with the military leaders who first destroyed Riftdremar. They'd rewritten history, buried the truth beneath layers of carefully constructed lies.

I needed air. Standing abruptly, I wandered into the maze of shelves, letting my fingers trail along the spines of books. At the end of one aisle, I noticed a blocked-off section in the back. A sign marked it as restricted, but the rope that usually barred entry had been moved aside. Curiosity pulled me forward.

As I rounded the corner, someone jerked upright, dropping their book with a dull thud. Raven stood there, dark hair falling into his eyes as he glanced around like a startled animal. Books lay scattered around the plush chair he'd clearly been lounging in.

"Erm—I was just—" He gestured vaguely at the mess.

I bit back a smile. "Hiding from Talon?"

His shoulders relaxed slightly, a sheepish grin replacing his panic. "You caught me."

"Don't worry, I won't tell anyone." I bent to pick up the fallen book, noting its worn leather binding and gold-leaf edges. "Your tether demonstration in the trials was impressive, by the way."

"That's kind," Raven said, accepting the book from my hands. "Though what I showed wasn't even the beginning of what I can really do. I couldn't exactly demonstrate their full potential easily in such a setting."

"Is that so?" I settled against one of the shelves, grateful for the distraction from my earlier discoveries.

"Well," he shrugged, absently straightening the books around his chair, "I suppose enchanting mirrors isn't exactly combat efficient. Not in the traditional sense, anyway."

"What exactly do you mean?"

His eyes lit up with enthusiasm. "The mirrors—I can form bonds with them, leave them places. Use them to communicate across distances, or..." he hesitated, glancing around before continuing in a lower voice. "Or observe what happens around them. Like looking through a window."

Something clicked in my mind. A tether like that would be invaluable to a military operation. No wonder the Umbra had placed him in the archives instead of dismissing him outright—his abilities weren't about combat, they were about intelligence.

"At least, I used to," he added, his enthusiasm dimming slightly. "Before everything started failing. Now it takes so much more essence just to maintain a single connection."

"That must be difficult," I said, thinking of how my own abilities had never weakened, even here. The guilt of that privilege sat heavy in my stomach.

He shrugged, clearly trying to shake off the moment of vulnerability. "So what's the realm's new Duskbound looking for in the archives? Besides catching Archivists breaking protocol, of course."

"Information about arcanite."

"Sounds thrilling," he said, lips quirking into a smile. "Though I suppose that's more useful than my current reading material."

I glanced at the book he still held. "And what exactly are you reading?"

"Well, I only just opened it, but—" he smiled sheepishly, holding it out to me, "my taste is less academic."

"*The Adventures and Life of Krayken Vindskald,*" I read from the ornate cover. "Sounds riveting."

"It might interest you actually. Vindskald was around before the crusades, when Duskbound were still *born in the wild.*" He laughed at his own phrasing.

Despite myself, I was intrigued. The history of Duskbound in Umbrathia was something I wanted to understand. "Haven't you just started it?"

"I've got about five hundred on my to-read list. I won't miss it for a while." He gestured to the scattered books around his chair. "Every time I figure out which one I'll read next, another draws my attention. I'll never make it through that many, but it's fun to think I might."

I tucked the book under my arm. "Well, thanks for this. And your secret is safe with me."

"Let me know when you finish it," Raven said, already settling back into his chair. "Not many people around here share my taste in literature." He paused, then added with a hint of mischief, "Well, not many who'd admit to it, anyway."

"I'm sure Talon would love to discuss historical fiction with you."

"Oh, absolutely. Right after he finishes lecturing me about proper preservation techniques." He grinned. "And proper posture. And proper breathing, probably."

I couldn't help but smile as I turned to leave. "I'll let you get back to your extremely important research then."

"Much appreciated. Very classified stuff happening here."

When I returned to the table, Aether looked up from behind his glasses, his brow furrowed. "Another fit?"

"You know, if you woke up one day and realized everything you'd ever been taught was a lie, I think you'd need some time to process that away from judgmental glances." I narrowed my eyes.

He simply nodded and returned to his reading, though something in his expression had softened slightly.

The afternoon stretched on as I poured over more texts, finding nothing of substance. Nothing that seemed like it would help stop this war. It wasn't until Aether stretched and stood that I realized how late it had grown, the eternal twilight somehow dimmer.

Before we could leave, Raven rushed up to me, pressing a small compact into my hand. "If you'd like to discuss any of your reading." He gave me a mysterious smile before disappearing into the archives.

We walked back to the fortress together, the silence heavy with everything I'd learned. My mind raced with possibilities, each one seeming more hopeless than the last. How was I supposed to present anything to Urkin when all of it lead to a dead end?

At the entrance, Aether paused. "I'm taking Nihr for a ride." He hesitated for a moment before adding, "Would you like to join with Tryggar?"

The invitation caught me off guard. We'd already spent the entire day together, albeit in silence.

"Not tonight," I said. "I need to..." I gestured vaguely at nothing.

He nodded once before heading toward the stables, leaving me alone with my growing sense of helplessness and the weight of Vindskald's book pressed against my chest.

CHAPTER TWENTY-NINE

THE COMPACT MIRROR Raven had given me sat on my desk, its surface reflecting the twilight that filtered through my window. I turned it over in my hands, wondering what exactly he had done to it, if he could see me right now through its glass. I snapped it closed before setting it aside. My muscles ached from sitting hunched over archive texts all day, and my mind still churned with everything I'd learned about arcanite. Or rather, what I hadn't.

It just felt like I was missing something. Arcanite seemed to be the common denominator between both the war in Riftdremar, and the one now being waged on Umbrathia. But I couldn't figure out the way the two connected. Had Sídhe taken the stores knowing they would begin draining Umbrathia nearly a decade and a half later? I knew there was more to it, but I had no idea where to look.

I changed out of the stiff uniform into sleeping clothes, but sleep felt impossible. My eyes kept drifting to the leather-bound book on my bedside table. Its gold lettering caught what little light remained. Perhaps a few chapters would force sleep to come.

I settled against my pillows and opened the book. The spine

crackled, revealing elaborate script that could only have been hand-written. *The Adventures and Life of Krayken Vindskald, Most Humble Servant to the Written Word and Observer of the Extraordinary.* I couldn't help but smile at the grandiose introduction.

My fingers traced the weathered pages as I flipped through, scanning for anything useful, until the word *Duskbound* caught my eye. The ink had faded slightly, but the words remained clear.

In this, the thirtieth year of my wanderings through our fair realm, and the second spent in the dubious company of certain gentleman bandits (whose names I shall withhold for the sake of discretion and continued breathing), fortune saw fit to grant me an encounter most rare indeed—a true Duskbound.

Such beings had grown scarce as winter roses since our noble King Thaddeus claimed his throne, His Majesty being, perhaps understandably, somewhat discomfited by those whose gifts so closely mirrored his own. Yet there one sat, in a modest tavern South of what was then the prosperous township of Croyg.

At first glance, he appeared no more remarkable than any other patron seeking solace in his cups, though he ordered them with impressive frequency. His true nature revealed itself only when one of my traveling companions (let us call him Dullard, for that is what he proved to be) made the grievous error of attempting to liberate the gentleman's satchel from his person.

In a display that shall haunt my dreams until my dying day, the man rose like smoke itself, darkness erupting from his very being. The shadows moved as serpents might, wrapping poor Dullard in their cold embrace until his face turned the most fascinating shade of purple. Most curious was the complete absence of void burns upon the man's skin—a detail that did not escape my notice, though I confess my attention was primarily occupied by Dullard's rather dramatic change in complexion.

Being possessed of both scholarly curiosity and a particularly robust sense of self-preservation, I took great pains to distance myself from my former companions' unfortunate choices. Indeed, once Dullard had been deposited rather unceremoniously upon the floor (still breathing, though with a newfound appreciation for personal property), I found myself drawn to this mysterious figure.

When at last he returned to his seat, I gathered what remained of my courage—bolstered, perhaps, by the remarkable quantity of ale in my belly—and approached. My inquiries regarding his service to the Umbra were met with surprising revelation, for he had never sworn allegiance to our realm's defenders. The Void, it seemed, had claimed him in childhood, the result of a foolish dare and the sort of bravado that so often leads young boys to their doom.

When I pressed him, with all the delicacy my profession demands, to speak of his time within that endless dark, a shadow passed across his face that had naught to do with his extraordinary abilities. He stared into the depths of his mead as though it might shelter him from memories that, even after so many years, seemed to plague him still. I did not ask again, for some horrors, I have learned, are best left unspoken.

I lowered the book. The Duskbound man had remembered everything, even years later. The Void's mark went deeper than just the shadows it stitched into him. Would I be the same? Would those visions haunt me forever?

I knew I should be focusing on my plan for Urkin—or something at least useful—like sleep, but something pulled me to keep reading. My fingers traced the next page, where elaborate script detailed another encounter.

I had been summoned, with no small measure of pomp, to document what Lord Sveinson assured would be a most historic achievement—the first successful domestication of those magnificent and terrible beasts known as Vördr. Had known then what bitter folly awaited, perhaps I might have found pressing business elsewhere in the realm.

The creature they had somehow managed to capture was a sight to behold, its coat as black as a moonless night, with threads of silver running through its wings like stars woven into darkness itself. They had constructed an elaborate holding pen of polished steel and precious metals, adorned with the family's finest craftsmanship—as if such a being might be impressed by our mortal displays of wealth and station.

"Today," Lord Sveinson declared to the gathered nobility, his voice carrying all the certainty of one who has never been properly acquainted with humility, "we shall prove these creatures can be bent to proper Kalfar will."

It was then I noticed her—a stable hand who kept to the shadows of the gathering, her face drawn with the sort of concern that comes from knowing something one's station forbids them to speak. As they brought forth elaborate harnesses of tooled leather and silver chains, I observed her desperate attempts to catch her master's attention, though protocol kept her silent.

What followed shall be forever etched into my memory, though I confess I sometimes wish it were not...

The beast's reaction was as swift as it was terrible. As Lord Sveinson's eldest son approached with his elaborate bridle, the Vördr's wings snapped open with such force that the very air seemed to crack. Those magnificent wings—how curious that they reminded me so of the darkness I had witnessed in that tavern years before, the way they seemed to drink in the light itself.

Indeed, I had heard whispers in my travels, tales told in hushed voices over too much wine, that these creatures were born of the Void itself. Some swore they had witnessed Vördr vanishing into that endless dark at strange intervals, as if answering some ancient call. Others claimed they returned to the Void to breed, though none could explain how such knowledge was obtained, if it held any truth at all.

Such thoughts occupied my mind for only a moment before chaos erupted. The Vördr's rage manifested in a display of savage grace that defied description. Steel bars bent like river reeds, chains snapped like thread, and Lord Sveinson's son found himself airborne in a manner most unflattering to his station.

It was then that the stable hand—that quiet girl who had tried to warn them—did something that changed everything. As the beast reared up, preparing to deliver what would surely have been a fatal blow, she stepped forward. And dear reader, I swear upon my very profession that shadows moved with her...

The shadows that danced around her were unlike any I had witnessed before—not the raw power of a Duskbound, but something more subtle, like ink spreading through water. Later, I would learn these were the marks of one touched by the Void, though she bore her burns with more grace than most.

The Vördr's reaction was immediate and extraordinary. Where moments before it had raged with the fury of a tempest, now it stilled, those terrible wings folding as it turned its attention fully upon the girl. The gathered nobility, many of whom had been scrambling for safety mere moments before, fell silent as death.

She approached the beast with neither fear nor pretense, extending her hand as one might to an equal, not a creature meant to be conquered. The Vördr lowered its great head, and I swear by all that is sacred, it bowed to her. Not in submission, as Lord Sveinson had so foolishly hoped to achieve, but in recognition. As though they shared some profound understanding that we mere viewers could never hope to grasp.

"They cannot be tamed," she spoke then, her voice carrying despite its softness. She turned to face her master, and though her station remained humble, something in her bearing had changed. "They are creatures of the Void, my Lord. They answer to it alone."

Lord Sveinson's face had turned a shade of purple that rivaled poor Dullard's from my previous tale, though for entirely different reasons. Yet even he could not deny what we had all witnessed. The Vördr allowed the girl to lead it from its elaborate prison, and I noted with no small amount of irony that it followed her without need of chains or bridles.

I learned later that she was elevated to master of the Sveinson stables —the first void-touched to hold such a position. A small victory, perhaps, but one that began to change how our realm viewed both the Vördr and those marked by darkness.

I closed the book for a moment, letting the words sink in.

Creatures of the Void itself. The thought sent a chill down my spine as I remembered Tryggar's reaction to me that first day—how he had claimed me before I'd even entered the Void, as if he'd sensed what I would become. Or perhaps what I had always been.

The memory of him standing between me and Aether in the courtyard took on new meaning. Had he known even then? Could these creatures truly see something in us that we couldn't see in ourselves?

Interest piqued, I turned to the next chapter.

After nearly fifty years of traversing our fair realm, collecting stories and memories I sometimes wished I could forget, I encountered something that defied all understanding. Something that, even now as I pen these words in my hundred and twentieth year, I have never witnessed again.

My wanderings had taken me to the Southeastern ridge of the Leidvra region, where villages grew sparse and the wilderness held secrets yet untamed. I had joined a group of warriors drawn by tales of some great beast haunting the rivers—a simple enough pursuit, or so I believed.

But what I witnessed that day far exceeded any mere beast. Indeed, dear reader, I scarce dare put it to paper for fear you might doubt my very sanity. A siphon.

My eyes fell upon the river as essence seemed to rise from its depths like morning mist, leaving the waters gray and lifeless in its wake. Yet this was not destruction—for as I watched, transfixed, that very essence redirected to the surrounding fields, where summer's cruel heat had left naught but ash. Before my very eyes, green burst forth from dead earth, life flowing back into land long thought barren.

Can you comprehend what I describe, dear reader? A force that could redirect the very flow of essence itself—

My heart thundered in my chest as I turned the page, only to find ragged edges where the rest of the chapter should have been. The pages had been torn out.

I shot to my feet, pacing the small confines of my room as my mind raced. A siphon? In all my studies in Sídhe, in all the texts I'd read in the archives today, I'd never encountered such a thing. But the implications... if something could redirect essence...

My eyes fell back on the book, its weathered cover suddenly feeling much heavier than before. This could be it—the missing piece I'd been searching for. The answer to everything.

CHAPTER THIRTY

I SHOVED the compact mirror into my pocket and bolted from my quarters. The discovery about the siphon burned in my mind as I raced through the fortress corridors, barely registering the surprised looks from those I passed. I burst into the courtyard just as Aether was dismounting from Nihr, nearly colliding with him in my haste.

His expression shifted from startled to annoyed to confused in the span of seconds. "What—"

"We have to go back to the Archives," I cut him off.

"I assumed we would return tomorrow." He began removing his riding gloves, studying me with that maddening calm.

"No. Now."

"What did you find?" He raised an eyebrow but started walking toward the Archives, his long strides forcing me to quicken my pace to keep up.

"Have you ever heard of a siphon?"

"Can't say that I have."

"In the book I was reading, it says there was an item—a siphon—that could direct essence. Actually direct it."

"What text did you discover this in?"

"It was in a memoir. *The Adventures and Life of Krayken Vindskald.*"

Aether stopped walking, turning to face me with lifted brows. "The drunk ramblings of a bard?"

"Just hear me out. Right now, the Umbra's only tactic is attacking the arcanite. But what if there's more to it? What if Sídhe is using a siphon?" The words tumbled out faster now. "And better yet, what if we could find our own—redirect the essence back into Umbrathia ourselves?"

He paused, considering my words with unexpected seriousness.

"Let's be honest," I pressed, "the current strategy isn't exactly working."

"What else does the book say?"

"That's the most intriguing part. The rest of the chapter about siphons is ripped out."

Aether's brow furrowed, but he continued walking. "I guess it's going to be a late night then."

I noticed how empty the streets were as we approached the archives, especially the area surrounding the building. When we reached the entrance, I pulled on the handle. It didn't budge.

"It's locked." I turned back to him.

"Well, of course. It's after hours." His tone suggested this should have been obvious.

"Then why did you let us walk all the way here?" Heat crept into my voice.

A smirk pulled at his lips. "Because you're going to unlock it for us."

"And how exactly am I supposed to do that?"

"Your spectre form. You can slide right through the door if you're quick enough."

"You're going to have to give a better explanation than that."

In an instant, Aether dematerialized before my eyes. Where he had stood, only misty shadows remained, twirling like smoke before dissipating completely. A breath brushed my ear from behind, making me jump. I spun to find him there, solid once again, standing far too close.

"Better?"

I crossed my arms. "Show-off."

"You used your shadows the other day for the void-letting. This isn't so different." His voice was steady, patient. "Instead of imagining them pouring out of you, imagine becoming them."

I took a step back, eyeing the door before closing my eyes. Drawing the shadows in was easy now, but this was different. Instead of letting them flow out, I had to let them consume me. I focused on becoming intangible, letting the shadows spread from my core outward until they filled every part of me.

The sensation was bizarre—like losing all my weight at once while still maintaining my shape. When I opened my eyes, everything looked slightly darker, edges bleeding into shadow.

I moved forward towards the door, bracing for impact that never came. Instead, I felt the grain of the wood pass through me—or maybe I passed through it, I couldn't quite tell. The smell of cedar filled my nose as I slipped past, and then I was on the other side, reforming into solid flesh with a strange tingling sensation, as if spider webs clung to my skin.

My heart thundered in my chest. I had just walked through a door. Actually *walked* through it.

"Impressive," Aether's voice came from behind me, his shadows still whipping around him.

I refused to give him the satisfaction of seeing how thrilled I actually was. "Let's find those missing pages."

Aether simply turned and began walking through the tall shelves.

The archives felt different after hours. The usual shuffle of feet and whispered conversations had been replaced by absolute silence. I pulled out the compact Raven had given me, studying its polished surface before snapping it open.

"I don't know how this works," I whispered to my reflection, feeling slightly foolish, "or if you can even hear me, but if you're interested in some late-night debauchery at the archives, we're waiting." I eyed the door once again, and twisted the lock.

I followed Aether through the maze until we found a table near one of the brass lamps, its light barely reaching the edges of the wooden surface. I set down Vindskald's memoir, the leather binding making a soft thud against the table as I opened it to the chapter about siphons.

Aether moved behind me, his chest nearly brushing my back as he leaned over my shoulder to examine the faded text. His breath stirred loose strands of my hair as he squinted at the pages, clearly struggling to make out the words.

"Do you require your spectacles?" I asked, trying to ignore how his proximity made my skin tingle.

Instead of answering, he reached around me to lift the book, his arm brushing mine. He turned and leaned his back against a chair, shooting me a narrowed glance from behind the pages. I couldn't help but notice how the lamp light caught the gold in his eyes, how it traced the sharp angles of his jaw. He was almost devastating to look at, that statuesque beauty almost too perfect at this angle, backlit and shadowed against the archives. The silence stretched as his gaze moved across the words, broken only by the occasional rustle of paper.

Eventually, he turned to the section that was torn out, a thoughtful *hmm* escaping his lips. The sound vibrated through me, reminding me just how close he still stood.

"It's something," I said, my voice soft, but I couldn't hide the eagerness creeping in. "I can feel it."

"It could be." His tone remained carefully neutral.

I snorted, ignoring his skepticism. "Where should we start from here?"

"If it's some kind of spelled or enchanted item, it would be somewhere along those shelves." Aether pointed to the back of the archives, where rows of books stretched into shadow. "Or," his voice dropped slightly, "it could be in the restricted section."

A creak of the door cut through the quiet. We both turned to find Raven in the entrance, one eyebrow arched as he took in the scene before him.

"You made it." I turned to Aether. "You remember Raven?"

Something in Aether's presence seemed to make Raven smaller, his easy confidence from earlier replaced by something more hesitant.

"Our new Archivist." Aether nodded before walking back to the section he had previously pointed to, running a hand through his dark hair.

"So," Raven said once Aether was out of earshot, "breaking into the archives after hours? I thought you were supposed to be the responsible one."

"Technically, I never said that. Simply an assumption on your part."

"Fair point." His eyes fell on the open book. "Found something interesting in Vindskald's memoir then?"

"Maybe. If we can find anything about siphons in the rest of these texts." I gestured to the towering shelves ahead of us.

"Well," Raven grinned, his confidence building, "you've got an Archivist on your side now. Where should we start?"

That first night stretched into early morning as we combed through dozens of texts. Raven's knowledge of the archives was a saving grace. He knew exactly which sections might hold relevant information, which authors had written about magical artifacts, which historical periods to focus on. But despite our efforts, we found nothing more about siphons.

Days blurred together as we established a routine. Mornings were spent in regular archive sessions, carefully maintaining appearances of normal research. Nights were dedicated to more thorough investigations, particularly of the restricted sections. Vexa and Effie had immediately volunteered to help when I'd explained what we'd found, eager for something more engaging than their usual duties. Rethlyn was too busy training the new recruits, though he gave me an apologetic smile on his way out of the dining hall.

"There has to be something," I muttered on the third evening, surrounded by stacks of books. My eyes burned from reading endless pages of faded text. "An item that powerful doesn't just disappear from history without leaving any trace."

"Unless someone wanted it to disappear," Aether said quietly from where he sat across the table, his glasses reflecting lamplight as he studied yet another tome.

"What do you mean?"

"If such an item existed, it would be incredibly dangerous in the wrong hands. Perhaps someone deliberately removed all record of it."

The thought settled uncomfortably in my stomach as I watched the twilight glimmer from outside. Time was running out. I had less than two days left before I had to present something to Urkin, and so far, all I had was a single page from a questionably reliable memoir and a growing pile of books that told me nothing.

"Maybe we're looking in the wrong place," Raven suggested, closing another useless volume with a sigh. "If someone did try to erase its existence, they wouldn't have left information in obvious locations."

"Then where?" I asked, frustration creeping into my voice.

But no one had an answer for that.

"I need air," I said, shoving away from the table. My head

throbbed from endless hours of squinting. "And time to think that doesn't involve being surrounded by useless books."

Aether simply nodded, already standing. He stayed quiet, pulling the door open for me as we filtered into the gray light. Days of searching, of hope building and crashing with each dead end, and all we had to show for it was exhaustion.

The walk to the stables was silent, both of us lost in our own thoughts. Maybe I'd been foolish, letting myself believe we'd found something significant. The siphon could have been nothing more than the drunken imaginings of a traveling bard, and I'd wasted precious time chasing it.

Laughter drifted across the lawn as we approached—a sound so unexpected it made me pause. Lael stood in front of the stables, practically bouncing with excitement as he ran his hands over a Vördr's coat. The beast had charcoal-colored fur marked with patches of pure black that spread across its wings like ink spills.

"Aether!" Lael called out, sprinting toward us with a grin that seemed too big for his face. Rethlyn followed at a more measured pace, though his easy smile seemed proud. "Look! She claimed me! Just now—she landed right in front of me during training and wouldn't leave!"

Despite my exhaustion, I couldn't help but smile at his enthusiasm. The Vördr watched us with intelligent eyes, its head tilted as if assessing newcomers.

"Her name is Nyx," Lael continued, practically vibrating with joy. "She's perfect, isn't she?"

"She suits you," Aether said, and though his voice remained steady, I caught the hint of warmth beneath it.

"Well the two of you have been spending an awful lot of time together in the archives," Rethlyn said, his tone casual but his eyes knowing. "After everyone else has called it quits for the day."

Aether ran a hand through his hair, letting out an irritated sigh. "Your perception skills are unparalleled."

"Urkin will wonder what you're up to," Rethlyn added, a slight grin pulling at his lips.

"Urkin is welcome to inquire about whatever he likes." Aether's eyes narrowed. "He knows he can request me any time he requires my presence."

"He just might." Rethlyn shrugged, his eyes playful. "Especially since you've missed the last two briefings."

"I've had more pressing matters to attend to."

"That may be." Rethlyn's gaze flickered between us. "Though I can't recall the last time you showed such... dedication to research."

"Rethlyn." There was a warning in Aether's voice.

"What *have* all of you been doing?" Lael asked, quirking an eyebrow.

"Nothing to concern yourself with," Aether replied, his expression closing off slightly. "Focus on your training."

Rethlyn ruffled the boy's hair. "He's so mysterious—"

"Don't you have somewhere to be?" Aether cut in.

"As a matter of fact, I do," Rethlyn sighed, shooting me a smile. "I have to go check in with Mira and Theron. I'll catch you two later."

Tryggar's silver form descended from the clouds as if summoned by my thoughts, landing with enough force to send dust scattering across the yard. His eyes immediately found Aether, and his wings flared slightly—a warning I'd come to recognize.

"Still holding that grudge, I see," Aether muttered, taking a careful step back.

Tryggar snorted, positioning himself between us. I couldn't help but laugh as he nudged me with his snout, nearly knocking me over in his enthusiasm.

"Yes, yes, I missed you too," I said, scratching under his chin. His purr of contentment vibrated through my chest. "And your instincts are correct, as usual."

Tryggar's only response was to wrap his wing around me like a shield, effectively blocking Aether from view.

"Mature," Aether said dryly. I heard him whistle, and moments later Nihr appeared, her dark form a stark contrast to Tryggar's silver coat.

The wind whipped through my hair as we soared above Ravenfell, its dark spires piercing the sky. Up here, everything seemed smaller—the problems, the pressure, even my own doubts. But they weren't gone, just muted by the altitude and the steady beat of Tryggar's wings.

"I wasted our time," I finally said, breaking the silence between our Vördr. "Three days of flipping through nearly every tome, book and scroll and we're no closer to stopping this war."

"You found a lead," Aether replied, guiding Nihr closer so we could hear each other over the wind. "That's more than we had before."

"A lead that goes nowhere." The words tasted bitter. "I have less than two days to present something to Urkin, and all I have is torn pages and theories."

"Sometimes theories are enough to start with."

I shot him a look. "Since when are you the optimistic one?"

"I'm not," he said, and I caught that ghost of a smile again. "But you seemed to be taking a break from it."

The laugh that escaped me was sharp, almost desperate. "I just thought... I don't know what I thought. That maybe there was a way to fix this without more death. Without having to choose sides."

"There might be," he said after a moment. "Perhaps we just need to get more creative."

CHAPTER THIRTY-ONE

"Two days from now," Rethlyn said, pushing his food around his plate. "Urkin wants the new recruits to cross the rip. See the Western territory of Sídhe firsthand."

I stared at my own untouched meal, my appetite gone. In two days, I was supposed to present Urkin with an alternative to war. Instead, I'd be watching the Umbra prepare their next generation to infiltrate my former home.

"It's just observation," Rethlyn continued, as if sensing my discomfort. "No engagement. They need to understand what we're facing beyond the rip, learn the patrol patterns."

"Am I not included in this run?" I asked, unable to hide the bitterness in my words.

Rethlyn's eyes glanced from Aether to me, a questioning look settling into his features. "I would assume," he finally said. "Although, I'm not sure Urkin cares either way."

"Yes. Because I've already given him exactly what he needs."

"The recruits deserve to see what they're up against. What they've committed their lives to." Rethlyn shrugged, but there was an apologetic look in his eyes.

"They've only been training for five days," I said, disbelief coloring my tone. "None of them are ready for this."

"They don't need to be ready," Aether replied, his voice carrying that familiar weight. "They just need to see."

"Besides," Effie cut in, barely glancing up from her nails, "the Guard never positions themselves that close to the rip. Flying through the Western border is nothing."

Her words hit like a physical blow, that old part of me flinching at the revelation. How many times had they entered Sídhe without anyone catching on?

"Will they be using... shadows?" I asked, though I already knew the answer. They were my shadows now—my power being used against my former allies.

"Just for concealment," Rethlyn said quickly. "Standard protocol for crossing the rip. We're not looking to engage anyone."

An uncomfortable silence fell over the table. Even Effie's rhythmic filing paused.

"Don't look so grim," she said finally, resuming her manicure. "It's not as if they're launching an attack. Though I suppose that will come soon enough if you don't produce this miraculous alternative you keep promising."

"Effie," Aether warned, but she just shrugged.

"What? We're all thinking it. The deadline is in two days, and so far all we have is a bunch of dusty books and—"

Vexa's hand slammed onto the dining table, rattling plates and startling several nearby soldiers. "I have an idea."

"Some of us are trying to eat here," Rethlyn grumbled, tugging his plate away from her fingers.

"It's risky," she continued, sliding into a seat with a self-satisfied smile, "but at this point, you don't have much of a choice, do you?" Her eyes found mine across the table.

"I'm listening." I leaned forward, trying not to let my desperation show. After days of dead ends in the archives, I'd take almost anything.

"I'm honestly surprised you didn't think of it earlier, Aether." Vexa shot him a disappointed look.

"Elaborate, please, dear," Effie said, examining her nails with disinterest.

Something passed between Vexa and Aether—some shared knowledge that made the air feel heavier. I glanced between them, hating how often I felt like I was missing pieces of the puzzle.

"We've been going about this the wrong way—trying to find information in the archives about siphons. Why did we waste all that time when we could have just spoken to the source himself?"

Effie scrunched her eyebrows. "The man's been dead for over a century."

"You're the only one who still knows how to find them," Vexa said to Aether, ignoring Effie completely. "What had you told me... some cave in the Blodfhal—"

"No." Aether's response was immediate as he leaned back, crossing his arms. The shadows around him seemed to deepen.

"The book was written by him, it carries his penmanship. It would work, I think." Vexa shrugged, but there was nothing casual about her tone.

"Vexa." Just her name, but it carried enough warning to set my nerves on end.

"What are you two talking about?" I asked, unable to keep the edge from my voice. More secrets, more half-truths.

"I'd also like to know," Rethlyn added around a mouthful of ricecake.

"When I was in prison, there were rumors about this fiend, or monster—something stereotypically horrifying, of course. Said it could speak in voices of the dead, as long as you had a personal item of the deceased." Vexa's lips curled into a smile. "Like, perhaps, a memoir."

Effie nearly choked on her drink. "Absurd."

I rolled my eyes, disappointment settling heavy in my stomach. I'd actually let myself hope for a moment, but this was ridiculous.

"I thought so too. Until this one here broke me out, and confirmed it was real."

The silence that followed was deafening as all eyes shot to Aether. Even Effie's disinterest cracked.

"Vexa, that's not even close to an accurate account of what happened." He sighed, but something in his voice made me pause. He wasn't denying it existed.

"I was telling you all the tales I'd heard whispered across those cells—"

"Quite loudly, and frequently, if I recall."

"So you do remember? Good." Vexa's smile turned sharp. "Anyway, I guess in an attempt to *quiet me*, he confirmed the existence of the Dread Sirens. Said he had encountered them nearly two decades before."

"And they were useless, which you'd remember, if you hadn't put away so much ale that evening." Aether's voice was flat, but his shoulders had tensed.

"Only because you didn't have any possessions." She held up the memoir, waving it like a prize. "But this time, we do."

Aether stayed quiet, jaw clenched as his gaze narrowed further on the wall.

"The two of you could go when the rest of us travel to the rip. Urkin would never suspect it," she whispered.

"Vexa, it's too early for these ridiculous heist aspirations. You're not in prison anymore." Effie's voice was sharper than normal. "You're simply asking for trouble."

"If we timed it right, we could leave and return at the same time. He'd never know you weren't with us." Vexa raised an eyebrow.

"It's not worth the risk." Aether wouldn't meet any of our eyes now, and that told me more than his words.

"We're running out of options," Vexa pressed.

"I said no." Aether stood abruptly, his chair scraping against stone as he strode toward the courtyard door.

I watched him leave, frustration burning through me. If there was even a chance this could work, how dare he dismiss it without discussion? Without letting me decide if the risk was worth it? Before I could think better of it, I pushed away from the table and followed. I didn't even know what Dread Sirens were, nor did I particularly want to find out, but if this was the only way forward, I was sure as Esprithe going to take it.

"So that's it?" I called after him. "You're just going to walk away? You're the one who said we need to get creative!"

He didn't slow his pace, forcing me to jog to catch up. "I already gave my answer."

"Without even discussing it? Without even considering—"

"There's nothing to consider." His voice was sharp as he rounded on me, shadows writhing across his void burns. "The cave is in Draxon territory. After what happened at the Void, you think Valkan wouldn't love to find you wandering right into his domain?"

"So you *have* thought about it." I stepped closer, refusing to be intimidated by his looming presence. "You've already mapped it all out in your head, haven't you? And you said nothing."

Something flickered across his face—too quick to read—before his expression hardened again. "It doesn't matter. It's not happening."

"Why? Because you said so?" Heat crept into my voice. "Last time I checked, you weren't in charge of me anymore. I'm not your prisoner."

"No," he said, his golden eyes burning with an intensity that made me want to step back. I held my ground. "But you are my responsibility."

"I don't need your protection."

"Clearly you do, since you're willing to walk straight into Valkan's territory on the word of a drunken bard."

"At least I'm trying to find a solution!" The words burst out louder than I intended. "While you're content to just let everything fall apart because what? Because it might be dangerous? Aether, *everything* about this is dangerous. The whole realm is dying, in case you hadn't noticed."

His jaw clenched, shadows deepening around him. "You think I don't know that?"

"I think you're scared." The moment I said it, I knew I'd struck something. His entire frame went rigid. "Not of Valkan, not of the Dread Sirens. You're scared of taking a risk that might actually change something."

"You have no idea what you're talking about." His voice had dropped dangerously low.

"Then explain it to me. Because right now, all I see is you shutting down our only lead without even—"

"Because I don't care to watch you die." The words exploded from him with enough force to make me stumble back. In the silence that followed, I could hear his breathing—heavy and ragged. "Not for this. Not for some desperate, idiotic gamble."

I stared at him, caught off guard by the raw emotion in his voice. His careful control had cracked, revealing something underneath.

"Aether..." I started, but he was already turning away.

"Find another way," he said, his voice steady again, though something in it still trembled. "Any other way."

As I watched him walk off, my rage nearly boiled over. If he wasn't going to help me, I'd find a way to these Dread Sirens myself.

And with that, I turned back towards the archives. I needed a map.

CHAPTER THIRTY-TWO

Vexa caught my eye as she adjusted Draug's saddle straps, giving me a slight nod. Even Effie shot me a meaningful look, though uncertainty flickered across her features. It was the day of the deadline. The day the Spectres would make the journey to the rip.

I still had nothing to show Urkin. But today, I was going to find it.

I busied myself with Tryggar's tack, trying to focus on the familiar motions instead of the guilt churning in my stomach. From a crack in the wood of the next stall, I could hear Aether's low voice as he helped Lael prepare Nyx.

"You'll stay in your spectre form as long as you can," he said, hoisting the saddle onto the charcoal Vördr. "It's the most assured way not to be seen. Do you understand?"

"I know," Lael urged, bouncing slightly on his feet. "Rethlyn's already told us. You don't need to worry—I've gotten really good at it."

"This isn't training anymore, Lael." Aether's voice dropped lower, meant only for the boy. "The Guard won't hesitate if they spot you. They won't see a sixteen-year-old boy—"

"I understand." Some of Lael's enthusiasm dimmed.

Something passed across Aether's face—pain, maybe, or regret as he straightened the collar of Lael's leathers. "And I don't care what happens over there. If something goes wrong, if one of the others engages—I'm ordering you right now. Don't fight. Don't even think about it. Just run. Get back across the rip as fast as you can."

"But what if someone needs help? What if—"

"No." Aether's tone left no room for argument. "Promise me, Lael."

The boy nodded, serious for once, and Aether gave his shoulder a few firm pats before turning away. My eye caught a glint of reflected light at his back. A solid gold longsword was sheathed down his spine, the hilt crafted with intricate patterns similar to those I'd seen on Vexa's creations. It was beautiful, and it fit him perfectly.

He ran a hand through his dark hair as he walked toward Nihr, and I couldn't help but notice how the movement pulled his leather uniform taut across his shoulders, how his shadows were already flickering around him. It was rare to see him show any kind of emotion. It made him seem more dangerous for some reason. When his golden eyes caught mine staring, I quickly returned my attention to Tryggar's saddle straps.

I ignored the stress slithering over my shoulders and hopped down from my stool, turning the corner into Lael's stall. He managed a warm smile despite the heaviness that had settled over him.

"I know you're not coming with us," he whispered, eyes fixed on adjusting Nyx's straps.

I shifted uncomfortably. "No, I'm not. There's something else I have to do." I watched him fiddle with the buckle for a moment before adding, "I wish none of you were going. This seems reckless and unnecessary. If I can find the answers I'm looking for—"

"Have you told Urkin this?"

I walked next to him, helping to tighten the strap of his saddle bag. "Obviously not. He won't listen to me. You know that."

He was silent for a few moments, seemingly deep in thought.

"I won't tell anyone." Lael nudged me, but not with the playful energy I'd come to expect. This was more solemn.

"I appreciate that."

He nodded and looked down at his boots. "I'm worried about you," he said finally.

I turned fully towards him. "Don't worry about me. Focus on the mission to Sídhe. And do exactly what Aether told you."

"Don't engage. Run. I got it." He took a deep breath, and for a second, I caught a flash of fear cross his face before that boyish grin returned.

"You don't have to go, you know," I said quietly. "None of you do. You could all just tell Urkin no."

"I know you don't want—" Lael hesitated, "well, I know you're trying to figure out a better way to end all of this. I hope you do, Fia. Really, I do. But the rest of us need to be ready in case you don't..." He trailed off, giving me an apologetic look.

The words hit me like a physical blow. He was right. If I failed, if this lead turned out to be nothing more than Aether suggested, then I'd have to face the reality of what was coming. War. More deaths, more destruction. Everything suddenly felt very real, very heavy.

Movement across the lawn caught my attention. Urkin approached the stables, flanked by two Sentinels, his stride carrying that familiar rigid authority.

Lael and I stood quickly, brushing hay from our leathers. I pulled him into a quick hug before he could move away. "Be safe," I whispered.

"You too," he replied.

I returned to Tryggar, anxiety coiling in my stomach. He

nudged me gently, his dark eyes carrying an understanding that made my throat tight. He knew something was different about today.

Around us, the other Spectres were mounting their Vördr. Lael settled onto Nyx, his earlier fear carefully masked. Rethlyn and Mira shared Raskr's broad back, while Vexa helped Theron adjust his position on Draug. And then there was Aether, already astride Nihr, his golden eyes fixed on me with an intensity that made guilt churn through me. I shot him a dismissive scowl, though my heart thundered in my chest.

Urkin's boots crunched against the gravel as he approached. "Recruits, this will be your first mission to Sídhe." His eyes fell on me, his lip curling slightly. "Well, for most of you."

"Learn what you can, and report back here," he continued. "I want updates on the state of the Guard's positioning, and any changes made to their strongholds. Especially in regard to the arcanite towers."

The sound of boots hitting ground drew my attention. Aether had dismounted Nihr, his movements controlled but carrying an edge I rarely saw in him. "That wasn't the agreement."

"The agreement changes as I see fit." Urkin's voice carried a warning.

"They're not ready for that kind of infiltration." Aether closed the distance between them, his shadows deepening. "The towers are heavily guarded. If we're caught—"

"Then you better not get caught," Urkin cut him off. "Or have you forgotten what's at stake here, Second?"

"I haven't forgotten anything." Aether's voice dropped dangerously low. "But sending untrained recruits into Sídhe strongholds is not the right move. You know this."

The air seemed to grow heavier as the two men faced each other. Even the Vördr had gone still, watching the exchange with unusual interest.

"Your concern is noted," Urkin said finally, though his tone suggested it was anything but. "Now get them in position. We've wasted enough time."

"Sir—"

"That's an order." Urkin's eyes narrowed. "Unless you'd like to explain to the Council why we've delayed gathering intelligence yet again?"

Something dark flashed across Aether's face, but he held his tongue.

Urkin turned away from him, making his way toward me. As he neared Tryggar, he lowered his voice so only I could hear. "If you pull anything, if you try to return to the enemy, you'll be damning us all."

"You're damning us all with this mission, sir," I whispered back, refusing to meet his gaze. "They've only been training for a week, and now you want to dangle them like carrots in front of the Sídhe Guard."

"This is war," he said coldly. "I shouldn't have to remind you of that." He turned and strode away, his guards falling into step behind him.

Vexa and Aether shared a quick, tense conversation before she turned to address the group. "Form up," she called out. "We fly in pairs. Stay above cloud cover unless ordered otherwise."

One by one, the Vördr took to the launch platform. I watched as Lael guided Nyx into position, his earlier reluctance carefully masked behind concentration. Rethlyn and Mira followed on Raskr, then Vexa with Theron on Draug. Each pair rose into the gray sky until they were little more than shadows against the clouds.

I waited until last, checking my saddle bag one final time. The memoir was secure, along with the map and Raven's compact. Tryggar shifted beneath me, sensing my anxiety. His wing brushed against my leg—a gesture that felt almost like reassurance.

"Ready?" I whispered to him, though the question was more for myself.

Just as we moved toward the platform, I caught Aether's gaze. He sat atop Nihr, his expression unreadable, but something in those golden eyes made my breath hitch.

I forced myself to look away, urging Tryggar forward until his wings snapped open and launched us into flight. We needed altitude before I could break from the group. Everything depended on timing this perfectly.

The wind whipped stronger as we climbed, carrying us above the fortress walls, past the twisted spires of Ravenfell. Ahead, I could see the others—my friends, though I still felt strange thinking of them that way—arranged in their careful formation. Somewhere beyond them lay Sídhe.

My chest tightened at the thought of what waited there. Raine. Briar. Nazul and Draven. People I'd trained with, shared meals and jokes and dreams with—now potentially facing off against these recruits I'd grown to care for. Facing off against Vexa. Effie. Rethlyn. And Aether... My heart sank.

Laryk...

I pushed that thought away before it could take root, before the ache that accompanied it could make me turn around. What I was about to do was risky—possibly suicidal if Valkan caught me in his territory. But if there was even a chance the siphon was real, I had to try.

Until then, I'd just have to believe that everything would turn out okay. That the Spectres wouldn't be seen. That no harm would come to any of them—on either side.

We broke through the cloud cover, and for a moment, everything was gray mist and silence. Then we emerged into clearer air, and I allowed myself one last look before I turned Tryggar toward Draxon.

CHAPTER THIRTY-THREE

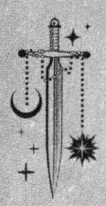

THE MAP of Draxon was clipped across my thigh as Tryggar flew, the parchment fluttering in the wind. Vexa had mentioned Blodfhal—a volcanic mountain range that cut through the center of Valkan's territory. According to the tome I'd found, it reached higher than any peak in Umbrathia. Easy to spot from the sky, I hoped.

I pulled out his compact mirror, flipping it open.

"Found anything new?" I asked my reflection.

His response came almost immediately. "A few more texts mention volcanic caves along the Eastern ridge. Something about the way the lava flows created natural tunnels. That's where I'd look."

I nodded, studying the range on my map. "Any idea about patrols in that area?"

"The terrain seems nearly impossible for horses to traverse, and I see no mention of roads that run through the mountains. Though I'd be more concerned about whatever's making Talon so nervous. He keeps pacing past my hiding spot, muttering about missing books."

"Maybe you should find a new spot."

"And miss all this excitement? Besides, someone has to make sure you don't get yourself killed looking for cave-dwelling death speakers."

"Your concern is touching."

"Just doing my part for the realm." His grin flickered in the mirror. "But Fia..." His voice turned serious. "Be careful. I still haven't found any mention of such creatures in the archives. And these texts are old. The landscape could have changed significantly since they were written."

"Will do." I snapped the mirror closed, tucking it safely away. What I knew about the Dread Sirens could be summed up in a few sentences: they could speak with the dead, they required a personal possession of the deceased, and they lived in the depths of a cave somewhere in Blodfhal. It wasn't much to go on, but it would have to be enough.

A shadow passed over me, massive and dark, making Tryggar's wings falter for just a moment. My heart stopped as Nihr's obsidian form dove through the clouds above, cutting through the air like a blade. Aether materialized from his spectre form as they descended, shadows rolling off him in waves. His golden eyes blazed with fury as Nihr banked hard, coming alongside us with enough force to make the air crack.

"You're absolutely insufferable," he snarled, his voice somehow carrying over the wind. The shadows around him were twisting violently.

"What are you doing here?" I had to shout over the wind. "Go back to them!"

"I'd rather we both went back." His jaw was set.

"I can't." The words came out harder than I meant them to. "But you can. They need you more than I do."

"There are six of them together, and you're out here alone," he growled. "That's not bravery—it's reckless stupidity."

"I don't care."

Something dangerous flashed in his golden eyes. "You just became hope for these people. The one person who might actually save them. And now you're going to throw your life away on some fool's errand?"

"We can't keep doing what the Umbra have been doing," I shot back. "It's not working—it never has. We have to try something different. This is how *I help*."

"And if Valkan finds you? If his men catch you in their territory?" His voice carried a dangerous edge. "The way he looks at you." Aether's eyes burned through me. "You have no idea the horrors he'd inflict."

"Aether, you're not going to change my mind." I shook off the images of Valkan.

"Then I am coming with you," he insisted.

"I guess you'll have to keep up."

His jaw tightened. "This isn't a game, Fia."

"No, it's not. It's about finding another way—any other way—to save this realm without destroying mine." The words came out sharper than I intended. "Unless you'd prefer we just keep killing each other until there's no one left to fight?"

Silence fell between us, broken only by the steady beat of Vördr wings. Below, the landscape had begun to change. Where there had been only gray ash and death, patches of brown and green now dotted the earth. Actual living plants. I'd never seen it in Umbrathia before. The sight made my chest ache—this was what the realm should be.

Finally, Aether broke through the quiet, his voice shifting into something harder, more precise. The soldier I'd come to know replacing the man who'd argued with me moments ago. "We'll need to stay high—above the cloud cover. Valkan's men patrol the main roads, but they're less likely to spot us if we come from above." He gestured toward a dark smudge on the horizon. "The range will be visible soon. We find the highest peak first, then work our way down. The cave..." He hesitated, something flickering across his face. "The cave will make itself known."

"What does that mean?" I asked, but he had already urged Nihr higher into the clouds.

"Follow my lead," he called back. "And go into spectre form if we see anyone on the ground. It'll just appear as a Vördr flying a bit too far South."

"What are they like?" I called over the wind. "The Dread Sirens?"

Something dark passed across his eyes. "Difficult to deal with. They might demand a price."

"What kind of price?"

"I don't know." His jaw tightened. "It's different for everyone."

"Why did you go to them before?"

He was quiet for so long I thought he wouldn't answer. Finally, he said, "Because I was young and desperate." The words carried a weight that made me hesitate to ask more.

Just then, the clouds parted, revealing a peak that seemed to pierce the eternal twilight itself. Its dark stone stretched impossibly high, edges jagged and cruel against the gray sky.

Aether signaled for us to descend, guiding Nihr toward a wide shelf of volcanic rock that jutted out from the mountain face. The ledge was barely large enough for both Vördr to land, forcing them to touch down one at a time.

Tryggar's hooves struck stone with surprising grace, though the impact still sent loose rocks skittering over the edge. I slid from his back, my boots finding the uneven surface. The shelf dropped away sharply on three sides, leaving us surrounded by nothing but air and distant peaks.

"We need to move," Aether said, already studying the rough cliff face that stretched above us. "The cave is higher up, but we'll have to go on foot from here."

I turned to Tryggar, who nudged me softly with his nose. "Stay out of sight, okay?" The beast pushed his head into my hands and I gave him a final scratch before turning to Aether.

He pointed to a narrow ledge about thirty feet above us. "There first. We'll have to move quickly—avoid plummeting to our deaths."

I swallowed the lump in my throat, but didn't allow myself to look down.

His form dissolved into shadow, rising like smoke before materializing on the ledge above. My heart thundered as I focused on my own transformation. The sensation was still new—that weightless feeling as my physical form became shadow. I pushed up through the air, forcing myself to move faster than natural. And just as I felt the shadows beginning to fray, I reformed on the ledge beside him.

"Good," he said, already scanning for our next landing point. "See that outcropping? The one that curves slightly to the left?"

I nodded, noting how the rock formed a small shelf about forty feet up. This jump would be longer—more dangerous if we didn't make it in time.

"Ready?" he asked, but he was already dissolving into shadow.

We continued like this, moving from point to point, each transformation draining more energy than the last. The higher we climbed, the harder it became to hold our spectre forms. One slip, one moment of lost concentration, and we'd fall hundreds of feet into the rocks below.

Finally, we reached a wider ledge that curved around the mountain face. The rough stone was littered with loose pebbles and debris that shifted under our boots. I pressed my back against the cliff wall, trying not to look at the dizzying drop beside us.

"There," Aether said, nodding toward an opening in the rock face about fifty feet ahead. The cave mouth was angular, its edges far too precise to be naturally formed.

"Last jump," he said, already gathering shadows around himself.

I followed his lead, pushing through the air as quickly as I could. My form began to waver just as I reached the cave entrance, and I stumbled slightly as I materialized on solid ground. Aether caught my arm, steadying me.

The entrance tunnel was pitch black, the darkness so complete it seemed to swallow the dim light from outside. A cold draft whispered from its depths, carrying a scent I couldn't quite place—something metallic.

For a moment, it reminded me of the Void.

I pulled out Vindskald's memoir, its leather binding worn smooth by time. "I guess this is it."

"Stay close," Aether said, his voice echoing slightly against stone walls. "The tunnels branch off in different directions."

We moved deeper, our boots scraping against rock despite attempts at stealth. The passage twisted left, then right, each turn taking us further from what little light remained. I pressed my hand against the wall, using it to guide me through the absolute darkness. My heart thundered in my chest—it was too fucking dark.

Then something strange began to happen. At first, I thought my mind was playing tricks on me, creating shapes in the dark. But the shadows around us started to shift, to separate into distinct shades of black and gray. The walls emerged from the darkness, their surface rough and crystalline, glittering with tiny fragments of some mineral I didn't recognize. The tunnel ahead became clear—curving sharply about twenty feet ahead, the ceiling dropping lower at the bend.

I stopped, stunned. "I can see everything."

"Another gift from the Void," Aether said, turning to face me. Even in the darkness, his golden eyes seemed to glow.

"Is this how you see all the time?" I asked, taking in details I shouldn't have been able to make out—the jagged patterns in the rock, the way certain crystals caught non-existent light, the subtle movement of air disturbing loose pebbles.

"Among other things." That ghost of a smile played at his lips. "Darkness becomes an ally rather than an obstacle. Though I suspect you're already familiar with that concept."

Before I could respond, a burst of warm air slammed into us from somewhere ahead, carrying the acrid stench of rotten eggs. I pulled my shirt over my nose, but it did little to help. Through my enhanced vision, I could see the passage ahead narrowing into what looked like a crevice—barely wide enough for one person to squeeze through sideways.

"Sulfur," Aether said, moving toward the gap. "We're getting closer."

The tunnel walls pressed in from both sides until my shoulders brushed against rock with each step. The ceiling dropped lower, forcing us to duck our heads. In the darkness, I could make out every jagged edge, every protruding crystal that threatened to catch on our clothing. The stone itself seemed to pulse with a dull heat.

"We'll have to turn sideways," Aether called back. "Watch your footing—the ground slopes here."

I pressed myself against the right wall, turning so my chest faced the left. The rock was uncomfortably warm against my back, and sharp edges caught at my leathers as I edged forward. My boots scraped against loose pebbles, each one threatening to roll beneath my feet.

"This is cozy," I muttered, watching as Aether navigated the narrow space ahead. His shoulders barely fit through the gap, forcing him to angle his body awkwardly. Another blast of hot air rushed past, stronger this time, making my eyes water. "Please tell me it opens up soon."

"Actually..." He stopped suddenly, and I nearly slammed into his back. Through the darkness, I could see his posture tighten. "Damn."

"What?" My heart skipped. "What is it?"

"The passage splits here." He gestured to where the crevice forked into two equally narrow paths. "And it gets narrower. Much narrower."

Heat seemed to pulse through the air, and the leathers suddenly felt suffocating.

"You should remove some of those layers," Aether said, as if reading my thoughts. "It's only going to get hotter."

"I'm fine." Even as I said it, I felt the beads of sweat forming across my forehead.

"Suit yourself." Fabric rustled in the darkness ahead. "But I'm not carrying you if you pass out."

"What are you—" I started, then stopped as I realized what he was doing. "Are you taking your shirt off?"

"Would you prefer I collapse instead?" The smirk in his voice was unmistakable as he pulled the leather uniform over his head. With my newfound vision, I could see every detail with frustrating clarity—the way his muscles moved beneath his skin, how the void burns traced down his frame. He tucked the shirt into his belt, completely unbothered by my presence.

"Suit *yourself*," I muttered, forcing my gaze to the tunnel ahead. Though my eyes kept betraying me, drawn back to the shadows that danced across his shoulders.

"Your pride is going to get you killed one of these days." He turned back to examining the split in the passage. I noticed how the heat had caused a sheen of sweat to form across his back.

I was about to respond when another blast of hot air hit us—but this time, something was different. The heat came with a deep rumble that vibrated through the stone around us. The crystals in the walls seemed to shiver.

"Aether—"

"I hear it." His voice turned sharp. "We need to move. Now."

"Which way?"

The rumble grew stronger, and loose pebbles began to rain down from above. The heat was becoming unbearable, pressing against us like an iron.

"Left," he said, already moving. "Stay close to me."

I followed, pressing myself against the wall as the passage narrowed even further. The rock was hot enough now to feel through my leathers, and I tried not to think about what that meant. Ahead, Aether's bare shoulders barely fit through the gap, the muscles in his back tensing as he navigated the tight space.

The rumbling intensified, and suddenly steam burst from somewhere above us with a deafening hiss. The hot vapor filled the passage instantly.

"Aether!" I called out, but the steam was too thick—I couldn't see him anymore. The hissing grew louder, and more bursts of scalding vapor shot from cracks in the walls. "Aether!"

It burned my throat as I tried to call out again, my voice lost. I pressed myself flat against the wall, the heat of it searing my leathers, but it was better than the scalding clouds billowing through the center of the passage.

Fuck. I was going to die in this Esprithe-forsaken cave.

"Fia!" Aether's voice came from somewhere ahead. "Don't move!"

"Wasn't planning on it," I said, though my heart still raced.

The steam shifted, creating gaps in the white mist. Through them, I caught glimpses of the passage ahead—how it curved sharply before disappearing into darkness.

"There's a chamber," Aether called out. "Follow my voice but stay against the wall."

I edged forward, keeping my shoulder pressed to the burning stone. The passage was somehow even narrower here. My chest scraped against one wall while my back pressed against the other as sweat dripped into my eyes.

"Still so certain about keeping those leathers on?" His voice was closer now, that familiar dry tone somehow reassuring.

"Shut up and tell me where you are."

A shape emerged from the steam—Aether's outstretched hand. I grabbed it without thinking, and he pulled me through the vapor into a small chamber where the air was clearer. I nearly collided with his chest, halting myself at the last moment.

"See? That wasn't so difficult." But there was tension in his jaw that hadn't been there before.

"Speak for yourself," I said, trying to ignore how the steam had plastered his hair to his forehead—how droplets of water traced down his chest. "Some of us don't enjoy crawling through volcanic death traps."

Another rumble shook the chamber, deeper than before.

"We need to keep moving." Aether's eyes fixed on something above. Following his gaze, I saw what looked like a narrow fissure cutting upward through the rock face. "That's our way forward."

"Up?" I moved closer to the wall, taking in the near-vertical climb. "You can't be serious."

"Unless you'd prefer to go back through the steam. I'll remind you that this was quite literally your idea." He was already testing handholds, his bare shoulders tensing as he pulled himself up slightly. "I'll go first. Watch where I place my hands."

"How reassuring," I muttered, but I found myself studying his movements as he began to climb. The rock face was slick with moisture, and several times his grip slipped before finding purchase. I could see every flex and strain of muscle, the way his jaw clenched when a handhold crumbled slightly. His back glistened with remnants of steam and sweat.

"There's a ledge about fifteen feet up," he called down. "The path continues from there." His voice echoed strangely in the vertical space.

I reached for the first handhold, testing my weight against it. The rock was sharp enough to cut, but at least it wasn't burning hot anymore. As I pulled myself up, my boots scrambled against the wall, finally finding a ledge that jutted out.

"You know," I grunted, "we could just shift into our spectre forms and float up there."

"In here?" His voice carried exasperation. "The steam's warped the air currents. One wrong move and we could materialize inside the rock face."

My hand slipped slightly at the thought. "Inside the—"

"Yes." Something dark crept into his tone. "These passages play tricks with depth. Better to do this the old-fashioned way."

"Wonderful." I pulled myself up another few feet, very aware now of how the moisture made the rocks shimmer. How the walls seemed to shift and ripple. "Any other horrifying possibilities I should know about?"

"Not at the moment."

"That's not actually reassuring." Another rumble shook loose debris that clattered past me into the darkness below. "At all."

The cavern trembled again, and I pressed myself closer to the wall, trying to become as flat as possible. Above me, Aether had paused his ascent, bracing himself.

"Almost there," he called down calmly. Of course he was calm right now. Just as we were inches from being swallowed up by some volcanic nightmare.

I glanced up as he pulled himself over the ledge, a relieved sigh escaping my lips. His form disappeared for a moment before his head peeked over, golden eyes finding mine in the darkness.

"Your turn." He reached down, arm extending toward me. "And try not to knock any more rocks loose. The sound carries."

"Yes, because I'm doing that on purpose." I stretched upward, fingers straining for the next hold. The rumbling had made everything less stable, and what had looked like solid rock now crumbled beneath my touch.

Oh Esprithe.

My right foot slipped, sending a shower of pebbles into the depths. For one terrible moment, my entire weight hung from my left hand, fingers sliding down the wet stone. I clawed at the structure with my other hand frantically, but there was nothing else to hold onto. *Fuck.* Panic seized my heart as my hold finally slipped.

Before I could even cry out, Aether's hand locked around my wrist.

"I've got you." His voice was steady, but his grip was almost painful.

Heart thundering, I let him pull me up the last few feet until I could crawl onto the ledge. We both sat there for a moment, catching our breath.

"Well," I managed finally, "that was fun."

"Your definition of fun needs work." But there was something almost like amusement in his tone.

The ledge opened into another tunnel, this one mercifully wider than the last. But as we moved forward, I noticed something changing in the air. The suffocating heat from below was giving way to something that made goosebumps rise on my arms.

"Temperature's dropping," Aether said, his bare shoulders tensing slightly. "We must be nearing one of the mountain's ice veins."

I was about to make a comment about him regretting the shirtless decision when the cold hit like a physical wall. My breath clouded in front of me, and the sweat that had soaked through my leathers suddenly felt like a snowstorm against my skin.

"Ice veins?" My teeth threatened to chatter. The tunnel ahead seemed to glitter—frost covered the walls.

"Underground rivers of ice," he explained, moving forward. "They run through the mountain like—" He stopped abruptly, causing me to nearly walk into him. "Well, that's unfortunate."

The passage ahead had narrowed again, but this time the walls were slick with ice. Crystals hung from the ceiling like jagged teeth.

"Of course," I muttered, wrapping my arms around myself. "Because this wasn't challenging enough already."

"You wanted to come here alone." His voice carried a hint of irritation, though I noticed he'd crossed his arms over his chest against the cold. "Since you were so determined to do this without help."

"You didn't exactly volunteer," I shot back through chattering teeth. "In fact, I distinctly remember you shutting down the entire idea."

His jaw clenched. "You could have at least waited. Made a proper plan."

"We don't have time for proper plans." Another violent shiver ran through me as we edged forward. The ice-slicked walls reflected our breath in the darkness.

"And you getting yourself killed would help how, exactly?"

"I can't just do nothing," I muttered, though the cold was making it harder to form the words. My soaked leathers felt like sheets of ice.

His eyes raked me over, taking in the gasps I was fighting against wholeheartedly. Even the heat of his eyes on me did nothing to fight the cold that clung to me in waves now.

"Can you continue?" he asked.

Another violent shiver wracked through me, and my legs nearly gave out. Aether caught my arm before I could stumble, his skin blazing hot against mine.

"You're freezing," he muttered, and before I could protest, he pulled me against him. The heat of his bare skin seared through me, and despite my pride screaming at me to pull away, my body betrayed me by pressing closer. My fingers found the ridges of his spine.

"What are you doing?" I managed through chattering teeth.

"Keeping you alive." The words vibrated through me where I was pressed against him. "Your leathers are soaked. In this temperature, that's deadly."

I wanted to argue, to maintain some dignity, but the warmth radiating from him melted any resistance. His arms tightened as another shiver coursed through me, and my breath stilled at the flex of muscle beneath my palms.

"Why are you so warm?" I asked, unable to help myself. Even in the freezing cave, he burned like he carried the sun inside him.

He was quiet for a long moment. "I don't know."

"Add it to the list of mysteries," I muttered, trying to ignore how perfectly I seemed to fit against him.

"Stop talking," he ordered, but there was no real bite to it. "Focus on getting warm."

Minutes stretched by as feeling slowly returned to my limbs. My world narrowed to the points where we connected—the steady rise and fall of his breathing, the occasional brush of his jaw against my hair, the burning heat of his skin seeping into mine.

"Better?" he asked finally, his voice low.

I nodded, not trusting myself to speak. *I should step away now.* The worst of the cold had passed. But neither of us moved.

"We should keep going," I said.

"In a minute." His arms tightened fractionally. "You're still shivering."

I wasn't, not anymore, but I didn't correct him.

A distant rumble shook the passage, reminding us where we were—what we were doing. The spell broke, and we stepped apart, though the ghost of his warmth lingered.

"The drop is just ahead," he said, his voice carefully neutral as he turned toward the ice-slicked tunnel. "Stay close to the wall. One wrong step and—"

"I know," I cut him off, already moving forward. "No need to paint me a picture."

The tunnel continued its descent, each step more treacherous than the last as ice coated everything. The path curved sharply, and my heart leapt at what lay ahead.

The passage simply ended, opening into a vast cavern that stretched down into absolute darkness. Even with my enhanced vision, I couldn't see the bottom. The edge was ragged, like something had torn the mountain apart from the inside.

"Please tell me we're not going down there," I whispered, though I already knew the answer.

Where else should I expect beings called *dread sirens* to reside?

Aether crouched at the edge, studying something I couldn't see. "There's a path. Narrow, but it's there." He pointed to what looked like a thin ledge spiraling down into the abyss. "We follow it counter-clockwise. The sirens' chamber is about halfway down."

I edged closer, trying to gauge the drop. "How did you even find this place the first time?"

His jaw tightened. "I followed the whispers."

A chill that had nothing to do with the cold ran down my spine. "Whispers?"

"The sirens call to those who are desperate enough to hear them." He straightened, shadows twisting through his void burns. "Ready?"

I nodded, not trusting myself to speak. Aether took the lead, pressing close to the wall as he began the descent. I followed, my fingers finding whatever handholds they could in the ice-slicked stone.

"Don't look down," Aether called, though it was too late.

"Thanks for the advice," I shot back. The cold seemed to deepen again as we spiraled lower, until my breath crystallized in front of me.

That's when I heard it—a sound so faint I thought I'd imagined it. Like hisses carried on wind that shouldn't exist this deep underground. They grew louder as we descended, until they seemed to come from everywhere and nowhere at once.

"That sounds welcoming—"

"I know." His voice was tight. "We're close."

The path curved again, and something glowed in the darkness ahead. A soft, phosphorescent light that seemed to pulse in rhythm with the sounds. As we drew closer, I could make out an opening in the wall—an arch carved from the stone itself.

Beyond it lay a chamber that defied explanation. The floor was black liquid that moved like silk in a breeze, though no wind stirred this deep.

Aether stopped at the chamber's entrance, his bare shoulders tense. "Last chance to turn back."

I stepped forward, the memoir clutched against my chest like a shield. "We didn't come all this way to—"

The whispers cut off abruptly, replaced by silence so complete it felt like the Void once again.

"The Realm Crasher returns." The voice wasn't spoken aloud, but resonated directly in my mind, clear as crystal and hauntingly beautiful. *"Twenty years since you last graced our depths."*

Realm Crasher?

"Still searching, are we?" Another voice, equally mesmerizing but touched with cruel amusement. *"Did you ever find what you sought?"*

Aether's jaw tightened. "We're here for a summoning."

Laughter echoed through our minds—three distinct voices harmonizing in a way that made my skin crawl. The black liquid rippled again, more violently this time.

"And what makes you think we'd help you again?" the first voice purred. *"After you left so... abruptly last time."*

"We have a personal possession," Aether said, his voice steady despite the tension I could see in his frame. "We seek to speak with Krayken Vindskald."

Something broke the surface of the pool—a pale, translucent form that seemed to hover between liquid and air. The creature was impossibly thin, almost skeletal, yet possessed an otherworldly beauty that made it difficult to look away. Its eyes were completely black, like holes cut into reality itself.

"Everything has a price," it spoke into our minds. *"Feed us, Realm Crasher. Let us taste the Void again."*

I stepped forward, but Aether's arm shot out, blocking my path. "I'll pay it."

The creature's mouth opened in a grotesque smile, revealing rows of needle-sharp teeth. It let out a long, rattling inhale—the first physical sound we'd heard from it. Dark tendrils began to seep from Aether's void burns, drawn toward the creature's mouth like smoke caught in a draft.

The shadows flowed into the creature's mouth for what felt like an eternity. Finally, it pulled back with a satisfied hiss, sinking partially beneath the black surface.

"The price is paid," the voices sang in unison. *"Present the item."*

I held out the memoir with trembling fingers. The book lifted from my hands, floating over the pool where it hung suspended in the air. The black liquid began to move, forming patterns that seemed to writhe and twist. The phosphorescent glow pulsed brighter, then dimmer, then brighter again.

A new voice filled our minds—drastically different from the ethereal tones of the sirens.

"What do we have here?" a vibrant tone questioned.

"Krayken Vindskald?" I asked.

"The very same! Though I must say, this is quite different from my usual audiences. The ambiance leaves something to be desired, but I suppose we must work with what we have." A pause, then: "But what's this? Such fascinating coloring you have, my dear. In all my years of documenting the realm's oddities, I never encountered a Kalfar with hair like starlight."

"I'm not—" I started, but caught myself. "That's not why we're here."

"No? Pity. I do so love a good mystery. And you, my dear, are certainly that. Though I suppose you have your reasons for seeking me out in this rather dramatic fashion. Not that I'm complaining—it's quite thrilling, actually. Being summoned by such an intriguing pair."

"I read your memoir," I said, trying to steer him back on track. "But some pages were torn out—the part about siphons."

"Ah, but surely we can spare a moment for proper introductions? The art of conversation is sacred, after all. And I find myself burning with curiosity about how someone so... unique... came to be asking about such matters."

"The realm is dying," I said, hoping the gravity of our situation might curb his curiosity. "Essence is being drained from our lands. Cities have been abandoned. Even the Kalfar's tethers are weakening."

"Dying?" All theatricality dropped from his voice. "Truly? Even Croyg? Those gardens were something to behold in their day..."

"Gone," I confirmed. "Everything's gone. Which is why we need to know what you saw that day by the river. What you wrote about in those missing pages."

A heavy silence filled our minds. When Krayken spoke again, his voice had lost its playful edge.

"I see. Though I must warn you—you're asking about dangerous business."

"We don't care about the danger," I said. "Please, just tell us what you know about siphons. How do we find such an item? Or how do we create one?"

Krayken's laugh echoed through our minds, but it wasn't cruel like the sirens—it was almost sad. "You have it all wrong. A siphon isn't something you find or create. A siphon is no item, no magical artifact. A siphon, my dear girl, is a person."

The words hit me like a physical blow. "What?"

"Like a tether?" Aether asked, tension evident in his voice.

"Precisely! Though far more rare, and far more... problematic."

"But that sounds like the ultimate power," I breathed.

"Exactly why it's the ultimate curse. Those who pull from the land itself, from their fellow Kalfar—well, I'm sure you're both familiar with how the Umbrathians feel about the corruption of essence."

Aether and I exchanged glances, the weight of his words settling between us.

"A siphon is an abomination," Krayken continued, his voice growing darker. "The one I saw by the river that day was swiftly killed once more realized what she was doing."

"Could a siphon drain the essence from an entire realm?" Aether asked.

"I never witnessed such a thing myself, though the theoretical implications are rather thrilling. Of course, the strain on the siphon would be..." He paused. "Well, astronomical, I'd imagine. Like trying to drink the ocean through a reed."

"But it's possible?" I pressed.

"My dear, in my experience, most things can be achieved. This, however..." Krayken paused for a few seconds. "I suppose if one could do it incrementally, store it over time, such a thing might be achievable."

The black liquid rippled violently, and one of the sirens emerged further from the surface. Its black eyes fixed on me.

"Time grows short," the siren's voice cut through our minds like ice. "The price only buys so many words."

"Wait," I said quickly. "Just tell us one more thing. How would one identify a siphon?"

Krayken's laugh echoed through our minds one final time. "Oh, you might never know. I'm sure one born of today would make sure to keep such a thing veiled in secrecy. But there could be clues—they are, *after all, beings of theft, feeling the pull of essence around them, always fighting the urge to reach out and take—"*

His voice cut off abruptly as the black liquid stilled. The phosphorescent glow dimmed, leaving us in near darkness.

"The dead have spoken enough," the sirens sang in unison. *"Leave now, Realm Crasher. And take your fair-haired friend with you."*

CHAPTER THIRTY-FOUR

My heart thundered in my chest as Tryggar carried us higher, the cold air whipping past until we broke through into cloud cover. The sirens' voices still echoed in my mind, but something else was taking shape—something that made dread coil in my gut like a serpent.

"The King of Sídhe," I called over the wind. "He must be a siphon."

Aether guided Nihr closer so we could hear each other. His expression was guarded, but attentive.

"I never knew what his focus was," I continued, the pieces falling into place faster now. "No one did. In all my time in the Guard, there were no stories about his power." My hands tightened on the saddle's horn. "But it's him. It has to be. He's been slowly draining Umbrathia, using the arcanite to store what he's stealing."

"If that's true," Aether said carefully, "destroying the arcanite towers won't solve anything."

"No," I agreed. "He could continue draining essence with or without them. And worse—if we destroy the arcanite, all that stored essence would be lost. It would never return to Umbrathia."

The implications hit me harder with each passing moment. All those years of prosperity in Sídhe, the abundant harvests, the thriving cities—it had all been built on stolen Essence. And the arcanite towers weren't just storage; they were proof of how long this had been happening. How long he'd been planning this. He had destroyed Riftdremar with this goal in mind.

"The towers are just the beginning," I said, my voice growing stronger despite the wind. "Think about it—he's had decades to perfect this. To figure out exactly how much essence he could take without completely destroying Umbrathia. Just enough to keep the Kalfar weak, but not enough to kill them outright."

"A slow death instead of a quick one." Aether's golden eyes had turned sharp. "But why? Why not just take everything at once?"

"Because he needs the realm alive, at least in some capacity," I realized. "If Umbrathia dies completely, there's no more essence to take. No more power to steal. Even as the essence is drained, the realm creates more—just not enough to make up for the loss. But perhaps, enough for him to take and store as it's created." The words tasted bitter. "He's farming the realm. Taking his time."

Tryggar let out a low sound, as if he could sense my growing anger. Below us, the fertile fields of Draxon stretched endlessly, the only part of the realm that was left untouched.

"We have to tell Urkin," I said. "The entire strategy needs to change. If we keep focusing on the towers while ignoring the real threat—"

"He won't believe it," Aether cut in. "Not without proof."

"Then we'll find proof. We have to." I met his gaze across the space between our Vördr. "Because if we don't stop him soon, there won't be anything left to save."

We flew on in silence, moments dragging by as clouds drifted around us. Without warning, both Vördr let out sharp hisses, Nihr's turning into a growl as they suddenly banked downward.

Through gaps in the mist, I caught glimpses of something large moving through the brush below. A deer.

"What are they doing?" I yelled, gripping the saddle horn as he dove faster.

"They rarely get fresh meat anymore," Aether called back.

"They're chasing that deer?" My stomach lurched as we plummeted toward the ground.

"Unfortunately. They'll eat anything."

The Vördr crashed through the canopy, branches snapping beneath their massive wings. We emerged into a living forest—actual green trees, not the twisted husks I'd grown used to seeing. Tryggar's hooves thundered against the earth as he gave chase, Nihr right beside him. The deer bounded ahead, weaving between trees until the thickness of the forest finally forced it out of sight. Both Vördr slowed, snorting in frustration before lowering their heads to the grass at their feet, tearing it from the earth.

"Doesn't take much for them to abandon their better sense," I breathed, trying to calm my racing heart now that there was ground beneath us.

"Food is certainly a motivator," Aether responded, adjusting his positioning on the saddle.

"What are you doing?" he asked as I slid from Tryggar's back. "We're still in Draxon. We need to leave."

I watched the Vördr devour the grass, their movements almost frantic. It hit me then—they probably hadn't eaten anything truly fresh in a long time.

"Let them eat. We can spare a few minutes." I started walking, taking in the vibrant forest around us. "Besides, we're in the middle of nowhere."

"Fia." His tone carried irritation.

"I'm sure they'll alert us if they sense anything close."

An audible sigh escaped him, but I heard his boots hit the

ground behind me. He followed as I wandered deeper into the trees, never straying too far.

I stopped at a bramble bush, leaning down to examine what looked like iridescent bubbles clustered on its branches. "What are these?"

Aether moved to crouch beside me, plucking one of the berries and popping it into his mouth. "Rainberries. Try one."

I watched as he grabbed a few more, then held out his hand. I took one, studying its translucent surface before tasting it. Sweetness burst across my tongue, followed by something lighter—like drinking fresh spring water on a hot day. After months of stale bread and rice, it was almost overwhelming.

"Esprithe," I breathed, grabbing a handful.

We settled onto the grass, and I felt the breeze stir my hair—actual wind, not the stale air of the fortress or the bitter cold of high altitude. The forest around us was a riot of life. Leaves rustled overhead, their edges tinged with amber and gold. Tiny purple flowers dotted the ground between tree roots, and somewhere nearby, water trickled over stones. It felt impossible that this could exist in the same realm as the wasteland we'd left behind.

"It's beautiful," I said softly, taking it all in.

"It is."

I glanced over to find his eyes fixed on my lips. We locked gazes for a moment before both quickly looking away. Heat crept up my neck as I focused intently on a nearby flower.

"It all used to look like this," he finally said. "This entire region."

"It reminds me a bit of Sídhe, actually. The forests surrounding Luminaria." I peeked over in his direction, noticing how still he had become.

"What did you do before the Guard?" he asked, twisting a blade of grass through his fingers.

"I worked in an apothecary." I couldn't help the smile that tugged at my lips. "For a woman, Maladea. We all called her Ma."

I felt his eyes on me again, studying me curiously.

"What?" I asked.

"Awfully mundane." He let out a laugh. "It surprises me."

"That used to be my whole life. Mundane monotony. It was safe and I was content." I looked down, remembering that girl. "Feels like a lifetime ago."

"Time does seem to have that effect." He shrugged.

"Life in Sídhe wasn't easy. Especially before the guard." I motioned towards my Riftborne branding.

"I heard you. What you said at the bonfire. I was staying in the shadows because it felt rude to interrupt such a tense moment." He laughed again. "But I heard everything."

Heat rushed across my cheeks. "You were spying on us?"

"Observing," he corrected, that ghost of a smile playing at his lips. "It's what I do."

"And what observations did you make?"

"That you're more interesting than I initially thought." His eyes met mine again. "Though still incredibly frustrating."

"Well, I wouldn't want to disappoint." I plucked a blade of grass and tossed it at him. "What about you? What profound mysteries lurk in your past?"

His expression closed off slightly. "Nothing worth sharing."

"Says the man who emerged from the Void with no memories, looking exactly as you do now, thirty-five years ago. That's a lot of time. A lot of life to live."

"Careful," he warned, though there was less edge to it than usual. "I'd hate to bore you."

Movement caught our attention—the Vördr had wandered further into the trees. We both scrambled up, following them through the thick brush until the forest opened into a clearing. What we found stopped me in my tracks.

An ancient shrine stood before us, open to the sky and partially reclaimed by vines. Statues lined its perimeter—their forms similar to the Kalfar—the Aossí, but unnaturally elongated, features carved with an otherworldly perfection. Their faces were too symmetrical, their limbs too graceful, stretched just beyond what seemed possible.

The Vördr halted at the shrine's edge, but Aether and I stepped inside.

"The Esprithe," I breathed, recognizing the figures from my studies.

"Looks like it." Aether's tone was distinctly unimpressed.

"They're painted on the windows of the archives too."

"Yes, they're inescapable, it seems."

"You don't sound like a fan."

"I've never given much interest to the idea of a higher power," he said flatly.

As we wound through the statues, an idea struck me. Without warning, I shifted into my spectre form, materializing behind one of the carved figures.

"It's hardly the time for games," Aether called out.

"Come on," I shot back, already moving to another statue. "This is all new to me. I need the practice, wouldn't you agree?"

I caught a glimpse of him shaking his head before I disappeared again, reforming behind a statue of Sibyl, her stone eyes fixed eternally on some distant point.

"You're not hiding very well." His voice carried closer.

"Then why haven't you caught me yet?" I taunted, slipping between Conleth and Niamh.

I heard him sigh—that familiar sound of exasperation—before I moved again, black mist blurring beyond my vision. Our game of chase continued through the shrine as leaves descended from the canopy above.

Finally, his hand caught my arm just as I reformed behind Fírinne. "Found you."

A smile tugged at his lips—small but real. Something in my chest fluttered at the sight.

"Your turn then," I said. "I feel like hunting."

His expression closed off immediately. "I'm afraid I can't." He released my arm, taking a step back. "The sirens... they took more than I expected."

I noticed then what I should have seen earlier—the void burns crawling up his neck looked different. Lighter somehow, almost faded.

"You can't shift?" The playfulness drained from my voice.

"Not until they replenish." He turned, already walking back toward the Vördr. "We should go."

I stepped toward him, my hand finding his arm before I could second-guess myself. The moment my fingers made contact, his head snapped around, but it was too late—I was already releasing the darkened tendrils. They poured from my skin into his void burns, and the sensation was unlike anything I'd experienced. His marks didn't just accept the darkness, they pulled at it, drawing my shadows in.

Aether's eyes went molten. His hand locked around my wrist with bruising force, and for a moment, I thought I'd made a terrible mistake. But instead of pushing me away, he pulled me against him, his other arm wrapping around my waist until there was no space left between us. Our faces were so close I could feel his breath against my lips. The shadows continued their transfer, and something about his reaction—the way his pupils had blown wide, the way his fingers dug into my skin—made heat rush through my veins. Heat that suddenly felt like something deeper. Something that meant more.

At that moment, Aether blinked as if returning to reality. He shoved me back, breaking the connection. "Don't ever do that again," he growled.

"What—" I started, confused by the cruelty of his response. "I was just trying to help."

He took several steps away, running a hand through his hair. The shadows now curled beneath his skin, restored but agitated.

"Aether, why are you—"

A snarl cut through the air. Tryggar's massive form shot past us, charging toward something in the distance. Nihr was already moving to follow.

"Stay here," Aether ordered, his voice leaving no room for argument as he raced after them.

I stood there, heart hammering, still trying to process what had just happened. And why did I feel like I'd crossed some invisible line I hadn't known existed?

I sat heavily on the ground, pressing my palm against my forehead. The intensity of Aether's reaction had startled me, but what scared me more was my own response. The way heat had flooded my veins, how my heart had raced at his touch. Guilt churned in my stomach as an image of emerald eyes flashed through my mind.

Time stretched as I waited, the forest growing quieter around me. Maybe I should look for them. But which direction had they gone? The trees all looked the same now, thick and towering.

"They ran into a small herd." Aether's voice startled me from behind. I let out a sigh of relief but kept my gaze down, still too uncomfortable to look at him directly. "Found a spring nearby too."

He held out his canteen. "Here. The altitude can be dehydrating."

I accepted without thinking, grateful for the distraction. The liquid hit my tongue in an instant, and the sensation was so magnetic that I pulled in several gulps before finally coming up for air. The water tasted off—like it had been sitting too long in the metal container.

It wasn't until I lowered the canteen that the silence registered.

No wing beats, no heavy hooves against earth. Where was Tryggar?

My vision swam slightly, and I blinked hard, trying to clear it. Had the altitude really affected me that much? Why did I feel like this? Finally, I looked up, and my blood turned to ice.

Golden eyes had turned milky white.

"You should have stayed in your tower, lovely." Aether's features twisted into something else entirely as darkness claimed me.

CHAPTER THIRTY-FIVE

My head felt wrong—heavy and disconnected. Fragments of memory slipped through my mind as I woke. Silk draping across my skin sent a wave of panic through me. Not my leathers. Something else. Something wrong. Ropes bit into flesh as I tried to move my hands, a wooden chair creaking beneath me.

Metallic taste. Burning throat. Golden eyes turning milky white. "You should have stayed in your tower, lovely." Darkness...

My eyes shot open.

A gown. I was in a gown the color of charcoal, red beading slithering up from the hem. Slowly, my vision crept up, taking in the grandeur around me.

A table stretched endlessly, covered in things that shouldn't exist in this realm anymore. Steam rose from fresh bread, dark and crusty. Wine-glazed meats glistened in the glowing candlelight. Actual fruit spilled from silver bowls, not the husks I'd come to know in Ravenfell.

Portraits lined the walls of the dining room—massive gilded frames housing generations of nobility. My eyes caught on one in particular. A younger Valkan, his eyes a startling blue instead of that milky white, standing beside what must have been his brother. The resemblance was unmistakable, though the brother's features were softer, less severe. Behind them stood an older couple—the woman's chin lifted with pride, the man's hand resting on Valkan's shoulder. A family portrait.

Panic raced through me as I realized where I was.

A soft step had my eyes flying to my right. Valkan moved down the length of the table, touching a flame to each candle. His eyes reflected the light as he turned, fixing on me.

"There she is." The words slid from his lips like honey.

"Let me go." I pulled against the ropes, ignoring how the room spun slightly.

"I intend to." He smiled, and my stomach turned. "Once I know you'll behave."

The shadows rippled just below my skin. They felt weak, muted by whatever drug he'd laced the water with, but they were there. And I could use them. Before I could think better of it, darkness seeped from my pores, curling through the air between us.

"Ah, ah, ah." Valkan clicked his tongue, moving forward with predatory grace. His fingers twisted through the black mist. "I know you're smarter than that."

My shadows wrapped around his wrist, coiling up his arm like smoke. He took a measured step back, though his smile never faltered.

"Think carefully, my dear," his voice dropped lower, "about what my men would do if they found their Lord in any condition other than how you see me now." His eyes sparked. "It would be quite disappointing if your first official act as a Duskbound was to plunge the realm into civil war."

Rage boiled through me, made worse by the smug satisfaction on his face. I kept my shadows coiled around me, no longer reaching for him but refusing to retreat entirely.

"You don't care about this realm," I hissed.

"Oh, quite the contrary." Valkan's smile widened. "I want to see it in its golden age again. But those in leadership are bound and determined to let us fall to ruin. I'm the only one willing to do what it takes to save us all."

"You're disgusting," I spat the words like venom.

"A foul mouth." He settled into the chair opposite me, crossing his feet on the table with casual arrogance. "That will have to be tamed, I'm afraid."

"Ever find your *own* shadows?" I seethed. "Since you couldn't produce them outside the Void?"

My words cut a slice through his satisfaction, but he recovered quickly.

"The Void may not have gifted me the powers of a Duskbound. But it left me alive, untouched." His eyes scanned the room. "I'd say that's rather fitting. Even the strongest force in this realm couldn't mark me, couldn't claim me."

"Or it simply rejected you," I shot back, still tugging at my restraints.

"Believe what you like, my love, but we both made history that day."

"Why am I here?" I finally asked, despite the nerves churning inside. I didn't want the answer, but I didn't know what else to say.

"Because I want to make a deal with you." He lifted a golden goblet, studying the liquid inside with exaggerated interest.

"And why would I ever make a deal with you?" The words came out as a growl.

"Because despite what you think of me, I see what you truly are." He took a long sip, watching me over the rim. "Someone willing to sacrifice everything for what they believe in. And I think with enough... persuasion, you could be made to see reason."

A bitter laugh escaped me. "Reason? Is that what you call it?"

"I think you're smarter than the others. I think you understand that sometimes difficult decisions must be made." His dead eyes fixed on me. "And I think, with the right motivation, you could come to see things from my perspective. Even share it, perhaps."

His words hit me like a physical blow, stirring something deep within me. All my life, people had tried to tell me who I was, what I should be. The Aossí who marked me as Riftborne, defining me by my past. The Guard who tried to shape me into their weapon. Even Laryk, who saw me as something to be molded, controlled.

But I wasn't that lost girl anymore, hiding in shadows and letting others write my story. I had found my own power, my own truth. And here was Valkan, another man trying to force his vision upon me, thinking he could bend me to his will.

No. I was done letting others define me. Done being what everyone else wanted me to be. I might be caught between two realms, but those parts of me—the ones that made me a weapon, an asset, something to be feared or welded or forged…

Those parts belonged to *me*.

"I would never, in a million years, allow you to unleash your forces onto Sídhe. That's what you don't understand." My voice shook. "I don't want more death and destruction, and that's all you offer. It's all your men know how to do."

"Sometimes," he said softly, "the end justifies the means."

My shadows pulsed wider, reaching for him again before I could stop them.

"Careful now." His voice dropped dangerously low. "I'd hate for this to turn into something ugly."

"You're delusional." I tried to hide the terror in my voice as my nails dug into the flesh of my palms. I needed to find a way out of this.

"I had hoped this conversation would go differently." He sighed, almost theatrical in his disappointment. "I truly hate being forced to take a firmer approach, but you leave me no choice."

I met his gaze with all the hatred burning in my chest, and his eyes lit with something dark. Something that made my blood run cold.

"Don't look at me like that," he growled. "Save it for our wedding night."

The words crashed into me. For a moment, I couldn't process what he'd said—what he meant. *Wedding night?* The web braided itself up my spine almost outside my control as panic clawed at my throat. My shadows morphed into a wall of darkness around me, ready to tear him apart.

"I've asked you quite nicely to keep those contained." His voice cut through my rising fury. "If the fate of the realm itself isn't enough to heed my warning, perhaps this will be."

Valkan slid something across the table, and my heart stopped. A clump of leather—torn and shredded in places, but unmistakable. Aether's name was still visible on the outer edge. The fabric was stained dark in places I didn't want to think about.

"If you care an ounce for his life, I suggest you start cooperating." His smile turned wicked as he watched the shock spread across my face.

"The Umbra will come for you," I managed, though the words felt hollow even as I said them. "If you hurt him, they will descend on Draxon—"

"Do you honestly believe that?" he cut me off.

The question hit harder than I wanted to admit. *Would they come?* With Urkin's attention fixed solely on Sídhe, with the Council in chaos... Only Vexa and Effie knew where we were. Would they assume we died at the bottom of that cave? My shadows trembled with helpless rage, but I forced them back, letting the web sink into the depths of my spine. Useless. I felt useless again.

"That's what I thought." Satisfaction dripped from his voice.

I stayed silent, jaw clenched so tight it hurt. Tears burned in the corners of my eyes. I knew it best to try and pacify him, at least for now, but I didn't know if I had the strength to do it. To not recoil any time his eyes fixed on me with that disgusting curiosity. To not unleash the stores of my power until he was no more than dust covering the floor.

Breathe.

"Would you allow me to remove your restraints now? I'm sure you're starving." He rose from his chair with fluid grace.

Just let him think he's winning. It's the only way you're getting out of here.

I gave a small nod, hating myself for it.

He approached with that satisfied smile, untying the ropes, making sure to graze my skin with his fingers before settling into the chair beside me. "Eat, darling."

I didn't move. The food's aroma filled my nose, making my stomach clench, but the memory of that metallic taste in the forest kept me frozen. My eyes darted between Valkan and the feast before us.

"You need to stay strong." He began filling my plate, movements deliberate and precise. "Look what I can provide for you."

Slowly, I picked up the fork, pushing the food around without bringing it to my lips.

"Together, we're going to conquer both realms." His voice took on a distant quality, like he was speaking to himself.

I watched him from the corner of my eye, trying to mask the hatred pulsing through my veins.

"If we don't intervene, this conflict will never end. It's not enough to quell Sídhe. It's not enough to restore Umbrathia." He leaned closer, and I fought the urge to recoil. "In order to maintain the peace we will carve across the rip, we will need to bring all to their knees."

My grip tightened on the fork until my knuckles went white, the end digging into the wooden table.

"Those guards are quite formidable, even I'll admit that. Your friends." His smile turned cruel.

Panic shot through me. "What are you talking about?" My voice came out clipped.

"The Umbra don't know everything that happens in this realm. Or across the rip." He shrugged, but there was nothing casual about it.

My heart thundered against my ribs as faces flashed through my mind. Raine. Briar. Laryk.

"You've been there," I whispered.

"So invigorating, their veins gluttonously pulsing with stolen essence." His tongue ran across his teeth. "The most exquisite feast I've ever tasted."

Something in me snapped. Before I could think, I drove the fork into his thigh.

His cry of pain turned into a snarl as he lunged for me, form rippling and growing impossibly large. His hand locked around my throat as he slammed me back against the table. Cold metal pressed against my lips, forcing them open. Metallic liquid flooded my mouth.

"Such a shame, I was really hoping to do this differently." His hand caressed my face, and I tried to pull away, but I was already losing my grip on reality.

"Tyreth, bring her to the chamber." His voice drifted above me as darkness claimed my vision. The sound of a door creaking open and boots rushing towards me was the last thing I heard.

CHAPTER THIRTY-SIX

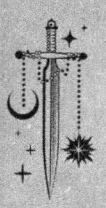

WAKE UP.

FIANDRIAL.

WAKE UP.

CONSCIOUSNESS RETURNED to me in fragments, like trying to piece together a shattered mirror. My limbs felt impossibly heavy, weighted. Even my eyelids refused to cooperate, leaving me trapped in a darkness that pulsed with each sluggish heartbeat.

Voices drifted through the haze—distant at first, then clearer. The sound of boots against stone. Whimpers from somewhere nearby. My mind struggled to make sense of anything beyond the fog that seemed to fill my skull.

When I finally managed to force my eyes open, the world refused to come into focus. Blurred shapes swam above me—

fabric hanging in sweeps. As my vision cleared, details emerged with sickening clarity. The bed frame beneath me felt wrong—too soft, too luxurious—with posts carved into twisted shapes that seemed to writhe in my peripheral vision.

I tried to move, to turn my head, but my body wouldn't respond. It was like being trapped underwater, every signal from my brain dying before it could reach its destination.

Blurs moved through my field of vision—men in gray uniforms pacing between rows of smaller beds that lined the walls. More whimpers drew my attention further to find other Kalfar forms laying motionless beneath fine linens. A scream caught in my throat as I begged my body to cooperate.

After seconds of straining my muscles so hard that tears formed in my eyes, my head lulled to the right. And my heart seized in my chest.

Valkan sat beside me, those dead eyes fixed on my face with an intensity that made bile rise in my throat.

I tried to reach for my web, for my shadows, for anything that might help me fight. But the drug held everything just out of reach, leaving me trapped in a body that wouldn't respond.

"Hello again." His lips curved into the most terrifying of smiles.

Terror shot through me at that voice—silky and wrong—as my drugged mind finally registered where I was. Who I was with. *Oh Esprithe. Oh no. No. No. No.*

I tried to scream but my mouth wouldn't work, wouldn't move, wouldn't do anything but let out a pathetic whimper that made Valkan's eyes flash with pleasure. My heart slammed against my ribs so hard I thought they might crack. I couldn't move. I couldn't *fucking* move.

"I must admit," he leaned in, so close I could feel his cold breath against my skin, "I was beginning to worry I'd given you too much."

He straightened, adjusting the cuffs of his perfectly tailored jacket. "But now that you're awake, we can have a proper conversation about the future." His milky eyes gleamed as he began to pace. "You see, there's something poetic about having a Duskbound here to witness what's coming. One of their precious chosen ones, watching as I tear down everything they've built."

He stopped, cocking his head to the side at an unnatural angle. "Tell me, little Duskbound, do they teach you the true history of our realm? Or just the convenient version the crown wants you to believe?"

My heart thundered against my ribs as he turned back to me, that cruel smile never leaving his lips.

"Centuries ago, the Syrndore line ruled Umbrathia. We were kings before your precious Valtýrs ever dreamed of wearing the crown." His voice carried centuries of inherited bitterness. "But they claimed the Void had chosen them, that only their bloodline could truly understand its power. And the realm, desperate for any sign of divine right, believed them. Three generations of my family were massacred, leaving only a child behind to rebuild our great line as they sat atop our throne and called themselves monarchs."

I tried to turn my head, to look away from those dead eyes, but my muscles wouldn't respond. The paralytic left me trapped, forced to watch as he continued his measured steps around the room.

"For generations, we waited. Played their game. Smiled at court while they squandered their power." His laugh was hollow. "And now look what they've become—the Valtýr's precious realm withers while the Queen remains hidden. While her sycophants cling to outdated traditions. At least I had the courage to take what was needed when the drought came.

"For generations, my family served faithfully in their court, all while remembering what was stolen from us." He ran a finger along the edge of a nearby table. "We watched as they grew complacent, soft. And now?" His milky eyes flashed. "Now their precious Queen sits in her tower while her people starve. While her realm dies."

A fresh wave of terror washed over me as his pacing brought him closer. My lips wouldn't move, but inside, I was screaming.

"The Skalvindrs will be the first to fall," he said, his tone shifting to something almost gleeful. "How quickly they changed allegiance when the drought worsened. One day bowing to the crown, the next supporting my innovation." His lip curled. "Such spineless creatures don't deserve their titles. I think I'll start with the children. Make the parents watch as I drain them, one by one. Show them the true cost of political games."

Bile rose in my throat. I wanted to vomit, to scream, to do anything but lie here listening to this monster's plans.

"And after that?" He spread his arms wide. "The other houses will fall in line. Those who don't... well, I have plans for their daughters. Strategic marriages to my most loyal followers. Nothing bonds men like sharing the same sins." His smile turned vicious. "Though I doubt many will survive the wedding nights."

My web strained against whatever was blocking it, desperate to reach out, to fight back, to do something. But there was only silence along my spine.

"As for Sídhe..." He leaned closer, his cold breath ghosting across my face. "I have something special planned for them. Your Guard won't expect an army that doesn't need to eat, doesn't need to rest. Imagine their faces when they realize their precious arcanite towers won't save them. When they see their own people turned into fuel."

Tears burned in my eyes as I pictured Raine, Briar, all of them facing an endless tide of Damphyres. The horrors they would witness before the end.

"I'll march their bloodless corpses through Ravenfell's streets in celebration." His voice dropped lower, savoring each word. "Stack their heads on pikes outside the palace. A reminder of who truly delivered salvation to Umbrathia."

Please, I tried to beg, but only a whimper escaped.

"Which brings me to your commander." Something shifted in his expression, turning darker, hungrier. "Would you like to know what's happening to him right now? In my dungeons?"

No. No. Please no.

"He's quite resilient," Valkan mused, examining his nails. "Most would have broken by now. But him? He just keeps asking about you. Even as my guards strip the shadows from his flesh."

My heart splintered at his words. Tears rolled freely down my cheeks now, and Valkan's eyes lit up at the sight.

"You see, that's the beauty of it. The torture of a vessel. When they run out of that delicious darkness you so lovingly provide, they're all skin and bones once more." He traced a finger through my tears. "And bones can be broken…" He closed his eyes as if savoring a fine wine. "The screams are exquisite."

The room spun as nausea clawed at my throat. I wanted to retch, to cry out, to beg him to stop.

"Soon, his mind will begin to fray. That's my favorite part. When they start hallucinating, calling out names, pleading with ghosts." His voice dropped to a whisper. "I wonder what secrets he'll reveal in those final moments?"

Stop. Please stop.

"Of course, that's assuming my men don't cut too deep." Valkan's eyes glittered. "My guards can be quite creative with their tools."

Rage burned through my paralyzed limbs, useless and devastating. But beneath the fury, guilt crashed over me like a wave, threatening to drown what little strength I had left. This was my fault. All of it. My arrogance in thinking I could enter this territory without conflict. My stupidity in flying to Draxon despite Aether's warnings. My weakness in getting captured so easily.

Aether had tried to stop me. Had begged me to find another way. But I wouldn't listen. Couldn't listen. And now he was paying the price for my stupidity. Being tortured in some lightless dungeon while I lay here, useless, unable to even scream.

The memory of his golden eyes flashed through my mind—how they'd looked when he'd made the decision to come with me. The way his warmth surrounded me in that cave. And this was how I repaid him. By leading him straight into Valkan's trap. By being the reason he might die in agony, alone in the dark.

I'm sorry, I tried to whisper, though my lips wouldn't move. *I'm so sorry.*

"But enough about him," Valkan cut through my thoughts, "I'd rather focus my full attention on you, lovely." His cold fingers traced my jaw.

Something inside me cracked at his words. My focus exploded outward in desperate, silent waves, but found nothing to grasp onto.

He inhaled deeply at my neck, making a sound that sent violent shudders through me. "Now that we're so close…" He trailed off, running his hand along my side. "I can smell how potent you are. How much essence flows through these veins."

My mind screamed at my body to move, to fight, to do anything. But I was trapped, forced to lie there as his fingers moved to my cheek.

"You have no idea how long I've waited for this." His voice lowered with need. "Since that first night in Stravene, when I caught your scent. The power in you... it's pure. Untainted." His eyes seemed to devour me.

A knife appeared in his hand and my mind exploded with panic. *No. Please no.* This couldn't be happening. I had to wake up. Had to get away. Had to—

The blade pressed against my throat and a sob caught in my

chest. Tears leaked from my eyes as he leaned closer, his face twisting into something grotesque.

"We could have been magnificent together," he breathed against my skin, and I fought the urge to vomit. "A true Duskbound and a Damphyre king. We could have restored Umbrathia to glory." His voice turned vicious. "Now you'll serve a different purpose." His free hand tangled in my hair, yanking my head back to expose my throat. "You'll be my own personal wellspring. My infinite source of essence. The tool I needed to conquer both realms."

He inhaled again, longer this time, like he was savoring a fine wine. "Though I must confess, it will be... difficult to show restraint—to not drain you completely each time. But that would be wasteful, wouldn't it? When I can keep you like this, suspended between awareness and oblivion, for as long as I desire."

The knife bit deeper and I felt warmth trickle down my neck. My mind shattered as his mouth sealed over the cut. The sound he made was obscene—pleasure and hunger mixed into something monstrous as he drank deeply, each pull of his lips sending waves of weakness through me. I could feel my essence draining, could feel him stealing pieces of me.

Seconds stretched into an eternity. My consciousness flickered as he fed, darkness creeping at the edges of my vision. Just when I thought I might pass out, he wrenched away with a gasp, blood staining his lips and chin. His milky eyes had gone wild.

"Oh," he moaned, running his tongue over bloodied teeth. "You're even more divine than I imagined. So much power. So much *life*." His fingers dug into my shoulders as he shuddered with pleasure. "Can you feel it? How your essence sings in my veins?"

I wanted to scream, to fight, to die—anything but endure the way he looked at me now, like I was something to be consumed. To be devoured. But I couldn't even turn my head away as he leaned in again, tongue tracing the wound he'd made.

"Your blood might save us all," he whispered against my throat. "Perhaps we should open you up, spill all of you onto the land itself, see if we can't restore the entire realm with what flows through these veins." His hand slid down to rest over my heart. "That's what you want, isn't it, my darling? To be the salvation of Umbrathia?"

"My brothers and sisters," he called out suddenly, his voice trembling with the most horrifying form of excitement. "Come taste her."

Gray uniforms moved toward the bed, knives glinting in their hands, their milky eyes all fixed on me with that same terrible hunger. My mind broke further as they surrounded me, blades catching the light. *No. Please no.* I thrashed internally against the paralysis, but my body betrayed me, refusing to respond as they descended.

Sharp pricks of pain bloomed across my arms, my shoulders, my wrists my ankles. Each new wound followed by the press of cold lips, the grotesque sounds of feeding. My essence was being pulled in too many directions, drawn out of me like poison from a wound. The room began to spin.

Valkan's laughter drifted somewhere above me. "Careful. We mustn't drain her completely. Not yet." His bloodied fingers traced my cheek. "She's far too precious for that."

The last thing I saw before consciousness fled was his face hovering above mine, those dead eyes gleaming with triumph as he whispered, "Welcome to your new life."

TIME LOST ALL MEANING. I drifted between darkness and horror, never fully gone, never truly awake. Each time awareness returned, new mouths fed from different cuts. The room spun endlessly, and my essence felt threadbare, pulled apart like a fraying rope. Sometimes, I could make out distant conversations, fragments of sentences.

"Sir, I just returned from Ilsthyre. You requested me?"

"Oh do tell, how is my dear brother? Still pouting over his newest title?" Valkan's voice cut through the mist swimming in my head.

"He seems to be having a hard time." The other man's voice sounded pained, almost fearful.

"Of course he is. He's always been dreadfully dim-witted. Always cowering at a simple conflict. Tell me, what's the status of blood rot?"

"They're uncontrollable. Lethal, and strong. But they do not discern between foe and friend, sir. It seems to be getting worse."

For a split second, I could have sworn Valkan's eyes settled on me.

"I have an idea, Frederick." His voice was touched by a smirk. "A recent discovery. It's made me rather curious." Valkan's hand slithered across my arm. "Bring me one of them. I wonder if they will respond differently to her." He found my hand and dragged it up against his lips.

"You want to bring one of them here, sir?" the voice questioned, a slight tremor in his tone. "Into the city?"

"Did I not make myself clear? Why do you still stand before me? Go."

"But–"

A scream shattered the quiet murmurs from the rest of the room. At first, I thought it might have been a figment of my imagination, but then there were more. They grew louder, more distinct. More victims in other rooms? No one would have volunteered for this if they knew what fate awaited them once Valkan's forces began their torture.

But it didn't seem to be. Both Valkan and the other Damphyre had gone eerily silent, their heads snapped in the direction of the door.

"How did he—" A man's voice rang from beyond the chamber, followed by more screams.

A deep vibration began to pulse through the stone floor. The crystal chandelier above swayed. One of the windows cracked—a thin line appearing in the glass that spread like a spider's web.

The pressure in the room shifted suddenly, violently. My ears rang and crackled, like being dragged into ocean depths. The walls seemed to groan under some invisible weight.

A massive crack split the air—the sound of wood and stone protesting against an impossible force. The bedposts splintered, pieces of ornate carvings raining down around me.

The Damphyre scrambled through the room, but it was too late. Their bodies jerked upward as if yanked by invisible hooks, boots scraping desperately against marble as they were lifted into the air. For one terrible moment, they hung suspended—their milky eyes wide with genuine fear for the first time.

The pressure in the room became suffocating as the Damphyre's bodies hung in the air, so still, even as chaos erupted around them.

In an instant, their forms began to contort.

The sound of bones snapping filled the chamber as they compressed, folding inward like paper crushed by a giant fist. Blood erupted from every orifice as the pressure increased. Their screams cut off in wet gurgles before their forms imploded completely, reduced to unrecognizable masses that rained down onto the marble floor.

"Careful now." Valkan's voice cracked as his body was lifted from the ground. "My followers will tear this realm apart if anything happens to me."

"You seem to think I care." The voice that cut through the chaos was familiar but wrong—darker, deadlier than I'd ever heard it.

Aether emerged from the shadows, and my heart nearly stopped. His perfect lip was sliced through, and purple bruises bloomed across his bare chest, weaving in and out of his void burns. His shadows writhed beneath his skin like living things. The very air around him seemed to bend and twist.

His fingers curled and Valkan's right arm snapped backward with a wet crack. Not just broken—shattered, the bone splintering in so many places it bulged beneath his skin.

A scream threatened to tear through my throat.

The air whipped, whistling through the cracked windows as Aether took another step forward. Above, the crystal chandelier swayed violently, its shadows dancing erratically across the walls.

"The realm needs what I offer," Valkan gasped through the pain, blood dripping from his lips. "It's the only path for survival."

Aether's fingers twisted again, and Valkan's left arm shattered. The sound was different this time—slower, more deliberate, like ice breaking across a frozen lake. Each crack echoed through the chamber as bone splintered into smaller and smaller pieces.

"Stop this while you still can, you idiot! You have no idea what awaits—" Valkan's voice was guttural, choking on blood as he croaked. But Aether simply cocked his head to the side and studied the Damphyre. Suddenly, Valkan's right leg twisted until bone pierced through flesh. His scream turned into a gurgle as Aether held him suspended in the air.

"I hope you have decent maids." Aether's voice dropped dangerously low as his eyes fell on the red-stained chamber.

"You're all going to die for this—" Valkan's growl was cut off in another scream as his left leg began to splinter, each break more excruciating than the last. The sound of grinding bone roared through my ears.

The temperature in the room plummeted as Aether stepped closer. "The thing about bone," he said, his tone unnervingly calm, "is how many pieces it can break into. Shall we count them?"

Another flick of his fingers and Valkan's ribs began to crack—one by one, methodically, each snap echoing through the chamber. The chandelier above shattered, crystal raining down around us but somehow avoiding my bed entirely.

"Is she worth another war?" Valkan's voice was just a hiss now, grunts of pain tearing through his words.

Aether simply lowered his chin as his fingers curled. Valkan's body snapped backward at an impossible angle, a piercing scream shattering through the room.

Valkan whipped his head to the left, blood trickling from his nose. His milky eyes found mine one last time. "You ungrateful cu—"

The rest of his words disappeared in a violent explosion that sprayed across the entire chamber. The pressure released so suddenly my ears popped again, and I could hear my own ragged breathing in the sudden silence.

I watched Valkan's shredded remains slide down the ornate walls, leaving crimson streaks across gilded paper.

Footsteps approached the bed.

My heart seized as Aether's form neared me, blood drenching his flesh, dripping from his hair and down that structured face in rivulets until it met his marked chest. His golden eyes burned into a liquid bronze as his stare raked over me. I could nearly feel every open wound pulsing as his eyes fell upon them. As his face twisted in disgust.

I tried to shrink away as he reached for me, but my body still wouldn't respond. A whimper escaped my throat as I was finally able to dig my fingers into the linens. His hands froze mid-air, and something flickered across his face.

This wasn't the controlled soldier I knew. This was something else entirely—something that had just turned a dozen bodies inside out with a mere flick of his wrist. Not with shadows, but by pure will.

"Fia." His voice was softer now, though it trembled. He moved slower, each motion careful as he reached for me again. "I won't hurt you."

His arms slid beneath me. Even through my muted senses, I could have sworn energy thrummed through him, like a brewing storm was lifting me—carrying me through the thunder. He pulled me against his chest, and I caught the scent of rain beneath the metallic tang of blood.

"I'm taking you away from here."

The world dissolved into darkness as consciousness finally, mercifully slipped away.

CHAPTER THIRTY-SEVEN

Light played out from beyond my eyelids. It was the first thing I registered. The second was the softness beneath me—unfamiliar but comfortable. Not my bed in the tower, nor the one in the Umbra lodging. My eyes shot open as panic clawed up my throat.

A piece of glass dangled from a string near me, causing patterns of muted rays to dance across rough-hewn logs, illuminating a small room with exposed wooden beams overhead. A stone fireplace was built into one wall, its hearth still warm with dying embers. My eyes traced the space, falling on a small table beside the bed.

It held various ointments and bandages, their herbal scent mixing with soap and woodsmoke. Everything about the space felt lived-in but sparse—a hunter's refuge perhaps.

Through a single window, I could see branches swaying in a gentle breeze, their leaves that strange, muted color that seemed to define everything in this realm. The isolation of the place struck me—no other buildings in sight, just dead wilderness stretching toward the gray horizon.

I was wearing an oversized white shirt that wasn't mine.

My heart still thundered as I tried to place where I was, who had—

The sound of Vördr wings beating against wind drifted in from outside, followed by their distinctive neighs, and a shred of understanding tore through me.

"You're awake." Aether's voice came from the doorway.

My body sagged with relief for just a moment before memories flooded back—cold lips against my skin, the endless pull of them feeding, Valkan's dead eyes as he—

I flinched involuntarily. Aether took a half-step forward before stopping himself, something flickering across his face as he registered my reaction. My gaze crept up to see him towering just a breath below the ceiling, his arms crossed tightly across his chest. His face had returned to that structured perfection, no sign of the cut or bruises I'd seen in Draxon.

"How long?" The words scraped against my throat, raw from disuse.

He held out his canteen. "Drink first."

The sight of it sent ice through my veins. I shook my head sharply, remembering metallic liquid flooding my mouth. Remembering his hand wrapped around my throat. How my back slammed into the wooden table.

A soft sigh escaped him as he settled into a chair across the room. His eyes fixed somewhere past my shoulder, deliberately avoiding direct contact.

"Two days," he said finally.

"Two days?" Panic surged through me as I swung my legs toward the floor. "The others—they're already back from the rip—"

"Don't." His voice carried no real force. "What's done is done. Urkin knows we diverted. A few more hours won't change anything now."

My gaze fell to my arms, taking in the bandages wrapped around my wrists, my forearms, scattered across my skin in stark white patches. Horror coiled in my stomach as I remembered each cut, each blade slicing into me. The way their lips felt pressed against my flesh, leeching me. I twisted the sheet in my fingers.

When I finally looked up, Aether's posture was rigid, troubled. He was still staring past me, jaw clenched tight.

"Where are we?" I asked softly.

"A cabin, about half an hour from Ravenfell."

"Whose cabin?" My eyes darted across the space again.

"Mine. I built it years ago," he said simply. "No one is supposed to know about it. However, I suppose Rethlyn does now."

"Why didn't you just take me back to the city?"

He paused, his void burns growing darker. "I didn't want you to be overwhelmed when you woke up."

I nodded, my chest heavy with everything that had happened. The silence stretched between us, thick with unspoken words.

"Draxon will retaliate," I said quietly.

"I know." His eyes traced patterns on the floor, slowly sliding up to the wooden beams.

"What are we going to do?"

"I don't know."

His gaze remained on the wall behind me, his brow furrowed with something I couldn't place. And he said nothing more.

Frustration gnawed at me. "Why won't you look at me?"

His head jerked slightly, gaze finally meeting mine before sliding down to my bandaged arms. The look in his eyes was pained, haunted and angry—a look I had never seen before, not on him. Finally, he shook his head, darkness bleeding from his void burns. "What they did to you..." His voice was strained, like he was fighting to contain something volatile. "I didn't get there fast enough."

"You should have gone back to Ravenfell."

His eyes went rigid. "And leave you behind? To those

monsters?" He nearly shot up from his chair, rage flickering across his features.

"It's better than starting whatever is going to happen next. The Umbra can't fight two wars at the same time." I looked down at my hands. "I would have found a way to escape, eventually..." Even I didn't believe the words.

"We will find a way to handle it," Aether said, taking another deep breath.

"What will the Council think?" I asked, a lump forming in my throat.

"Draxon will need time to make their plans," he said. "They're not going to attack outright. And he's already lost most of their support."

"But what we did," I whispered, "it was an act of war."

"And I'd do it again," Aether growled, and my eyes found his once more. Heat rushed through me at his stare—dark and desperate. Longing. I found myself taking a shallow breath.

"They will come for all of us."

"They will. At some point."

Another silence fell, heavy with the weight of what we'd started. What we couldn't take back.

"How did you escape them?" The question had been nagging at me. "After the Vördr ran off?"

His jaw tightened slightly. "About twenty of them surrounded me in that clearing when I finally returned. I told Tryggar and Nihr to go—I didn't want his men to try and harm them." A shadow of something crossed his face. "I figured you'd already been taken, since you were gone and Valkan was nowhere in sight."

"You let them capture you?" My voice was laced with quiet shock.

"Seemed the quickest way to find you." His voice was carefully neutral. "Though I hadn't counted on them forcing that sleeping tonic down my throat."

My stomach turned at the memory of metallic liquid. "How long were you out?"

"Hard to say. Woke up in their dungeons." His eyes fixed on some distant point through the window. "Found my way out." He cleared his throat and tilted his head to the side as if digesting a thought. Whatever he'd done to escape that cell, he clearly didn't want to discuss it.

"They tortured you," I said softly, noting the purple patches had disappeared from his neck.

"I'd hardly call it that." His lips quirked into something that wasn't quite a smile. "As soon as the drugs wore off, they found their branding irons lodged in their throats."

Fire rushed through me, followed by a surge of rage that caught me off guard. My shadows responded instantly, pulsing outward as my vision tinged with darkness.

"Careful," Aether said, but there was something else in his voice now—something almost like wonder as he watched my shadows coil through the air. "Conserve your energy."

"They hurt you." The words came out like steel.

"They're dead now," he said it simply, but his eyes had turned sharp again. "All of them."

I forced my shadows back, trying to understand why his pain affected me so viscerally. Why the thought of them hurting him while he was defenseless made me want to tear the castle apart all over again.

"What exactly did you do to them?" The question had been burning in my mind since I woke. Even through the haze of what had happened, the memory was so vivid that it made dread settle in my gut. How the very air had cracked, how their bodies had twisted and broken without him laying a hand on them.

Aether's shoulders tensed, but he didn't turn to face me. "Does it matter?"

"You ripped them apart from the inside." The words were soft on my tongue. "I didn't even know that was possible."

His jaw tightened. "You're wondering why I never used it before." It wasn't a question. "In Sídhe."

"The thought crossed my mind."

He shifted in his chair, and for a moment I thought he wouldn't answer. When he finally spoke, his voice was strained. "Whatever I did... it's not something I can control. Not really." His fingers curled slightly against the armrest. "Once I start using it that way, it's hard to stop. And despite what you think about me, I don't want to murder hundreds in the blink of an eye."

I studied his profile, noting how carefully still he held himself. Like he was containing something that wanted to break loose.

"But you did use it. For me."

"What I did in that chamber..." He looked away again, but not before I caught something dark flash across his face. "That wasn't a tactical choice. It wasn't strategic."

"Then what was it?"

He paused. "Seeing what they were doing—" His voice caught, and he had to take a breath before continuing. "I lost control. Completely. And that's exactly why I never let myself use it. Not like that."

I remembered the calmness in his voice as he'd torn them apart, how the very stones of the castle had groaned under the force of his rage. It should have terrified me. Instead, I felt something else entirely.

"We need to get back to Ravenfell," I finally said.

"You need to rest."

I shot him an irritated look. "We don't have time for that."

"We'll have to face Urkin once we're back. He's going to be furious." His voice carried an edge of concern. "I have no idea how he will handle our deviation. You need to gather your strength."

"We need to tell him what we discovered about the siphon. About the King," I hissed.

"I already told you, he's not going to believe us without proof."

The silence that followed felt charged. I traced one of the bandages on my arm, remembering. "Valkan said something. When he was..." I couldn't finish the sentence.

Aether's jaw went rigid, his knuckles turning white, but he stayed silent.

"He said he wished he could open me up and spill my blood onto the land. That maybe that would restore the essence." I took a deep breath. "I'd never thought of something like that before."

His eyes locked onto me. "What are you trying to say?"

"Talon suggested that I create essence within me. I just wondered..." I shook my head, gathering courage. "What if I could transfer my essence to the land? What if I could imbue arcanite?" I peeked up at him.

"We don't have arcanite."

"What if we could get it?"

"How?"

"Riftdremar."

Aether leaned forward, resting his elbows on his knees. "It was destroyed, Fia. You know this."

"But we don't know that *all* of the arcanite stores were destroyed. It's been over twenty years, for all we know, they just took what they needed and left the rest."

He sat back, deep in thought, eyes distant.

"You want to go to Riftdremar on another whim?"

"I was right about the siphon." I met his gaze. "Can't you try to start trusting me?"

He studied me for a few moments.

"I know it's not proof," I said into his silence. "Or the *proof* that will make Urkin believe us about the siphon. But it can buy us time. If we can start feeding essence back to the land, even in small amounts, wouldn't it be worth it?"

Aether sighed, running a hand through his dark hair. "You're sure you want to do this?"

"Time is our biggest enemy at the moment. Let's tackle that battle first."

"Time." He nodded, his face unreadable.

"Let's get back to the city." I pushed myself up, but the moment I put weight on my left ankle, pain shot through my leg where a deep cut remained. I stumbled, the room tilting dangerously.

Aether was there in an instant, his arms steadying me. But even after I found my balance, he didn't let go. The heat of him seeped through the thin shirt, and I became acutely aware of how close we were.

"I'm sorry," he said finally, his breath warm against my ear.

"It's not your fault." The words came out barely above a whisper as moisture formed in my eyes.

We stayed like that, neither moving away, and I realized it was the first time since entering this realm that I felt truly safe. The first time the constant weight in my chest had lifted, even just a little. I didn't know how long we stood there, but I knew that something had shifted between us—something I wasn't ready to name.

CHAPTER THIRTY-EIGHT

Our boots hit the worn stone path as we left the stables. Vexa burst through a side door, looking nothing like herself. Her violet eyes were glassy from lack of sleep, and she was missing several of the piercings that typically dotted her features—something I'd never seen from her before, even at her most casual.

"Where have you two been?" Her voice came out hoarse, as if she'd been shouting. "Urkin is furious."

"Well, he's about to be even more furious once we speak to him." Aether was already striding toward the Citadel.

"You can't right now, he's been called into a Council meeting in Stravene. He left an hour ago." The words tumbled out as she tried to match his pace.

Aether stopped and we shared a knowing look as my stomach twisted. The Council already knew. *Fuck.* Aether trudged back over to us and I noticed how he positioned himself closer than before, his tensed forearm grazing against me.

Vexa's tired eyes darted between us. "Did something happen? In Draxon?" She lowered her voice. "You were gone way longer than we agreed on. And Aether, you could have let us know you were going with her."

I tugged at my sleeve, trying to cover the bandages that wrapped my arm, suddenly aware of how exposed I felt. "There were, erm, complications."

Her gaze locked onto the movement, then shot to Aether. Understanding dawned on her face, followed immediately by rage.

"What did he do?" The words came out as a growl, her hands curling into fists.

I opened my mouth, but how could I even begin to explain? The feeding, the darkness, the way Aether had torn them apart? The political chaos we'd just unleashed?

"We can't discuss it here." Aether's tone left no room for argument. "Later."

Vexa's fingers tapped against her weapon belt, but she nodded, though the anger didn't leave her eyes.

"What happened at the rip?" I asked, desperate to change the subject.

Her expression shifted from fury to something that made my stomach drop.

"That's the other thing." She gave Aether a pained look before turning toward the medic's wing, her steps dragging against the path. "Come with me."

THE INFIRMARY DOOR creaked open to reveal two occupied beds. Effie and Theron sat propped against pillows, their faces drawn and pale. I rushed to them, questions tumbling out before I could organize my thoughts.

"We're fine," Effie managed, but her eyes darted past me, exchanging a look with someone I couldn't see.

I turned to find Mira and Rethlyn seated in an alcove near the entrance, both looking like they'd been dragged through something unimaginable. Rethlyn met my gaze and gave a slight nod, but something in his expression made my stomach clench.

My eyes swept the room again, counting faces, and understanding hit me like a physical blow.

Aether's dark form cut through the room toward the back. I followed without thinking, my feet carrying me forward even as dread built in my chest. He reached a privacy curtain, yanking it back with enough force to rattle the rod above.

A lanky figure lay face-down on the bed, a white sheet draped across his lower half.

Lael.

Aether knelt beside the bed, his shoulders rigid as he examined the boy. The skin across Lael's back was raw and blackened, split open in places where something had torn through flesh. Some areas had begun to blister and weep, while others remained blackened and tight. The damage continued down his arms, disappearing beneath the sheet.

Aether shot to his feet, pacing back to the center of the room. "What happened?" The words came out as a growl.

I heard shifting as a few seconds dragged past.

"It's like they were waiting for us," Rethlyn's voice finally carried from behind.

"They were on us in an instant, faster than any of us could even think," Vexa snarled. "And something was different this time. They didn't respond to the shadows in the same way. Like being robbed of their breath was no longer a deterrent."

Her words sent daggers straight through me. That's what Laryk had meant when he said the Guard had a new strategy. I caught my balance on the railing beside Lael.

"The breathing tonics," I whispered as I turned back to the room.

"What?" Vexa asked as all eyes fell upon me.

"Something that Sídhe was developing." I swallowed hard, wanting to leave Ma out of it. "It's how I was able to break out of your holds on the lawn in Emeraal."

Everyone stared at me in silence. Everyone except for Aether, who kept his back to me as his shoulders rose and fell in ragged fashion.

"I guess they've been able to mass-produce them," I said again, my eyes meeting the floor as guilt slammed through my chest. I stepped back a few feet.

"What do these tonics do?" Effie asked, her voice having dropped a few octaves.

"They allow one to go for much longer periods of time without needing to breathe."

Realization washed over the group as the silence stretched on. No one moved, and Aether still never turned to look at me.

"Thank you for telling us," he finally said, his voice so low I almost missed it.

A gurgling noise came from Lael, and I rushed back to his side, Aether trailing close behind. But he lay unchanged, his chest rising and falling slowly, a peaceful expression on his face which remained untouched by the damage.

"The medics don't know why he hasn't woken up yet," Effie's voice cracked.

"What do we do?" Something dark threaded through Aether's words.

I could practically hear the desperation churning in the air, mirroring the hollow dread that now filled my veins. But no one answered for a long moment.

"I don't know." Vexa's response was heavy with exhaustion.

"The scars..." Mira trailed off. "The medics aren't strong enough to erase them. Those types of burns..."

"Burns?" I gripped the bed frame as I stood, turning to face the room.

The others had shifted closer together. Effie perched on the edge of her bed while Theron held his head in his hands. Mira remained in her chair as Rethlyn stood, but Vexa now separated them from Aether, her fingers working anxiously at her weapon belt.

"They came at us with everything," Rethlyn said, drawing his arms up in submission. "But we saw the fire first."

The name formed in my mind before I could stop it.

An ex-team V member. A fire-wielder. And a bigoted asshole.

Baelor Soleil.

"Lael lost control of his spectre form," Effie choked out. "He turned to run, to get back to the rip."

He had done just as Aether had instructed. My eyes blurred and I tried to blink away the tears, but it was to no avail, they already slid down my face. I returned my gaze to Lael as a sob threatened my chest. If we had been there...

"We carried him out, rushed back here." Vexa's voice cracked. "The entire thing was pointless and reckless. We didn't get any of the information we were sent to retrieve. We should have never gone. Urkin should have never made that call."

"We're having an emergency meeting. First thing in the morning." Aether shoved past them all, the door slamming behind him with enough force to rattle the glass. Silence fell as a few of them raced off after him. I wasn't sure who still remained in the room, if anyone. I could hear nothing apart from the steady sound of Lael's breathing.

I pulled a chair close to his bedside after a few moments. As I reached up to brush his hair back, my fingers caught on something. A leaf, vivid green against the white pillow.

I scanned my eyes along his hair, down his shoulders and back to his neck, peeking under his chin to find a few more leaves sticking out from under him.

That's when I noticed the marks on his neck, like something had been wrapped around it. Ligature marks, partially hidden by the burns but clear enough on the unmarred skin. He had been strangled.

I looked down at the leaf again, and my entire body went still.

Briar.

The leaf crumpled in my fist as understanding crashed through me. My friends had been a part of this. And Baelor Soleil was back on team V.

SLEEP WASN'T JUST ELUSIVE—IT was fucking impossible. Every time I closed my eyes, Valkan's milky gaze was there, watching me bleed. My skin crawled with phantom sensations—steel biting into flesh, blood running down my arms, that sickening *drip drip drip* onto stone floors as hungry mouths leeched me. I paced my room like a caged animal, but the memories followed. They wouldn't leave.

Aether.

The thought hit me like a whip, stopping me mid-stride. His quarters weren't far—just up a few levels. But the idea of appearing at his door, of admitting I couldn't handle this on my own... My chest constricted, shame burning hot beneath my skin.

He'd been so devastated earlier after what we saw in the infirmary. What if he rejected me, needing to be alone? That would be fair. It's not like he owed me anything. But even worse, what if he blamed me for what happened to Lael—for abandoning the mission and taking him with me? If it weren't for me, he'd have been there, and none of that would have happened. Lael wouldn't be hurt. I bit my lip, eyes drawn to the stone floor beneath my feet. He must think it. Because I was beginning to think it, myself.

Beyond that, I didn't want to *need* him.

I'd spent my entire life convincing myself I didn't need anyone. Proving I could survive without being dependent on another person. And now what? I was going to go running to him because I couldn't close my eyes without re-living those horrors? Others had suffered far worse.

My vision blurred, and I slammed my eyes closed. *No.* I wouldn't cry.

A blade dragged across my collarbone—sharp, cold, *real*. I stumbled back, crashing into the wall as my hands flew to my throat. The metallic scent of blood filled my nose, but when I pulled my fingers away, they were clean. My heart slammed against my ribs as I stared at my trembling hands. *Not real not real not real.*

I can't. I can't do this.

The corridors were silent except for my bare feet against stone. Each step up to his quarters felt like admitting defeat, and I almost turned around twice. My heart wouldn't slow down, wouldn't let me catch my breath properly, but I'd rather die than let anyone see me like this. Anyone except—

When I reached his door, I stood there like an idiot, hand raised to knock. *This is ridiculous. You're ridiculous.* But before I could retreat, the door swung open.

Aether filled the doorway, and for a moment, my racing thoughts stilled. He looked different without the Umbra uniform —just simple dark sleep clothes, his hair pushed back from his face. Those golden eyes widened slightly as they found mine, and I saw the exact moment concern replaced surprise.

"I—" My voice came out shaky and small, and I hated it. Hated how my hands wouldn't stop trembling, how the walls felt like they were closing in. I tried for something witty, something to prove I wasn't falling apart, and I even opened my mouth in an attempt, but no words came.

"Come in," he said quietly, like he understood everything I couldn't say.

Heavy black curtains blocked out the eternal twilight, wrapping everything in darkness that should have been suffocating but somehow wasn't.

The whole space smelled like him—rain and smoke, with hints of weapon oil. Something in my chest loosened slightly at the familiar scent. I wrapped my arms around myself, trying to stop the trembling that wouldn't quite go away.

"I don't usually..." I started, then stopped. *Don't usually what?* "I'm sorry," I finally managed.

"Why are you here, Fia?" His voice was quiet, but there was something else there. Concern, maybe. Or understanding.

The question hit harder than I expected. I stared at the weapons on his wall, unable to meet those golden eyes. "I can't sleep." My voice came out smaller than I meant it to. "I didn't want to disturb you, with Lael and everything, but..."

I couldn't finish. Couldn't admit that every time I closed my eyes, I was back there. In Draxon. That I'd spent hours trying to convince myself I was being ridiculous, that I was stronger than this. That I'd only come when the alternative became unbearable.

Something shifted in his expression. He didn't move closer, didn't offer empty comfort. He just nodded.

"I can sleep on the floor," I added quickly. "I just... can't be alone right now."

"You're not sleeping on the floor. Take the bed," he offered, striding over to a worn leather couch in the corner of the room. "I'll sleep here."

I watched as he grabbed a pillow from the bed, his massive frame making the furniture look impossibly small.

"That couch is barely long enough for me, let alone you."

He sat down anyway, the leather creaking under his weight as his legs stretched well past the armrest.

"This is ridiculous." I moved closer, my arms crossed. "The bed is huge. We can share."

He stilled, and I could see the hesitation in his posture.

"I don't want to make you uncomfortable," he said quietly.

"More uncomfortable than watching you try to fold yourself onto that thing?" I shook my head. "Come on."

He moved toward the bed slowly, like he was still unsure. I slipped under the covers on the far side, trying to make the decision easier for him. The sheets were soft, carrying that same scent that seemed to follow him everywhere.

After what seemed like forever, the mattress dipped under his weight. He stayed on the very edge, maintaining a careful distance. The silence felt heavy.

"Any word about Lael?" I asked into the darkness.

Aether's sigh was heavy. "No change. The medics are doing everything they can, but..." He trailed off. "I should have been there. For both of you."

"You can't be everywhere."

"Tomorrow, everything changes." The words came out rough, almost like they pained him. "Urkin can't keep making these decisions."

I understood the frustration in his voice. The rigid hierarchy of the Umbra had nearly gotten both Lael and me killed. But I didn't know how to respond, so I stayed quiet.

I was drifting off when the flashes hit—not just Valkan this time, but everything. The burns on Lael's skin. The blood on the floor. That damned smile with too many teeth. My body went rigid, heart slamming against my ribs as I tried to remember where I was. My lungs wouldn't work.

"Fia?" Aether's voice cut through the panic.

I managed a shaky breath. "I'm fine." The lie was automatic.

The mattress shifted as he sat up. For a moment, neither of us moved. Then slowly, carefully, like he was afraid I might bolt, his hand found my shoulder.

"You're not." His voice was quiet in the darkness. Then his arm slid around my waist, drawing me back against his chest. The heat of him crept through my clothes, and something inside me shifted. I should have resisted, should have maintained some pretense of dignity, but the solid warmth of him broke down the last of my defenses.

Esprithe, this felt good. Dangerous, probably—letting myself need him. But as his heartbeat thrummed against my back—as his breath stirred my hair—I couldn't bring myself to give a damn about the implications. For the first time since Valkan, since everything, the darkness didn't feel like it was trying to swallow me whole.

Sleep came easier then, wrapped in his arms, surrounded by his scent.

And I dreamed of the twins again.

I was in a garden, my hands sticky as I cut back thick, dark vines that seemed to weep a black substance into the bucket at my feet. The sound of running made me look up as two women burst through an archway—the twins, though years had passed since the courtyard scene.

One wore a violet gown, a delicate tiara nestled in her dark hair, her pregnant belly visible beneath the fine fabric. A golden band glinted on her finger as she gestured wildly. The other wore simple gardening clothes, dirt staining the knees. "Leave me alone!" The one in the tiara's voice cracked as she spun to face her sister. Tears streamed down her face, ruining the careful paint around her eyes.

"Please, just let me explain—" The other woman reached for her arm, but she jerked away.

"Explain what? That you've always been in love with him?" Her words echoed across the lawn. "That while I was preparing for our wedding, you were—" She choked on the words.

"I've always wanted the best for you," the woman pleaded. "Everything I've done—"

"Don't! I've always protected you, been there for you, through everything!" The sister's hands cradled her stomach protectively. "You've always been jealous of me. Ever since the Void rejected you—"

"This isn't about the Void! This is about father, about how he's always pitted us against each other. Can't you see what he's done to us?"

"What he's done?" The noble sister's laugh was bitter. "He made me strong. He gave me everything, while you—you chose to waste away in these gardens, pretending to be something you're not."

"I didn't have a choice!"

Silence fell between them.

"Lord Skaldvindr chose me," the one in the gown said finally, though her voice trembled. "Remember that."

"He didn't."

She took a few steps towards her sister, but the woman turned and fled across the lawn, her skirts billowing behind her, the golden ring refracting the sunlight as she disappeared. Then, the remaining sister stood alone, frozen, watching her go. Slowly, she walked back to where I stood among the bleeding vines and sank onto the ground beside me. Her shoulders shook as she buried her face in her hands.

I felt my own hands move to comfort her, and she fell into my lap, body convulsing with sobs.

CHAPTER THIRTY-NINE

"Valkan is dead."

Aether's words fell into the cramped meeting room like stones into still water. I watched the ripples spread across each face—Vexa's sharp intake of breath, Effie's fingers stilling against her sleeve, Rethlyn's shoulders going rigid.

"How?" Vexa finally asked.

"I killed him." Aether's tone was flat, matter-of-fact. "Along with a dozen of his Damphyre."

"You did what?" Effie shot up from her chair. "Have you lost your mind?"

"The only fertile region we had left," Theron rasped from his corner, "and you murdered its Lord?"

"There must have been a reason," Rethlyn said, but uncertainty drenched his tone.

"Of course there was a reason," Vexa snapped.

"Do you have any idea what you've done?" Mira cut in. "The political chaos this will cause? The Council will demand—"

"I don't care what the Council demands." Something in Aether's voice made them all fall silent.

"Then explain it to us," Raven said quietly. "Why?"

Aether's jaw tightened, and for a moment I thought he wouldn't answer. Then his eyes found mine, something dark and violent crossing his face. The others followed his gaze, and suddenly I felt the weight of every stare in the room.

Effie was the first to notice the bandage peeking above my collar. Her eyes widened, then narrowed to slits. "He didn't."

I tried to shrink away from their scrutiny, but it was too late. Understanding bloomed across their faces, followed immediately by horror, then rage.

"That monster," Effie breathed, all color draining from her face. "He actually—"

"He deserved it. That's the last I will say on the matter. We have other things we must discuss," Aether cut in, though his voice still carried that dangerous edge. "Because we have a plan to move forward, but Urkin won't go along with it."

"What do you mean, won't go along with it?" Vexa asked, though her eyes kept darting to my collar, her fingers still tight on her weapon belt.

"I'm done taking orders from him." Aether's words seemed to press against the walls. "He's served this realm well for thirty years, but he's stuck in the past, unwilling to listen to new approaches. If we continue down his path, we'll destroy everything we hope to save."

"You're talking about desertion," Rethlyn said carefully.

"I'm talking about survival." Aether's gaze swept the room. "The arcanite towers—we have to stop trying to destroy them."

"Stop destroying them?" Theron pushed himself straighter in his chair. "That's our entire strategy."

"A strategy that will fail." Aether's voice hardened. "Because if we destroy those towers, all of that stored essence will either be destroyed or lost to Sídhe forever."

"How do you know this?" Mira asked.

"Because we found something in Draxon." Aether paused, his eyes finding mine again. "Something that changes everything we thought we knew about this war."

"What exactly did you find?" Raven leaned forward.

"What we found was information about something called a siphon," Aether said, his voice carrying weight that made everyone lean forward. "A person who can redirect the flow of essence through the realm."

"I've never heard of such a thing," Rethlyn said, scrunching his eyebrows.

"You wouldn't have." Aether's jaw tightened. "Throughout history, they've been erased from existence. Viewed as an abomination."

"But why?" Vexa asked.

I stepped forward, drawing their attention. "Because they don't just redirect essence—they can steal it. Pull it from the land itself, from other people."

"That sounds like a Damphyre," Mira said quietly.

Aether stepped closer, his voice taking on a grimmer tone. "There are similarities, yes, but a Damphyre is created—twisted into existence through the murder of another Kalfar. Their ability to drain essence is unnatural, forced. A siphon is born with this power. It's their tether, as much a part of them as breathing." His eyes fell on me again. "But while Damphyres can only feed on their fellow Kalfar, a siphon's reach extends to the land itself. They can pull essence from one place and channel it to another. Both abilities corrupt the natural flow of essence—which is why our people have always viewed them with such... extreme vitriol."

"So what does this have to do with the arcanite towers?" Theron asked.

"Because we finally know how Sídhe's been doing it," Aether said. "How they've been draining our realm."

The room went quiet, waiting. I stepped forward.

"The King of Sídhe is a siphon."

"The King," Raven breathed, scribbling something into a notepad. "Is this common knowledge in Sídhe?"

I leaned against the stone wall, eyes tracing a pattern on the floor. "No one has ever known what his focus—tether is. It's always been a mystery."

"It would make sense," Vexa said, pacing now. "The way the drought spreads, how they're able to drain specific regions while others remain untouched..."

"How long?" Mira asked, her voice sharp. "How long has he been planning this?"

"Decades," I said. "Ever since they started farming arcanite in Riftdremar. This was the goal all along."

"So what do we do? Assassinate the King?" Theron asked.

A chill ran across my skin at the thought, but I couldn't say I hadn't considered it myself. "We don't know, but this changes everything. We have to come up with a new plan to approach this."

"In the meantime," Aether cut in, "we have an idea that might help restore some of what's been stolen, but we're going to need help from everyone in this room."

Rethlyn leaned forward. "What kind of idea?"

Aether nodded to me, and I stepped closer to the center of the room. My heart thundered against my ribs—what I was about to suggest wasn't just dangerous, it was probably impossible. But after everything we'd learned, we had to try something.

"I believe that if I can get my hands on arcanite, I might be able to imbue it with essence."

"That's quite an assumption." Mira narrowed her eyes.

"Talon—when he examined me—said that essence seemed to flow through me in a way that was different than a tether. There was no connection between me and the land." I paused, collecting myself. "He said that I create my own essence. That its self-sustaining. Valkan seemed to think the same thing."

I looked down as another silence fell across the room.

"And where exactly do you propose we find arcanite?" Effie finally asked, though something in her tone suggested she already knew the answer.

I met her gaze steadily. "Riftdremar."

And once again, all eyes fell in my direction.

"That's impossible," Theron said. "Riftdremar was destroyed. Everything was burned—"

"But what if it wasn't?" I pressed. "What if they only took what they needed? There could still be stores left, forgotten after all these years."

"It's worth trying," Vexa said, surprising me. "What other choice do we have? Valkan's men will retaliate at some point. We need to be as strong as we can before they descend on Ravenfell—our tethers at their peak."

"We'll need to move fast," I said. "Before the Council has time to reorganize, before Draxon's forces can mobilize. Raven, you could be our eyes and ears here in Ravenfell."

He looked me over and nodded, that mysterious glint returning to his eye.

"And what happens if we're surrounded by Sídhe forces the second we find these mines?" Theron asked.

"Then we die trying to save our realm," Aether said simply. "Instead of watching it wither away to nothing."

The room fell quiet again as they considered his words. I watched their faces as doubt warred with hope, fear with determination. Finally, Vexa stepped forward.

"I'm in."

"Me too," Effie said, "though I'd prefer not to die, if we can help it."

"The archives might have maps of Riftdremar from before the burning," Raven offered. "Details about where the arcanite stores were."

Mira exchanged a look with Theron before nodding. "After what happened to Lael... I'm done watching us lose people while we wait for orders."

"We'll need to move carefully," Rethlyn said, already shifting into tactical mode. "Scout the territory first, plan our approach—"

"No time for that," Aether cut in.

"When do we leave?" Vexa asked.

"Tomorrow night." Aether's voice left no room for argument. "The Council will still be in chaos from Valkan's death. Urkin won't be back from Stravene. It's our best chance."

"That's... soon," Effie said.

"It's not soon enough," Aether countered, and for a split second, I could see the leader that the Council had wanted all those years ago. The tone of his voice, the determination written across his forehead, the commanding presence that nearly seeped off of him.

A moment passed as they all considered what they were agreeing to. What it would mean to desert their posts, to go against direct orders. To risk everything on a theory that might not even work.

"You're right," Vexa finally said.

The others nodded, and something settled in my chest—something laced with fear, but also something lighter, something that blazed through me. We had a plan. It wasn't much, but it was something. A chance to actually make a difference.

"Get some rest," Aether said.

As the others filed out, I caught Raven's arm at the door. "Stay." My eyes found Vexa and Aether, still murmuring in the corner of the room. Effie sat alone, her head in her hands.

I walked towards them, my boots scraping against the stone floor.

"There's something you all need to know."

The heaviness in my voice must have carried weight, because Raven closed the door immediately and took a seat in front of me.

"I haven't exactly been transparent about all of my abilities," I said, feeling the anxiety clawing as all of their eyes fell on me and darkened slightly.

"Beyond controlling minds, beyond seeing them behind barriers..." I drew in a breath, forcing myself to continue. "There's something else. Something I've barely begun to understand myself."

Aether sat back in his chair, crossing his arms over his chest and giving me a look that nearly made my mouth go dry. "Go on."

My fingers twisted together as I searched for the right words. "I dream. But not normal dreams. I see through other people's eyes, experience their memories, their moments. Sometimes they're from the past, sometimes they're happening right now. And I can't control when they come, or why they show me what they do."

I turned to Vexa, whose violet eyes had narrowed. "Last year, I lived through someone forging a dagger. Every strike of the hammer, every marking carved into the blade." My gaze fell to her weapons. "Your markings."

Her hand drifted to the hilt at her side, fingers tracing patterns she carved herself.

"And you," I said to Aether, whose golden eyes had gone sharp with interest. "I saw your eyes in my dreams months before I crossed the rip. Before I even knew this realm existed." The words came out softer than I meant them to, and heat crept up my neck as his gaze locked onto me with an intensity that made my heart stutter. For a moment, the others in the room seemed to fade away.

The silence that followed pressed against my skin, but I pushed forward, before the weight of his stare made me lose my nerve completely.

"Lately, I've been seeing two sisters. Twins, I think. Young girls, born into nobility—maybe even royalty—here in Umbrathia." The memory of the first dream flickered through my mind. "Their father took them to the Void when they were barely more than children. Their mother..." I swallowed hard, remembering her desperate pleas. "She begged him not to."

"But, I've seen glimpses of their life as they grew up. One of them later married a Lord from the Skaldvindr family—that's what made me realize that these people were real, and relevant, perhaps. They had a child together." The words felt heavy as they left my mouth, though I didn't understand why. I could still feel Aether's gaze on me, but I kept my eyes fixed on the floor.

Raven stepped closer, something shifting in his casual demeanor. "The current Queen was married to Lord Skaldvindr before his death."

Slowly, my eyes crawled up to Raven, who was studying me intensely. Vexa and Effie exchanged a look that made my skin prickle.

"She also had a sister," Raven said quietly. "What was her name?"

"Vilda. Her twin." Aether's voice had lost its earlier warmth, replaced by something vacant. "She died not long after Skalvindr. Not long after their father, in fact." He looked towards Raven.

"Some say that was the catalyst. Why the Queen's mind began to slip into madness," Vexa breathed, clutching the chair beneath her with white knuckles.

"And then her son died of a rare illness, which only made matters worse," Effie said quietly.

Silence pressed against the walls as I absorbed this. The Queen. I was dreaming of the Queen and her family. But why? How did all of this connect? I could feel in my bones that there was a reason. That it was going to end up being important, but I still couldn't connect the dots.

My heart thundered against my ribs as I forced myself to continue. "There's one more thing."

Their attention snapped back to me.

"In these dreams, sometimes..." I wet my lips, suddenly unsure.

"Sometimes I hear a voice. It calls me by a different name." The words caught in my throat. "Fiandrial. I think it might be my real name."

Aether went completely still. Not the practiced stillness of a soldier, but something deeper, as if he'd been frozen in place. Raven and Vexa looked confused, but Aether...

He stood so abruptly his chair scraped against stone. "There's something I have to do." His voice was tight, controlled, but I caught the tremor beneath it. "I'll be back later."

The door closed behind him with a force that stopped my heart for a beat.

I CRAWLED INTO BED, tugging Aether's shirt closer around me. The fabric still carried his scent—rain and woodsmoke. It should have felt strange wearing it, but instead it felt... Right. Safe. Though safety seemed like a cruel joke now. Just like the night before, every time I closed my eyes, I was back in that horrendous chamber.

Aether still hadn't returned from wherever he'd run off to. I was going to have to face this alone tonight.

My eyes traced down my skin to the stark white bandages, too clean, too pristine against my flesh. They felt like a lie—like covering the truth of what had happened in that castle, making it seem neat and contained when it was anything but. Before I realized what I was doing, my fingers were already tearing at them, ripping them away until the shallow cuts beneath were exposed. Maybe it was worse, seeing the evidence of what they'd done to me, but something about facing the truth of it felt better than hiding it away.

A knock at the door made me jump, Valkan's face flashing

through my mind before I could stop it. I had to remind myself that he was dead, that I'd watched him torn apart, that his blood still stained the walls of that chamber. Still, my heart thundered as I approached the door.

When I opened it, Vexa and Effie stood there with pillows and blankets tucked under their arms. The sight of them made something in my chest crack.

"We're staying with you tonight," Vexa said, already pushing past me into the room. Effie followed, both of them dropping their bedding onto the floor as if this was the most natural thing in the world.

It wasn't until they turned back to me that I remembered my state—Aether's shirt hanging loose, the cuts now visible across my arms and legs. I watched understanding dawn in their eyes, watched as Vexa's face transformed with a rage that looked lethal. Shock spread across Effie's features.

"I had no idea..." she breathed, and I'd never seen her look at me like that before—like she might cry. The pity in her eyes made me want to cover myself.

"Any of us would have done what Aether did." Effie's voice was fierce.

My first instinct was to hide the evidence of what they'd done to me. But something in their expressions—the raw honesty there—made me pause.

The tears I'd been holding back all day finally spilled over, and once they started, I couldn't make them stop. It felt like everything I'd been containing since that castle was suddenly breaking free.

Vexa crossed the room and pulled me into a hug. The gesture surprised me. "Tell us what we can do." Her voice was softer than I'd ever heard it, and somehow that gentleness made it harder to keep myself together.

"Thank you for coming," I managed between shaky breaths. "I didn't know how I was going to sleep tonight." The admission was difficult, but it felt good to say it aloud. To acknowledge the fear that had been building all day as I thought about laying in my bed, trying to find sleep again. Alone. Without Aether.

"Do you want to talk about it?" Effie asked gently.

I considered it for a moment, wondering if speaking the horror aloud would help me move past it. But the thought of describing those cold lips against my skin, of reliving the helplessness as they fed from me... Maybe I wasn't ready to move past it. Maybe I wanted to hold onto that anger for a while longer. Or maybe I just couldn't bear to say his name, to speak the word *Damphyre* again. It felt like giving them back some small piece of power, and they'd already taken enough from me.

I shook my head as fresh tears fell. They guided me to the bed, sitting on either side of me until the sobs that wracked my body finally began to quiet. Their presence felt like an anchor, keeping me from drifting too far into those dark memories.

Moments passed, I wasn't sure how many, but finally, my body stilled from the sobs that had been tearing through my chest. The tears became less and less.

After my breathing steadied, Effie broke the silence. "I have to be honest, Fia." She paused, and when I looked up, there was a familiar glint in her eye. "I'm rather offended that you never dreamed about *me*."

The laugh that burst from me surprised us all. It felt strange in my throat, almost foreign after everything that had happened, but also necessary—like breaking through ice to find air.

"I found it quite interesting..." Vexa said, and something in her tone made me tense. "The manner in which you dreamed of us. Or, more precisely, the fact you've been dreaming about Aether's *eyes*."

Heat rushed to my face as Effie let out an undignified snort. I hadn't expected them to focus on that detail, though maybe I should have. The memory of those dreams flooded back—how his golden eyes had haunted me long before I knew what they meant, who they belonged to.

"Quite the romantic, Fia." Effie's voice carried a teasing lilt that would have been annoying if it wasn't such a welcome distraction from darker thoughts.

I nudged Effie, trying to ignore how my stomach flipped at their implications. "It's not like that." But the words felt hollow, even to me. When had that changed?

"Don't think we haven't noticed how he acts around you," Effie said, and my stomach did an odd flip. I wasn't ready to examine what they might have noticed, what I myself had been trying desperately not to notice.

"At first, I had never seen him so irritated, never seen someone get under his skin like you did. Or get a reaction out of him at all, really." Vexa shrugged, but there was something knowing in her violet eyes. "He's always been more statue than man."

My mind flashed to days before, how he'd held me against him in that ice-filled cave, the way his shadows had danced beneath his skin when I'd given him more. The way his eyes had burned when he found me in Draxon.

And then there was last night. When he saved me from the ghosts plaguing my every thought. When he'd held me against his chest, our heartbeats echoing through each other.

"Yes, well," I muttered, trying to hide the blush creeping across my cheeks, "we seem to have that effect on each other."

"But it's different now." Vexa's voice carried a weight that had me pausing.

The silence seemed to stretch on, and I found myself unable to meet their eyes. *Different.*

"It's not," I said quickly, though my voice betrayed me. "We just learned how to work together."

"Whatever you say." Effie's tone dripped with suspicion, and I could feel the heat creeping up my neck.

Was I really that transparent?

We talked late into the night. The conversation drifted to lighter topics—Effie's perfume line she'd started before the drought began, Vexa's stories from her time in prison. Slowly, the weight in my chest began to ease. The cuts still stung, and I knew the memories would return, but for now, surrounded by their warmth and laughter, I felt almost whole again.

At some point, I drifted off to sleep, Aether's shirt still wrapped around me, their voices a gentle murmur in the background.

Although I could have sworn, sometime during the night, that I'd seen a pair of golden eyes peeking into the room.

Or perhaps I'd imagined it.

CHAPTER FORTY

Maps of Riftdremar were sprawled across a table in the archives, their edges curling from age. I traced the faded lines with my finger, trying to memorize every detail, every path that might lead us to what we needed.

"Here." Raven tapped a spot near the Western border. "Old mining tunnels."

I leaned closer, studying the careful notations around the area. "You think they were harvesting the arcanite there?"

"The geological markers match." He shuffled through some loose papers. "And look at this—the Guard kept these sections heavily fortified, even after mining operations officially ceased."

"Why protect empty mines?"

A slight smile played at his lips. "Exactly."

We worked in comfortable silence for a while; the only sound was the rustling of parchment and the scratch of Raven's pen as he made notes. I'd grown to appreciate these quiet moments with him. His steady presence, his careful attention to detail.

"I lived in Draxon for a while, you know." His voice was gentle, still focused on his notes. "I worked as a carrier. We maintained communication channels across the Southeastern territory."

I set down the map I'd been studying.

"Things changed slowly at first," he continued. "So slowly you almost didn't notice. Messages started getting intercepted. Certain communications were... altered." His pen stilled against the parchment. "Then people began disappearing. Other communicators. Merchants. Anyone who spoke against the changes happening in the region."

"When did you leave?"

"After the network collapsed." He looked up, and something in his expression seemed haunted. "But I should have left sooner. Should have seen what was really happening. The signs were there, in the fear that started creeping into people's eyes, in the way they'd hurry inside when his men passed by." He shook his head. "Sometimes I dream about the ones who vanished. Wonder if I could have warned them somehow."

"You couldn't have known," I said quietly.

"Neither could you." His response was gentle but firm, and I realized this was why he was telling me now. Not to burden me with his past, but to tell me I wasn't alone in what I'd survived.

We returned to our work, the silence now comfortable in a different way. Raven's pen scratched against parchment as he made more notes about the mining tunnels. I was studying a detailed section of the Eastern border when he suddenly stopped writing.

"Oh, and nobody knows about—" He trailed off as footsteps echoed through the archives.

"No. Not yet." I kept my voice low as Raven slid two compacts across the table. I barely had time to slip them into my pocket before the doors burst open.

Three Sentinels strode toward us, their expressions grim beneath their darkened eyes.

"We will be escorting you to General Urkin's office immediately."

My stomach dropped.

Fuck. We're too late.

"For what purpose?" Raven's casual demeanor had vanished, replaced by something sharper.

They ignored him completely, rough hands grabbing my arms as I stood. For a moment, I considered reaching for my web, for my shadows—anything to break their grip.

"Your accomplice is already waiting."

Aether.

I let them lead me into the empty street towards the Citadel, through its winding corridors, their fingers digging into my arms with unnecessary force. Even from a distance, Urkin's voice carried through the stone walls, each word dripping with fury.

The door opened, and suddenly I was falling, shoved forward with enough force to send me sprawling across the floor. Before I could even catch my breath, there was a blur of movement and a sickening crack.

Aether had the Sentinel pinned against the wall, his hand locked around the man's throat. The Sentinel's eyes rolled back as he slumped, unconscious. The other guard retreated instantly, pulling the door closed behind him.

"Have you gone mad?" Urkin's voice boomed through the room.

"Have you?" Aether's earlier rage had vanished, replaced by something colder, more controlled. His face was a mask of perfect neutrality as he turned from the unconscious Sentinel and offered me a hand. The gesture sent warmth coursing through me as I let him pull me up, my hand lingering a beat too long in his.

"You murdered a Lord of Umbrathia." Urkin slammed his fist on the desk. "Do you have any idea what you've done? The entire realm will burn for this."

"We found something," I said, straightening my clothes. "If you'd just listen—"

"Listen?" He let out a bitter laugh. "To more of your schemes? Your *theories*? While Draxon's forces gather at our borders?"

"We're going about this war in the wrong way—" I started, but he cut me off.

"We will continue as we have been doing. It's the only way to end this war." His voice cracked with an emotion I hadn't heard from him before. "I lost my son to these monsters. Watched him die defending our realm from Sídhe. And now you want me to consider another way?" He slammed his fist on the desk again. "There is no other way."

Understanding washed over me. Finally, I saw the man beneath the General's mask—a father whose grief had hardened into something unbreakable.

"We can restore the essence," Aether said quietly. "Without destroying everything in the process."

"There is no other way." Urkin's voice had lost its edge, replaced by something hollow. "I won't let his sacrifice be for nothing."

"Then you'll doom us all." Aether's words carried a weight that made the air feel heavy.

"Listen to what we found," I pressed, stepping closer to his desk. "The King of Sídhe. He's a siphon."

"A what?" Urkin's attention snapped to me.

"Someone who can redirect essence itself," Aether explained, his voice steady. "Pull it from one place and channel it to another. The arcanite towers aren't draining the essence from Umbrathia—they're *storing* it."

"Even if what you're saying is true," Urkin's voice was tight, "how does this change anything? The towers still need to be destroyed."

"No," Aether stepped forward. "If we destroy them, all that stored essence will be lost forever. The realm will never recover."

"We have a plan," I added quickly. "A way to potentially restore what's been taken. But we need time—"

"While Draxon's forces gather?" He shook his head. "Your theories about siphons and stolen essence don't change the fact that you've started a war we can't afford to fight."

I exchanged a glance with Aether. "If war comes to Ravenfell, then we need to be as strong as possible to face the Damphyre." I paused before continuing. "We need our own arcanite. We need to go to Riftdremar."

Urkin went still. "Riftdremar was destroyed."

"The surface, yes," Aether said. "But the mining tunnels could still be intact. And if there's any arcanite left..."

"You want to walk into a wasteland on the chance that something survived the burning?" Urkin's laugh was hollow. "For what purpose?"

I stepped closer to his desk, keeping my voice low. "Because I can *create* essence. Not channel it from the land like a tether, but generate it within myself. If we can find arcanite, I might be able to imbue it. Start replacing what's been stolen."

"You've lost your mind." But there was something else in Urkin's voice now—a crack in his certainty. "Even if you could find arcanite, even if you could somehow restore essence to it, it wouldn't be enough. Not against what we're facing."

"It's a start," Aether said.

For a moment, Urkin looked down, face strained as though we could physically see him coming to terms with what we offered. But just as that realization pulled at his features, he simply looked up.

"I can't allow any of you to leave while Draxon's forces mobilize."

I felt Aether's attention on me now, and I turned to look at him. Something had changed in his expression. We locked eyes for a few seconds, as if he was making a decision, something I wasn't aware of. Finally, his gaze left mine, and he faced Urkin once more.

"I'm afraid you can't command her." Aether's voice carried an edge. "Not anymore."

Urkin's jaw tightened. "She's a member of my unit, under my direct authority—"

Aether took a step forward. "Tell me, when was the last time Tryggar chose a rider?"

Urkin's face twisted in exasperation. "What does that have to do with—"

"Nearly half a century, not since *him*," Aether continued, his voice growing harder. "And now, after decades of refusing every soldier who approached, he chooses her."

Something in Urkin's expression shifted.

"Her power alone should have been our first clue." Aether's eyes narrowed. "A Duskbound, appearing from across the rip. When that gift hasn't manifested outside one bloodline for over a century."

My heart thundered in my chest. What was he doing?

"Her appearance is so strikingly different from ours, the white hair, the opalescent eyes, yet she shares our darkened features, our perpetual shadows."

"Make your point, Aether. I'm beginning to lose my patience," Urkin muttered.

"The Void showed Fia a couple, an Aossí and a Kalfar right before they were engulfed in flames—flames that would come to destroy Riftdremar. I believe those to be her parents."

Urkin's eyes sliced through the air in my direction, so quickly it made my heart jump.

"At first, I thought it was just coincidence." Aether's attention fell to the floor. "That her birth in Riftdremar was simply the result of some forbidden affair between realms. An Umbra soldier who'd crossed the rip and fallen for an Aossí woman."

Urkin had gone very still.

"We were together that day," Aether's voice dropped dangerously low. "When Riftdremar burned. When he refused to leave. The public might believe he died of illness, but we know the truth, don't we?"

"That's enough." Urkin's voice shook.

"I returned to the archives to take another look at reports from that time. Nine months before her birth, he filed notice that he'd be splitting his time between the realms." Aether's golden eyes burned. "Convenient timing, wouldn't you say?"

Then he turned to me, and something in his expression confused me more than his words. "And then there's the name she spoke last night."

My heart stopped.

"The royal family has followed the same tradition for centuries," he continued, "every heir's name, a testament to the parent with shadows in their blood." His eyes locked onto mine. "There's a reason you dreamed of this family, Fia."

Urkin's attention shot between Aether and me, coming to some realization that I hadn't yet put together. "It couldn't be…" he stammered over his words as he rounded the desk, taking a few steps in my direction, his eyes alive with questions.

"It's because you belong to it," Aether said, a look of wonder spreading across his face. "Your father was Prince Andrial Valtýr, son of Andrid, our ruling Queen."

Andrial?

The name echoed through my mind like a bell toll, ringing so loudly that the world seemed to tilt beneath my feet.

"You've never been simply *Fia Riftborne*."

I grabbed the back of the chair, my knees threatening to give out as the revelation washed over me. My eyes traced patterns on the floor, unable to process what he was saying. What it meant.

Everything I thought I knew about myself, about my past, began to crack and reshape itself.

Slowly, I lifted my head to meet Aether's gaze, but he was already turning back to Urkin.

"So you tell the Council. You tell them that what Valkan did was an act of war. You tell them that he captured and fed from the heir to the throne of Umbrathia."

CHAPTER FORTY-ONE

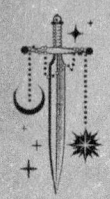

The war room was drenched in nervous energy as I stepped through the door. Vexa paced near the windows while Effie perched on the edge of a chair, fingers drumming against her knee. Theron and Mira huddled in quiet conversation, their shoulders tense. Rethlyn stood alone, arms crossed, watching everyone else with wary eyes. Only Raven seemed calm, lounging in a chair, face buried in a book.

"Finally," Vexa breathed, stopping mid-pace. "Urkin sent orders for all of us. I thought for sure—"

"What happened?" Effie was already walking towards us.

Raven shot up. "The Sentinels practically dragged you out of the archives."

My mind still reeled. I wasn't even sure if I could form coherent words.

"They're going to strip us of rank, aren't they?" Theron's voice carried an edge of panic.

"If we're lucky, that's all they'll do," Mira muttered.

"We're still going to Riftdremar," Aether said, his voice steady beside me. "Tonight, as planned."

"Have you completely lost your mind?" Theron pushed away from the wall. "Urkin is back now. He will never allow it."

"He already has." The words felt strange leaving my mouth, like I was speaking from somewhere far away.

"That's not possible." Mira shook her head. "After what happened in Draxon–"

"Something's changed," Raven said quietly, studying us with sharp eyes. "Hasn't it?"

"What exactly happened in that meeting?" Vexa's eyes darted between Aether and me, her usual confidence wavering.

I sank into the nearest chair, the weight of everything pressing down on me. My father. A prince. The implications scattered my thoughts every time I tried to grasp them.

"We told him about the siphon," Aether said, moving to place a hand on the back of my chair. "About the King of Sídhe."

"And he just... believed you?" Effie's brow furrowed. "Just like that?"

"There were other factors," Aether replied carefully.

"What factors?" Rethlyn asked, speaking for the first time. "What aren't you telling us?"

The door opened before either of us could respond. Urkin entered, and the room fell silent. Some form of tired determination ringed his eyes, and his rigid posture had softened with exhaustion. He surveyed us all before speaking.

"I'm leaving for Stravene within the hour to address the Council." His voice lacked its usual command. "The rest of you will proceed to Riftdremar as discussed. Raven will remain here to maintain communication between realms."

The confusion in the room was palpable. Effie's mouth fell open, while Vexa's eyes narrowed with suspicion.

"Two others will join you," Urkin continued. "A Sentinel whose tether allows manipulation of stone and minerals, and an Archivist skilled in cartography. They'll meet you at the stables this evening."

Without another word, he turned and walked out, leaving the room in stunned silence.

"What in the Void just happened?" Mira's voice shook slightly.

"How did you manage this?" Vexa asked, taking a step toward me. "One minute the Sentinels are dragging you off, and the next Urkin's giving us permission to desert?"

Questions buzzed around me like insects, but I couldn't focus on any single voice. My attention kept drifting to absurd details—the way Effie's fingers twisted her rings, how Rethlyn's shadow stretched across the floor, the slight tremor in Mira's hands. Anything to avoid processing the weight of what we'd learned in Urkin's office.

"A mineral specialist will help with the arcanite," Mira said, "but why send an Archivist?"

"It's a huge continent. That type of skillset will certainly help us navigate it," Rethlyn said, though his brow was still creased in confusion.

"How are we all going to get there?" Effie said, slumping back down in a chair.

"I have my Vördr now. Right before the meeting, Easkath claimed me." Mira hid a grin that threatened her lips.

Rethlyn shot her a proud smile. "Excellent, Mira—"

"I'm more concerned about why Urkin suddenly supports this," Theron cut in. "He was ready to have us all arrested this morning."

"Something changed his mind." Vexa's eyes hadn't left my face.

"Whatever it is," Theron's voice turned sharp, "it better be worth risking our lives over. Some of us don't have the luxury of running off on secret missions whenever we feel like it and keeping things from the rest of the unit." His eyes fixed on me.

Aether's form shifted, shadows writhing beneath his skin as he advanced on Theron. The air seemed to still around him, and when he spoke, his voice carried a viciousness I'd never heard before. "You will never speak to her that way again."

The threat in his words made my pulse quicken, though I wasn't sure if it was from fear or something else entirely.

The room stilled. Even Theron seemed to lose his earlier bravado, confusion washing over him.

"Aether," Vexa said carefully, "what's gotten into you?"

Everyone's attention shifted to me, questions burning in their eyes. The truth sat heavy on my tongue, but I couldn't make the words form.

Aether's golden eyes found mine, carrying an intensity that made my chest tight. He was waiting for me to decide—to either reveal everything or keep it hidden. But my mind felt trapped behind a mist.

"Fia?" Vexa's voice had lost its edge.

I opened my mouth, closed it. The silence stretched uncomfortably.

"They need to know," Aether said quietly, though something in his tone suggested he understood my hesitation.

"She's the daughter of Prince Andrial Valtýr," he said finally, his voice carrying weight but not dramatics. "Heir to the throne of Umbrathia."

"How can that be?" Vexa's voice cracked. "Prince Andrial died of illness before bearing any heirs, before he even had the chance to marry."

"No." Aether's eyes had turned sharp. "That was the story we told the public. Urkin and I were together that day, when Riftdremar burned. When the Prince refused to leave." His jaw tightened. "The reports show he'd been splitting his time between realms in the months before. Nine months before her birth."

The room stilled as understanding rippled through them. My heart thundered in my chest as I watched their faces transform—confusion giving way to shock.

"A forbidden affair," Raven breathed. "Between realms."

"You're both—at the same time," Vexa said, studying me with new eyes. "Aossí and Kalfar."

"She is," Aether finished.

"How long have you known?" Vexa asked, her voice barely above a whisper. The question seemed directed at both of us.

"Since this morning." Aether looked back at me once more, a softness in his eyes.

"That's why Urkin..." Rethlyn trailed off, understanding dawning on his face.

"You outrank him, Fia," Effie managed, her voice barely there.

"So what should we call you now... Princess?" Rethlyn furrowed his brow as his eyes scanned the room.

"Of course not," I said a bit too quickly, my voice not as confident as I would have liked. "I'm still me. Fia... just Fia."

"The Council will have to listen now," Mira said. "With Valkan's attack on the heir to the throne—"

"If they believe it," Theron cut in, though his earlier hostility had vanished. "This changes everything."

"It changes nothing." The words came out sharp. Suddenly, I felt as though I could move, breathe. I stood from my chair and walked to the center of the room. "We still need to get to Riftdremar. We still need to find that arcanite. My blood doesn't make our mission any less urgent."

"No," Aether said quietly. "But it gives us an edge we didn't have before." His golden eyes met mine across the room. "And right now, we need every advantage we can get."

Raven advanced towards me, that familiar glint returning to his eye despite the weight lingering in the room. He gave me a slight nod, something both playful and serious in his expression. "Well then. Let's go steal some arcanite."

The stables were electric with bodies rushing to prepare for the journey to Riftdremar. A woman in sentinel's armor stood near Vexa, her dark hair pulled back in a severe knot. The Umbra insignia glinted on her chest as she introduced herself as Dannika. Beside her, a thin man in Archivist robes shifted from foot to foot, looking distinctly uncomfortable among the Vördr. He gave a slight bow when Vexa introduced him as Tamir.

"Right," Vexa said, eyeing the two newcomers. "Dannika, you'll ride with me. Tamir..." She glanced around at the remaining Vördr.

"He can ride with me," Rethlyn offered, though his expression suggested he wasn't thrilled about it.

Tryggar huffed impatiently beside me, his wings rustling. The other Vördr seemed equally restless—Nihr pawing at the ground while Draug and Raskr shifted their massive forms.

I noticed the change in Dannika and Tamir's posture as I approached—how they straightened, their eyes dropping briefly before meeting mine again. The sentinel's earlier rigid demeanor softened into something like deference, while Tamir's nervous energy transformed into careful attention. News had spread quickly, it seemed.

Of course it had.

"Your High-" Tamir began, but Vexa cut him off with a sharp look.

"Just Fia," she said, and I shot her a grateful glance. At least my friends still saw me as myself.

"The rip hasn't been used in nearly two decades," Tamir said, clearing his throat and turning back to his map. "But based on the old records, it should be about an hour Northeast of Ravenfell, if we're flying, of course."

"Should be?" Theron asked sharply.

"The landscape has... changed since the records were made." Tamir's fingers traced a line on the parchment. "The drought has altered many of the landmarks we'd normally use for navigation."

"Wonderful," Effie muttered, adjusting her position on her Vördr. "So we're basically flying blind."

"Not *completely* blind," Tamir said, his voice turning scholarly. "The geological formations will still be there, even if the vegetation has changed. We're looking for a specific rock formation—three peaks that form a triangle when viewed from above."

Dannika mounted behind Vexa with so much ease, one might have thought she'd ridden a Vördr hundreds of times, but Tamir eyed Raskr like he might bite him.

"They can smell fear, you know," Rethlyn said seriously, and I had to bite back a smile as Tamir went pale. At least I was in on the joke this time.

"He's kidding," Mira called out, already astride her newly-claimed Vördr, Theron sitting calmly behind her. "Mostly."

One by one, the Vördr took to the sky. The familiar sensation of leaving the ground behind settled in my stomach as Tryggar lifted us higher. Below, Ravenfell's twisted spires grew smaller until they were little more than dark shapes. For a moment, I wondered if I'd ever see them again, and that sent a pang through my heart I wasn't expecting.

We flew Northeast, following Tamir's directions as he clung to Rethlyn, knuckles white against his leathers. The world stretched endlessly before us—an expanse of muted grays where vibrant forests should have been. Where they would again grow if we were successful.

Everything felt different now. Each wing beat carried us closer to Riftdremar, to the place where I took my first breath, where my parents drew their last. I'd spent years avoiding any thought of my past in fear of the pain it would bring. Now, the tiny fragments Aether had managed to piece together held weight. My father hadn't been just another casualty of war—he'd been a prince who chose love over duty, who gave up a throne to stay with my mother as flames devoured their world.

What would I find in those ruins? Part of me wanted to discover something that might help me understand who they were, who I was meant to be. But another part dreaded what those answers might mean. It was easier being Fia Riftborne, the orphan who carved out her own place in the world, albeit how small and suffocating that once was. Being Fiandrial Valtýr, heir to a throne I never knew existed... that felt like drowning in someone else's life.

The wind whipped tears from my eyes, though I couldn't tell if they were from the cold or something deeper. Ahead of me, Aether's form cut through the sky, while Vexa and Effie flanked us on either side. They still looked at me the same way, still treated me like the person they'd come to know. But how long would that last? How long before the weight of my bloodline changed everything?

I thought of the Queen, my grandmother, lost in her own madness in that towering castle. Was that my destiny too? Was there something in our blood that turned power into poison? That caused the destruction of those around us?

"There!" Tamir's voice broke through my thoughts. He pointed toward three jagged peaks rising from the wasteland, their formation unmistakable even through the haze.

Had we really been flying for an hour?

Rethlyn signaled for us to descend. The Vördr banked sharply, and through gaps in the clouds, I caught glimpses of what waited below. Dead vegetation sprawled in every direction, the skeletons of nature slowly reclaiming what had once been carefully maintained paths. My heart lodged in my throat as we dropped lower. This was it. This was where it all began.

We landed in what might have been a clearing once, though it was hard to tell through the ashen overgrowth. Dead vines crept up the remains of stone markers, their surfaces worn smooth by decades of neglect.

"The rip should be nearby," Tamir said, sliding awkwardly from Rethlyn's Vördr. He pulled out his map again, but the paper seemed useless against the reality of what time and abandonment had done to this place.

We spread out, searching. Fragments of old structures peeked through the tangles of dead growth—hints of the civilization that had thrived here before the drought.

Minutes stretched into what felt like hours. The others called out occasionally, marking their positions, but finding nothing. Doubt began to creep in. What if the rip had closed? What if we'd come all this way for nothing?

Then I felt it. A shift in the air, subtle but unmistakable. Like the moment before a storm breaks, when everything goes still and heavy. I followed that sensation, pushing through thorny vines until I found myself in a smaller clearing.

The rip hung there, barely visible. A shimmer cutting through reality, like heat rising from hot pavement. But this wasn't heat. This was a tear between worlds, a gateway to everything I'd spent my life running from.

I turned back to the others, my stomach in knots. They gathered slowly, forming a loose circle around the phenomenon. No one spoke. What was there to say? We were about to step into a graveyard of my past, searching for something that might not even exist.

The weight of their gazes pressed against my back as I studied the rip. A flash of movement caught my attention, and then Aether was there, right by my side, close enough that I could feel the heat radiating from him.

"Are you ready?" His voice was low, meant only for me.

I turned to face him, struck by how the muted light caught his square jaw, how it danced along his high cheekbones. How strands of onyx hair fell perfectly across his forehead. And then there was the look in those golden eyes, one that made me feel vibrant among all of the death. I tried to ignore how his shadows seemed to reach for mine across the space between us, and the treacherous feeling that accompanied them.

"Does it matter if I'm not?"

Something softened in his eyes. "We don't have to find all the answers today."

"Just the ones that might save us all." I tried to smile but couldn't quite manage it.

His hand moved as if to touch my arm, then stopped, fingers curling at his side. "I'll be with you. Always."

The words were careful, but warmth bloomed in my chest all the same. Because I believed him. Because I wanted him there, despite any of the judgement that should have plagued me. Doing any of this without him seemed impossible now.

Finally, I nodded, not trusting my voice, and turned back to the rip. One breath, then another, and I stepped through.

CHAPTER FORTY-TWO

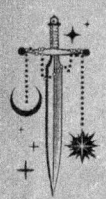

THE AIR CHANGED FIRST. Gone was the stale, ashen taste of Umbrathia, replaced by something so rich with life it nearly overwhelmed me. Sunlight—real sunlight—filtered through a canopy of leaves above, casting dancing shadows on ground that seemed to pulse with vibrant green. My knees nearly buckled at the sight.

This was Riftdremar. Not the burned husk I'd always imagined, but something wild and alive. Nature had reclaimed everything, transforming the ruins of my birthplace into a tangled paradise. Vines thick as my arm wrapped around chunks of blackened stone. Moss carpeted what might have once been streets, broken here and there by saplings that had fought their way through old foundations.

The others stepped through behind me. Someone gasped, maybe Effie or Mira, but I barely registered it. My attention caught on a half-standing wall where delicate purple flowers bloomed from cracks in the ancient mortar.

"Time does wonders," Tamir breathed, clutching his maps tighter. "Nature always prevails."

I forced myself forward, letting my fingers trail across stone still blackened from decades-old flames. Life had returned here with a vengeance, but beneath the beauty lay the bones of a massacre.

I pulled out one of the mirrors Raven had given me before we left. "Made it through. No Guard in sight, the entire place seems to be abandoned."

Raven's reflection appeared, that familiar glint in his eye. "Disappointed? I know how much you enjoy a dramatic entrance."

"I'll try to contain my disappointment." I shifted the mirror, giving him a view of the verdant chaos around us. "I guess we'll head towards the mining tunnels now."

"Far North, near the Western border." He shuffled through some papers. "Though I should warn you, these maps are old. Might be slightly less reliable than my usual work."

"Well, that's why we have Tamir, after all."

"Now I truly feel invaluable to the operation, Your Highness," he said sarcastically, then his expression softened slightly. "Stay safe out there."

"You too." I tucked the mirror away, shaking my head as I turned back to the group.

"We'll need to follow the Western ridge," Tamir said, spreading his map across a fallen column. "The mining operations were concentrated near the mountains, tucked away from the main settlements." His finger traced a path through faded ink. "If we keep the peaks to our left, we should reach the entrance to the valley in about three hours."

One by one, we mounted Vördr that were already tearing grass up by the roots. Tamir's earlier hesitation returned as he settled behind Rethlyn.

"Hold on properly," Rethlyn said, amusement lacing his words. "Unless you fancy a long fall."

The Vördr took to the sky in pairs, their massive wings sending ripples through the canopy below. Tryggar followed, and I found myself holding my breath as we rose above the treeline. Riftdremar spread beneath us in a riot of green I hadn't seen since leaving Sídhe. But this was different—this was wild, untamed. Twenty years of nature reclaiming what flames had tried to destroy.

The further North we flew, the more the landscape changed. Dense forest gave way to rolling hills, then jagged cliffs. Massive rock formations thrust up through the greenery like bones breaking through skin. Time stretched on as we navigated the sunlit clouds.

"There!" Tamir finally called over the wind, pointing to a narrow valley cutting between two peaks. "The mining complex should be just beyond that pass."

Tryggar's wings caught an updraft, and my stomach lurched as we soared higher. Below, something glinted among the trees, maybe metal, or glass glinting in the sun. Evidence that this wasn't always wilderness, that people had once lived and worked here.

"We'll need to find somewhere clear enough to land," Dannika shouted from behind Vexa. "Those trees look too dense for the Vördr."

She was right. The valley floor was a tangle of vegetation, broken only by the occasional jutting rock or fallen tree. But then I spotted it, a break in the canopy where something massive had collapsed long ago, leaving a rough clearing in its wake.

Rethlyn signaled, and we began our descent. The Vördr landed in stages, their hooves finding purchase on ground that hadn't felt such weight in decades. As I slid from Tryggar's back, my boots crunched against something that wasn't just leaves or twigs. I looked down to find fragments of dark glass scattered across the moss, its surface still bearing strange, swirling patterns.

I crouched to examine the glass, but Dannika's sharp voice cut through the clearing. "Movement in the trees."

Everyone froze. My shadows coiled beneath my skin, ready, as

I scanned the thick foliage surrounding us. The Vördr shifted uneasily, Tryggar's tail flicking with agitation.

"There," Mira whispered, pointing to our left where branches swayed against the wind.

Aether moved first, his form dissolving into shadow as he glided toward the disturbance. The rest of us spread out, weapons drawn. Even Tamir had produced a small knife from somewhere within his robes.

A flash of white darted between trees—too fast to make out any details. My heart thundered. Had the Guard somehow known we were coming?

The creature burst into the clearing, and we all staggered back. Not Guard. Not Aossí at all. A massive stag stood before us, its coat pure white, antlers branching toward the sky. It regarded us with no hesitation. Even the Vördr seemed locked in place, a drastic contrast to the last time they'd chased a deer through Draxon's territory.

"Esprithe," Effie breathed.

The stag's gaze swept over our group.

"Fascinating," Tamir said, his tone tinged with awe. "The white stag is the symbol of Riftdremar."

"I've never seen anything like it," Vexa whispered.

The stag's head tilted slightly, as if considering Tamir's words. Then it turned, taking three deliberate steps toward the cliff face before looking back at us.

But the stag was already moving, picking its way through the undergrowth. Without thinking, I started after it.

Aether's arms caught me before I could follow, my eyes tracing the path it took until it disappeared into the thick brush. "It's best we don't separate," Aether hummed against my hair.

"Of course—I don't..." I stammered. "I don't know what I was thinking."

Aether helped balance me, his arm lingering on my back.

"The mining entrance should be nearby," Tamir said, unfolding his map again.

"Well that was interesting," Dannika muttered, scanning the treeline where the stag had vanished. Her hand hadn't left her weapon. "But we should move quickly. Daylight won't last forever."

She was right. Though Riftdremar's sun blazed bright compared to Umbrathia's endless eclipse, it had begun its descent toward the Western peaks.

"This way." Tamir pointed toward a ridge of dark stone jutting through the foliage. "The main shaft should be just beyond that rise."

We moved carefully through the undergrowth, boots catching on twisted roots and remnants of what might have once been a path. Every sound seemed amplified—branches creaking overhead, leaves rustling in the breeze, the occasional snap of twigs beneath our feet.

"That looks promising," Tamir called out softly, pointing to where two weathered pillars emerged from thick vines.

Dannika stepped forward, pressing her palm against the stone behind the pillars. Her eyes went distant for a moment. "It's stable. The tunnel should be structurally sound, at least near the entrance."

"How far down do they go?" Mira asked, peering into the darkness beyond.

"The records mention three main levels," Tamir said, squinting at his notes. "But there could be more. These operations weren't exactly... transparent."

"We should split into teams," Vexa said, already pulling out her weapons. "Cover more ground."

"Agreed." Aether's voice carried authority as he assessed our group. "Vexa, take Dannika and Effie. Mira and Theron together. Rethlyn, you're with Tamir. I'll go with—"

"Me," I finished. No one argued.

"The rest of you start with the upper levels," he continued. "We'll take the lowest tunnel. If anyone finds anything—"

"Or runs into trouble," Vexa added.

"Three sharp whistles," Aether said. "That should echo through the tunnels."

Dannika and Tamir lit their torches, the flames casting an uneven light across the carved pillars. The rest of us wouldn't need them. Our eyes could navigate the darkness easily enough. I took a deep breath, trying to ignore how the shadows beyond the entrance seemed to dance with something more than just absence of light.

The lowest level opened into a vast expanse, empty save for abandoned mining equipment scattered across the floor. Support beams stretched up into darkness, their weathered wood creaking softly in the stale air. No sign of arcanite yet. I tried not to let my disappointment show.

"Well," I said, trying to distract myself, "at least this cave isn't trying to freeze us to death."

Aether's lips twitched. "No ice veins to rescue you from this time."

"Rescue me?" I raised an eyebrow. "I seem to recall handling the cold just fine."

"Is that what you call chattering teeth and blue lips?"

"I think you're being a bit dramatic."

"Of course." His voice carried that dry tone I'd come to recognize as amusement. "Though you seemed rather eager to accept my help at the time."

Heat crept up my neck as I remembered what it felt like with his arms around me, his warmth rushing across my skin. "Yes, well. Life or death situation and all that."

"Indeed." Something flickered in his golden eyes before he turned away, scanning the chamber. "Three tunnels. Any preference?"

I stepped into the path in the middle as a silence fell between us, broken only by the distant drip of water echoing through stone. I studied his profile in the darkness.

"Were you ever planning to tell me?" I finally asked. "About who you thought I was? Or were you waiting for the perfect moment to throw it at Urkin?"

His shoulders tensed slightly. "I wasn't certain. Not until you mentioned the name Fiandrial."

"But you suspected." It wasn't a question.

"There were... signs." He turned to face me, something almost careful in his expression.

"And you didn't think I deserved to know?"

"Would you have believed me?" His voice was quiet, but it carried weight. "I wasn't even sure myself until you told me your name."

"Princess was the first name you ever called me," I shot back.

He was full on smirking now as he ran his hand through his hair, causing it to fall in messy wisps over his forehead. "I wish I could say I'd known all this time. But truly, I called you a *Princess* because you were acting like one."

I stopped, turning to him and narrowing my eyes. "Seriously?"

"You were in some monstrous version of a ballgown, your hair was in perfect little tidy ringlets, and you began pouting immediately upon waking. What was I supposed to think?" He raised an eyebrow, but that same insufferable amusement had returned to his face, a dimple cracking his features.

"You had quite literally just stolen me away from my home and locked me in a tower. I wasn't pouting—I was *enraged*. I wanted to kill you," I countered.

"The thought crossed my mind as well." His smirk grew into a smile as he took a step towards me and whispered. "Several times."

I shoved him back a few feet and continued walking, hiding a grin as he chuckled from behind.

"And then you isolated me for weeks, were rude to me any time we dared some semblance of a conversation, assaulted me with your shadows." I carried on as we moved through the tunnel.

"See, that sounds like pouting again," he said as he stepped in line with me, arm brushing against mine. "*Princess*."

I jabbed him in the side with my elbow. "Don't start that. I might have preferred it when it held no meaning." My eyes found the ground and I couldn't help the sudden onslaught of discomfort that title now brought. The weight of it.

"I know this was never what you imagined for yourself. That you've been held at a certain expectation for far longer than crossing into Umbrathia. And this only brings more of that." I felt his eyes on me, the lightness of the previous conversation now falling into something more serious. "But for what it's worth, you're more deserving than most."

"Why do you think that?" I asked, my voice quiet.

"Because you put others above yourself. It's a rare quality."

"I don't know if I do that." The words fell out before I could stop them. "Maybe I just find myself in situations where it's convenient to do so. Maybe it's not really my choice, in the end."

Aether stopped, his fingers sliding around my arm as he turned me towards him. "You saved Lael," he said, his eyes piercing through me.

"He appeared on the ground before me. I wasn't seeking him out," I argued back, shrugging my shoulders. Suddenly, the intensity of his stare was too much, and I looked away as his fingers began traveling up my arm.

"Most people would have left him there. You didn't. Most people would have never signed up for the Void—to face something so horrible for an entire realm they didn't know." His hand was moving across my shoulder, guiding my eyes back to his. There was a certain determination in his whisper that nearly made my knees weak. "Everything you've done since you've been in

Umbrathia has been selfless. I've never wanted to know someone so much."

His hand slid up to my neck, thumb grazing my jaw, and everything else faded away. The simple touch sent electricity down my spine, making my breath catch. His eyes darkened as they dropped to my lips, and something molten rushed through my veins.

I'd never wanted someone's touch like this—like my skin was starving for it, like every point of contact was both too much and not nearly enough. The intensity of it blindsided me. A month ago, I would have run from this feeling, from the way my body seemed to recognize his touch before my mind could catch up. Instead, I found myself leaning into his hand, craving more.

I wasn't sure who moved first. His fingers slid into my hair as I pressed closer, erasing what little space remained between us. My hands found his chest, feeling the shadows writhe beneath his skin, feeling his heart racing as fast as mine. He exhaled against my lips, the sound nearly undoing me, and then he was leaning down, his forehead touching mine—

Three sharp whistles cut through the darkness.

We jerked apart, reality crashing back. My heart thundered in my chest as we both turned toward the sound, instantly alert.

"Upper level," Aether said, already moving. I followed close behind as we raced back through the tunnel, taking the spiral steps two at a time. The whistles came again, more urgent.

We burst into the main chamber just as Vexa's voice echoed down the corridor. "Over here!"

The passage opened into a vast cavern, and I stopped dead in my tracks as my eyes fell upon the back wall. Dozens of crystals jutted from the rock face. Their violet-blue light cast strange shadows across the chamber.

Arcanite.

CHAPTER FORTY-THREE

"We'll need to break it down," Dannika said, examining the crystalline formation. She reached out to touch one of the smaller pieces and it separated easily from the larger mass, like a magnet releasing its hold. "That's... interesting."

"What is it?" Vexa moved closer.

Dannika pressed the piece back against the formation and we watched in fascination as it seemed to meld seamlessly back into place, the crystal structure realigning itself. "The arcanite—it wants to stay together. Like it's drawn to itself."

"Of course," Tamir breathed. "That's how they were able to construct such massive towers. The crystals naturally reform once they're in contact. It's not just a mineral, it's almost..."

"Alive," I finished, watching as Dannika separated another piece, larger this time.

"This makes things much simpler," she said. "We can break it into smaller pieces for transport, then reconstruct it once we're back in Ravenfell."

"The Vördr can handle that weight if we distribute it properly," Aether said. "But we'll need something to secure them with."

"We can use some of these old support beams," Theron suggested, gesturing to several fallen timbers. "Fashion makeshift harnesses, spread the load between them."

"Let's not get ahead of ourselves. We don't even know if I can actually imbue it yet," I cut in, suddenly feeling another pressure weigh me down.

Piece by piece, we carried the arcanite out of the mines, laying each crystal in the clearing where we'd left the Vördr. As the fragments touched, they pulled together seamlessly, rebuilding themselves into their natural formation. Soon, a structure nearly as tall as me and twice as wide rose from the ground, its violet-blue light even more breathtaking in the dying sunlight.

"That's... a lot more than I expected," Vexa breathed, circling the formation.

"Quite the haul," Rethlyn said, wiping sweat from his brow. "Though I suppose that's what happens when no one's mined here in decades."

"It's beautiful," Effie whispered, reaching out as if to touch the crystals before pulling her hand back.

"But will it be enough?" Theron asked, his voice tight with something between hope and doubt.

I studied the formation, watching how the light seemed to move within each crystal, like something alive trapped beneath the surface. The sun had nearly set now, painting the sky in deep purples that made the arcanite's glow even more pronounced.

"Even if I can do this," I said carefully, "we don't know how much essence it will take. How much I can give."

"You don't have to do it now," Aether said, moving to stand beside me. His entire frame was silhouetted by the last fragments of the setting sun, so stark and bright that it was nearly impossible to take in the sight, as if the two were one in the same.

"No." I shook my head. "We should know if this will work before we transport it back to Umbrathia."

I stepped closer to the formation, my fingers hovering over its surface. The crystals hummed with their own strange energy, but I had no idea how to actually transfer essence into them. I pressed my palm against the arcanite, its surface cool. Nothing happened. No surge of power, no transfer of energy—just smooth crystal against my skin, as lifeless as any common stone. A knot formed in my throat as I pulled my hand back.

What had I been thinking? That I could just touch it and somehow fill it with essence? Everyone was watching, waiting, their hope almost palpable in the fading light. Hope that probably died a little more with each passing second of failure.

"Maybe try..." Vexa started, but fell silent as I exhaled sharply.

I placed both hands on the formation this time, pressing harder, as if force alone could make this work. The violet-blue light pulsed steadily, mockingly unchanged. Sweat beaded on my forehead as I tried to push essence through my palms, the way I'd learned to channel shadows. But essence wasn't darkness—it wasn't something I could see or grasp or control. It just existed within me, as natural and unreachable as my own heartbeat.

"I don't know how to do this," I whispered, more to myself than the others. The admission felt like failure, like letting down not just my companions but an entire realm. My realm, according to some accident of birth I still couldn't quite wrap my head around.

"Take your time," Rethlyn said from somewhere behind me. But we didn't have time.

I stepped back, running trembling fingers through my hair. How many people in Ravenfell were starving right now? How many children like Lael lay wounded because their realm's essence had been stolen? And here I stood, supposedly carrying the same power that could restore it within me, but unable to do anything with it.

I closed my eyes, trying to focus on that well of energy Talon had described— this endless essence that supposedly flowed through me. But it was like trying to catch rain with a sieve. Every time I thought I felt it, it slipped away.

Relax.

It didn't feel like my own thought, but I decided to go with it. I turned back to the formation, desperation clawing at my throat. There had to be a way. I'd felt power before—when my web braided itself up my spine, when it filled my skull with its iridescence.

Almost instinctively, I reached for that deeper part of myself. The web responded instantly, but instead of letting it climb to my head as it always had, I focused on drawing it down my arms.

The web resisted at first, like a river trying to flow uphill. My fingers trembled against the crystal as I fought to redirect that familiar power. Every instinct screamed at me to let it rise, to let it fill my skull as it always had. But something about this felt right.

My breath came in short gasps as I concentrated. The web pulsed through my veins, searching for its usual path, but I held firm, channeling it down, down, through my shoulders, my elbows, into my palms. The sensation was foreign, almost uncomfortable, like wearing a glove on the wrong hand.

"Fia?" Someone's voice seemed distant, concerned. I couldn't tell who had spoken. Everything had narrowed to this moment, to the feeling of power coursing through me.

Please, I thought, pressing my forehead against the cool crystal surface. *Please work. We need this. They need this.* I closed my eyes.

The web thrummed stronger now, no longer fighting its new direction but flowing freely. It felt different than when I wielded shadows or touched minds. More raw. Or Fundamental. Like I'd tapped into something that had always been there.

A gasp cut through my concentration and my eyes flew open.

White light blazed within the crystals, so bright I had to squint. It spread from where my hands touched, transforming the violet-blue into something impossibly pure. The glow pulsed outward through the ridges like veins of starlight, each crystal refracting and magnifying the radiance until the entire structure seemed alive with its own blinding moon.

"Esprithe," Effie breathed behind me.

I stumbled back from the formation, my legs weak. The white light continued to pulse through the crystals, a stark contrast to their earlier violet-blue glow.

"Incredible," Tamir whispered, his eyes wide and glassy in the light. He reached toward the formation but stopped just short of touching it, as if afraid it might shatter under his fingers.

I felt Aether's presence before I saw him, that familiar warmth as he moved to stand beside me again. When I finally looked up at him, the white light from the arcanite reflected in his golden eyes, making them almost silver.

"You did it," he said quietly.

"Let's try and get these strapped to the Vördr," Rethlyn said, running his hand along one of the makeshift harnesses they'd been fashioning from the support beams. "Though crossing the rip might be tricky."

"We should get moving," Mira cut in, "It's already dark."

And so they began preparing the Vördr.

"Careful with that piece," Vexa called out as Theron and Rethlyn secured another section of arcanite to Draug's harness. The Vördr shifted, adjusting to the weight as Dannika moved to fasten the final straps.

"Talon should be able to tell—when you bring it back to Umbrathia," I began, nerves setting in. "I can feel the essence flowing through it, but I don't know how you will reform it." Only Mira seemed to be paying attention. "Talon should be able to sense the direction in which it flows. He should be able to tell you how to place it in the ground so that it releases it into the land."

Mira simply narrowed her eyes. "Why are you telling us this?"

I watched as Aether approached Tryggar with the last fragment. My heart thundered against my ribs as I made the word form: "Wait."

It came out sharp and direct, making everyone pause. Their eyes found me, confusion evident in their expressions.

"I'm not going back to Umbrathia." The words felt like stones in my throat, but I forced them out. "Not yet."

"What?" Vexa's brow furrowed.

"I have to return to Sídhe." I looked at each one of them individually. "If we want any chance of winning this war against the King, we need to start by unraveling the lies he's woven throughout the Isle."

"You want to go back?" Effie's voice carried disbelief. "After everything that's happened?"

"That's suicide," Theron cut in. "You can't just walk back into—"

I pulled out the compacts Raven had given me, turning them over in my hands. "I have friends there—contacts. People who might listen." I held up the mirrors. "People who could help us expose the truth. People on the *inside*."

Aether stepped towards me, his eyes burning. "This was not a part of the plan," he nearly growled.

Dannika rounded his side. "Your Grace, I'm afraid we cannot allow you to do that, as noble as it sounds."

I took a careful step back. "There are blood oaths. Sworn by anyone who enters the Guard. They keep everyone within it muzzled, unable to speak about anything that happens in the West. As long as they stay in-tact, we'll be facing an army of thousands every time we go across the rip." I scanned the group, determination set in my tone. "And now they have an advantage we didn't plan for. The breathing tonics."

Aether's gaze shifted from burning rage to slight consideration, but he still crossed his arms over his chest, glaring at me with narrowed eyes.

"Respectfully, Dannika. I'm not asking for your permission. I'm telling you what I'm doing. And if anyone tries to stop me—"

"Fine," Aether growled, and something sliced through me. I opened my mouth, and closed it.

"You can't be serious..." Tamir managed, peeking out from behind Dannika.

Theron stepped forward. "She's the future of our realm, this is a ridiculous idea."

"She also no longer answers to us. To Dannika or Urkin." Aether's eyes locked onto mine, and although I could tell he was not overjoyed by my sudden announcement, understanding flickered across them. "If this is what she wants, then none of us can stop her." He paused, coming to stand beside me. "But I'm going with you."

Murmurs ran through the rest of the group as I turned to him. "Are you sure?" I asked.

"I already told you." His voice was low, dangerous. "I'm with you. Always."

CHAPTER FORTY-FOUR

Vexa pulled me into a hug that nearly crushed my ribs. "I still think you're insane," she muttered, but her arms tightened. "Try not to get yourself killed."

When she finally released me, Effie was there, tears already forming in her eyes. "We just got you back," she said, wrapping her arms around me. "And now you're walking straight into their territory again."

"I'll be fine." I tried to sound more confident than I felt. The weight of what I was about to do pressed against my chest—return to Sídhe, to the Guard I'd once learned to be proud of.

Vexa's violet eyes narrowed at Aether. "You better bring her back in one piece."

His jaw tightened, but he gave a slight nod. I watched as the others mounted their Vördr, the arcanite secured between them in makeshift harnesses. The crystals' white glow pulsed steadily, a reminder of what we'd accomplished. What we still had to do.

As they took to the sky, the reality of my choice settled over me. I was choosing to return to the realm I'd been taken from, to face the very people I'd once defended. But watching the Umbra disappear into the darkness, their forms growing smaller against the stars, I knew I'd made the right choice.

"We should find a better place to make camp," Aether said, scanning the darkened landscape. "Somewhere more defensible."

I nodded, already moving toward Tryggar. The silver Vördr lowered his massive form, allowing me to climb onto his back with far more grace than my first attempts. A small victory, but one that made me smile despite everything.

Aether mounted Nihr beside me, and we took to the sky, keeping low enough to study the terrain beneath us. Moonlight caught the waves in the distance, and I realized we were nearing the coast. As we flew closer, a cliff came into view, its face dropping sharply to a sandy beach below.

"There," I called out, pointing to the ledge. The elevation would give us a clear view of any approach, and the ocean at our backs meant one less direction to watch.

Aether guided Nihr down, and Tryggar followed, his wings sending bursts of cool air across my skin as we landed. The cliff offered a strange sort of beauty—wild and untamed, like everything else in this place. Below, waves crashed against the shore in a steady rhythm that felt almost hypnotic.

I slid off Tryggar's back and began unloading the supplies Raven had managed to find for me—a few blankets, some dried meat, a worn leather pouch filled with basic survival gear.

Before I could finish, Aether appeared at my side, his hands already gathering the supplies from my arms. "I'll handle this."

I couldn't help but notice the flex of muscle in his forearms as he collected everything, the way his shoulders stretched beneath his leather uniform.

"Careful now," I said, fighting a smile. "One might mistake you for a gentleman."

He shook his head, but I caught the semblance of a grin playing at his lips as he brushed past me and began setting up camp. After arranging the blankets, he dragged a few fallen logs from the treeline, arranging them near the cliff's edge before handing me the fire starter.

"I'll be back," he said simply, already heading down the slope toward the beach. "Think you can handle it?"

"I'll manage."

I rolled my eyes and began positioning the logs, working to create a proper fire pit. As I struck the flint against steel, my gaze drifted to the path he'd taken. I told myself I was just being vigilant, keeping track of his location, but then he pulled his shirt over his head and my eyes widened.

Heat slid across my face as he stripped off his leather pants, leaving him in only black undergarments. I told myself to look away. *I should definitely look away.* But I couldn't tear my eyes from him as he waded into the water, sword in hand.

The fire crackled beside me, finally catching, and I forced myself to turn back to it. A laugh escaped my lips as I arranged more kindling, wondering what the others would think if they could see the fearsome Umbra warrior now, hunting for fish in his underclothes.

Some time later, the sound of boots on grass made me look up. Aether stood there, fully dressed again, his sword skewered with four decent-sized fish.

"What?" I managed, taking in the sight.

"We're not wasting the opportunity to eat something recently alive," he said, giving me a knowing look that made my stomach flip—though that might have been from the thought of actual fresh fish after months of dried grains.

I could barely contain my excitement as he knelt by the fire and began preparing them, his movements practiced as he cleaned and gutted each one.

"Where did you learn all of this?" I asked, watching him work.

"You've seen my cabin." He positioned the fish over the flames. "It's where I spent most of my time before the drought."

I turned toward the coast, where the darkness of the ocean met the star-filled sky. Somewhere beyond that horizon lay Sídhe, and whatever awaited us there. The thought sent a chill down my spine that had nothing to do with the night air.

The smell of cooking fish drew me back to the present. Aether pulled one from the fire, testing its flesh with his fingers before handing it to me in a cloth. Steam rose from the crispy skin, and my mouth watered at the sight. This entire night felt surreal, sitting under the stars, the ocean air swimming in my lungs, the feeling of solitude—of being free in this untamed land.

I took a careful bite, and warmth flooded through me. The meat was flaky and perfect, seasoned with nothing but smoke and salt from the ocean. A sound escaped my throat—something between a laugh and a moan of pleasure.

"Good?" Aether asked, and when I looked up, that dimpled smile had returned.

I was too busy taking another bite to respond. We ate in comfortable silence, the crackling fire and rhythmic waves our only company. I couldn't remember the last time I'd tasted something this fresh. It felt like being alive again after a very long sleep.

My eyes drifted to Aether as he ate, watching how his jaw worked, the way his full lips pressed together between bites. The firelight caught his features, dancing across the sharp planes of his face, and I found myself remembering the mines. How close he'd been, his fingers sliding into my hair, his breath warm against my mouth. How for one charged moment, he'd almost kissed me. How I'd almost let him. How I'd *wanted* it.

Heat rushed to my face and I forced my attention back to my food. What was wrong with me? We had bigger concerns than whatever this thing was between us—this pull I couldn't quite understand or ignore. And yet I couldn't stop my gaze from finding him again, couldn't help but wonder what would have happened if those whistles hadn't echoed through the tunnels.

When we finished, I leaned back on my hands, staring into the flames. "Thank you," I said softly. "You're a terrific cook."

"When you live alone in the woods, you learn to make do." He tossed another piece of wood onto the fire. "But I'll take that rare compliment."

"Is that what you prefer? Being alone?"

His golden eyes found mine across the flames. "For a long time, yes."

Something in his tone made my heart skip. "And now?"

"Now..." He seemed to consider his words carefully. "I'm not so sure."

I pulled my knees to my chest, wrapping my arms around them. "It must have been peaceful though. Before all of this."

"It was quiet," he agreed. "But I'm learning there's a difference between peace and emptiness."

The waves crashed below us, filling the silence that followed. I watched as shadows danced beneath his skin, wondering if he was even aware of them anymore.

"Did you ever get lonely?" The question slipped out before I could stop it.

"Loneliness requires knowing what you're missing." His voice was soft, almost distant. "And I didn't, not then."

A part of me wanted to push further, but something held me back as we prepared the bedding for sleep. I wasn't sure how much time had passed as we lay there, side by side, staring up at the endless expanse of stars. A strange tension hummed between us, but beneath it was something else—a feeling of safety I hadn't experienced since being taken from Sídhe. Maybe even before that.

"Is it strange?" Aether asked, his voice low. "Being here, in Riftdremar?"

I considered his question, watching as clouds drifted across the moon. "It's different from what I imagined. Seeing all this regrowth, all this life..." I paused, letting out a breath.

The words had barely left my mouth when guilt churned in my stomach. Here I was, finding comfort in this deserted paradise while his realm withered, while his people suffered in overcrowded streets.

"I just realized how insensitive that sounded."

"It's not," he said quietly. "Just because Umbrathia is dying doesn't mean the rest of the world should."

I turned my head to look at him, studying his profile in the starlight. "I feel like such a fool." The admission came easier than I expected. "When things began changing in Sídhe, when the realm started prospering, I never questioned it. Not like I should have."

"I don't know why you would." He paused, and I could hear him choosing his next words carefully. "At the bonfire, when I overheard you... it didn't exactly sound like your life there was that great to begin with."

"No, it wasn't." The memory of that night, of spilling my secrets to people I'd barely known, made something twist in my chest. "But it was nothing like what the Kalfar are experiencing. I was privileged compared to that."

Aether reached over, taking my hand in his. He turned it palm-up, studying the Riftborne branding in the firelight. "I'm sure this made it rather difficult."

"Well, it served its purpose." I smiled wearily. "But we wore gloves most of the time."

"We?" His eyes found mine, a curious glint crossing them.

"Osta and me." Warmth spread in my chest at the memory. "My best friend. Well, I guess she's more like a sister than anything else. We grew up in a group home. Then when we finally moved out, we got an apartment together. Stayed that way until she got a job with a noble family and I was stationed out West." I let out a small sigh. "You'd like her. Everyone does."

"I'm not sure I trust your judgment." He laughed softly.

I shot him a look. "Wise observation. I'm here with you, after all."

We both laughed, and a comfortable silence fell between us as we returned our gaze to the stars. The fire crackled beside us, sending sparks dancing into the night air.

"You know, I haven't seen the stars in years," he said after a while.

"Not in Sídhe, when you cross the rip?"

He paused. "We were never there for long, and I've never looked up."

I studied his face, the way his golden eyes reflected the starlight, an almost childlike wonder softening his sharp features.

"There's something I've been curious about," I said, breaking the silence.

He turned to look at me. "What's that?"

"The sirens called you 'Realm Crasher,'" I said carefully, "and it made me remember that first night in the tower. You said something about crashing down into this realm." I paused, watching his expression. "I hadn't thought about it much until that day when they said it in the cave."

Aether looked up again, twisting his mouth. For a moment, I didn't think he would answer.

"I told you I only had one memory of my past life," he finally said. "But that's not entirely true. I remember falling. For a long time."

"Into the Void?" I asked, something tugging at the edges of my memory.

"The darkness was overwhelming. I thought for sure I'd die in there, but death never came for me."

I sat up, realization hitting me. "I dreamed that," I whispered, the memory suddenly clear.

"Exactly how many times have you dreamed about me?" That familiar smirk played at his lips, but something in his eyes remained serious.

Heat rushed to my face and I turned away. "It is strange," I admitted.

Neither of us said anything for a long moment.

"I have that dream nearly every night." His voice had lost its teasing edge, replaced by something almost haunted.

"And you know nothing else about where you're from?"

"Sometimes I feel things, like I'm being pulled somewhere, but it vanishes quickly."

Silence settled between us, broken only by the crackle of the fire and the distant sound of waves.

"Why did you not take the position as commander?" I asked, wondering if I was pushing too far.

Aether's expression turned thoughtful, his brow furrowed as he stared up at the stars.

"Wherever I'm from..." he finally said, his voice low, "I was cast out. There must have been a reason for that. Something I did." A flicker of pain crossed his face, gone so quickly I almost missed it. "A part of this life feels like a chance at redemption." He paused, taking a deep breath. "I don't think someone like that should be leading others."

"You speak of redemption like it's religious," I said quietly. "I thought you didn't give much interest to the thought of a higher power."

"Not all redemption is for the sake of the gods, Fia." He turned to look at me, and something in my chest fluttered at the way he said my name.

"The gods?" I arched a brow.

"The Esprithe, I guess."

"For an instant in Draxon, I wondered if you were one of them." The admission slipped out before I could stop it. "I'd never seen anything like that. What you did."

"I've never done that before." Something dark passed over his face. "Not in this life, at least."

The weight of his words settled between us, and I realized how much guilt he carried, how much uncertainty about his own past plagued him.

"So none of the others know?" I asked softly.

"They know I can manipulate matter, but they don't know the extent."

"It felt like more than that. The pressure inside that room changed completely. Like I was being dragged under the ocean."

"I'm sure you've seen greater gifts," he said, deflecting. "The Sídhe Guard seems to have no shortage of them."

"Not like yours," I said, thinking back to my time in the Guard. "There were some unique gifts in the team I'd been part of. One of my friends can create lightning. Another can paralyze people with just a drop of his blood."

Aether went quiet for a moment. When he spoke again, his voice was flat. "Is that the one you were talking about at the bonfire?"

My eyes widened as I recalled everything he'd heard me say about Laryk that night. "No. Not him."

"He sounded like a prick."

"Coming from you?" I laughed, though it felt awkward in my throat.

The silence that rolled past felt heavier than before.

"Have you dreamt of him?" Aether finally asked.

I contemplated how to answer, a sinking feeling settling in my stomach. "I have," I said softly, then paused. "He thinks I'm still alive."

Something violent crossed Aether's eyes, all trace of amusement draining from his face. And suddenly, I felt like we were entering dangerous territory.

"Are you in love with him?" His voice was cold.

The question shocked me, and before I could even think it through, I heard myself whisper, "I thought I was."

"And now?" His words were clipped, but there was an undercurrent of something in his tone that I couldn't ignore. Something that sounded like hope.

Guilt churned in my stomach as I thought about it—about how distraught Laryk had seemed in my dreams, how certain he'd been of my return. I hadn't let myself think about any of this in so long, and now that I did, I found myself more confused than ever.

"I don't know," I finally said.

The silence that followed felt barren. The wind sent a chill across my skin and I tucked my hands beneath my head. A part of me wanted to be closer to him, to absorb that endless warmth, but I couldn't bring myself to move. Something had changed. I could feel the energy shift between us, and for a moment, I regretted answering his question at all.

Aether turned over, his back to me. "We need to get some rest."

A strange panic fluttered in my chest at his withdrawal. Suddenly, I wanted to be back in Ravenfell. In his bed, with his arms wrapped around me like armor. An armor that, perhaps, I'd just broken with an admission I wasn't even sure was true.

That feeling followed me into a restless sleep.

CHAPTER FORTY-FIVE

The scent of woodsmoke pulled me from sleep. I blinked away the heaviness in my eyes to find Aether already awake, crouched by the fire. Dark clouds churned across the horizon where sea met sky, their edges bleeding into each other until I couldn't tell where one ended and the other began.

It seemed the tension from the night before still lingered in the air. I could feel it in the careful way he moved, in how his shoulders stiffened when I sat up. Even his shadows seemed more contained, pulled tight against his skin like armor.

"Looks like it might rain," I said, the words falling flat in the heavy air.

Aether's eyes flicked up from the fire, scanning the sea. "Looks like it."

I lowered myself to sit across from him, watching the way his fingers gripped the makeshift spit with more force than necessary. Last night's conversation hung between us like a mist.

He pulled a fish from the flames and handed it to me first. "Careful, it's hot."

Thunder rolled in the distance as we ate, the sound echoing off the cliff face. Neither of us spoke. I found myself counting the seconds between lightning and thunder, anything to fill the silence.

"Will rain affect the Vördr?" I asked, watching as Aether tossed pieces of fish to Nihr and Tryggar. The massive beasts tore into their breakfast with none of the discomfort that plagued their riders.

"They love it," he said as he finished his own meal, gaze fixed somewhere, anywhere other than me. "For the journey, it won't matter so much. We can fly above it."

I nodded, tracking another flash of lightning as it split the sky.

Aether stood abruptly, adjusting the straps of his leather armor. "When you're finished, there's something we need to do before we leave."

"We shouldn't waste time," I countered, but something in his posture told me this wasn't up for debate.

"I know you think we're going to go do all of this without struggle." His fingers worked at his weapon belt, checking each blade. "But I need you to be prepared for any outcome."

"What do you mean?"

"You've never used your shadows in battle. At least not intentionally." His eyes finally moved toward me, but settled somewhere over my shoulder. "You need to learn how to fight with it *intentionally*."

I pushed myself to my feet, brushing dirt from my leathers. "I'm all ears."

Angry waves crashed against the shore as Aether began to explain, his voice taking on that familiar commanding tone I remembered from my first days in the tower. "Going in and out of spectre form can disorient your enemy. When you're pure shadow, you're resistant to physical damage. You need to use that to your advantage." He moved toward the center of the cliff, keeping well away from the edge. "But it requires speed, precision. Complete awareness of your surroundings."

I followed him, feeling the electricity in the air as another burst of thunder shook the ground beneath us.

"Try to attack me." The words were clipped.

I hesitated for only a moment before lunging forward. But where Aether had been standing, there was nothing but smoke. Before I could turn, his hands locked around my wrists, pulling them behind my back.

"You see how it can be extremely useful in a fight," he said, his breath warm against my ear. Then he released me just as quickly, and I felt cold in all the places his hands had touched.

Lightning split the sky as I spun to face him, my own shadows coiling beneath my skin in response to his challenge.

"Again," he commanded, circling me slowly. "This time, don't just attack blindly. Feel the shadows around you. Use them."

I closed my eyes for a brief moment, letting my awareness expand. Shadows were everywhere, cast by the clouds above, by the rocks scattered across the cliff, by our own bodies. They called to me.

This time when I moved, I let myself dissolve just as he had. The sensation was exhilarating—being everywhere and nowhere at once. Nothing more than black mist. I reformed behind him, but he was already turning, his arm blocking my strike with infuriating speed.

"Better." His golden eyes had darkened, shadows writhing beneath them. "But you're still thinking too much. Let instinct take over."

Thunder cracked overhead as we began to move. Aether's form blurred into darkness, and I matched him, our shadows dancing around each other like smoke. Every time I thought I had him, he would slip away, reforming just out of reach. But I was learning, watching how he moved, how he used the environment to his advantage.

I caught a glimpse of his solid form and struck, my fist connecting with his shoulder. The victory was short-lived as he grabbed my arm, using my momentum to flip me. I dissolved before I hit the ground, reforming on my feet several paces away.

"Now you're getting it," he said, and for the first time that morning, there was something other than careful distance in his voice.

We continued to spar as the storm drew closer, lightning illuminating the cliff in stark bursts. Each flash cast new shadows for us to bend and manipulate. I was beginning to understand what he meant about letting instinct take over. It was as if my body knew what to do before my mind did.

My next attack caught him off guard. I feinted left before dissolving, reforming low and sweeping his legs out from under him. But instead of falling, he turned to smoke, reappearing behind me. His arm locked around my waist, pulling me back against his chest.

"Creative," he murmured, his breath stirring my hair. "But you left yourself open."

The next clash came faster, more intense. I caught a glimpse of Aether's form through the shadows and moved instinctively, arm shooting out to grab him. But everything happened so quickly, movements blurring together, and in my flustered state, I felt my shadows begin to flow into him without permission.

Aether immediately solidified, his eyes burning. "Fia," he snapped, yanking his arm away.

"What's your problem?" Heat rushed to my face, whether from embarrassment or anger, I couldn't tell.

He laughed darkly, shaking his head as he turned away from me. "That's not how it's done. You're aware of that."

"But why? Does it hurt you?" I asked, watching as the muscles in his back tensed beneath the leathers, how his fingers curled into fists.

He remained silent as the first raindrop splashed against my shoulder. The storm had finally reached us.

"We didn't get to do the transfer before we left. I know you must be getting close." My voice was barely audible over the growing wind.

"If you had told me about your plan before leaving Ravenfell, this wouldn't be an issue." His voice was low, almost a growl.

"I understand that. But it's not an option anymore." I watched as rain began to darken his hair, how droplets traced paths down his neck.

He turned back to me slowly, something unreadable crossing his face. "It makes it more difficult," he said, finally meeting my eyes. "For me."

My heart thundered against my ribs as I moved closer, drawn by the rawness in his voice. "What does that mean?" But something in his expression told me more than his words could. The way his eyes darkened, how his breath seemed ragged as I stepped nearer.

"Do you remember when I gave you shadows on the lawn that day, how it felt?"

The memory rushed back—that moment when his darkness had filled me, how it had felt like drowning in the most exquisite way. How for one terrifying, beautiful moment, I'd almost lost myself to the sensation. How a part of me had wanted to.

I nodded, suddenly feeling flushed despite the cool rain beginning to fall.

"What I gave you is a fraction of what you just transferred to me." He took a step closer, and something in his voice made my stomach flip. His eyes burned into mine.

"Why is it difficult?" The words caught in my throat. My better judgment was roaring for me to step back, to retreat from whatever was building between us. But something treacherous in me wanted to move closer.

He paused, conflict written across his features. Rain dripped from his dark lashes as he seemed to wrestle with himself. "It makes things confusing for me." The words were careful, like they weren't the ones he really wanted to say.

"I'm confused too." The admission slipped out before I could stop it. I looked down, pushing away the guilt that came with those words—guilt about what we weren't saying, about everything I thought I knew about myself. But I could feel him closer now, feel the heat radiating off him despite the rain. His presence seemed to fill all the space around me, making it hard to think clearly.

"I felt nothing for decades." His voice was rough. "Existed, but barely lived. Hiding from no one other than myself, but hiding all the same. And then you showed up. And now..." His voice trailed off, pain crossing his face as he tried to collect himself. A dark familiarity tugged at me. "I've tried to go back to that place. But I can't find my way there. I'm not sure it even exists anymore. Not since you showed up and destroyed every wall I'd built."

His words struck something deep within me, a truth I'd been trying to ignore, but that had become so glaringly obvious over the last few days that I felt it in my bones. Laryk had been the first person to see what I could become, to believe in my potential. But Aether... Aether was the first person who understood who I'd always been. In that deep, unexplainable way that only two souls who had existed by hiding could ever truly understand.

My mind drifted to that first night in the tower, when something had sparked between us in the darkest and most confusing of ways. That connection had terrified me then. Maybe it still did. But I couldn't deny it anymore.

Rain streamed down my face as I looked up at him, my heart

thundering in my chest. "That's why I'm confused, Aether. Because you've been tearing my walls down too."

Suddenly he was moving, and my world narrowed to nothing but him. His arms wrapped around me as my lips found his, and the sky split open.

Rain poured. Thunder cracked. But all I felt was the sun.

The heat of him burned through my wet clothes, searing every place we touched. I wanted more. Needed more. My fingers tangled in his hair as my shadows slipped free, seeking his darkness. The groan that tore from his throat sent lightning through my veins, and he deepened the kiss with a hunger that matched my own.

His hands slid down, gripping my thighs, and the world tilted. My back hit the wet ground, and then he was everywhere—his weight pressing me down, his heat seeping into my bones. More shadows poured from me, seeking him, needing him.

He broke away, breathing hard. Raindrops clung to his lashes as he stared down at me, his golden eyes molten. His fingers threaded through my soaked hair, and something in his gaze made my heart stutter. Like I was both salvation and damnation. Like I was everything.

Darkness crept into my vision as our shadows merged, dancing beneath our skin. Every touch sparked something deeper. Every brush of his fingers left trails of fire. The pleasure of it was devastating—this giving and taking, this sharing of darkness. I couldn't tell where I ended and he began.

His mouth found my neck, tongue tracing paths that burned despite the cold rain. Another wave of shadows passed between us and I moaned, the sound raw and desperate. His answering groan vibrated against my throat as his teeth grazed my skin.

My head fell back, eyes fluttering as pleasure threatened to consume me. Through the rain, through the haze of desire, my eyes widened.

And my heart stopped.

Fear crystallized in my veins, sharp and sudden as a blade. There, through the storm—a ship. The Sídhe crest billowed on its sails.

And it was heading straight for us.

CHAPTER FORTY-SIX

"Aether." My voice cracked on his name. Something in my tone made him freeze, golden eyes finding mine before following my gaze across the water.

We moved as one, shifting to shadow form in an instant. My heart thundered as we rematerialized beside the Vördr, urging them deeper into the forest. *Had we already been spotted?* The thought sent ice through my veins.

"We need to be close when they come ashore." Aether's voice had shifted, all traces of intimacy replaced by tactical precision. "Find out what they're doing here."

I nodded, still tasting him on my lips, still feeling the ghost of his touch on my skin. But there was no time for that now. We dissolved into darkness once the Vördr were hidden, moving silently toward the shore.

Through the mist, the ship emerged like a ghost—first just a shadow, then taking solid form. Water churned white against its dark hull, and the Sídhe crest snapped in the wind, gold thread catching what little light penetrated the clouds. Fire licked through my veins as I noticed a second flag beneath the Sídhe crest—a roaring sun with crossed swords.

It can't be.

But I knew that symbol. The Soleil family crest.

The ship's anchor splashed into the water, chains rattling as smaller boats were lowered into the choppy waves.

"I'm going to see how many are on board." My voice sounded steadier than I felt.

I'd never tried using my focus while in shadow form, but the web responded instantly, braiding through my darkened mist. Silver orbs of consciousness lit up across the ship like stars. Four on the upper deck. Six below.

"Ten," I breathed.

"We have two options." Aether's voice cut through the rain. "We can wait for them to come ashore, to see what they're here for, or we can cast darkness and take out everyone on the ship."

"Cast darkness?" The words felt foreign on my tongue.

"Don't worry, I can handle it." There was something deadly in his tone.

Two figures appeared at the ship's bow, their forms blurred by the mist. They lifted what looked like brass spyglasses, methodically scanning the shoreline.

"They're looking for something," I whispered, but the words died in my throat as one of the men suddenly pointed behind us, shouting to his crew.

My stomach dropped as I turned. Tryggar stood on the cliff's edge, his silver form unmistakable against the storm-dark sky.

Fuck.

Options raced through my mind, each worse than the last. We couldn't run— they'd already seen Tryggar. And if these were Soleil's men... I didn't let the thought go any further. If they even got a glimpse of my Riftborne branding, I'm sure some sort of torture would await us. But letting them return to Sídhe with news of us could destroy everything we'd planned.

"We need to make a move, Fia." Aether's voice was low, urgent. "It's your call."

I swallowed hard, tasting bile. "We take them out." The words felt like glass in my throat.

The crew had begun loading into the smaller boats when we moved. We shot across the water like living smoke, materializing on deck just as impenetrable darkness descended over the ship. Panicked shouts erupted around us.

I lunged toward a guard in Sídhe colors, shadows coiling around my fist—then I froze. Through the darkness, a flash of honey-blonde hair.

My heart stopped.

"Aether," I choked out. "Stop. Aether, stop!"

The darkness dissolved, and suddenly I was staring into aquamarine eyes I knew better than my own. Osta stood before me, terror morphing into shock as recognition dawned. Tears welled as she threw herself into my arms.

I couldn't move. Couldn't breathe. This couldn't be real. The last time I'd seen her, her eyes were wide with horror as a scream broke her throat. When they took me away from Emeraal. Now here she was, on a ship in Riftdremar, tears streaming down her neck. My Osta had always been sunshine and terrible jokes, not this trembling, broken thing.

Something cracked open inside me—a dam I'd built months ago, holding back every memory of her that hurt too much to face. Osta, who had been my sister in all but blood, both of us marked as Riftborne, both of us surviving on the edges of a society that never truly wanted us. We had found each other when we needed it most, two outcasts who turned their tiny flat into a sanctuary of laughter and warmth and safety.

I had dreamed of this moment so many times in my tower in

Ravenfell. Imagined all the things I would say, how I would explain everything. But now, holding her, feeling her shoulders shake with sobs against mine, words seemed impossible. How could I tell her that while she thought I was dead or worse, I had discovered the truth about our birthplace, about who I really was? That I had found answers to questions she'd whispered about late at night, wondering about our parents, about the war that made us orphans?

My Osta. The piece of my heart I'd left behind in Sídhe. She still smelled like vanilla and warmth, still felt like coming home. But we were both different now—changed by time and trauma and the weight of secrets I wasn't sure how to share–

"Well, that was almost quite the tragedy," a distantly familiar voice cut through my thoughts.

I pulled Osta behind me, looking up to find Lord Soleil watching us, Lady Soleil at his shoulder. *Not the General. Not Baelor.* Movement behind me drew my attention—Aether stood surrounded by guards, perfectly still, hands clasped behind his back. Though weapons were trained on him, his eyes remained fixed on me.

"Enough," Lord Soleil commanded. "Leave the man alone."

The instant the weapons lowered, Aether vanished, reappearing at my side like a shadow made flesh.

Rain pearled on the worn deck planks, each drop reflecting the sky above. The wood beneath my feet was smooth from years of boots and salt, dark patches showing where the sea had claimed its territory.

"What are you doing here?" I turned to Osta, but her wide eyes were fixed on Aether.

"Who's he?" she whispered, tears still tracking down her face.

"Osta, focus. What are you doing here?"

Her gaze slid to the Soleils, and something in her expression made me follow it.

Lady Soleil stepped forward, a gentle smile gracing her features. "I've been looking for you, Fia. Ever since you disappeared from Emeraal."

"Looking for me?" The words felt hollow in my throat. "What do you mean?"

Lord Soleil moved beside his wife. "That night, when we met, I realized immediately that you were not like us. Do you remember?"

The memory rushed back—his curious gaze, the weight of his words. *I'm glad you're on our side.* My heart skipped as understanding began to dawn. My eyes darted between the Soleils and Aether, who looked as confused as I felt.

"My wife, her focus allows her to see premonitions." Lord Soleil's voice carried a note of pride. "Sometimes they're just feelings, other times they're full-blown visions. She's an absolute marvel—"

Lady Soleil stopped him with a look. "As I said, I've been looking for you since you disappeared. And yesterday, I felt your presence back in this realm."

"I don't understand." I turned to Osta, whose tears hadn't stopped. She looked both exactly the same and completely different. Her honey-blonde hair still curled rebelliously in the damp air, but it had grown long past her shoulders now. New lines creased the corners of her eyes. She wore one of her old dresses, the blue one with tiny flowers that she'd sewn back when she still worked for Thearna, but it hung looser on her frame.

"I thought you were dead," her voice cracked. "When you disappeared... I became a mess, I couldn't function after that." She kept doing this thing with her hands—twisting her fingers together until the knuckles went white, then letting go. It was new, this nervous habit. Just like the dark circles under her eyes were new, and the way her smile seemed to tremble at the edges before fully forming. And I'd left her alone, drowning in grief while I discovered my own truths across the rip. The weight of it pressed against my chest until I could barely breathe.

"The Soleils," Osta continued, gesturing to the couple, "they saw how much I was suffering. And they finally told me the truth."

I looked back at them as Lord Soleil gripped the railing separating us.

"We never believed you to be dead. We never thought they would harm one of their own. Just like we knew no harm would come to us that night." He turned his eyes to Aether. "None of you have ever targeted civilians, despite what those in the Guard might say." Lord Soleil's tone grew serious. "I was young when Riftdremar rose up against Sídhe. Young, but vigilant. I knew the narrative they spun was a lie. Many knew back then, but few cared."

The rain seemed to let up as he spoke. "So when we began experiencing *attacks* on our Western borders, I allowed myself to get close to the Guard, allowed them to exploit my focus. And once I traveled to Emeraal, to Stormshire, and saw those towers of arcanite, I realized that this was yet another lie, folded beneath layers of carefully constructed propaganda and nationalism." He paused, collecting his thoughts. "But I still didn't know all of the details."

Lady Soleil stepped closer, her eyes finding mine. "We didn't know who this supposed enemy was, so I began searching after Henrick told me of his suspicions. And you all do well, keeping yourselves hidden. It took nearly a year before I was able to see anything at all through that darkness." Her gaze flickered to Aether.

"Eventually, I saw glimpses of a dying realm, green turning to ash." Her words hit me like a physical blow. I thought of my first sight of Umbrathia—the eternal eclipse, the withered crops, the hollow eyes of its people. How different would things be now if others in Sídhe had seen what the Soleils had seen? If we could make them believe past all of the lies.

The Soleils shared a meaningful look before Lord Soleil continued. "Since then, we have begun forming a small resistance, some normal citizens, some within the Guard, those that were willing to destroy their blood oaths. Much like you, I assume." His eyes were on me, but then they stretched past my shoulder, and I heard footsteps behind me.

"It's been a long time." The voice sent a jolt through me. I spun to find a man with shaggy blonde hair and familiar brown eyes—eyes of the Riftborne boy I'd grown up with in the House of Unity. Who had been one of my true friends in Sídhe. The last time I'd seen him, it had been outside of the Compound, when he looked at me like I was a stranger.

"Eron." His name came out as barely more than a breath as I walked toward him.

"When I saw you had joined the Guard, I didn't know what to think. How to talk to you. Because I was already a part of this, and..." He trailed off, uncertainty creasing his brow. "Well, I didn't know if I could trust you."

He offered a tentative smile and held out his hand. I looked down at it for a moment before pulling him into a hug instead.

When I turned back to Aether, his face was unreadable, but one eyebrow lifted slightly—a silent question. *Can we trust them?*

I sighed, taking in the scene around us. They made an odd collection on the rain-slicked deck—base guards in their uniforms standing beside civilians in travel-worn clothes. The Soleils seemed almost ethereal in their fine garments, Lady Soleil's silk dress rippling like water in the wind, while Lord Soleil's coat was punctured with buttons that matched the ship's brass fittings.

"Well, you found me," I said finally, turning back to Lady Soleil. "What did you want with me?"

"Can we discuss it over lunch?" Osta broke in, her voice

wavering slightly. "All of these emotions have left me dreadfully hungry."

Despite everything, I couldn't help the smile that tugged at my lips. Even after everything that had happened, she was still so perfectly *Osta*.

"Lunch would be splendid," Lord Soleil agreed. "Shall we exit the boat and discuss everything?"

My eyes found Aether's again, searching for guidance. Just moments ago, we'd been lost in each other, sharing shadows and secrets in the rain. Now here we stood, surrounded by people from my past, the lines between enemy and ally blurring as the sun peaked out from behind a cloud. His face remained carefully neutral, but I could see the shadows filtering through his void burns, ready to protect us both if this turned out to be anything other than what it seemed.

CHAPTER FORTY-SEVEN

Soleils' men had really outdone themselves.

A proper feast laid out on the cliffside, complete with linens that probably cost more than our old apartment. The spread was impressive—fresh bread, fruit I hadn't seen since leaving Sídhe, even wine in delicate glasses that looked hilariously out of place among the ruins. The ocean crashed against the rocks below, sending up spray that occasionally misted our faces.

Just the six of us sat at the table—me sandwiched between Osta and Aether, with Eron and the Soleils across from us. The rest of their people had spread throughout the ruins, giving us privacy while keeping watch. Every time I caught Osta stealing glances between me and Aether, she'd quickly look away.

"Before your disappearance," Lord Soleil began, breaking the awkward silence, "we had a decent network in place. My people in the Guard could create small gaps in patrols, moments where the Umbra could slip through unnoticed. With Kalea's visions guiding the timing..." He gestured to his wife.

Aether looked up from his untouched plate. "Am I supposed to be grateful for that?"

"I understand it's the bare minimum," Soleil said carefully. "But we are working with what we have."

Aether's golden eyes fixed on him, the silence stretching uncomfortably long.

"Why are you helping us at all?" I asked. "Your family must benefit from everything Sídhe has gained. You have no ties to Umbrathia, no reason to care about what happens to their people." I leaned forward, studying his face. "So what's in it for you?"

Lord Soleil's expression shifted, something darker crossing his features. He shared another look with his wife before responding, but I cut him off.

"The nobles in Sídhe have never been richer, never held more power. Yet here you are, risking everything to help the very realm you're stealing from."

Lord Soleil's expression hardened. "Prosperity built on the suffering of others isn't prosperity at all—it's parasitism. And it can't last." He set down his wine glass carefully. "People like my brother may be content watching our realm grow fat while another withers, but I've seen where this path leads." He shook his head. "What happens when there's nothing left to drain from Umbrathia? Where do you think the King will turn next?"

Lady Soleil reached for her husband's hand. "The nobles think they're untouchable in their golden towers. But they're just as blind as everyone else. This isn't sustainable—and when it falls apart, it won't matter how rich or powerful anyone was."

"Balance has been completely disrupted throughout the realms," Lord Soleil went on, "I know many do not follow the teachings of the Esprithe, but I've always been a devout follower of their wisdom. And this crime cannot go unpunished."

I watched Aether fight back a scoff, but something at Soleil's words tugged at me, and I wasn't sure why.

"Which is why we need something bigger than sneaking people across the border," Lord Soleil continued, refusing to wilt under

Aether's stare. "We've been gathering support, slowly. Carefully. We've even managed to turn a few officers within the Guard. But there's only so much we can do with that level of influence." He paused, sharing a look with his wife. "What we need is someone higher up. Someone with real power."

"A General," Lady Soleil added softly.

I felt Aether go still beside me.

"Osta mentioned how close you and Laryk Ashford had become," Lord Soleil said.

Heat rushed to my face. I shot a look at Osta, who suddenly found her plate fascinating. Then I felt Aether's eyes on me.

"Ah," he said quietly. "So that's him."

"What exactly do you expect me to do?" I asked, my fingers curling around my untouched wine glass.

"Ashford has always been... unpredictable," Lord Soleil said carefully. "He openly despises my brother, which is a point in his favor. But more than that, he's always been the one to question things. The only General who ever pushes back against direct orders." He leaned forward slightly. "If any of them could be convinced of the truth, it would be him."

Aether's eyes went dark as he pushed his plate forward a bit too forcefully. Osta leaned back in obvious fashion now, eyes darting between us, her head tilting slightly.

"The blood oaths have to come first," I said, trying to redirect the conversation. "It doesn't matter who we convince in the Guard if they can't speak about what they know."

"I couldn't agree more." Lord Soleil nodded. "The blood oaths must be destroyed."

"It was one of our plans," I admitted.

"A few of my guards work the front gates of the Compound," he offered. "They could grant you access—"

"We won't need that," Aether's voice cut through the air,

carrying a distrusting tone. "It'll only draw attention. Better to enter our own way."

"The place is heavily fortified," Lord Soleil countered.

Aether scoffed, still refusing to touch the food in front of him.

"But... whatever method you prefer," Soleil conceded, clearly noting Aether's darkening mood.

"They're all kept in Luminaria, right?" I asked. "Even the ones from other regions?"

"Yes, all stored at the Compound."

"Then that's our first priority," I said firmly, before turning to Lady Soleil. "Have you ever seen anything about the King? About his focus?"

Lady Soleil looked at her husband before responding. "I've never been able to see anything regarding him. I can only see clear visions of people I've actually interacted with." Her fingers traced the rim of her glass. "And I've never met him personally. Rather frustrating, actually."

"We learned something in Umbrathia." I shifted forward, lowering my voice though there was no one close enough to hear. "A tether—I mean, a focus. Called a siphon. One who can transfer essence from one place to another."

The table went silent. Even the waves seemed to still.

"It would make sense," Eron finally said, his eyes lighting up. "We've never known exactly how they're managing it. We thought it must have something to do with the arcanite towers."

"The arcanite is just storage." I watched their faces as understanding began to dawn. "But the King has to come second to all of this. His people need to be told the truth before we can do anything about him. They need to be given the opportunity to choose their own side in this war."

"You're right." Soleil nodded. "That has been our strategy all along. To cause disruption from within." His eyes found mine again. "And having the support of a General would be invaluable."

I shifted uncomfortably as Aether's leg pressed against mine under the table. "I wasn't planning on speaking with him," I said quietly.

"He's in Stormshire, with the rest of your old unit." Lord Soleil's words hit me like a physical blow.

My eyes snapped to Osta. "Does Nazul know anything about this?"

Osta's face fell, and she shook her head. "No. I haven't spoken with him much recently. Since... everything."

Another wave of guilt whipped through me.

"If you could infiltrate Stormshire, convince Ashford..." Soleil leaned forward. "It would be the turning point we all need."

I felt Aether go rigid beside me.

"We could help you, of course. I know it's late notice, but tomorrow night, all of the Generals will be attending a conference in the central control room. If you could find your way into his quarters, unseen—"

Aether stood so suddenly the table shook, shadows rippling around him like waves. "It's not happening." His voice was barely more than a growl.

I watched Osta's eyes go wide as she dropped her fork, the metal clanging against porcelain. Her gaze shot to me, but Aether was already too far gone.

"You have no idea who she is." The darkness in his voice made even Lord Soleil lean back. "To us. How important she is."

"Aether, stop." I pushed to my feet beside him.

"She may trust all of you, but I don't." Shadows writhed beneath his skin. "And I will not stand by while the heir to the throne of Umbrathia is led into a death trap."

Silence crashed over the table like a wave. Osta's wine glass slipped from her fingers, red liquid seeping into the white linen like blood. Her mouth opened and closed several times before she managed, "I'm sorry, you're a *what* now?"

Lord Soleil had gone completely still, his composure cracking around the edges. Even Lady Soleil seemed frozen.

"The heir to..." Eron managed. "But you were raised in Sídhe. In a group home. With—" He gestured at Osta, clearly struggling to make sense of it.

"Fia." Osta's voice had taken on that familiar tone she used when she seemed close to passing out. "Are you telling me that on top of being some sort of shadow-wielding, mind-controlling, prisoner-turned-not-so-prisoner, you're also *actual royalty?*"

"It's a recent discovery," I said quietly, shooting a narrowed glance towards Aether.

"Oh, well that makes it *so* much better." She let out a slightly hysterical laugh. "Here I was, thinking you were dead for months, and you're casually discovering you're the heir to an entire realm." She paused, then added, "Though I suppose this explains why you've always been so terrible at folding laundry."

"Osta," I started, but she was on a roll now.

"Does this mean I have to curtsy? Because I've been practicing, you know, working for the Soleils and all, but I'm still quite terrible at it. Though I suppose you are too—"

"The political implications alone—" Lord Soleil began.

"Oh please," Osta interrupted, rolling her eyes. Then she froze, horror spreading across her face. "Wait, should I not say things like that anymore? Are there rules about insulting foreign royalty? Am I going to be arrested? Because I have so many incriminating stories—"

"Osta!" But I was fighting back a smile now, grateful for her ability to cut through tension. But nothing about Aether's posture had changed, if anything, he seemed more riled than before.

"Excuse us for a moment," I managed, grabbing Aether's arm and dragging him towards the treeline.

"Can you simply not help yourself?" I seethed once we were out of earshot.

"They were going to send you into Stormshire," he growled, turning to face me. "Like some kind of liaison."

"That wasn't decided—"

"That's precisely what their plan depends on." His shadows writhed beneath his skin. "And now they know who you are, and the implications that come with that."

"You had no right to tell them" The words came out sharp.

"I had every right." His voice dropped dangerously low. "You're not just some soldier they can send on a suicide mission anymore. You're more—"

"I don't even know what I am!" The outburst surprised us both. "I've barely had time to process any of this myself, and now you've just announced it to everyone like it's some sort of shield you can use to protect me."

"Of course I'm going to protect you against those with nefarious intentions." Something flashed in his golden eyes.

"I can think for myself." I stepped closer, anger making me bold. "Make decisions for myself. You were going along with that quite nicely before. What changed?"

He didn't answer, but his eyes narrowed.

"Is this because of Ashford?" I raised an eyebrow. "Because I was already planning on finding my friends in the West, the ones I was in a unit with. I told you this last night."

"I don't understand why you should be the one to speak with him," he said, running a hand through his hair and looking off towards the ocean.

"Because they're right. He might not listen to anyone else," I admitted quietly, taking a step toward Aether. "If he could join this resistance that they've started, it could change everything."

I slipped my hand into his and the rigidness in his posture melted as he pulled me towards him, my face pressing against his chest.

"I don't want anything to happen to you." His chest vibrated with the words. The fear in his voice could have been about my safety, but something told me he was more afraid of losing whatever this was between us. This fragile thing we'd only just begun to understand.

CHAPTER FORTY-EIGHT

The waves crashed against the cliff as we finalized our plans. Despite the Soleils' new hesitation about my involvement—now that they knew exactly who I was—we'd agreed to move forward, confirming that once a fortnight, we would each send representatives to Riftdremar to exchange information and any new advancements. My stomach churned at the thought of returning to Sídhe, but we needed allies. We needed the truth to spread.

"It's about four hours by ship," Osta's voice cut through my thoughts as she approached, her familiar presence already soothing some of my anxiety. "Please tell me you've gotten over the seasickness. Remember that time we took the ferry to—"

Before she could finish, Aether let out a sharp whistle. Tryggar and Nihr emerged from the treeline, their massive forms casting shadows across the clearing. I caught Osta's expression shifting from confusion to terror as she stumbled backwards. Even the Soleils took a few steps back, their earlier composure cracking.

"We actually have our own ride," I said, fighting back a smile.

"On *that*?" Osta's voice cracked on the second word, her eyes wide as she watched Tryggar's wings flex in the sunlight.

"They're not so terrifying." I took Osta's hand and nearly dragged her towards the Vördr. Tryggar immediately pressed his head into my palm as we approached, his dark eyes gentle. Osta stood frozen beside me, clearly torn between fascination and fear.

She took a hesitant step forward, not taking her eyes off Tryggar. "Who *are* you?" Osta asked quietly.

I paused, not quite sure how to answer her question. "A lot has happened," I finally said, the words feeling inadequate even as they left my mouth.

"I can see that." Her eyes finally found mine. "You're different."

"You can pet him, you know," I teased, stepping aside to give Osta room to advance. She shot me a look that reminded me of all the times she'd tried to convince me to do something questionable and I'd refused. Eventually she sighed, taking a tentative step forward, reaching out to run her hand along the Vördr's neck.

"His name is Tryggar," I said as he nudged her gently, drawing a nervous giggle from her throat.

"Well you're just a big baby, now aren't you?" Osta cooed, her confidence growing with each stroke of his fur.

I glanced behind me, finding Aether at the cliff's edge. He stood perfectly still, staring out at the sea, hair being tousled by the wind. It had stopped raining, but the salt air and humidity had done marvelous things to his onyx waves, causing the ends to curl just above his shoulders, and at his temples.

"What's going on with the two of you?" Osta's question snapped my attention back. Heat rushed to my face as I realized she'd caught me staring.

"I don't really know," I managed, but Osta's knowing look told me she wasn't buying it.

"Come on, Fia. You know you can't lie to me about these things." She lowered her voice, though Aether was too far to hear. "If I thought Laryk's looks were intense..." She shook her head.

"The way that man watches you—it's like you're the only person who exists." She paused. "It's actually terrifying."

The heat in my cheeks spread down my neck, guilt and something else tangling in my chest.

"He's... protective," I offered weakly.

"And awfully brutish." Osta scrunched her nose. "Also quite rude, if I'm being honest." But then her eyes took on a mischievous glint, her voice dropping to a conspiratorial whisper. "But Esprithe if he isn't the most gorgeous man I've ever seen." Her eyes lingered on Aether's distant form.

I let out an awkward laugh. "I mean, he's okay."

"Those legs, those arms..." Osta continued, shaking her head. "He's huge. I'd be destroyed."

"Please stop." I nudged her, but couldn't help laughing at her typical lack of filter. Some things never changed, even when everything else had.

"Fine. You don't have to divulge all the dirty details." Osta pouted, crossing her arms. "But one day, you're telling me exactly how all of this happened."

I turned to her then, sliding a compact mirror into her hand before I could second-guess myself. Her fingers closed around it instinctively.

"When I return to Umbrathia, this is how we can communicate," I explained quietly. "We can't use it often, only for emergencies. But if you speak into it, I can hear you, and vice versa."

"That's brilliant." Osta turned it over in her hands, examining the delicate engravings. "Are you wanting me to keep this a secret?"

"For now." I nodded, glancing toward the Soleils. "I know you trust them. I want to, but I'm not there yet."

Osta slipped the compact into her pocket without further question. A silence built between us as I busied myself securing Tryggar's saddle, though I could feel the weight of what she wanted to ask.

"So... you're a Princess, then?" she finally managed, trying and failing to sound casual.

"I'm not sure how I feel about that word yet." I winced, turning to face her. "But technically. Yes."

"Does that mean you found out about your parents?" The excitement drained from her voice, replaced by something more fragile.

A pang of guilt hit me. Osta had always been the one desperate to know more about our past, about where we came from. She'd spent years wondering, hoping, while I'd tried to forget. And now here I was with answers about my own history, but nothing to offer her about hers.

"Yes," I said quietly. "Before Riftdremar fell, the Umbra were here." I looked around, suddenly aware of the weight of this place —where both our stories began. "Negotiating an alliance against Sídhe. My father... was the son of the current Queen. He died here when the continent burned."

"I'm sorry, Fia." The sadness in her eyes was almost too much to bear.

"I didn't know him," I cut her off with a look, shaking my head. "But this," I gestured toward Tryggar, who was watching us with those ancient, knowing eyes. "This was his Vördr."

Osta nodded, taking in the giant beast again with new understanding.

"And your mother?" she asked quietly.

"I don't know anything about her."

Osta bit her lip, and I couldn't tell if the look she gave me was understanding or sadness. Maybe both. But before either of us could say more, her eyes fixed on something behind me. I turned to find Aether approaching, his expression carefully neutral.

"We should leave soon," he said.

"I'm Osta." She extended her hand, the bubbly energy I remembered so well returning to her voice. "We were never officially acquainted."

I rolled my eyes as Aether stared at her outstretched hand for a moment too long before taking it in his, giving it an awkward shake.

"Pleasure," he managed.

"I'm sure you've heard all about me." Osta's eyes found mine, a knowing glint in them.

I couldn't help but laugh at the absurdity of this interaction—my best friend and the man who'd turned my world upside down, attempting small talk.

"I've heard things." The corner of his mouth twitched, that dimple threatening to appear.

"All good things," I assured Osta quickly.

She raised an eyebrow at me. "What else is there to report?"

"Nothing, of course." I laughed, but my attention had shifted to Aether. He stood there, clearly uncomfortable with the social niceties, making no attempt to hide it. No false smiles, no practiced pleasantries. Just him, unapologetically himself. Something warm took root in my chest at the realization—how he never pretended to be anything other than what he was. Even now, when diplomacy might serve him better.

I pulled Osta into a tight hug, trying to convey everything I couldn't say. "I promise we'll speak soon."

She whispered against my hair, "I love you."

"I love you too," I said, but the words caught in my throat.

When we pulled apart, Osta merely turned towards Aether and patted his chest. "Take care of her," she said, like he wasn't the most lethal person she'd ever met. Like he wasn't a warrior who could tear armies apart. I watched his expression shift at the touch, his shoulders going rigid, and had to bite back a laugh as Osta simply skipped back toward the Soleils, completely unfazed.

Aether cocked his head to the side, and I merely shrugged.

"So that's the best friend?" he asked, still looking slightly stunned.

"The very one."

"I'm still doubtful about your judgment." But when I nudged him, he finally broke into a full smile. My breath caught—he was devastating like this, all sharp edges softened by that dimple, those golden eyes bright with amusement. Perhaps he truly was the most gorgeous man I'd ever seen.

We mounted the Vördr as Lord Soleil took a few steps forward.

"Good luck," he said with a solemn nod, which Lady Soleil mirrored. Eron offered a simple wave.

As we guided the Vördr to a clear spot for takeoff, my mind raced with everything that awaited us in Sídhe. But as Tryggar's wings spread wide, preparing to launch us into the sky, I felt Aether's presence behind me like an anchor. Whatever came next, at least we were in this together.

Of

RADIANTHIAN MOUNTAINS

Fort Agate

Aedenvale

MYLITHIAN EXPANSE

Campgrounds

STORMSHIRE REACH

Emeraal

THE TEAR

CRESCENT TOWER

OBSCURA MARSH

YAELAREND

Kiltdremar

BLOODTHORNE HIGHLANDS

Pathora Estate

PRAELYTHIAN KEEP

Luminaria

Aithroain Sea

SCARLET COAST

CHAPTER FORTY-NINE

TRYGGAR'S WINGS cast rippling shadows across the forest floor as we descended into the Grove. The ancient trees reached toward us with gnarled fingers, their branches still bare from winter's touch. I paused, taking everything in—the smell of fresh flowers, the cool breeze rolling in from the Highlands up North. I glanced over at Aether, whose eyes had fallen to the ground, some unreadable expression crossing his face.

"This isn't anywhere near the Western border," he said quietly, dismounting Nihr beside me.

"No." I ran my hand along Tryggar's neck, feeling his muscles twitch beneath my palm. "But it's where the Compound is—where they keep the blood oaths. All of them." I turned toward the city sprawling beyond the trees, its towers piercing the morning sky. "This is Luminaria."

"The Grove stays relatively empty outside of solstice celebrations," I explained, but my voice faltered as memories flooded back—Bekha and Jordaan, their silent screams echoing through these very trees as my focus tore through their minds. Laryk's face when he found me, his eyes observing me with something dark—understanding, maybe. Or pity. That was the moment everything changed.

Now I stood in the same spot, a different person entirely.

I turned to Tryggar, pressing my forehead against his. "Stay hidden," I whispered. "No more curious impulses like in Riftdremar." His dark eyes held mine, and I felt an unfamiliar ache—wondering if my father had once spoken to him like this. "Stay safe."

Nihr was already melting into the treeline, but Tryggar lingered for a moment, nudging my hand before following.

"There's somewhere we need to go first," I said, turning to Aether. "The Apothecary."

His brow furrowed. "The one you used to work at?"

"Yes. There's someone I need to see." I moved toward the city's edge, where shadow met stone. "Someone important."

Aether fell into step beside me as we dissolved into darkness, flowing from tree to tree until forest became alleyway. Luminaria sprawled before us in all its glory—white marble and gilded towers reaching toward the clouds, streets paved with stones that sparkled in the sunlight between all of the vines and moss, canals breaking the city into pieces. Once, I'd found it beautiful. Now I saw it differently—every shimmering surface seemed to mock the ash-covered streets of Ravenfell.

"So this is how the other half lives." Aether's voice carried a dry edge as we melted between shadows, going in and out of our spectre forms. "Rather gaudy, isn't it?"

I glanced up at the towering domes, their golden caps catching sunlight. Everything gleamed with an artificial brightness that made my eyes ache. "It does feel... different now."

"Different how?"

We pressed against a wall as a merchant cart rattled past, the sound of its wheels against cobblestone almost deafening.

"Like a mask," I whispered once the street cleared. I led us down another alley, this one darker, safer. "When I lived here, I thought the city was beautiful."

Aether's shadows curled around mine as we moved. "And this Apothecary— it's worth the risk of being seen?"

"Ma runs it. We can trust her." The words caught in my throat. "She's... she took me in when no one else would. Gave me work when others saw nothing but my branding. She's family." I paused at the mouth of another alley, checking for passersby. "She never saw me as anything but Fia. Never wanted me to be anything else."

"Until now?" Something in his tone made me turn to him.

"What do you mean?"

"When she learns what you are. Who you are." His golden eyes found mine through the darkness. "Will she still see you the same way?"

The question hit harder than I expected. "I don't know what's happened since I've been gone," I admitted. "But I need to find out."

A group of nobles passed by, their silk robes rustling against stone. We waited, pressed into the shadows of a doorway.

"And if she alerts the Guard?" Aether's question was barely a breath against my ear.

"She won't." But even as I said it, a sliver of doubt crept in. She had been mass-producing the breathing tonics for the Western strongholds. Just as I had asked her to. Guilt churned through me as my eyes found the cobblestones. "Ma's different. She sees past what others can't. Or won't."

We emerged into another alley, this one achingly familiar. The Apothecary's worn sign creaked in the morning breeze, herbs painted in fading gold across weathered wood. My pulse began to race as we approached.

Not so long ago, I'd stood in this very spot, desperate to warn Ma about the Wraiths devouring the Western border. Now I was back with one of those supposed monsters, trying to undo everything I'd once believed. The girl I'd been then wouldn't recognize me now—wouldn't understand how I'd become this.

"No one's inside," I whispered, reaching out with my focus to confirm what I already suspected. "Just Ma, in the back room."

Aether's form shifted beside me. "I'll stay in the shadows."

I nodded, my hand already reaching for the handle. The familiar bell chimed as I stepped inside, and for a moment, everything felt wrong. The usual herbs and spices that had once perfumed the air were gone, replaced by the sharp tang of brine. Dust coated the shelves where dried flowers once bloomed, and bottles sat askew, their contents looking dull and far past their expiration date.

"I'll be right with you!" Ma's voice called from the back, and my throat tightened at the sound. I turned the lock on the door with trembling fingers.

My boots scraped against the floor as I moved toward the back room, each step feeling heavier than the last. Ma stood at her workbench, her silver-streaked hair falling loose from its bun and the sight alone tugged at my heart in a ferocious way. Somehow, there were hibiscus stains dotting the back of her work robe in places that seemed impossible to reach. I took a step closer as she stirred something in a cauldron, the motion seeming mechanical and strained.

"Just a moment," she said, still not turning.

"Ma."

The glass vial slipped from her fingers, shattering against the floor. She spun around, her face draining of color as our eyes met.

"Fia?" Her voice cracked on my name, and suddenly I was moving, crossing the space between us as tears blurred my vision.

Ma's arms wrapped around me with crushing force, and I buried my face in her shoulder, breathing in the familiar scent of burning rosemary. Her whole body trembled as she held me, or maybe I was the one shaking. I couldn't tell anymore.

"I thought—" Her voice broke. She pulled back, her hands moving to cup my face, eyes searching mine as if she couldn't quite believe what she was seeing. "I thought..." Fresh tears spilled down her cheeks. "How is this possible? How are you here?"

"I'm so sorry," I whispered, the words feeling inadequate. "I wanted to tell you I was alive, but I couldn't—"

"Where have you been?" Her voice cracked again, hands still trembling against my face. "All this time, I thought those monsters had—" She stopped, unable to finish the thought.

I caught her hands in mine. "Ma, there's so much you need to know. Everything we thought... it's not what we believed. None of it is."

Her eyes searched mine, confusion creasing her brow. "What do you mean?"

"I just came from Riftdremar." The words fell between us, and Ma's eyes went wild.

"What?"

"There are tears between realms—rips, we call them." My voice shook despite my efforts to keep it steady. "When I was in the Guard, we only knew about the one in the West. But there's another. In Riftdremar."

"You've been in another realm—this whole time?" Her hands trembled as she removed her hand from mine and pushed her hair back from her face.

"The Wraiths I told you about last time..." I swallowed hard. "That's just how they hide themselves—they're not monsters, Ma. They're people, just like us. A race called Kalfar." The words tumbled out faster now. "They've been attacking the Western border because they're desperate. The Isle has been stealing essence from them for a decade. Their entire realm is dying because of Sídhe."

Ma dropped onto her stool, but her eyes never left my face. I recognized that look—the one she got when she was putting pieces together.

"Tell me everything," she said quietly.

I nodded, relief crashing through me, washing away any doubts. "It's a lot," I warned her.

"I can handle it."

"First, we were in Riftdremar looking for arcanite. We found the old mines where—"

"Arcanite?" She blinked, as if recalling a memory.

"That's what started all of this." I let out a breath, the weight of everything I needed to explain suddenly crushing. "Sídhe stole the arcanite from Riftdremar. Then they burned it to the ground to hide what they'd done."

"But why?" She leaned forward. "Why did they need it so badly?"

"There's this ability—a focus that can steal essence and move it somewhere else. It's called a siphon." I gave her a knowing look. "Remember your plants, Ma? How the arcanite killed them when you thought it would help them grow?" Something flickered in her eyes. "They lied to us about what it does. It doesn't create essence—it stores it. It can take or give to the land, based on how the energy in it is directed..."

Ma's eyes were darting back and forth now, across the room.

"The King of Sídhe. We think he's a siphon," I finally finished.

Ma leaned back, running both hands through her hair until it fell completely loose from its bun. After what felt like forever, she let out a laugh that sounded more like defeat. "I always knew the Guard was pure fucking evil."

"I was wrong about them." I moved closer, meeting her eyes. "I should have trusted your gut. It's always right. But there's so much more to it. The King—he's lying to everyone. Most people in the Guard believe they're defending our realm. We have to get the truth out somehow. It's the only way to end the bloodshed."

"I guess..." She trailed off, her eyes finding mine again. "I don't understand. Why you?"

I pressed my lips together, choosing my words carefully. "They recognized me," I finally said. "You know I've never fit in here."

"Recognized you?" The shock was back in her voice.

"I'm one of them." My eyes darted toward the front room. "Well, in part... My father was Kalfar, my mother Aossí. They both died in Riftdremar when it fell."

Ma looked around the room like she might find answers written on the walls. "Esprithe be damned," she whispered.

"There's another thing, actually..." I took a deep breath. "I didn't come here alone."

Her eyebrow shot up. "One of the Wraiths is here?"

"He's not a wraith, Ma." I couldn't help but smile.

"He's in this shop right now?" Her eyes narrowed as they swept across the space. "Where?"

"Aether," I called softly.

Shadows writhed beside me, and suddenly Aether was there. It nearly flipped my world upside down to see him standing so close to the desk I had worked at for years before even knowing he existed—with his void burns trailing up his neck like dark veins, disappearing into his raven hair. The metal of his piercings reflected the firelight beneath the cauldron, the fire that Ma had probably started with her own hands.

His golden eyes assessed Ma carefully, but to my surprise, she didn't flinch. Her gaze lingered on the way his arm wrapped around my waist, and heat rushed to my face.

A moment passed in excruciating silence as the two merely observed each other.

Aether finally nodded, face neutral. "Nice to make your acquaintance."

Ma's eyes drifted from me, to Aether, then back to me, her expression completely unreadable. Finally, she let out a sigh.

"Well, that's a real man if I've ever seen one." Ma chuckled, raising her arms as if to surrender.

I caught Aether's gaze, mortified, but there was that damn dimple threatening to show as he fought back a smile.

"What an improvement." Ma let out a sigh of relief before slapping me on the shoulder. "Good job, kiddo."

The laugh that burst from Aether caught me off guard—deep and genuine. He looked irritatingly pleased with himself as he cocked his head to the side. "I tend to agree."

"And a sense of humor." Ma nodded approvingly. "Yes, I like him."

"Okay, well that's just about enough pleasantries, I think." My face felt like it was on fire.

Ma turned back to her cauldron, lifting the lid to peer inside. "I assume you want me to stop making this then?" She asked, stirring the contents.

I glanced up at Aether, taking his hand. "Remember the breathing tonics I told you about?"

His eyes fixed on the cauldron before finding mine again. He nodded once, understanding dawning in his expression.

"Ma is the one who created them," I said, the words tasting bitter. "For me. When she thought I might need them in the West. It was my idea for her to make more for the Guard."

Aether's body went rigid beside me, but he nodded once. "I suppose that makes sense," he managed, though his words were stilted.

"Yeah, those arms are going to come in handy." Ma broke through the slight tension, eyes fixed on the leather stretched across Aether's bicep. "I have a lot of crates in the back."

That dimple finally appeared as Aether grinned. I couldn't help but laugh, shaking my head at both of them.

"You can't stop making them." I walked over to where she stood. "There's already a resistance forming in Sídhe. I don't believe the King is aware of it. But there are people who know the truth, who want to help. If you suddenly stop production, it might draw suspicion that we can't afford right now." I paused, considering. "Though if you could make them weaker..."

Ma sighed, running a hand along the rim of her cauldron. "And here I was hoping my shop wouldn't have to smell like fish guts anymore." She shook her head. "But you're right." Then her eyes narrowed, that familiar calculating look crossing her face. "Though that brings me to my next question."

I raised an eyebrow.

"What are we going to do about the King?" She shrugged like she was asking about the weather. "Seems like the simplest answer, doesn't it? Take him out, the draining stops."

"We have to work from the bottom up," I said, catching Aether's slight nod of approval. "Let the truth spread first. If the King dies and people don't understand why..." I trailed off, letting her fill in the blanks.

"That sounds complicated." Ma scrunched her nose.

"It's the best way. Besides, the royal guards are nearly impenetrable. We don't have access. Not yet."

Ma nodded, but something flickered behind her eyes—a thought she wasn't sharing. Finally, she asked, "So are you leaving again? Going back to—?"

"Umbrathia," Aether supplied.

"Right." Ma's eyes fixed on me, seeing too much as always.

I glanced at Aether, caught between two worlds again. How could I explain that I belonged to both now? That I couldn't simply choose one over the other?

"I have to. At least for now—"

"For now?" The edge in Aether's voice made my heart sink. We hadn't discussed this—what would happen after. After the truth spread, after the King was dealt with. After everything changed.

Ma looked between us, crossing her arms. The tension in the

room had shifted. "What are you not telling me, Fia?" Her eyes held that knowing look I'd seen a thousand times before. "Keeping secrets has never worked out well for you in the past."

I pressed my lips together. "My father was important there." I tried to sound casual, but my voice wavered. "Someone with power."

Ma tilted her head, and I knew she wasn't buying it. "Important how?" she asked.

"You're going to want to sit down," I said, finding my own chair.

The words poured out then—everything about my father being Prince Andrial Valtýr, about being a Duskbound and what that meant. I told her how I'd essentially joined the Umbra forces, which earned an eye-roll that was so perfectly *Ma* I nearly cracked a smile. I explained the Void, about shadow wielders, about Tryggar choosing me. With each revelation, Ma's expression shifted between disbelief and that furrowed brow. When I finally finished, the silence felt heavy with everything I'd just dumped on her.

Ma simply looked at me for a long moment, then nodded once. "Well, I know you're royalty and everything." She stood, turning back to her desk and grabbed something. When she faced us again, she held out a pair of garden shears. "But can you go fetch some peakroot from the greenhouse? If we're going to take down this kingdom, we'll need to dull down this potion."

I accepted the shears with a smile, grateful for her casual acceptance—the way I was hoping she'd react. The way I'd hoped everyone would react—like I was still me.

Ma winked before turning to Aether. "And you." She motioned toward him. "Follow me. I've got some shipments to bring in, and my back is not what it used to be." She started toward the storage area, and Aether followed, a smile quirking on his lips as he disappeared through the doorway.

Night crept over Luminaria, casting long shadows through the shop windows. The familiar scent of burning herbs intermingled with something sharper—whatever Ma was brewing in the back room. She had closed the shop for the rest of the day so that we could prepare. I leaned over a map spread across the counter, the parchment worn at the edges from when I'd tried to escape last summer.

"Here." I traced a path with my finger, feeling Aether's warmth as he stood close beside me. "We can head North, find somewhere to stay in Obsidia."

"A farming village?" His eyes followed my hand across the map.

"Small, quiet. If we get there late enough, we shouldn't draw attention." I glanced up at him. "Plus, there's dense forest surrounding it. The Vördr will have plenty of cover."

He nodded, studying the route. "And then?"

"We go around the North side of the central range, into Aedenvale."

"Through the mountains would be faster."

"The Guard uses a campground there when they travel West." The words rushed out before I could stop them. Memories flooded back—that night in the mountains, discovering I could walk through dreams. Heat rushed to my face as I remembered the dream of Laryk's I'd stumbled into. The one about me.

Aether's eyebrow lifted slightly, but he said nothing more.

"Besides," I added quickly, "approaching from the North gives us an advantage. Most forces will be further Southwest, near the tear." I traced the final stretch of our route. "I've never been to Stormshire before, so once we're there..."

"We'll have to improvise," he finished, though I caught the reluctance in his tone.

The shop had grown dark enough that Ma lit the lanterns, their flames casting dancing shadows across the walls. She emerged from the back room, carrying a wooden crate that she handed to Aether.

His confused look shifted between the crate and me.

"Healing potions," Ma said, dusting off her hands. "For your realm."

"Ma—" I started, but she cut me off.

"It's not much, but it's something." She shrugged, although I saw the weight in her eyes. "With a realm dying, I highly doubt you still have access to the resources to make them."

Pain flickered across Aether's face as he looked down at the crate. "No, we don't." When he met Ma's eyes again, his voice was rough. "Thank you."

"We can't exactly carry these with us to the Compound—" I began.

"I'll leave them in the back, behind the greenhouses." Ma was already moving, motioning for Aether to set the crate down. "You can collect them before heading North."

"I'll take them out there." Aether's voice was soft as he lifted the crate again, disappearing through the back door.

Ma sank into her chair with a sigh, rolling her shoulders. "I'm sorry I can't be of more help, kid."

"You've done plenty, Ma." I moved to stand beside her chair, my eyes already beginning to mist over.

"Honestly, I feel a bit helpless just sitting around while all of you go off on these missions." Her smile was small, sad in a way that made my heart ache. "I didn't take enough initiative when I was young. Didn't go on these kinds of adventures."

I reached into my bag, pulling out one of Raven's compacts. Ma's eyebrow raised as I placed it in her hands.

"And this is?"

"We can use it to communicate while I'm gone." I watched as

she looked at it with reluctance. "We'll need all the eyes and ears we can manage over here. So Ma, you're not useless. You're our spy."

She turned the mirror over in her hands, examining the delicate engravings. "Well this is some fancy sorcery." She shook her head. "I don't really understand how talking to my reflection somehow connects me with you. But I'll take your word for it."

I couldn't help but laugh.

"We should get going," I managed. Ma set the mirror down carefully, like it was something precious, and stood.

For a moment, we just looked at each other. The shop seemed to close in around us, heavy with memories—countless afternoons spent grinding herbs, early mornings re-organizing shelves, late nights preparing tonics for the Sídhe elite, laughing at the absurdity until we nearly cried. She'd given me everything when I had nothing. A home. A purpose. Love without conditions.

"You know," Ma's voice was rough as she pulled me into a hug, "I always wondered why you seemed so different from us." Her arms tightened around me. "But now I think maybe you were meant for something bigger than Sídhe could offer."

"Ma—" My voice cracked.

"No, listen." She pulled back, her hands on my shoulders. "I've spent years watching you try to make yourself smaller, trying to fit into boxes that this realm forced you into. But you never could, could you?" Her eyes were bright with tears. "Because you're not meant to be small, Fia. You never were."

I broke then, tears spilling down my cheeks as I fell back into her arms. She smelled like home—like rosemary and fire. "I'm scared," I whispered against her shoulder.

"Good." She stroked my hair. "Fear keeps you sharp. Keeps you from doing anything too stupid." She paused. "Well, more stupid than usual."

The back door creaked open, and I knew Aether had returned. Ma pulled back, wiping her eyes with the back of her hand.

"You take care of my girl," she said to him, and though her voice shook, there was steel beneath it.

"Always," he said it like a vow.

Ma nodded once, then turned back to me. "Go change the world, kid." She pressed a kiss to my forehead. "Just try not to burn it all down in the process."

I laughed through my tears, and then she was shoving us toward the door, muttering about how she wasn't good at goodbyes. But as we slipped into the darkness, I caught one last glimpse of her through the window—standing alone in her shop, holding that mirror like an anchor.

CHAPTER FIFTY

A BLOCK FROM THE COMPOUND, we pressed against the cold stone of an alley wall. The fortress-like building stretched countless stories into the sky, its black stone walls reflecting the moonlight. Guard towers punctuated each corner, though only the front entrance was lit by iron lanterns that cast pools of yellow light across the cobblestones.

"I'm following your lead," Aether said, his voice low beside me, "but we're sticking to the plan. We destroy the blood oaths, then we leave. Nothing more."

I nodded, watching the main gates where two guards in crisp white shirts lounged against their posts. Their silver badges gleamed as they chatted, clearly relaxed in the quieter evening hours. Before, the entrance would have been flooded with personnel, but with everyone stationed out West, it looked like a ghost of its former self.

"This way." I pulled us toward the Eastern wall where the healers' wing jutted out from the main building. Our forms dissolved into shadow as we approached. A simple metal door broke up the otherwise smooth surface.

I reached out with my focus, tracking the minds within. One silver orb of consciousness passed by on the other side, growing fainter as footsteps echoed away.

"Now," I whispered, and we slipped through like smoke.

Inside, rows of storage rooms lined a narrow hallway, their oak doors marked with brass plaques. The air smelled of herbs and antiseptic—so different from the metallic tang of the training gyms. No minds glowed behind these doors, thankfully. I led us right, our shadows hugging the walls until the corridor opened into a wider space. There, several minds were clustered in a room with light spilling out from under the door.

The infirmary. We were close.

"It's there." My pulse quickened as I spotted the heavy iron door at the end of the hall—the blood oath chamber.

Multiple locks lined the door's edge, but they meant nothing to us now. We shifted through like mist, materializing in a chamber that remained unchanged from the last time I'd broken in. Hundreds of glass vials lined the walls from floor to ceiling, each one containing tiny papers dotted with crimson. Black vines writhed between them, weeping a sticky sap that dripped onto the floor. The whole room felt wrong—like walking into something alive and hungry.

In stone planters along the walls, shards of arcanite glowed with that familiar violet-blue light. The same ones I'd seen months ago, when I'd come here to collect my own vial.

Aether paused beside me, tension radiating from his frame. "Bloodweep," he said, his voice tight. "We used it in Umbrathia too, before the Queen banned it. She called it barbaric."

"Well, she wasn't wrong." I remembered how the sap had coated my arm that first time, how it had seemed to reach for me with a mind of its own.

"The vials mean nothing without the plant." Aether moved closer to one of the planters, studying the twisted vines. "Kill it, and the oaths dry up. They might not notice for weeks, maybe even longer."

"Better than smashing everything." I glanced at the thousands of vials. "So how do we kill this thing?"

"Like any other plant." He stepped up to the first planter, holding his hand over the dark soil. "We destroy it from the inside out."

I watched, transfixed, as the vines began to tremble. Beneath the surface, something cracked—the sound of roots snapping echoing through the chamber. Aether moved methodically from planter to planter, that deadly grace in every movement as the bloodied leaves shook beneath his touch.

"Impressive," I whispered as he finished the last one.

"I can be gentle when the need arises." That dimple appeared as he smirked.

Heat rushed to my face at his insinuation.

"Not every use of my ability has to be a massacre," he added, cocking his head. I bit back a smile as I knelt down, examining one of the vials at eye level. The bright crimson that had stained the paper inside was already dulling, turning an ugly brown.

"It's working," I breathed, adrenaline flooding me.

Without thinking, I was moving—reaching for him. His arms surrounded me as I pulled his face down, our lips meeting with an urgency that surprised us both. The kiss tasted like victory, though we still had a long road ahead.

"We need to go," he nearly groaned against my mouth, but his hands tightened at my waist.

We made it to the door before I stopped suddenly, causing Aether to collide with my back. His arm slid around me, pulling me against his chest. "What is it?" he murmured against my hair.

I turned in his embrace. "I have an idea."

"Fia." My name was a warning on his lips, his golden eyes sharpening. "That was not part of the plan. We have to leave. Now."

"But we're already in here..." I pressed my hands against his chest. "What if we could get more information on Stormshire? A layout, or maps?"

Frustration creased his features as he looked down at me. "What did you have in mind?" His voice was flat.

"I think I know where to look. And it should be empty."

"Empty?"

Before he could protest further, I reached out with my web, scanning the hallway. A few minds moved about, but as soon as they turned into their respective rooms, I shifted into shadow form. We raced through the healers' wing like smoke, emerging into the circular lobby just before the social area. A set of spiral stairs beckoned from the left. I felt Aether's darkness brush against mine as we rushed up them, staying close to the walls.

At the top, I found the door I was looking for. One quick check confirmed it was empty, and we slipped through.

The office was exactly as I remembered—walls of rough gray stone stretching up to meet dark wooden beams. A massive mahogany desk dominated one side, its surface meticulously organized. On the other, leather furniture sat arranged on a cowskin rug, looking barely used. Everything about the space spoke of rigid control. *His* rigid control.

I flew to the desk, yanking open drawers and rifling through papers.

"Where are we?" Aether asked, leaning against the wall.

I ignored him, pulling out scrolls and spreading them across the desk's surface. Maps of Fort Agate and Emeraal—fortresses, just not the right one. My hands moved faster, opening another drawer.

Aether's form moved toward the hallway, immediately going still as he peered into one of the rooms—Laryk's bedroom. One I'd never entered before. "How did you know it would be empty?" he asked, his voice taking on a dark quality.

My fingers brushed something small and jagged. I pulled out a piece of red jasper—the one I'd given Laryk months ago during training, on a day when his mind seemed elsewhere. The stone felt warm in my palm, heavy with memories I couldn't afford right now. I returned it quickly to its hiding place.

"It's got to be here somewhere," I muttered, turning to the cabinets behind me.

"It's his, isn't it?" Aether's voice had gone completely cold.

I stilled. "Yes."

In my periphery, I saw Aether's form dissolve into shadow, reappearing near the exterior door, as if he was dying to get out of here. Frustration mounted as I searched faster, knowing we'd stayed too long.

Footsteps echoed in the hallway.

"We have to leave," Aether's words cut through the silence.

The footsteps paused outside. I reached out with my focus—someone stood just beyond the door. My hands moved frantically through the remaining drawers as the knob began to turn. *It couldn't be him, could it?*

"Now, Fia." The edge in Aether's voice was dangerous.

The door creaked open just as my fingers closed around another set of scrolls. I grabbed them, praying that one of them held the layout to Stormshire—that this hadn't been for nothing. Quickly, just as footsteps rounded the corner, I shifted into darkness, catching a glimpse of an emerald uniform before following Aether through the wall and into the night.

Why was a royal guard in Laryk's room?

We raced across rooftops and through alleyways until we reached the familiar street behind the Apothecary. The greenhouse loomed ahead, its glass panels reflecting moonlight. Behind it, nestled between herb gardens and storage sheds, we found the crate of healing potions.

Aether lifted it easily, and we made our way through the city toward the Grove. My heart didn't slow its frantic beating until we reached the trees, their branches offering welcome cover as we began searching for the Vördr.

"Tryggar?" I whispered into the darkness, scanning between the trees. Beside me, Aether moved with lethal silence, but the tension rolling off him was almost palpable.

Unable to stand the weight of it any longer, I pulled out the scrolls with trembling fingers. *Please let it be here.* The first two were supply lists, the third a report on Guard rotations. But the fourth—I nearly gasped as I unrolled it. Stormshire's layout spread before me in precise detail, every corridor and chamber carefully marked.

"I have it," I breathed, a smile breaking across my face.

Aether said nothing. His jaw was set, eyes fixed ahead as we waded deeper into the forest.

"I know I cut it close," I admitted, "but it was worth it. Now we're not entirely blind."

He gave a single nod, but the movement looked pained, like he was barely containing something darker.

I rushed forward, placing myself in front of him. He stopped just before we collided, but wouldn't meet my eyes.

"What's wrong?" I asked. His jaw tightened further as he stepped back, running a hand through his hair and letting out a long, slow breath.

The silence stretched between us, broken only by leaves rustling overhead. When he finally looked at me, the intensity in his eyes made me feel like I was drowning in molten gold.

"I'm happy you found what you were looking for," he said, his voice carefully level as he brushed past me.

I turned to follow, catching sight of Tryggar's silver form materializing through the trees. Aether walked straight for Nihr, and Tryggar let out a warning growl as he passed. Aether ignored it completely.

"Not now," I whispered as Tryggar stomped excitedly at my approach. "Someone's in a mood." I watched Aether mount his Vördr in one fluid motion, his shoulders rigid beneath his leathers.

The forest opened up ahead, giving the Vördr enough space to spread their massive wings. We took to the sky in silence, climbing until we disappeared into the clouds. For an hour we flew, the tension so thick I could barely breathe. Anger radiated from Aether's direction, but I didn't dare press him further.

The clouds provided excellent cover, but they also obscured the land below. I dipped beneath them briefly, my eyes falling onto a silver ribbon cutting through darkness—the Sprithe River. My heart dropped as memories rushed back—watching helplessly as my friends drowned in those currents, victims of the very Guard I'd later joined. I forced the thoughts away, scanning North until I spotted Obsidia's windmills turning lazily in the night air, thick forests sprawling behind them.

We landed in those woods without being seen, then moved like smoke through the sleeping village. The inn appeared ahead—a weathered two-story building at the edge of town, warm light spilling from its windows.

"I'll get us a room," I said, already pulling up my hood to hide my distinctive hair. "Stay out here."

Aether's expression darkened. "That's not—"

"You'll draw too much attention," I cut him off. Those golden eyes and void burns would be impossible to hide. People would certainly have *questions*. After a moment of clear internal struggle, he melted back into the shadows.

I pushed open the heavy wooden door, a bell chiming softly overhead. The common room was mostly empty—a few farmers nursing ales in the corner, an old man dozing by the hearth. Worn tables and chairs filled the space, and the whole room smelled of pipe smoke and cooking meat.

Behind a scarred wooden counter, a woman with gray-streaked

hair looked up from her ledger. Her eyes narrowed slightly as she took in my cloaked figure.

"Need a room?" she asked, her voice carrying that Northern lilt I remembered from those that visited Luminaria for solstices, filtering into the apothecary for tonics to *boost* their experience.

"Just for the night," I said, keeping my head slightly bowed. "We'll be gone before first light."

Her eyebrow lifted at *we* but she didn't comment. "Two silvers," she said, already reaching for a key. "Up the stairs, last door on the right. Extra blankets in the chest if you need them." She paused. "No funny business, mind. These walls are thin as paper."

I felt heat rush to my face as I handed over the coins. "Of course not."

She gave me a knowing look that only made me blush harder, then turned back to her ledger. I clutched the key and hurried toward the stairs, painfully aware of how the old wood creaked beneath my feet.

The room was small but clean, with a narrow bed, a decent sized chair by the hearth, and a window overlooking the forest. Perfect for a quick escape if needed. I moved to the glass and just as I was about to open it, Aether materialized beside me, still radiating that careful distance that made my chest ache.

Whatever was brewing beneath his controlled exterior, I had a feeling we wouldn't be able to avoid it much longer.

CHAPTER FIFTY-ONE

AETHER STOOD at the window like a statue, staring into the darkness beyond. I found a small door tucked into the corner of our room and peeked inside—a washroom, if you could call it that. Someone had turned an old barrel into a makeshift tub, and beside it sat a bucket of water, still warm from the hearth. Perfect.

Given how distant Aether had been since leaving the Compound, a moment alone seemed wise.

The warm water was a blessing after everything we'd done today. I washed quickly, then wrapped myself in one of the worn towels left on a hook. My leathers lay in a heap on the floor, and the thought of putting them back on made me cringe. My clean clothes were in my satchel—which I'd left by the window. By Aether.

When I stepped back into the bedroom, he hadn't moved an inch. He glanced over his shoulder at my footsteps, then turned away just as quickly. But not before I noticed the dark stubble shadowing his jaw, a sight that had me biting back a smile. If he was lovely before, this was maddening.

"Are we ever going to discuss what's bothering you?" I asked.

Aether turned, leaning against the wall but still avoiding my eyes. He shook his head as his gaze found the floor. "I don't want to be cruel to you," he said, dragging a hand over his mouth. "I'm just trying to process this."

I moved to sit on the edge of the bed. "Talk to me."

"I haven't done this before. Felt things like this." His voice was rough. "Not that I can remember, at least." He looked almost pained, like each word was being torn from him.

"I know I can't blame you for anything that happened before," he added quickly. "I'm just trying to rationalize why it affects me this way."

I watched him struggle, could practically see the thoughts racing behind those golden eyes. "Aether..." I trailed off, searching for the right words. "Laryk and I—it's not what you're thinking. I had been alone for so long, and he showed me I could be something other than what I was. I never thought I could attach myself to someone so quickly, someone that I was never even sure liked me for me, or liked me for what he thought I could do."

Aether stayed quiet for a long moment. "You thought you loved him," he finally said. "It seems deeper than that, and it's difficult to imagine competing with that history."

"*History* makes it seem like something far more than it was." I nearly laughed at the truth of it. We'd spent so little time together —a whirlwind built on my insecurities.

"But it was real, for you," he continued, his voice tight. "I'm trying Fia, I just don't know how to be what you need. I'm fumbling my way through this."

I shook my head. "I didn't know him, Aether. Not like I know you."

Our eyes finally met, and for the first time, I saw real vulnerability in his, the golden irises melting in the firelight. But just like that, he broke away, moving to sink into the chair by the hearth. He buried his face in his hands.

"I don't want to mess this up," he said simply.

I shifted on the bed to face him, my heart aching at how lost he looked.

"We don't need all the answers right now," I said softly. "We're working through this together."

He peered up at me. "For so long, I closed off every part of myself that could feel." His voice took on a strained edge. "I feel like I'm drowning. Sometimes it's incredible, like this morning on the cliff." He paused, exhaling slowly. "Other times, it feels like I'm going to burst out of my own skin. And in the middle of all that, is you."

I couldn't stand seeing him like this. Before I could stop myself, I was standing in front of him, taking his hands in mine, feeling the callouses that plagued them. The same hands that had shuffled through countless pages to figure out exactly who I was—the same hands that had carried me out of Draxon. *His* hands. Aether's hands. They were warm, almost burning.

"Do you know what it means to me?" I asked softly. "That you think about these things?"

My fingers found their way into his hair, and he leaned into my touch, those golden eyes finally meeting mine. Something had cracked open in him—no pretenses, no evasion, just pure honesty reflected in his irises.

"Sometimes I just need..." He struggled with the words. "Time. To process everything. The last thing I want is to say something in anger, something I can't take back."

His forehead pressed against my towel-covered stomach as my hands worked through his hair. The simple touch felt more intimate than anything we'd shared before.

"I've never met anyone like you," I said, meaning it more than I could express.

He turned his face against me, breathing me in. His hands found my bare legs, fingers pressing into my thighs as he drew me closer. "I want to know every part of you," he murmured into the fabric. "To breathe in every. single. piece."

Heat pooled in my stomach at his words. I wanted that too, with a ferocity that terrified me as much as it thrilled me, made me feel free and alive. This man. I wanted him to know me completely. No walls.

"I'm done hiding," I whispered, my voice low against the cracking of the fire. His head tilted back, creating a devastating distance between us.

And I let the towel fall to the floor.

Aether went still, his breath slowing as he took me in. The way he looked at me—like I was something sacred—made my skin flush, made me feel like I was burning from the inside out. Like I was the only thing in his world worth looking at.

His hands found my hips, and when he tilted his head to drag his mouth across my ribcage, the rough stubble on his jaw sent chills across my skin. His lips pressed right under the swell of my breast, golden eyes still locked on mine, and the intensity of his stare nearly undid me right then and there.

He nipped at the curve of my waist, then his mouth was on my stomach, his grip tightening like he couldn't bear to allow anymore distance between us. His hands slid down the backs of my thighs, barely touching—light and as intoxicating as a feathers edge, making me shiver despite the fire's warmth. Then suddenly his hands gripped the backs of my knees, and he yanked me forward onto the chair—onto him.

My arms wrapped around his neck as I pulled his mouth to mine, and the air in the room became electric. Something dark and terrifying rushed through me at the feel of him hard beneath his leathers, at how his hands seemed to burn everywhere they touched.

One arm curved around my back while the other gripped my hip, guiding me against him. I couldn't get enough—of his taste, of the impossible heat of his skin, of the way his shadows surrounded us—how they seemed to reach for mine.

His lips found my jaw, then my neck, and the sound that tore from his throat was almost pained as he shifted beneath me. Every brush of his stubble against my skin sent lightning through my veins.

I wanted him to feel what I felt, wanted to watch this carefully controlled man come undone completely, wholly, for me and me alone.

Heat coiled in my stomach as I watched the burning in his eyes. For a man who had spent decades feeling nothing, the raw hunger in his expression made my heart race. His hands raked over my body, leaving trails of fire in their wake, and when they reached my hips, his fingers pressed into my skin like he was afraid I might disappear.

"I've never..." His voice was rough, strained. "I don't want to hurt you."

The vulnerability in his tone made my chest ache. This was Aether—the man who could tear armies apart—who could bend matter to his will in an instant—now trembling beneath my touch.

I leaned down, pressing my lips to that perfect jaw. "You won't."

His breathing hitched as I rolled my hips against him. Even through his leathers, I could feel how hard he was. When my fingers found the fastenings, his whole body went rigid.

"Fia." My name was a warning on his lips, but I could hear the desperation beneath it—the longing.

"Let go," I whispered against his mouth.

Something snapped in him then. His hands tangled in my hair as he pulled me in for a kiss that stole my breath. Gone was the hesitation, the careful distance. This was pure need.

His mouth moved to my neck, teeth grazing sensitive skin as his hands explored every inch of me. Each touch felt like an iron, like he was branding me. I couldn't help the sounds escaping my throat as his nails trailed against my flesh.

"You're so beautiful," he breathed against my collarbone. "So perfect."

His hands found my breasts, and the sound that escaped him was almost feral. The guarded warrior I knew was unraveling beneath me.

"I've imagined this more times than I can count," he confessed against my skin. "Of touching you, tasting you."

My fingers worked faster at his leathers, desperate to feel his skin against mine. When I finally freed him, we both gasped. He was larger than I'd imagined, and heat flooded my face as I drank in the sight.

An ache radiated up from my center, my body crying out for more.

I lifted myself, sliding my hand between us to position him at my entrance. My eyes met his the moment I began to sink down, his size robbing me of my breath as I adjusted. The pain and pleasure were exquisite. Aether exhaled sharply, looking as if he was having to hold himself back. Allowing me to work myself down until his cock was fully buried within me.

"You're trembling," he whispered, his golden eyes searching mine.

"So are you," I managed, my voice shaky.

His hands slid up my back, pulling me closer until there wasn't a breath of space between us. "Thirty years," he groaned. "Thirty years of feeling nothing, and now..." His words dissolved into a moan as I shifted against him. "You're destroying me."

I pressed my forehead to his, our breaths mingling. "Good."

But I was already seeing stars. My body moved on its own, hips slowly rocking forward before sinking down again.

Aether's head rolled back against the chair, eyes looking dazed but never leaving mine. His plump bottom lip was trapped between his teeth, nearly drawing blood on the next roll of my hips.

I leaned down, wanting to bite his lip myself. I kissed the edge of his mouth and he turned to meet my lips with barely contained restraint. My tongue moved across the cut he'd created, sucking on it slightly as my hips continued to move at a slow place, building up the pleasure with every movement.

I knew it was treacherous then, the speed at which I was taking him. But something about every drawn-out moment, feeling every inch of him at this devastating pace, was like savoring the deadliest of wines—knowing it could kill me but craving it all the same. And a slow, free-fall of a death was exactly what I wanted with him.

Every movement sent waves of pleasure through me. His hands seemed to be everywhere at once—in my hair, on my breasts, gripping my thighs. Like he couldn't get enough, like he wanted to memorize every inch of me.

"Look at me," he commanded, his voice rough with need. When I met his gaze, his golden eyes were molten. "I need to see you."

And in an instant, he was pulling me down, down, down. So far that I couldn't tell where I ended and he began—the sensation of feeling him fully, wholly, unimaginably inside of me nearly had me coming apart at the seams.

I let my head lull back, exposing every delicate piece of me. My eyes wanted to roll, to dissolve into this perfect moment, searing this feeling into my mind—my body—forever. But as he thrust upwards and sank back down, relieving me of the most divine pressure, I found myself suddenly alive once again, my head whipping back to his, my desperate stare a rival to his own, and my lips found his.

"You're holding back," I breathed against his mouth.

His hands tightened on my hips. "Because if I don't..." His voice was strained.

"What?" I challenged, rolling my hips slower, drawing a groan from deep in his chest.

And in an instant, he was everywhere—filling me again, driving his cock into me with a force that seemed to disturb the delicate foundations of the chair beneath us, its creaking echoing through the room.

"Careful," I whimpered, "These walls are paper thin."

His expression told me everything he couldn't say with words as he plunged into me again, a cry escaping my lips just as his hand came down on my mouth, suppressing the noise from my throat. I tasted his flesh, the salty—smoke ridden delicacy of his fingers.

"You want everyone to hear what you do to me?" he breathed against my ear.

I bit down on his fingers in response, and his whole body shuddered. The chair protested beneath us as our movements grew more primal. And I wanted more.

More.

I arched my back in response, crashing back down around him as he moved for another thrust, our bodies colliding in a storm of fury.

The chair groaned beneath us once again, the wood straining with each movement. His eyes met mine, something dangerous flickering in their golden depths. His hand slid from my mouth, returning to grip my thigh, and without warning, he stood—the sudden movement making me gasp.

For a moment we were suspended, my legs wrapped around his waist, his hands gripping me as his muscles flexed. Then he took three measured steps, each one deliberate, making me feel every shift of his body against mine. When my back finally met the cold stone, I arched away from it instinctively, pressing closer to his burning heat.

One of his hands left my thigh to cover my mouth again as a cry threatened to escape, as he buried himself so deeply in me that

I thought I might just lose myself. His other hand supported my entire weight, keeping me pinned against the wall. The position left me completely at his mercy, trapped between the icy chill of the stone and the oblivion his eyes were promising.

"Better?" he growled. The word ghosted across my skin, making me shiver. When I nodded, he slowly removed his hand from my mouth, replacing it with his lips in a kiss that was all teeth and desperation.

"Think you can stay quiet on your own?" he breathed after pulling away, and there was nothing innocent about the smile at his lips.

"Probably not," I admitted, gasping.

"Good. Because I want to hear you scream my name."

And then he began filling me—over and over, each thrust harder than the last.

His name fell from my lips easily. A plea for more of him. I was sure I could never get enough.

A bead of sweat rolled down his temple as his muscles strained. The sight of him—this careful warrior, golden eyes almost black with desire—made something wild stir inside me.

My legs tightened around his hips, entire body tensing. "Aether, I–"

I could barely get the words out but he seemed to know I was reaching my peak, my insides squeezing him tightly. It didn't slow his relentless pace, and I crumbled around him, my shadows filling the room in an instant before flowing back into our bodies, the ecstasy almost blinding.

He didn't give me a moment to catch my breath, his rhythm working me through the earth-shattering orgasm that was already building into another.

"You have no idea what that does to me," he growled against my throat, his stubble scraping against my sensitive skin. "Watching you fall apart."

His shadows circled tighter around us as his breathing grew ragged against my neck. The arm supporting my weight flexed, adjusting his grip to drive even deeper. The movement had my mind going blank, my head falling back against the stone.

"Not yet," he growled, voice rough with restraint. "I'm not done with you."

Despite the trembling in his muscles, despite the desire I could feel building in him, he maintained that devastating rhythm. Each thrust was perfectly calculated to drive me higher, to push me toward that edge again. His self-control was maddening—even now, completely undone, he wouldn't let go until he'd wrung every ounce of pleasure from me first.

My fingers dug into his shoulders as that familiar tension began building again. His eyes had gone completely feral, watching my every reaction with an intensity that was almost predatory. When his name fell from my lips once again, his shadows whipped faster, but still he held back.

My nails raked down his back as he drove into me again, drawing a harsh sound from his throat that was somewhere between pleasure and pain. His hair was slick with sweat now, muscles trembling.

"Do that again," he commanded, voice rough against my ear. When I obliged, dragging my nails across his shoulders, his whole body shuddered. The movement sent sparks through me.

His rhythm shifted, each movement more devastating than the last. When his muscles flexed beneath my hands, I leaned forward, teeth sinking into the curve of his shoulder. The taste of salt and smoke filled my mouth as he let out a low growl that vibrated through his chest.

"Fia," he groaned. His shadows writhed, matching the building pressure between us. But still, he was holding back.

I bit down harder, drawing another harsh sound from his throat. His arm trembled beneath my thigh, but his pace never faltered. If anything, each thrust became deeper, harder, threatening to send me into free fall.

And finally, at the very moment I was losing myself all over again, his control shattered. The shadows surrounding us pulsed wildly as his rhythm gave way to something slower as he slammed his body into mine, driving himself to the hilt.

My name escaped his lips like a prayer as our shadows merged completely, dancing together in perfect synchronization. The darkness amplified everything—every touch, every movement, every shared breath between us.

"Fall with me," he growled against my throat, his voice breaking. The sound of it, of him finally letting go, sent ecstasy through my veins. My vision started to darken at the edges, erasing my entire world until all I could see was Aether's eyes mirroring my own, filling with those inky tendrils until there was nothing left. And then we were falling—tumbling down into that delicious oblivion together.

For a long moment, we stayed there against the wall, his face buried in my neck as we caught our breath. His arms held me securely, neither of us wanting to move, to break this perfect moment of connection. When he finally shifted, I couldn't help the small sound of protest that escaped my lips, my arms tightening around him.

His grip softened into something tender as he carried me to the narrow bed, laying me down. His lips traced a path from my temple to my cheek before finding my mouth. Then he moved to lie beside me, pulling me against his chest.

The night air was cool against our heated skin, but neither of us moved away. If anything, I pressed closer, memorizing everything about this moment—the steady rhythm of his heartbeat, the way his fingers traced patterns on my side, how perfectly we seemed to fit together.

We lay there in comfortable silence, neither wanting to be the first to pull away, to acknowledge that the world still existed beyond this room. I wasn't sure when I drifted off to sleep.

I FOUND myself walking down a long corridor, the stone walls draped in dark fabrics. People in black clothing pressed past me, their faces streaked with tears, whispers echoing off the walls. The scent of funeral incense hung heavy in the air.

My feet carried me toward a door at the end of the hall—ornate and heavy, carved with symbol I now recognized as the Valtýr Royal Family—as my family. As I reached for the handle, it swung open, and I came face to face with Vilda—the woman who would have been my great aunt. She startled at my presence, and for the first time, I saw her clearly. Her face was all sharp angles and striking features, framed by that familiar dark hair that fell in waves down her back. But it was her eyes that tugged at something inside me—black as onyx, a tear developing along her lashes.

She placed a hand on my arm, the touch sending a chill through me. When she lifted her chin to meet my gaze again, something apologetic flashed across her features. She gave a single nod before turning away, disappearing into the crowd of mourners like a shadow melting into darkness.

My feet moved forward of their own accord, through the doorway she'd just exited. The chamber beyond was large and circular, lit by iron chandeliers that cast strange shadows on the walls. And there, sprawled across the floor, was a man—the same one who had taken those two little girls into the Void. The King of Umbrathia lay dead.

CHAPTER FIFTY-TWO

"How did the King die—my great-grandfather?" I asked Aether as we soared above the clouds. The wind was calmer today, so we were able to hear each other easily. Nihr's wing hovered just above Tryggar's as we flew West.

"Something to do with his heart," Aether responded, arching a brow at me. "Why are you asking?"

"I had another dream."

"Last night?" he asked.

I glanced over at him, noticing the glint in his eye. "Yes."

"I'm surprised your mind could function enough to do so." He cracked a wicked grin.

"I guess you'll have to try harder next time." I shrugged, smiling as heat spread across my face.

"Tell me about this dream, then."

"It wasn't much, honestly. Short and more confusing than anything. The Queen's sister—"

"Vilda?"

"Yes—her. The corridors of the castle were filled with Kalfar in mourning clothes. And Vilda—she was walking out of a room…

looking quite shaken, or angry, maybe even sad. It was difficult to tell."

Aether nodded, digesting the information.

"As soon as she left and blended into the crowd, I looked into the chamber to see the King laying on the floor. He wasn't moving."

Aether's eyes were on me now, his brow furrowed. "The King did die on the day of Lord Skalvindr's funeral," he said, "perhaps she was the one to discover him."

"Perhaps," I echoed just as towers broke through the clouds in the distance. We dropped down, finding a place to land the Vördr in a thick brush of trees.

I scanned the perimeter as we moved through the dense growth. We'd flown for most of the day, only landing every few hours when the Vördr needed a break.

The sun was setting in the distance, in the West just beyond Stormshire. It had been too far to make out clearly, but it was Stormshire alright. Another hour of traversing the woods, after leaving the Vördr tucked into the forest at the base of the mountain, and we'd be there.

My fingers trembled slightly as I pulled out the scroll I'd stolen from Laryk's office, spreading it across a fallen log. I needed to find his quarters first, then figure out where team V would be stationed after that. The thought of seeing him again had my stomach in knots, especially after last night.

I glanced over at Aether, who was adjusting the saddle on Nihr. His hair fell into his face as he worked, and suddenly memories from the inn came rushing back—how that same hair had felt twisted in my fingers, how his golden eyes had—

Focus.

I forced my attention back to the layout. Each General had their own wing of the fortress, though they weren't labeled by name. My eyes found the smallest section, and I knew it must be his. Laryk's unit was deadly, not for the sheer size of it, but for the powerful focuses it housed. There were around fifty soldiers in faction venom, if memory served me, hundreds less than the others—it had to be his wing.

The fortress itself was a nightmare—corridors that doubled back on themselves, hidden passages between wings, multiple escape routes from every major chamber. The outer walls alone were twice as thick as any I'd seen before.

"This isn't going to be like breaking into the Compound," I sighed, turning back to Aether. "We're basically walking into the most heavily defended, most lethal part of Sídhe. Laryk's unit is..." I paused, swallowing hard. "Well, let's just say we cannot afford to be seen. Especially you."

Aether moved away from Nihr, coming to stand beside me. His presence felt different now, intimate in a way that made my face flush, and I had to force myself to focus on the map between us.

"Tell me about his unit," he said, his voice was that of a soldier again.

"If we ran into the wrong people, it could be catastrophic." I traced the path to Laryk's wing. "Mostly elemental abilities—fire, water, air, lightning even." I hesitated, remembering the ones I'd heard about when I joined the guard. "One has blood that can melt straight through flesh."

"And Laryk?"

Something in his tone made me look up. His expression was unreadable, but he seemed to have lost that edge of concern from the day before.

"He can anticipate people's movements even before they know their next step, whether it's in battle or negotiation." I turned back to the map, unable to hold his gaze. "He's never lost a fight."

"Until now." The words were quiet, almost to himself.

"Aether. We are not here to fight Laryk. We're not here to fight anyone."

I rolled my eyes, focusing instead on the task ahead. "The problem isn't just getting in. It's navigating the fortress without alerting them. One wrong move and—"

"Then we don't move wrong." His hand found the small of my back, the touch sending warmth through me despite the gravity of our situation.

"Soleil said that the Generals would be in a conference for most of the evening. And since there have been no attacks in months, they might have dropped their guard. We'll have to take advantage of that. They're not going to be expecting any infiltration. If anything, those on patrols will be most heavily stationed around the arcanite towers."

"And what's the likelihood they've moved things around since this map was drawn?" Aether asked, his fingers tracing the corridors.

"I don't know." The confirmation tasted bitter. "But the basic structure has to stay the same. The middle of war isn't exactly the time for renovations." I pointed to several marked passages. "These have the greatest chance of being empty. They're on the Northwestern side, furthest from the training yards and the arcanite."

A rustling in the trees had us both tensing, but it was just a bird taking flight. Still, the interruption served as a reminder of how exposed we were, even in the deepening twilight.

"We should move closer," Aether said, already rolling up the map. "Get a better view of the guard rotations before dark."

I nodded, but something was nagging at me. "There's another thing we need to consider." I caught his arm before he could turn away. "If we do run into anyone... you can't kill them."

His golden eyes narrowed slightly. "Fia—"

"I mean it. They're clueless right now—they don't know what's actually happening. And some of them were my friends." The words felt heavy. "If we're discovered, I will take care of it, try and wipe their memory. We do nothing more."

His eyes raked over my expression for a few seconds before he nodded.

"Also," I said, moving closer to him, feeling that familiar pull. I took his hand in mine, trying to ignore how my skin tingled at his touch. "If this is going to work..." I met his eyes, watching as they darkened slightly. "You cannot reveal yourself, no matter what. I need you to trust that I can handle it. I need you to trust *me*."

His jaw tightened, conflict clear in his expression. "I do trust you." His fingers interlaced with mine. "But if anything happened to you—"

"Nothing will happen." I squeezed his hand. "But you showing yourself might ruin this entire plan. If they see you, I don't know how they will retaliate, but..." I reached up, touching his face. "They won't hesitate."

"And if Laryk tries to hurt you?" The words came out rough, almost a growl.

"He won't." But even as I said it, uncertainty crept in. I knew he'd never physically harm me, but I had no idea how he'd react to the truth—not just about Umbrathia or the King, but about how I wasn't his. Not anymore. "Just... promise me. Promise you'll stay hidden unless there's absolutely no other choice."

His eyes searched mine for a long moment before he let out a slow breath. "Fine." The word seemed to physically pain him. "But the moment—"

"The moment there's real danger, you can go full 'Realm Crasher' on everyone." I tried for humor, but his expression remained serious.

"I won't watch you die." His voice dropped lower, that dangerous edge returning.

A twig snapped in the distance and we both tensed, instinctively moving closer together. When nothing emerged from the growing darkness, I turned back to find his eyes still fixed on me, burning with an intensity that made my heart skip.

"I'm not planning on dying," I said softly. "But I need to do this my way. He needs to hear the truth from *me*." I paused, choosing my next words carefully. "And if he sees you first... he'll never listen to anything I have to say."

Aether simply nodded, taking a step towards me, his eyes piercing.

"We should go," I said, glancing over at Tryggar chasing some small rodent through the trees in the distance. I turned for my satchel—

But before I reached it, Aether caught my wrist, pulling me back against him. His other hand tangled in my hair as his mouth found mine, and suddenly nothing else mattered. The kiss was deep, hungry—full of residual desire left over from the night before

My back hit rough bark as he pressed me against a tree, his body caging mine completely. Heat flooded through me as his hands slid down my sides, gripping my hips. When his teeth grazed my bottom lip, I couldn't help the small sound that escaped my throat.

"We shouldn't—" I managed between kisses, but my hands were already pulling him closer, betraying my words.

His stubble scraped against my jaw as his mouth moved to my neck, making me shiver. "I know," he breathed against my skin.

Nihr's hooves crunched on leaves beside us, reminding us where we were, what we were about to do. We broke apart, both breathing hard. His golden eyes had gone dark, void burns leaking black mist.

"We need to focus," I whispered, though my hands still gripped his leathers.

He pressed his forehead to mine, taking a steadying breath. "Later," he promised, his voice rough in a way that made heat surge through me.

The fortress emerged from the darkness like a beast, all jagged edges and shadows, its black stone seeming to devour what little moonlight remained. My heart sank as we drew closer—something was wrong. The walls crawled with guards, their silver badges winking like stars as they moved in perfect synchronization. Far too many.

"Fuck," I breathed, watching another patrol pass.

"They're everywhere," Aether said.

We shared a look of hesitation before melting into darkness, moving through shadows like mist. Each guard we passed made my heart stutter, though I knew they couldn't see us. Their conversations echoed off the walls as we slipped past.

"—third sweep tonight. General's orders."

Their words left ice in my veins.

I pulled out the scroll again after we materialized in a supply closet, checking our position. The layout was exact—each corridor where it should be—but the security was nothing like we'd expected. Guards posted at every major intersection, patrols moving within formations. This was nothing like I expected. This was an army preparing for war.

The guards weren't the only problem. Every alcove, every darkened corner that could have provided cover was illuminated by torches burning far too bright for this time of night.

We followed the map's path toward Laryk's wing, our darkness flowing like water through the corridors—shifting and adapting to any shadows we could find. The sound of boots against stone echoed everywhere. My web picked up dozens of minds moving through the fortress, all following the same patterns.

Finally, we reached the corridor leading to Laryk's quarters. I reached out with my focus, scanning the space ahead. No minds glowed within his chamber, but the hallway crawled with guards.

"Wait here," I breathed to Aether as we pressed into a shadowed corner. "Watch the corridor."

I could feel the tension rolling off of him at my words, but he didn't move. We'd discussed this. He had to trust me.

"Be careful," I heard him hiss from behind me.

I slipped through the wall like mist, materializing in Laryk's quarters for the first time, all sounds from beyond the door now completely silent behind the thick layers of stone. The space was larger than I'd imagined—a massive desk on one side, weapons displayed on the walls, a training dummy positioned in the corner. My eyes caught on something that wasn't on the layout—a fresh stone arch had been carved into the far wall, leading to what appeared to be a grand bathroom. The stone dust still lingered in the crevices.

The room felt empty, but something prickled at the back of my neck. Wrong. It felt wrong. I moved toward his desk, noting the tactical markers scattered across maps, the half-empty wine glass beside them. It was stained with a faint mark of lipstick at the rim.

I whipped around, scanning the room as my heart raced. That's when I felt it—cold steel against my throat, an arm like iron around my waist. The sharp, metallic scent of blood filled my nostrils, making my stomach turn.

"Hi there, Riftborne." A woman's voice was silk against my ear, but her blade pressed harder. "Welcome home." Something wet seeped into my leathers where her arm gripped me. And then there was only pain.

Narissa.

CHAPTER FIFTY-THREE

My side burned where Narissa's arm gripped me, so sharp and intense that I nearly doubled over. The acid had melted through the fabric, searing into my flesh as her blade pressed harder against my throat.

"You know," she purred against my ear, "when they said you were alive, I almost hoped it was true. *Almost*." The knife edge bit deeper. "Laryk was so... devastated when you disappeared. It took weeks to help him forget."

I dissolved into shadow just as her blade sliced air where my throat had been. The acid burn in my side screamed as I reformed across the room, but there was no time to assess the damage. Narissa was already moving, her daggers gleaming as she spun.

"Did you really think you could just walk back in here?" She drew one blade across her palm, letting blood pool in her hand. "After everything?"

She flung the crimson spray where I stood. I shifted again, but not fast enough—drops caught my shoulder and I cried out as they began eating through leather and skin.

"He's mine again," she said, circling slowly. "Has been for months. Did you think he'd wait for a ghost?"

I reached for her mind with my focus, trying to latch onto the silver glow, but she was too fast. She anticipated my stillness, flinging another arc of blood that forced me to dive behind Laryk's desk.

The desk began to sizzle as her blood ate through the wood. I rolled away, coming up in a fighting stance just as she vaulted over the dissolving furniture. Her dagger caught my arm before I could fully dodge, and I felt the bite of steel followed by the familiar burn of her blood.

"He told me everything about you." She slashed again, forcing me back. "About your powers. Your weakness." Her smile was cruel. "How desperate you were for his attention."

I shifted to shadow, materializing behind her, landing a solid kick to her spine. She stumbled forward but turned it into a graceful roll, coming up with fresh blood coating her blades.

"Tell me," she said, flicking crimson drops in a wide arc, "did you really think he loved you? Or were you just an entertaining diversion from me?"

The taunt struck deeper than her blades, but I pushed the feeling aside. I needed to focus, needed one clean shot at her mind. But every time I tried to concentrate, she was there with another attack.

My leathers were in tatters now, burns spreading across my skin wherever her blood had landed. The pain was making it hard to think, hard to maintain shadow form for more than a few seconds. I could barely breathe.

"The best part?" She advanced, cutting her arm to gather more ammunition. "When he finally stopped mourning you, when he came back to me..." Her eyes glittered. "He was better than ever."

My side screamed in protest as I dove under another spray of blood, rolling to my feet behind the training dummy. The leather target sizzled as her acid found it instead.

"You want to know what he said?" She stalked closer, her arm dripping fresh blood onto the stone floor, eating small craters into its surface. "When he finally stopped whispering your name in his sleep?"

I dissolved just as she struck, reforming by the weapon wall. My fingers closed around a short sword, but she was already there. Her dagger sliced through my thigh before I could block. The pain was instant, sharp, but it was nothing compared to the burning that followed as her blood seeped into the wound.

"He said you were nothing but a lost little girl." She pressed her advantage as I stumbled. "Playing at being a soldier."

My sword met her next strike, the clash of metal echoing through the chamber. But she was ready, using her free hand to fling blood at my face. I barely turned in time, feeling it sear across my cheek.

"Your problem," she continued, spinning away from my counterattack, "is that you never knew what he really needed." Another slash, another burn. "What he deserved."

I tried to focus on her mind again, reaching for that silver glow, but she was moving too fast. Every time I got close, she'd force me to shift or dodge, breaking my concentration.

The pain from her acid was becoming unbearable, spreading like fire across my skin. It built and built, the pain consuming my entire mind like a poison until something inside me snapped. The shadows around us began to pulse with my rage, darkening the room until it became the Void.

I let the darkness take over, becoming pure shadow as I moved. Narissa's next spray of blood passed harmlessly through my mist. And before she could even move, I materialized behind her, my elbow connecting with her spine. She stumbled forward and I pressed my advantage, dissolving and reforming in quick succession.

"What's wrong?" I taunted as she spun wildly, trying to track my movements, her eyes going wide in the darkness. "Can't hit what you can't see?"

"You're one of them," she snarled, slashing her own arm again, but I was already gone. The shadows bent to my will now, responding to my fury. I appeared at her side, sweeping her legs out from under her. Her head cracked against the stone floor, but she rolled away before I could pin her.

Narissa's eyes darted around the room, her confidence finally cracking. She flung blood in desperate arcs, but I was everywhere and nowhere at once. My boot caught her wrist, sending one of her daggers skittering across the floor.

This was my opening—the slightest hesitation as she struggled against my hold. I let the web flow out of me, dancing through the darkness like waves of stars in the night sky. It surged forward, latching onto her mind before she could move again.

But instead of finding the usual resistance, instead of having to carefully work my way in, I crashed through her mental barriers with shocking force. Like a door splintering beneath too much pressure.

Memories rushed past like leaves in a storm, and suddenly I wasn't in Laryk's quarters anymore. The world tilted and shrank around me, my perspective shifting until I was seeing through different eyes. The table before me seemed impossibly tall, the ceiling so far away it made me dizzy.

I watched as my small feet carried me forward. Blood-red hair cascaded down my shoulders, catching on the delicate lace of a green dress. The dining room stretched before me, military insignias and lieutenant badges glinting from their place on the walls.

A woman sat at the massive table, her shoulders trembling as she pressed a handkerchief to her face. She looked up as I approached, and I saw Narissa's features echoed in her. In her mother. She quickly wiped her tears away, straightening in her chair.

"He's not coming back, is he?" I felt my lips move, but the voice was small and sad. "From the island across the sea?"

The woman stood, crossing to kneel before me. Her perfume smelled of jasmine and salt, like she'd been standing by the ocean. "No, my darling. He's not."

"Is he dead?" The child's voice cracked. The woman shot to her feet, gripping the table's edge as her composure shattered.

"No," she finally managed, her voice raw. "But I wish he was." She turned away, her steps unsteady as she fled the room.

Through Narissa's young eyes, I watched her mother stumble into the living room, catching herself on furniture. "I wish they were both dead," she sobbed, "him and that whore." Her legs gave out and she crumpled to the floor, her cries echoing off marble.

Reality crashed back like a wave. I was in Laryk's quarters again, and Narissa stood before me, swaying slightly, her eyes unfocused. I lunged forward before she could recover, my focus surging through our connection again.

Leave, I commanded through the bond, feeling her resistance fade like smoke. *Clean yourself up. Go to bed. Forget what you saw here tonight.*

My hands moved without thought, wiping blood from her face with my sleeve, smoothing her dark hair. When I finally released her mind, she stumbled backward, blinking in confusion. I dissolved into shadow as she turned, watching her walk out the door as if in a daze.

I dropped to my knees, catching my breath and wiping sweat from my brow. After a few moments, Aether materialized from the shadows, his golden eyes wild.

"What happened? I didn't even hear anything." His voice was

frantic as his eyes scanned over me—my tattered leathers, the acid burns across my exposed skin. In an instant, he was moving, helping me up from the floor. And then his hands were on my face, jaw tense as he assessed my injuries.

"I'm fine. I thought no one was in the room," I whispered, allowing him to pull me against him.

The sound of a key turning in the lock had us springing apart, but not before Aether's hand gripped my arm.

"Aether, you have to disappear *right now*." He hesitated for a heartbeat. "I'm fine, Aether. *Go*," I hissed, and he narrowed his eyes before vanishing.

The door swung open.

General Laryk Ashford sauntered into the room, slamming the door behind him. He ran a hand over his face, dragging it down before shaking his head. His shoulders sagged with exhaustion as he walked toward his desk, his crisp black uniform now bore wrinkles. He looked older somehow, worn down by the months since I'd last seen him.

He took three steps before freezing. His eyes caught the damage to the desk first, then tracked across the room—taking in the blood-painted walls, the melting training dummy, the scattered weapons. Finally, his gaze fell on the floor, leading to where I stood. I'll never be able to put into words the look that crossed his face as his eyes found mine.

"Fia?" The word was barely a whisper as he moved towards me in a flurry.

CHAPTER FIFTY-FOUR

LARYK SWEPT me up into his arms with the force of a storm, his mouth crashing into mine. The familiar scent of burnt amber and vetiver wrapped around me like a ghost—training sessions that nearly had me coming undone, heated glances across rooms, things whispered in darkened corridors. My body went rigid, waiting for that spark, that raging wildfire that had consumed me every time he'd touched me before. But where there had once been an inferno, now there was only hollow space. Not even embers burning in the distance.

A shadow writhed in my periphery and I winced, the weight of golden eyes pressing against my skin as I tore myself from Laryk's grasp.

Confusion shattered his features before his gaze caught the acid burns scoring my flesh.

"What happened?" His eyes went dark.

"Narissa." Her name tasted like poison on my tongue.

"She was in here?" Annoyance flickered across his face, breaking through that careful mask of command he usually wore. "That's the third time this week."

"Don't worry. I sent her to bed. She won't remember anything."

"She hurt you," he growled, eyes scanning me. "There will certainly be repercussions for that."

"I'll be fine." I tried to assure him, tempted to bring up her claims but deciding against it.

"I knew you were alive," he breathed, and suddenly the exhaustion that had haunted his eyes when he entered transformed into something like hunger.

"I have so much to tell you, but I can't stay long." The words rushed out before I could stop them.

His brow furrowed. "What do you mean? You're here now." He moved toward me with that predatory grace I remembered, but I took a step back. The movement stopped him cold, his head tilting as he reassessed the situation. "You're home, Fia."

"I'm here," I said carefully. "But I can't stay."

"Why?" The word carried an edge of offense.

"I'm trying to explain all of it to you. Let me—"

"How did you escape?" he cut me off.

I shifted uncomfortably. "I didn't escape, Laryk. I came here on my own."

He looked me up and down, brow creasing.

"I'm here," I said carefully, measuring each word. "But I can't stay."

"Why?" His voice carried the weight of months of searching, of grief. Confusion rippled across his features. He reached for my face, but I turned away from his touch. Something dangerous flickered in his emerald eyes.

"I have to talk to you about something important."

"Fine." The word was soft, but his jaw was set. "Continue."

"Riftdremar—the uprising, this war. The Wraiths. None of what we've been told is true." The words sounded mad even to my own ears, and I forced myself to breathe slower.

"Where are you getting this from?"

"The arcanite," I said, watching his eyes sharpen at the word. "It doesn't create essence—it *stores* it. Those towers—in Emeraal and Stormshire—were mined in Riftdremar. That's the entire reason the uprising happened in the first place."

He blinked, and for the first time since I'd known him, genuine surprise cracked through that careful mask. But wariness still lingered in the set of his shoulders.

I took a deep breath, watching him process. "Have you ever heard of a siphon?"

"A siphon?" The word rolled off his tongue like he was tasting it. "No."

"A person who can control the flow of essence." I lowered my voice. "Tell me, what is the King's focus?"

His eyebrows shot up at the direct question, but he leaned back against his desk, crossing his arms. "He can turn water to ice."

"Have you ever seen him do it?"

He went still, and I could almost see him rifling through years of memories. Finally, he shook his head. "No."

"Have you ever questioned the fertility of the Isle?" I pressed. "How not long after the rebellion, things started to change? For years, more miraculous occurrences after the last."

Something shifted in his expression then.

"I'm almost positive the King is a siphon."

"Why?"

"Where I just came from, where I was taken to that night in Emeraal—it's being drained." The words tumbled out faster now. "There is mass devastation, families suffering, land rotting—no food for the people."

"The people?" His eyes narrowed dangerously.

"Yes. They aren't Wraiths, Laryk. They're just like us." I stepped closer, willing him to understand. "The shadows are just a way to hide and protect themselves. All this time, they've thought destroying the arcanite was the answer, but it's not. None of this will end until the siphon stops."

"I knew I saw a figure," he muttered, almost to himself. He began pacing, running a hand through his copper hair.

"They're not some monsters filtering in from another world. They have lives, possessions, land. Children."

He stopped abruptly. "So you believe the King is pulling essence from their realm and depositing it into Sídhe?"

"It's not happening all at once. It's being done systematically—over the last decade at least." I watched his face carefully. "He's storing the essence in the arcanite and distributing it to Sídhe."

Laryk's hand moved down his face, dragging his sharp features in frustration. "I don't understand."

"I know it's a lot—"

"Why did they take you?" His voice hardened, emerald eyes flashing. "What do you have to do with any of this?" Anger blazed across his features. "They took you away from me."

"You saw what I did that night." I met his gaze steadily. "You hesitated," I added quietly, looking away.

Suddenly he was there, gripping my shoulders, scanning my face with new intensity. "I only hesitated because I thought I saw something—someone—through the darkness. A figure beside you." Desperation bled into his voice. "You have no idea how I've played that moment over and over in my mind—the regret that I feel. I should have run to you, should have fought through all of it to get to you."

"Don't feel sorry." I stared at the floor. "If you had tried to intervene, we wouldn't know anything that we know now. We'd still be clueless to what's really happening—the atrocities our King is committing."

He paused, and I could feel him searching my face for answers.

"They took me..." I swallowed hard. "Because I'm one of them."

Laryk stared at me for a long moment before reaching up to tuck a strand white of hair behind my ear. "I don't care."

"We have to do something, Laryk. We don't have much time until the entire realm dies."

"They've killed us by the hundreds," Laryk nearly growled, eyes digging into mine.

"What would you have done, if you were them?" I asked, nearly begging him to understand—to grasp the weight of what was occurring.

He stilled, eyes strained as he shook his head. "This is a lot of information."

I leaned against his desk and sighed. "I know," I whispered. "But it's true."

"How can you be sure?" he asked, coming to stand beside me, never removing his gaze from my face.

"Because I've seen it. I've seen the devastation there." I tried to keep my voice from cracking but failed miserably. "This is the realm my father was from, Laryk. And it's all going to be dust soon. An entire half of me that I never knew until now."

He took my hand, fingers tracing over the Riftborne branding as a tear slipped down my face. "And your mother?" he asked.

"From Riftdremar. Both of my parents were killed because of greed—*his* greed. The King. I won't lose anything else to it." I turned towards him, my eyes burning.

He studied me, eyes scanning me up and down in the quiet as my thoughts raced. The seconds slipped by, then minutes. And I was going to drown in the silence if he didn't say something.

"I won't let that happen," he finally said, and there was something ragged in his voice as he reached up to wipe a falling tear from my cheek.

"Really?" I asked, my heart feeling like it might burst or crack, I couldn't be sure which.

He nodded slowly. "We can work together. We can find a way

to stop this." He turned, pacing again with renewed energy. "It will be difficult—"

"I've already destroyed the blood oaths in Luminaria." The words stopped him mid-stride.

"All of them?" His eyebrow arched.

"All of them."

A smirk tugged at his lips—the one I used to know so well. He strode back to me. "You're brilliant." He neared me, something soft shifting in his expression. "It's why I fell in love with you."

The words struck something hollow in my chest, leaving only distant sadness in their wake.

"The two of us together, think of what we could do, Fia." His voice dropped lower, more intense. "We can tear down this Kingdom and rebuild it however we want. Stop this theft, bring life back to that dying realm." His fingers traced my jaw. "Your power, Fia. Imagine what you could do."

I looked into those emerald eyes that had once meant everything to me, and I finally understood. Those words on *those* lips would have melted me months ago, they would have filled the void in me that years of isolation had carved out. Laryk did love me, in his own way. But his love was shaped by potential, by power, by what I could do for him. And I knew with a certainty it wasn't going to be enough anymore—perhaps it could have been, before, but not now. I deserved a different kind of love.

And so I took a step back, feeling the air between us turn to ice. "I need your help, Laryk. I need your help to right this, to bring balance back to this world, but not like that." My voice was barely above a whisper.

Pain flashed across his face before anger leaked in. "What are you saying?"

"I have to go back there. To Umbrathia."

"No." He nearly growled. "I just got you back, Fia. I can't allow you to leave again. You don't know what it did to me."

"I'm sorry, Laryk," I said, my voice a plea. I opened my mouth, then closed it. I didn't know what else to say—how to make the words form.

"Why are you behaving this way?" His eyes narrowed to dangerous slits.

"Because..." I trailed off as he raced forward, pulling me against him again.

"Stop, Fia. Nothing has to change between us." His arms wrapped around me, securing me against his chest. "I'll do whatever you need me to." The look in his eyes—the desperation caused guilt to churn through me.

Because it wasn't him. It was me. I was the one who changed.

His face lowered, breath heating my face right before his lips seared into mine once again.

Then shadows erupted.

Aether materialized in a surge of darkness, tearing me from Laryk's grasp and stepping in front of me in one fluid motion. But Laryk had anticipated the movement—his dagger already pressed against Aether's throat. The two men stood nearly chest to chest, Aether's towering frame forcing Laryk to look up, golden eyes meeting emerald in a clash of wills.

CHAPTER FIFTY-FIVE

THE TWO MEN remained locked in their deadly stance, neither willing to yield first. Slowly, Laryk's emerald eyes slid to me, and I watched realization settle across his features. The dagger lowered as he took a step back, his gaze darting between Aether and me.

Then he threw his head back and laughed, the sound sharp as it echoed through the chamber. "Oh, this is *rich*." His smile didn't reach his eyes. "Well, it all makes sense now. Your sudden shift in allegiances."

"That's not what this is about." I moved to stand beside Aether, my shoulder barely brushing his arm.

Laryk's eyes tightened at our proximity, but his smirk only grew crueler. "Although, I suppose I shouldn't be surprised. You seemed so passionate about your place in the Guard after that night in Emeraal. So eager to please once you'd been satisfied." The look in his eyes had me burning at the accusation. "You do remember that night, don't you, Fia? I certainly do—in vivid detail."

Aether surged forward, shadows pouring out of him, but Laryk didn't flinch. He simply twisted the dagger through his fingers and cocked his head to the side. "He makes quite the guard dog, I'll give you that."

"Better than the last man meant to protect her," Aether's voice was deadly smooth despite the rippling of his tightened muscles. "The one who hesitated, who watched as she was taken."

"Let me guess…" Laryk's voice dropped lower, that dangerous edge returning. "You're the shadow I saw that night. The one standing beside her." His eyes fixed on Aether with renewed interest. "The one who took her."

"Took her?" Aether's shadows pulsed. "Or saved her from a realm that would have killed her once they discovered what she was?"

"And what exactly is she?" Laryk's gaze cut to me. "Since you seem to know so much about her now."

"More than you ever did." The words carried ice.

Laryk's hand tightened on his dagger. "I trained her. Shaped her into—"

"Into a weapon." Aether's interruption was sharp. "Into something you could use."

Laryk barked out another laugh, but this one held no humor. "I *cared for* her. Which is more than I can say for whatever this is." He gestured between us. "Tell me, Fia, did they break you? Turn you into *their* weapon instead?"

"That's enough," I demanded.

"Is it?" Laryk's emerald eyes burned. "Because from where I'm standing, it looks like you've simply traded one wielder for another."

The shadows in the room darkened at his words, and I felt Aether's rage building beside me. The air grew thick with it.

"Both of you, stop." My voice tore through their posturing. I wanted to say more, to tell them I wasn't a weapon for anyone to wield, at least not anymore. But it wasn't the time—not if we were going to convince him to work with us.

I stepped between the two men, turning to face Laryk. "This is bigger than all of us. Personal feelings aside, I've seen what's happening beyond these borders. I've watched children starve, families lose everything. This is life or death."

His eyes bore into me, and behind the mask, I could see the pain—the grief of what he was witnessing, of losing something he had been searching for. He was lashing out like a wounded animal, but I had to try everything to get through to him. To get us back to that place where we were only moments ago.

"You said to me once that you believed Sídhe made mistakes in the aftermath of the uprising." I studied his face, searching for any reaction. "So it leads me to believe that if they were doing something terrible, you would not stand for it. Would fight against it."

He looked away, jaw tightening.

"You've always known something was off. Even before you saw the figure through the darkness in Emeraal, even before you argued with Mercer, argued with the King—"

"You saw that?" His head snapped back to me.

"Yes." I took a step forward. "I saw you trying to tell the others that there was more to this war. But nothing about it has ever sat well with you. The scar on your face, your ability to anticipate their moves—you've always known something was wrong, Laryk. And you were *right*. This whole time."

He stared at me, something breaking in his expression before that careful mask slipped back into place.

"I know you probably hate me right now. But don't let that interfere with doing what's right."

His jaw tensed, a muscle ticking beneath the skin.

"Could you really go back, now knowing what you know?" The words came out as a plea. "You could keep helping Sídhe drain a realm who has done nothing to provoke such a theft?"

"I have no proof of that." The growl in his voice betrayed the look in his eyes.

"Laryk," I began, my eyes glossing over, "You believed me only moments ago. What changed?"

"How am I to be certain you haven't been manipulated?" His eyes cut to Aether. "That all of this isn't some elaborate lie?"

"I don't have any way to prove it to you other than my word. You can't even get into my mind—you think I'd let anyone else do that to me? I didn't want to believe it at first either. I fought the truth with everything inside me. But then I saw it. *Lived it.* It's real, and it's only going to get worse." My voice steadied as I continued. "All the pieces are there, Laryk. You just have to want to see them."

Heat filled my voice as the words poured out, "It will continue, this greed, this oppression. The King is never going to stop. Not unless we break this cycle."

Doubt flashed across his face as he turned away, dragging a hand through his copper hair.

"I want us to work together. Because if we don't..." I swallowed hard. "If we don't, then real war is on the horizon. Not these attacks on arcanite. Real. Bloody. War. The kind that destroys continents."

He spun back toward me, head tilted. "Is that a threat?"

"It's not a threat. It's an inevitability." My voice carried steel now. "Umbrathia is growing restless, people are becoming desperate. There's not many other ways for this to end."

Laryk's emerald eyes moved to Aether, studying him.

"You understand the weight of what you're asking me to do." His words hung heavy in the air. It wasn't quite a question.

"I do." I met his gaze. "And I wouldn't be asking if I thought there was any other way."

He stared at me for the longest time, his face morphing slightly as something warred within him. A part of me wanted to reach out and comfort him, to save him from the pain he was feeling, but the thought of it was selfish and cruel. Not when it would mean something to him that it didn't for me.

Finally, he nodded.

"If I agree to this, all attacks from your realm must cease. Immediately," he spat the words in Aether's direction.

"We haven't attacked in months. Not since the night we found her." Aether's voice was deadly calm.

Laryk's lip curled. "You want an alliance, yet you continue to lie."

I turned to Aether, but his expression mirrored my confusion.

"The last one was quite horrific." Laryk's voice dropped lower. "Different than your normal game of shadows. An entire settlement wiped out, throats slit, drained of blood, their bodies left coating the ground. *Civilians.*"

The realization hit me like a physical blow. Draxon's soldiers. Valkan hadn't been lying. They had been here.

Aether's jaw went rigid as our eyes met in silent understanding.

"That wasn't us." His voice was a low rumble.

"Valkan—a disgraced Lord. He led an army of rebels who sought to end this war themselves, by any means necessary," I said. "He does not represent the views of the rest of Umbrathia."

"A brutal massacre, nonetheless." Laryk's hand tightened on his dagger, his eyes never leaving Aether. "Committed by monsters from *your* realm."

"They're taken care of." Aether took a dangerous step forward. "Their leader is gone."

"Convenient." Laryk matched his advance.

Shadows deepened beneath Aether's skin. "I killed him."

"And I'm supposed to take your word for it?"

"He did it to save me." The words rushed out before I could stop them.

"To save you?" Something changed in Laryk's voice as his eyes swept over me, falling on my neck. His gaze caught on the scars beneath Narissa's fresh burns—evidence of Valkan's torture still etched into my skin.

Something cracked in his expression before rage flooded his features. He whirled on Aether. "You let this happen to her?" The words came out as a snarl, his knuckles white around the dagger's hilt.

The accusation struck Aether and I could see him physically recoil as his golden eyes fell to the floor.

"Laryk." I moved between them again. "It's not his fault. And we are running out of time. You don't have to worry about Valkan's men anymore. We will take care of them. And if you agree to work with us, there will be no more attacks. You have my word."

Laryk sighed, turning to grip the edge of his desk. "Even if I wanted to believe you, you can hardly make promises for the actions of an entire realm. An entire army. You don't have that kind of authority."

For the first time, I felt the weight of my birthright settle over me like armor. "Yes. I do."

Confusion rippled across his face.

"She outranks our Generals." Aether's voice flowed past me, settling on Laryk.

"My father, the Kalfar I told you about?" I took a steadying breath. "He was the son of the ruling Queen."

Laryk simply blinked.

"I'm his heir." The words felt both strange and right on my tongue.

Aether moved to stand beside me. "She will inherit the throne of Umbrathia and become commander of the realm's forces. All of us answer to her, and her alone."

Laryk was stunned to silence, his gaze raking over me with a newfound respect that made me want to roll my eyes. *Perhaps we should have led with that.* The revelation seemed to shift something in him. He was a strategist, after all.

He paced the room, attention focused on nothing in particular as he rounded the desk, placing his palms down on the wooden surface.

"So, what exactly did you have in mind?" All emotion had drained from his tone, leaving behind the calculated General I'd come to know so well.

Relief washed over me, but I didn't hesitate. "We need to destabilize Sídhe from the inside out," I said, matching his tone. "The Guard is unaware of what's really happening. People need to see the truth, to be given the opportunity to decide for themselves—whether they will continue risking their lives for a King who has done nothing but lie to them."

"It's going to be difficult with such few allies on this side of the tear," Laryk pressed.

"There's more than you think," I countered, glancing at Aether. "A resistance already grows in Sídhe."

Laryk's brow raised.

"Both civilian and those within the Guard. People who have been able to see through the lies."

"Is that so?" he asked, tongue sliding over his teeth. "And who is the leader of this rebellion?"

"They'll be in contact soon," I said, "to strategize."

"The strategy is clear." Laryk shrugged. "Whispers are dangerous things after all. Especially now that the blood-oaths are destroyed."

I looked over to Aether, who simply nodded despite the skepticism in his eyes.

"Placing doubt in the right minds, taking advantage of the frustration that's already begun simmering throughout the factions." He laughed. "I control the deployments. I can keep them all here. If you're true to your word, and no attacks descend on our Western strongholds, that frustration could easily be bent to something stronger. Something sharper."

He gestured around the room with his hands, almost flippantly.

"I can play my part—causing fractures in the foundations that hold this place together, turning loyal soldiers against the crown. That part will be simple—you can leave the specifics to me," he said, "It is, after all, my greatest gift. The art of manipulation."

I nodded, fighting back the hope now coursing through me.

"You can tell no one else. For my seeds of doubt to develop organically, you have to leave now, go back to Umbrathia, and wait for my signal."

"But Raine, Briar—"

"You cannot tell them anything. Not only does it put them at risk of being named as traitors if things go badly..." He trailed off. "But you also have no idea who you can truly trust. I know they're your friends, but when it comes to matters such as this, you'd be surprised how fickle people can be."

A part of me wanted to fight back, to demand that they be told the truth, but something stopped me. I didn't want to doubt them, but what if he was right? I thought of Briar's odd behavior back in Luminaria—his possessiveness over Raine when it came to our friendship. And then I remembered how Raine hadn't kept my secret about private training with Laryk. Even if I thought I knew them, could I be sure of what they'd do in the face of their entire worlds being turned upside down?

Guilt gnawed at me.

Laryk paused, eyes fixed on something just over my shoulder for a few moments before his gaze slid to me, his emerald eyes growing deadly serious.

"You need to understand the gravity of what it means to overthrow a kingdom, Fia. It's not going to be easy. Difficult decisions will await all of us. But if we're going to prevail, we can never doubt one another. No matter what happens, you have to trust me. Trust that I'm doing what I must."

I matched the intensity of his stare. "I do trust you."

Laryk stood then, taking a few slow steps around the desk until he was facing me. In the corner of my eye, I saw Aether shift closer, but he stopped himself from intervening.

Those emerald eyes settled on me again, something sad crossing them as he reached out and tucked a stray curl behind my ear. "But I want you to know that I'm not doing this to save a realm. I'm doing it because you asked me to. Because it's what you want."

His hand lingered on my jaw, his fingers trailing across my skin softly. The touch sent memories of shivers across me.

"I'll prove myself worthy of you."

CHAPTER FIFTY-SIX

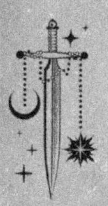

We slipped out of Stormshire in our spectre forms. Laryk's careful orchestration of the Guard's movements created the perfect cover for our escape—patrols strategically positioned just far enough apart to leave us a clear path to the rip. It felt like a victory, like the first real step toward change.

The flight back to Ravenfell was long, but my heart soared with every beat of Tryggar's wings. We'd done it. Not only had we destroyed the blood oaths, but we'd secured an alliance that could shift the tide of this war. Laryk's commitment to our cause meant more than just an allegiance—it meant hope. Real hope for both realms. *Real fucking hope.*

I'd sent word ahead through Raven's compact, requesting the team gather for an immediate briefing upon our arrival. I hadn't expected to find all four Generals waiting in the war room, Urkin's eyes narrowing as I entered. The disapproval radiating from him was palpable—clearly my unauthorized excursion to Sídhe hadn't earned me any favor.

Aether moved past me, handing the crate of healing potions to

Rethlyn. "Get one of these to the infirmary immediately," he said. "To Lael."

Rethlyn nodded, already turning toward the door, but his eyes caught mine for a moment—a flash of relief crossing his features.

"Well?" Urkin's gruff voice drew my attention back to the table. "What did you find?"

I approached the center of the room, feeling lighter than I had in weeks. The weight of their stares didn't intimidate me now—not when I had such promising news to share.

"We've secured an alliance with General Laryk Ashford," I began, watching their expressions shift from skepticism to interest. "He's already positioning his forces to weaken the crown from within. And the blood oaths—" I couldn't help the smile that tugged at my lips. "Destroyed. All of them."

Vexa let out a low whistle from her position near the wall. "You actually did it."

"There's more," I continued. "A resistance is already growing in Sídhe. People who have seen through the lies, or those who had suffered their own misfortune at the hand of the crown, who want to help restore balance. Who want real change." The words carried all the hope I felt burning in my chest. "We're not alone in this fight anymore."

Urkin's jaw tightened. "And you trust these... allies? This... General?" His voice carried decades of skepticism. "The same people who've benefited from the theft of our essence?"

"These are people who have woken up. Who have been told of Sídhe's deception. Who *believe* it," I countered. "Once others learn the truth—"

"If they learn the truth," Theron cut in, his analytical mind clearly running through every possible outcome. "How many will turn against their own King?"

"I don't know," I answered honestly, "but they deserve to have the knowledge before they make their decision. We would be the monsters they claim us to be if we needlessly kill the blind," I said, the command in my voice a shock to me.

Urkin's eyes met mine, but I didn't find resistance.

"We want the truth to spread so that we can create cracks in the undying fealty to the crown. Because the more people we have on our side, the better. But do not mistake my hesitation for weakness. Or ignorance," I continued, taking a few steps towards the Generals. "Those who choose to stay loyal to the King will suffer the same fate as their monarch. I know that this won't end in some pretty, perfect solution devoid of violence. I understand the weight of our goal. We're going to overthrow a Kingdom that's been established for centuries."

The room was silent, all eyes focused on me. Slowly, I turned to Aether, who was looking at me with that same expression from the trials—sitting back, his eyes black and narrowed, his jaw set, and mouth curved into something like a smile. Pride. Of the darkest variety.

Urkin stood then, gazes shifting to him as he approached the front of the room. The familiar creak of his leather boots seemed louder in the sudden quiet.

"I returned from Stravene this morning," he said, his rough voice carrying an edge I couldn't quite place. "The Council was... interested in the evidence Aether collected regarding your lineage."

General Karis rose then, his expression unreadable. "The Umbra forces find the evidence to be indisputable." His tone carried the weight of authority, but his face morphed into something more gentle as he looked at me. "All of the General's agree on this—that we find your claim to be legitimate."

"Her knowledge of Sídhe has been invaluable," Talon added from his corner, fingers drumming against the stack of archives before him. "The risk she took infiltrating their Guard—"

"A Duskbound has always sat on the throne in Umbrathia,"

General Taliora cut in, shaking her head as if alluding to something obvious. "Always."

"As you can see, you have our support." Urkin's jaw tightened slightly. "However..."

"What is the hesitation?" Aether's voice was sharp as he rose from his seat.

I watched as Taliora and Talon shared a look that made my stomach twist. Whatever was coming, it was clearly not what we were hoping for.

"The Council," Urkin cut in, "are wary."

"Of course they are." Vexa's exasperation cut through the tension as she drove her dagger into the wooden table before her.

"Fia did not grow up here." Karis's voice was measured, diplomatic. "She's spent very little time with our people. They question her ability to lead."

"Every ruler has descended from this single bloodline." Rethlyn stepped forward, something like pride coloring his face. "It's her right."

"Well, that presents another issue entirely." Urkin's eyes found mine. "They understand the evidence is compelling, however, they do not believe it to be enough to solidify your claim."

I should have felt the same indignation that flashed across my companions' faces, but I couldn't summon it. The truth was it still didn't feel real even to me. The Council's doubts merely echoed my own—how could someone who'd spent their whole life as an outsider suddenly claim to be heir to a throne they'd never known existed?

"There has to be a way to convince them." Raven's voice broke through my thoughts. "Something we missed in the archives, tethers that work with blood magic, *something*."

"They assured me they would be looking into it," Karis offered.

"She was the one who discovered the truth about siphons. She's the one who imbued the arcanite." Effie's eyes blazed. "They will have to reconsider once they—"

Urkin silenced her with a raised hand. "We will present all of this to them. And we will find a solution. But until then, there are bigger things to be concerned over." His gaze settled on me again. "The threat of Sídhe and the threat of Draxon, all spiraling towards us at once. Even with Fia's accomplishments across the rip."

"The Council," Urkin continued, shifting his weight as he leaned against the table, "deemed it my decision how much authority you should hold over the Umbra forces."

Anxiety coiled in my gut as glances were exchanged around the room. Even Vexa's blade had finally stopped thrumming.

"I think," he said, measuring each word, "that if you agree to stop going rogue on missions, and actually communicate effectively with the rest of us—the Generals and the spectres—we can work together. Your say will be equal to our own."

My breath caught as he straightened, his weathered face softening slightly. "Because despite the Council's hesitation, we believe you to be the heir to the throne. And it will only be a matter of time before you ascend." He gestured around the room. "Until then, we have battles still to be fought. And I think we'll be better for it if we're doing this with you by our side."

Relief swept through me as Urkin nodded, the ghost of a smile playing at his lips.

"We need to plan," he said, "but the hour is late, and you all need your rest." His eyes swept the room one final time. "You're dismissed."

As the others filed out, Urkin held me back with a raised hand, Karis lingering behind him. Aether stayed by the door, his golden eyes sharp in the candlelight.

"There's something else." Urkin's voice dropped low. "Ilsthyre, South of Draxon. It was supposed to be abandoned, but our scouts report increased military presence."

"How increased?" Aether moved closer to study the map Urkin had spread across the table.

"Double the guard rotations we'd expect from Valkan's forces. Supply wagons moving in under heavy escort, but nothing comes out." Urkin's finger traced the settlement's location. "And it's all continued after Valkan's death. If anything, security's gotten tighter."

"Who's giving the orders?" I asked.

"His brother, Verick, we assume." The name stirred something in my foggy memories of Draxon.

My head ached as I tried to grasp at the fragments—a conversation I'd overheard through a haze of pain and blood loss. Something about Verick... about him struggling with a new position.

"What do we know about him?" I asked, frustrated by the gaps in my mind.

"Not much." Urkin shared a look with Aether. "He's always been in Valkan's shadow. Never showed much interest in politics or military command."

Something else tickled at the edge of my consciousness. A word that made my skin crawl, though I couldn't remember why. *Blood rot.*

"Whatever it is, they're guarding it fiercely." Urkin's voice carried an edge of concern. "A weak leader desperate to prove himself, with access to whatever resources Valkan left behind..."

"Could be even more dangerous than his brother," Aether finished quietly.

I studied the map, trying to ignore the growing unease in my gut. "We have to keep watching," I said. "Every wagon, every guard change. The smallest detail might matter."

Urkin nodded, but his expression remained grim. "Despite these new developments, the situation remains... volatile but unchanged." Urkin's fingers traced the edge of a marker on the map. "His supporters haven't made any moves against us. But we've doubled our Sentinels around our borders in preparation. They are ready to defend Ravenfell."

"Our scouts move through the wasteland between territories," Karis added, his scarred face grim. "In endless circuits, watching for any sign of retaliation against the capital."

Urkin's jaw tightened. "They're waiting for something. Building their forces, perhaps. Or looking for the right moment to strike." He shared a look with the other Generals. "But when they do..."

"They'll find us ready, Your Grace." Karis turned to look at me, eyes deadly serious.

Urkin straightened, and when our eyes met, his stern expression had softened. "Any disturbance at our borders, any whisper of movement from Draxon—you'll know immediately."

CHAPTER FIFTY-SEVEN

FIVE DAYS HAD PASSED since our return from Sídhe. After the adrenaline wore off, the pain from Narissa's acid burns had set in with a vengeance. The first few attempts at cleaning the wounds left me gritting my teeth, fighting back screams that threatened to wake the entire medical wing. I'd turned down the healing potions—we needed to save those for more dire situations. The medics had offered to use their tethers, but I refused that too. Their powers were already stretched thin enough.

Now I sat in one of the infirmary beds, watching Lael's peaceful face as he slept. The medics had done remarkable work with his burns. Though evidence of the injury remained, the angry red had faded to pink, new skin already forming at the edges. He looked so young in sleep—a sight that still unsettled me. Despite all of his training, despite all of his dedication to the realm, he was still just a boy caught in the midst of forces beyond his control.

Aether occupied the chair between our beds, his golden eyes distant as he stared at nothing in particular. The creases around his eyes had deepened over the past few days, though he refused to admit he needed rest.

"What's on your mind?" I asked softly.

Aether's gaze shifted to me. "I've been thinking about your conversation with Laryk." He paused, choosing his words carefully. "You mentioned something about his tether—focus, whatever you call it. How it doesn't work on you."

I nodded slowly. "It doesn't."

"Are you sure?"

The question caught me off guard. "Yes, I'm sure. Why?"

He was quiet for a moment, that familiar crease forming between his brows. "I just wonder if it's a strategy."

"What do you mean?"

He looked towards the window, running a hand through his onyx hair and letting out a slow breath. "Perhaps," he finally said, "you're easier to manipulate if you think you can't be manipulated by him."

Irritation heated my face. "I don't…" I countered, shaking my head. "He protected us when he could have had us surrounded in seconds—"

"I know." Aether's voice was gentle, but something lurked beneath it. "It just seemed odd how quickly you decided to trust him in the end."

No. It couldn't be. I trusted Laryk because I *chose* to do so. I'd loved him because–

Movement from Lael's bed caught my attention before the thought could finish. His fingers twitched against the sheets as his eyes fluttered open. Aether was on his feet instantly, and I couldn't help but notice how the hardness in his expression melted away as he approached the bed.

Lael blinked several times, confusion clouding his features before recognition dawned. When his eyes found Aether, a goofy smile spread across his face.

"Did I miss training?" His voice was scratchy from disuse. "Everything feels… fuzzy."

That rare dimple appeared as Aether smiled. "You've been asleep for over a week."

"A week?" Lael tried to sit up, wincing slightly. "But the last thing I remember..." His brow furrowed as he struggled with the memory. "There was fire everywhere..."

"Don't push yourself," Aether said, helping adjust his pillows. "You're safe now."

Lael's eyes widened when he noticed me. "Fia? What are you doing here?" He glanced between us, questions evident on his face.

"Just keeping an eye on you," I said softly. "Ma's healing potions seem to be working well."

"Ma?"

"A friend from Sídhe. She created these." I gestured to the bottles beside his bed. "They've been helping with your recovery."

"Sídhe?" His eyes went wide. "But how—"

"It's a long story," I said, sharing a look with Aether. "There are good people everywhere, Lael. Sometimes in places we least expect."

He absorbed this, his young face thoughtful. "Is that where you two went? To Sídhe?"

"Among other places," Aether said carefully.

"So did it work?" Lael pressed, his enthusiasm breaking through his exhaustion. "What you guys did? Did it change anything?"

Aether looked down at him, finally letting that full smile show. "Why don't we go find out? First thing tomorrow. After you can get some strength back."

The gates of Ravenfell groaned as we passed through them, Lael leaning slightly on Aether for support. I could have sworn a slight breeze whispered across my face as the dead field came into view.

"If you're going to mother me the whole way there," Lael grumbled as Effie fussed with his collar, "I'm turning around."

"You can barely walk," Effie retorted.

"Can someone just tell me where we're going?" He shot a pointed look at Vexa, who was spinning one of her daggers through her fingers.

"Patience, little necromancer." Vexa smirked. "Keep complaining and I'll make you walk faster."

"Shall I find a dead wolf again?" Lael asked, but his lips twitched into a smile.

"Awfully sharp since waking, Lael." Rethlyn laughed, shaking his head. "You've been spending too much time with this lot."

"I do prefer the company of the dead sometimes," Lael countered. "At this point, they probably have more energy than I do."

"At least the dead know when to be quiet." Raven shrugged, and we all laughed.

The arcanite formation emerged from the gray earth ahead, essence burning bright within its crystalline structure. Though its glow had dimmed since I'd imbued it in Riftdremar, the power still pulsed steadily.

Lael's eyes went wide. "What is that?"

"Arcanite," Aether said.

"No way."

He moved forward on his own now, drawn to the crystal's light. We all felt it—that pull, that desperation for evidence of some kind of change. But it was Lael who noticed first. He dropped to his knees so suddenly that Aether moved to catch him, but then we saw what had brought him down.

"Grass," he whispered, voice cracking on the word. His fingers hovered over the delicate green blades pushing through dead earth. "Real grass."

Vexa's dagger stopped spinning, falling silent in her grip as she knelt beside him. Among the green, spiny flowers bloomed—their crimson petals and delicate stamens reaching toward the endless gray sky.

"Spider-lilies," Rethlyn said quietly to Lael.

"They're exactly as I remember," he finally managed. "They grew near the creek beds in Croyg." His eyes misted over. "I never thought I'd see them again."

I moved toward the crystal. As my hand met its surface, I allowed the essence to pool in my spine before directing the flow into the arcanite. The process hadn't left me light-headed before, but this time the drain hit me. Perhaps it was the weakness from my injuries taking over, or maybe I was just exhausted, but I swayed slightly. Immediately Aether was there, one hand steady on my waist while the other rested on my back, fingers intertwining with my white hair.

"Well, well," Vexa's voice cut through the silence, making us all turn. Her eyes were wide as she stared at Aether's grip on me. "*This is new.*"

Aether didn't move away, if anything his hold tightened slightly.

"Seems like a lot changed on your little journey through the realms." Effie raised an eyebrow, looking between us with a knowing grin.

"I knew it." Raven smirked, gaze falling on me. "It was the glasses, wasn't it?"

I bit back a smile, but a laugh managed to escape my lips. I couldn't help it. I had entirely no idea what to say to any of them.

"You're telling me," Vexa stepped closer, her eyes locked on Aether's face, "that our brooding commander actually—"

"Vexa," Aether warned, but that damned dimple appeared.

"No, no." She held up a hand. "Let me savor this moment."

Lael simply eyed us, a shy grin creeping across his face. When he noticed me looking, his attention turned back to the flowers.

The murmurs dissolved into silence as we all took in the sight —the first blooms of life this realm had seen in years.

"There has to be more out there," Vexa said, her eyes finding the horizon where the rip lay hidden in the distance. "More arcanite, buried in the ruins." The heaviness returned to her voice. "We just have to find it."

"And then what?" Lael asked, his young face serious again.

"Then start preparing," I said, leaning into Aether. His arm tightened slightly around my waist. "For whatever Draxon decides to unleash on us."

"Lael," Effie stepped forward, though her eyes kept darting between Aether and me with poorly concealed delight, "that's enough time out here. You're looking pale again."

"But—"

"Don't argue with her, it only makes it worse," Rethlyn sighed.

Aether reached out and ran a hand through Lael's messy hair. "You can come back tomorrow, if you're up for it."

"Promise?" the boy asked, a soft glint in his eye.

"Promise," I said softly.

We watched as the others headed back toward Ravenfell, their voices carrying on the breeze. Only Vexa remained behind.

"I've been waiting for the right moment," she said, reaching into her leather pack. "Though knowing you two, there probably won't be one." Her violet eyes sparkled as she pulled out a black cloth bundle.

With careful movements, Vexa unwrapped the fabric, revealing two daggers that made my breath catch. The memory of another ceremonial presentation flashed through my mind—standing before the Sídhe Guard as they bestowed their emerald-hilted dagger, a symbol of everything they wanted me to be. Everything I wasn't. But these—they were the most beautiful things I'd ever laid eyes on.

Their obsidian hilts were wrapped in dark leather, worn spots already pressed into the grip as if they'd been waiting for my hands. Intricate sigils had been carved into the pommels. And the blades were made of solid gold, just like Aether's sword. What drew my eye, though, were the small violet shards embedded just above the crossguards, glinting in the dim light.

"Vexa..." I breathed, recognizing the crystalline fragments. "Those are from—"

"The arcanite? Yes." She held them out, keeping the black cloth between her skin and the weapons. "Each one's been marked with a bonding sigil. Once your flesh touches the hilts, they'll recognize you as their wielder." There was something in her voice I'd never heard before—a mixture of pride and nervousness, as if she wasn't sure how I'd receive this gift.

"What does that mean exactly?" I asked, unable to take my eyes off the blades. They seemed to pulse with their own life, so different from the cold, ceremonial weight of my Sídhe dagger.

"They'll always return to you in battle. You can throw them, lose them, have them knocked away—doesn't matter. They'll find their way back." Her smile widened. "They'll call to you too, like a whisper in the back of your mind. No one else will be able to use them against you. They're yours, completely and truly yours."

My throat tightened at her words. In Sídhe, everything had come with conditions, with expectations. But this...

"Vexa, this is too much—"

"You've earned them," she cut me off, her tone brooking no argument. "Besides, I needed a challenge. Been too long since I've forged something worthy of a proper warrior."

Something I'd read in the archives suddenly clicked into place. "The arcanite stones..." I looked up at her. "A century ago, they used to forge weapons with them here. Warriors could somehow connect their tethers through the crystals."

"I wanted to test that theory." Vexa winked. "There's a reason I forged two daggers instead of a sword." Her eyes flickered to Aether. "He helped me find the old texts about crystalized weaponry. The techniques had been lost since the drought began."

I glanced at Aether, who stood watching us with quiet intensity, that familiar warmth in his golden eyes. Of course he'd been part of this. My chest tightened at the thought of them working together in secret, planning this gift.

"Well?" Vexa held the daggers out. "Let's see if it works."

With confident fingers, I took a blade in each hand. The moment my skin touched the hilts, I felt it—like two new heartbeats settling into rhythm with my own. The weapons seemed to sing against my palms, their weight perfect.

I called to my shadows, letting them curl around the blades. At the same time, I reached into the depths of my spine, pulling that familiar iridescent web.

The response was instant. Violent. Beautiful.

The right crystal exploded with light, flooding with pearlescent energy that matched my eyes. Pure starlight, captured in stone. The left crystal devoured all light around it, filling with writhing shadows that seemed to breathe.

Light and dark. Balance.

"By the Void," Vexa breathed. "Look at them, Aether."

"They're responding to both sides of her," he said softly, moving closer to examine the blades. "Incredible."

"Just like their wielder." Vexa's smile was fierce with pride, but I caught the glimmer of mist in her eyes. "No more borrowed weapons. These are yours, made for exactly who you are."

"Try throwing them," she added quickly, blinking away the emotion.

I hesitated only a moment before I turned, launching both daggers at a dead tree thirty paces away. They struck true, burying themselves deep in the trunk with a satisfying thud.

Then I felt it. A pull. Like invisible threads connecting us.

With a single thought, the daggers ripped free, spinning through the air like deadly stars before slamming home into my waiting hands. The sensation was electric—like finding limbs I never knew were missing.

Fucking. Incredible.

"Now *that*," Vexa grinned, "was worth all those sleepless nights in the forge."

"I don't know how to thank you," I managed, my own vision blurring. I tried to remember the last time someone had given me something so meaningful. If I had *ever* been given something so meaningful.

"Just put them to good use." She clasped my shoulder, her grip tight with emotion. "And try not to get yourself killed before I can forge you a matching set of throwing knives." She paused, then pulled me into a fierce hug. "You're one of us now," she whispered.

With a final wink at Aether, she turned and headed back toward the fortress, leaving us alone in the field. I watched her go, the daggers warm against my palms, feeling for the first time like I truly belonged somewhere.

"So…" I turned to Aether, still mesmerized by how the crystals pulsed with dual energy. "You were in on this?"

That dimple appeared as he smiled. "Vexa spent every night in the forge while you were healing. I searched the archives for anything that could help." His golden eyes held mine. "We wanted you to have something worthy of what you are."

"And what exactly am I?" The words came out softer than intended.

"The Blade of the Realm, of course." He moved closer, his fingers trailing over one of the arcanite shards. "It's what we call our leader, our Queen." He shook his head, something like wonder crossing his features.

"You make me sound much more impressive than I am."

"Do I?" His expression turned serious. "You survived Valkan's torture. Saved my life. Discovered the truth about siphons and arcanite. You connected us to a growing resistance in Sídhe. And now…" His eyes swept across the field where tiny blades of grass pushed through dead earth. "Now you're bringing life back to a realm that so many had given up on."

Heat flooded my face. "I didn't do any of that alone."

"No," he agreed. "But you gave us something we'd lost. Something even I had forgotten was possible."

"What's that?"

"Hope." He smiled down at me as he took my hand and pulled me through the dead field, our boots crunching against brittle grass.

"There's still so much work to do," I admitted.

"Valkan's troops are the immediate threat," Aether finally said, his voice low. "We expect his brother to claim his title soon."

"I know." I watched the wind breathe across the gray earth, stirring dust into the air. "And we need to give our allies in Sídhe time to plant their seeds. To grow their numbers."

"You trust Laryk to follow through?"

The question held no judgment, just quiet concern. I considered it carefully before answering.

"I trust that he'll help us," I said slowly. "Even if his reasons aren't entirely pure."

"Two wars," Aether said quietly. "One brewing in the South, another in a realm a world away. Both with the power to destroy everything."

The weight of it settled over me. Months ago, I would have crumbled under such pressure, would have run from any whisper of responsibility. But as I looked across this dead field toward the fortress that had once been my prison, I realized how much had changed.

I remembered all those times in Sídhe when I was terrified of everything around me, but mostly of myself. Of allowing myself to want things, to desire, to hope. I never used to let myself do it. But now, it burned so brightly in me that I couldn't deny it had taken permanent residence.

My eyes found the eclipse above us, the sun's rays reaching out from behind the moon's attempt to hide them, as if mirroring my thoughts.

The sound of a blade sliding against leather brought me back. I turned to find Aether drawing his sword, but his eyes were fixed on the expanse beyond.

"You know," he said, his voice taking on an odd tone, "there's an old tradition in Umbrathia. One that's faded in and out of history, I've been told."

He turned to face me, his expression somehow more serious than before. "If there was ever a moment that deserved it, it would be now."

Before I could process his words, Aether dropped to one knee before me, resting his sword across his lap.

"What are you—"

"I've never understood devotion to higher powers," he said, cutting me off. "Never grasped why people pray to gods who remain silent while realms die." His jaw tightened. "I've never given myself to anything like that. Never felt the pull."

"Aether—"

"Thirty years I've been here," he continued, "trying to make sense of this world. Why I found my way here. Whether I even had a purpose, or if this was some form of punishment for whatever atrocities I committed in my first life."

"I believe I understand now." Aether's eyes swept across the field, falling on the arcanite where essence pooled just beneath its crystalline surface. "All of those decades spent here, all of the sleepless nights searching for any kind of meaning to my existence —it was so that I could find you."

The wind caught his hair, dark strands falling across his face as those golden eyes found mine again. My heart thundered in my chest at the raw honesty in his gaze.

"I give myself to you," he said, voice deadly calm. "My life, my shadows, my loyalty—they belong to you now. Not because you're the heir to this realm, but because you're the only thing I've ever wanted to believe in."

I sank to my knees before him, suddenly feeling unworthy of such devotion. This man who could bend armies to his will, who could tear reality apart with a thought, who had completely pulled me into his orbit, even as we both fought it—offering himself to me like I was something sacred.

I reached out to brush the hair from his face. "I don't need a servant. I need you."

The intensity in his eyes nearly stole my breath as he looked at me. And I couldn't hold myself back anymore. I lunged, tangling myself around him—dragging my lips over his neck, across his cheek until they met his own.

"Fia," he murmured against my lips before pulling back and taking my face in his hands. "It's terribly rude to interrupt a man when he's swearing his life to you."

"I can think of other ways to get the point across," I whispered, leaning in against his grip and nipping at his bottom lip.

He studied me briefly, running his hands through my hair before his lips pressed against my throat. "Now?" He murmured dangerously.

"Unless you think your vow can wait—"

The flex of his body surrounding mine cut me off, and in seconds, I was in his arms as he carried me through the field and into the depths of a broken, gnarled forest.

CHAPTER FIFTY-EIGHT

We hadn't made it to the bed yet. Not even to the front door of his cabin before his lips found mine again.

"I meant what I said," he murmured against my skin. "Every word."

My fingers traced the void burns along his neck, feeling his muscles tense beneath my touch. "I know you did."

He pressed his forehead to mine, our breaths mingling. "I've never wanted anything the way I want you."

"Then have me," I whispered.

His hands found my waist as he guided me through the doorway. When my back met the wooden planks, he paused, eyes searching mine. "In any way I like?" His face held a dangerous curiosity.

Instead of answering, I pulled him down for another kiss. His shadows curled around us as we moved together through the darkness until my legs reached something solid.

He lifted me onto the bed with a gentleness that contrasted sharply with the hunger in his eyes. Dim light trickled in through the window, catching on the metal of his piercings, making them gleam against his skin.

"You're staring," he said, that dimple appearing as he smiled down at me.

"And you're still wearing too many clothes." My fingers found the fastenings of his leathers.

His laugh was low and rich as he caught my hands in his. "You're going to have to be quicker than that." He pressed a kiss to my palm. "Because I have plans for you tonight."

"Plans?" I raised an eyebrow, trying to ignore how my pulse quickened at his tone.

"Mhmm." He lowered himself over me, careful to keep most of his weight on his forearms. "I made a vow, remember? Now I must worship you properly."

Heat flooded my face. "Aether..."

"Starting here," he murmured, pressing his lips to my throat. "And here." Another kiss at my collarbone. His mouth traced a path lower as his fingers worked at the buttons on my shirt. Before I knew it, he was pulling it back, exposing me to him.

"Divine," he breathed, his hands moving to the clasp on my trousers. Soon enough, I was rid of those too.

My back pressed into the fabric, completely bare as he drank in the sight of me. He gently lifted my foot before kissing my ankle, making me squirm. "You're certainly taking your time," I whispered.

"Patience." Aether's teeth grazed the skin at my calf. "How else can I prove that I'm devout?" He raised an eyebrow, his lips already twitching at the corners.

I rolled my eyes as a laugh escaped me, but it didn't stop my arms from reaching for him again. I wanted to wipe that smirk off his face—preferably with my mouth. He merely smiled down at me shaking his head, continuing his maddeningly slow ascent up my legs.

When his lips finally reached my hip, I couldn't help the small sound that escaped me. His eyes found mine, dark with desire. That look should be illegal. The way it made me feel certainly was.

"People worship at altars, correct?"

I nodded, feeling almost dizzy.

"Your hips can be mine." I could feel his wicked grin as the words vibrated against my inner thigh. My legs fell open willingly.

His teasing had my body nearly vibrating for more. I tried arching my hips towards his wandering mouth but he tsked, arm pressing me firmly into the mattress, keeping me in place. His teeth bit into my inner thigh, causing me to whimper before moving to my other leg, leaving a trail of heat in his wake.

I was going to lose it.

"Aether," I breathed, my voice ragged with desperation.

"Yes?" His breath ghosted across my skin, making me shiver. "Tell me what you want."

I could barely think straight, every nerve ending alive with anticipation. The way he held me down, the control in his movements despite the hunger in his eyes—it was maddening. This was so different from our first time when desperation and need had driven us. Now he seemed determined to take his time, to reduce me to nothing but want.

I'd spent my life running from power, from desire, from anything that threatened to consume me. But the way he touched me now made me want to burn.

"I..." The words caught in my throat as his lips brushed the sensitive skin of my inner thigh again.

"You what?" That damned dimple appeared as he smiled against my skin. "Use your words, Princess."

The title that had once been a taunt now held something else entirely—reverence, maybe. Or possession. My fingers tangled in his hair as he continued his torturously slow path.

"You're enjoying this far too much," I managed, though the accusation lost its bite when it came out as more of a whimper.

His low laugh vibrated against me. "Of course I am." His teeth grazed my skin. "I love seeing you like this, flushed and writhing beneath me."

I wanted to respond with something clever, but then his mouth was moving higher, and all coherent thought fled my mind. His breath whispered over my clit, sending shivers across my skin.

"Is this where you want me?" His lips brushed over my center. He took my answering moan as confirmation and his tongue finally pressed against me.

My body had been wrung so tightly in anticipation that the sudden movement had my eyes rolling back. Another sweep of his tongue and I was on fire. It was almost too much. My thighs began to close and he pushed them open again with a force.

Aether seemed to be memorizing my every move and reaction, noting each gasp and shiver, learning exactly what made me cry out for him. His hands held me firmly in place as his mouth worked against me, refusing to let me squirm away.

His rhythm never faltered as he worked, his determination growing with each sound that escaped my lips. Dark tendrils began seeping from his void burns, curling through the air like smoke. They brushed against my heated skin until they paused, sweeping across my nipple and causing me to gasp at the new sensation. The shadows felt like silk and ice all at once, trailing paths of delicious torture across my flesh.

It was different now—the way our darkness merged. No longer two separate forces colliding, but something inevitable. Like our very essences were reaching for each other, recognizing their other half.

"Look at me," he commanded between movements. When I met his gaze, I could have sworn a smile touched his lips as he paused.

His shoulders shifted as his hand left my thigh. I let out a labored breath as he slid a finger inside me.

My back arched in response, my head falling against the mattress again.

"Don't hide now, Princess." His breath teased my sensitivity. "I want to watch you."

I allowed my arms to drag across the sheets, lifting myself enough so that my elbows supported me, and just as we locked eyes again, his mouth was back exactly where I wanted it—his tongue resuming that devastating dance from before.

The intensity of his stare combined with the pressure of his fingers sent waves of pleasure coursing through me. The shadows grew bolder, wrapping around my limbs, seeping into my very being.

Everything else fell away until there was nothing but the edge of that sweet oblivion once again, and I was spiraling towards that edge—his mouth working, his fingers pushing deeper as shadows flooded me, filling me with that intoxicating darkness I'd come to know so well. My vision went black for a moment as I absorbed them, the pleasure almost too much to bear. The combination was the most exquisite torment, unlike anything I'd ever experienced.

The pressure continued to build into something devastating, the assault threatening to shatter me completely. My vision started to blur at the edges, my world narrowing to just this moment, just us.

"Come for me," he murmured.

And then I was dragged off the cliff's edge.

Waves of pleasure crashed over me. The shadows around us pulsed wildly, matching the rhythm of my release as Aether worked me through it, his movements gentling as I came down from the high.

He lifted himself up, settling back on his knees. In one fluid motion, he pulled his shirt over his head, giving me a moment to admire the way his muscles shifted beneath his void-marked skin—the way they tapered down to a perfect *V*. The burns traced smoke-like patterns across his chest and arms, black mist still wafting from them like vapor.

"See something you like?" That dimple appeared as he caught me staring.

"You know exactly how beautiful you are," I breathed, reaching for him.

He lowered himself over me, the heat of his skin against mine drawing a gasp from my lips. "Beautiful?" He pressed a kiss to my throat. "That's not typically how people describe me."

"Lethal, then?" I suggested, my fingers trailing down his chest. "Mysterious, brooding?"

"Much better."

"Whatever you learned in your past life is clearly paying off," I teased, though my voice was breathless. "Maybe losing your memories wasn't such a tragedy after all."

His laugh was deep and rich as his muscles flexed against my skin. "I assure you, this is all instinct where you're concerned." The heat of his body against mine drew a gasp from my lips. "Though I do enjoy watching you come undone."

"Smug isn't a good look on you," I managed, though my fingers couldn't help but trace the defined ridges of his chest.

"No?" His golden eyes sparked with amusement. "And yet you can't seem to keep your hands off me."

"I could stop," I threatened, but my hands were already finding the waistband of his leathers.

"You wouldn't dare." He caught my bottom lip between his teeth.

My heart raced as I helped him shed the remaining barrier between us. When his mouth captured mine again, the kiss was deep and hungry, full of promise. The feel of him against me had my legs wrapping around his waist instinctively, drawing him closer.

"Slow and steady this time?" he murmured against my lips, though I could feel him trembling with restraint.

"You've tortured me enough," I managed, reaching between us to wrap my hand around his cock.

His response was a deep groan as his hips moved towards my touch.

"Look who's eager now," I teased, increasing the pressure of my grip as I stroked my hand up his length.

"Fia," he breathed against my neck. "You're going to be the death of me."

"What a way to go, though," I whispered, drawing another rich laugh from him before I moved my hand back down his cock. As he raised his head, something behind his eyes seemed to crack.

Suddenly, he was sitting up, his fingers digging into my flesh as he pulled my leg up over his shoulder and dragged me towards him. A predatory look had replaced the humor from seconds ago.

His grip tightened on my thigh, his other hand between my legs, positioning himself at my entrance. "You're so wet for me," he breathed, voice raw.

A whimper escaped my throat as he pushed the head of his cock inside me—just enough to make me crave more. I opened my mouth to beg, but he simply stared down at me, something feral in his expression. Then he pulled back with a groan. Everything about the angle of his frame was raw and unrestrained, teetering on the edge of something dangerous. He continued this silent torture, his eyes darkening with every movement until he stilled.

"I plan on ravaging you," his words came out rough as his hand tightened on my ankle, "until you can't remember anything but my name."

And in one fluid motion, he slammed into me, rocking my body against the sheets as I cried out. A groan rumbled through him as his hand found my hip. He pulled back, only pausing for a few seconds before he buried every single inch inside me.

Again.

And Again.

His movements were relentless, each thrust driving deeper than the last. The position left me completely at his mercy, my leg hooked over his shoulder as control began snapping behind those golden eyes.

The bed frame protested beneath us, the headboard slamming against the wall with each devastating motion. His fingers dug into my hip, keeping me exactly where he wanted as my body trembled beneath him. If this was how stars died—in fire and fury and perfect destruction—then let me blaze with them until there's nothing left but the endless dark.

The shadows flowing from him seemed to pulse with our shared need, dimming the room until there was nothing but us, nothing but this perfect moment of connection.

"The sounds you make," he growled, his voice ragged. "I want to hear more." His grip tightened on my leg, adjusting the angle until a feral moan tore from my throat, and he locked himself in place, pounding into me faster.

"That's it," he breathed, watching my reaction with those impossibly dark eyes. "But you're still not screaming yet." Liquid fire flooded me as he grabbed my free leg and hooked it over his other shoulder. His thrusts never eased as he pressed his hands against my thighs until they nearly touched my chest.

The pressure was building to something almost unbearable, each movement pushing me closer to that perfect edge.

"Aether," I gasped, my fingers clawing at his arms.

"I know," he groaned, the last vestiges of his control starting to fray. "I can feel how close you are." The shadows around us rushed through me, matching his increasingly urgent pace until I halted them, my mind going sharp as I redirected them back into his void burns.

The moan that escaped him nearly had me coming undone.

We were both monsters in our own way, both touched by darkness and marked by powers neither of us understood, not fully. Maybe that's why this felt so right, so perfectly and completely fated. Like finding the missing piece of a shattered blade.

The sight of him above me, completely lost in pleasure, had me spiraling toward that precipice. His usually pushed-back hair fell in his face, sweat glistening on his chest as he pressed my legs back even further, leaning over me until I was gasping.

The new angle had me seeing stars, each thrust hitting deeper than before. Every inch of me felt electrified, burning wherever his skin touched mine. My body sang for him in ways I never knew possible, like some part of me had been waiting for this. Exactly this.

"You're perfect," he breathed, voice strained with effort. "So perfect—taking all of me like this."

His voice, usually so controlled, was *so* rough with need. It did things to me I couldn't explain. Maddening, intoxicating things. It made me want to prove him right.

My hands grabbed for his arms, feeling his muscles flex beneath my fingers, my nails digging into him. The pressure built to something almost unbearable as he slammed into me.

Over.

And *over*.

"Please," I begged, though I barely recognized my own voice. "Aether, I need..."

"Tell me," he demanded, though his own voice was ragged. "Tell me what you need."

"Fall with me," I breathed, and suddenly, he slowed, replacing speed with pure force. It was beautiful, electrifying torment as I felt every glorious inch of his cock invade me, taking my sanity with it. I was trembling on the edge of that oblivion again. Every nerve ending felt like it was on fire as his hands tensed around my thighs—as a low groan rumbled through him.

"Come for me," he growled, his golden eyes burning into mine. "I want to feel you lose yourself."

My back arched off the bed as pleasure tore through me, my toes curling, my mind going deliciously blank. Ecstasy raked across my core, each wave threatening to pull me under. The sensation of darkness flooding me while he filled me was devastating—like being consumed and remade all at once. The shadows seemed to splinter through my veins until I was falling apart around him. Let me shatter. Let me break. He would catch every piece.

Aether's control snapped completely then. His movements grew erratic, desperate, as his own shadows smothered out the rest of the light, glass shattering somewhere beyond as he followed me into that perfect oblivion.

We stayed like that for a long moment, shaking and breathless. When he finally moved, it was to brush the hair from my face. He carefully lowered my legs from his shoulders, his hands gentle now as they massaged the muscles that had been stretched taut.

His fingers trembled slightly against my skin as our breathing slowly steadied. I wondered if he knew that his hands shook, if he realized how much of himself he revealed in these quiet moments. Then he was lying next to me, eyes scanning the room. The destruction around us became apparent—shattered glass from the window scattered across the wooden floor, sheets torn from the bed, furniture askew.

"I didn't mean to..." he started, but I silenced him with a kiss.

"Worth it," I breathed against his lips.

"I think you broke my bed," he murmured beneath a smile.

"Pretty sure that was your doing." I shifted to face him better. "Though I'm not complaining."

His laugh was deep as he pulled me against his chest. "I'll just have to build a stronger one."

"Planning on making this a regular occurrence then?"

"Clearly." He raised an eyebrow. "I take my vows very seriously."

I rolled my eyes as I settled in against him, lulled by the sound of his heartbeat before realizing how late it had gotten.

"We should probably get back to the fortress," I murmured, kissing his chest.

But he held me against him, blocking my movements.

"Tomorrow," he whispered into my hair. "I want one perfect night with you before the world crashes back down around us."

And with those words, I was already closing my eyes, sleep pulling at me from all directions, blissful and lovely.

Until the dream began.

CHAPTER FIFTY-NINE

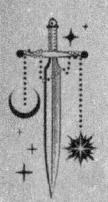

The sound of boots echoed through vaulted corridors, a steady rhythm against polished stone. My eyes remained trained on the marble floor, only lifting as we approached an ornate doorway. Beyond it stretched an elaborate throne room, golden light filtering through stained glass windows high above.

The body I inhabited moved with the familiarity of someone who had walked these halls a thousand times before, each step confident. My spine stayed straight as I took position near the throne, turning to face the gathering crowd. Other guards stood at attention around the perimeter, their faces as immobile as the stone walls surrounding us.

I watched as the room bowed in perfect unison, feeling a presence fill the space behind me. The eyes would not turn to look, no matter how I willed them.

"As some of you know, there is a war brewing on our Western Border." A strong female voice echoed through the chamber, each word cutting through the silence like a blade. "The countless casualties have been devastating to the Isle."

Something about that voice tugged at my memory, but I couldn't quite place it.

"But now we find there is a traitor in our midst. Working against our plans for peace. Harboring a hatred for the very ones who offered them sanctuary." She paused, letting fear ripple through the crowd before continuing.

"Her name is Fia Riftborne."

What?

Murmurs erupted, growing louder with each passing second.

"She has joined the enemy, escaping through a tear between worlds, into the realm of monsters, seeking their asylum before we even knew what traps she had laid in her wake."

The voice grew colder with each word. "She has already committed her first act of treason, and one so dark that it's difficult for me to even put into words. One meant to wound us deeply. To annihilate our spirit."

"Traitor!" Someone shouted from the crowd, sparking a wave of angry voices.

"Be vigilant, my friends," the voice purred, "because she has not acted alone."

There was the sound of shuffling, metal scraping against stone. Finally, the eyes tracked the movement, and confusion flooded through me at what they found. Ma stood between two men in emerald uniforms, their gloved hands locked around her arms as they dragged her forward. Her silver-streaked hair had fallen loose from its knot, and hibiscus stains still dotted her hands as they forced her to her knees below the throne.

I wanted to run, to scream, to move—to do anything to stop what was about to happen. But I remained frozen, trapped in this body that wouldn't respond to my desperate commands.

"Maladea Thiston. State your crimes against the Crown." The voice dripped with malice, almost gleeful in its accusation.

Ma's face twisted into a scowl as she looked up, then spat in the direction of the throne. The glob of saliva landed inches from the pristine marble steps.

The room gasped. Steel hissed against leather as swords cleared their sheaths.

"If the traitor won't accept or deny her charges, then I'm afraid she leaves me no choice." A pause hung in the air, heavy with anticipation. "Maladea Thiston. You are hereby charged with the murder of King Sydian."

Shock rippled through the crowd like a wave before the room went deathly quiet. My heart thundered so hard I thought it might break free of this borrowed ribcage.

"You were tasked with providing the Sidhe Guard with tonics meant to ease their fight against our enemy. We trusted you with our lives, our people, and the future of this realm. And yet, you were pulled into the darkness by the young girl who used to work for you."

Ma's jaw clenched, but she remained silent, defiant.

"You slipped a bottle of poisoned wine into our most recent shipment, one addressed to the King himself."

Gasps tore through the crowd, voices crying out in horror and rage. But Ma just glared toward the voice, unmoving, her shoulders straight despite the guards' grip.

"For such an offense, I have no choice other than to sentence you to death."

My blood ran cold, veins turning to ice.

No. No. No.

Cheers erupted throughout the room, bouncing off marble and glass until they became a deafening roar.

Rage threatened to burn me alive.

"Those who stand before the throne, turn to face me." The voice cut through the chaos. "Who will volunteer to carry out the deed?"

Slowly, each guard, including the one whose body I inhabited, turned toward the throne. As my borrowed eyes lifted, time seemed to still.

The woman perched on the golden throne wore Queen Ophelia's crown, draped in the familiar emerald silks of Sidhe royalty. Her blonde tresses cascaded down her shoulders exactly as I remembered from the palace halls.

But those eyes.

Haunting. Onyx. Eyes.

No.

Staring down at me, was the face of Vilda Valtýr, as young and vibrant as she'd appeared in my last dream.

I thought back to the girl that was never allowed to attend balls, who was always sinking into the shadows of her Duskbound sister.

And then I thought of how I'd never learned what her tether was.

The realization hit me like a blow to the chest. My mind refused to accept what was right in front of me, even as the pieces crashed together with devastating clarity.

Oh Esprithe.

Vilda Valtýr wasn't dead. She was the siphon.

The shock of it rippled through me, and even in this borrowed body, I felt my control slipping. Laryk advanced forward from the line of guards. Every step he took tore silent screams from my throat.

No.

The Queen extended an emerald encrusted sword towards him, and nausea flooded me.

The voices around me became deafened, muffled, as if I were sinking underwater. Through the haze, I heard someone calling my name, but it seemed to come from another world entirely.

The body I inhabited remained motionless as Laryk disappeared from view.

No! I begged the mouth to scream, begged the body to move, to stop whatever was happening behind me. But it wouldn't move. It wouldn't fucking move.

When Laryk returned seconds later, the pristine blade had been replaced with crimson, and something inside me shattered completely.

My eyes flew open to wooden beams inches from my face. Darkness erupted around me like a tempest, furniture splintering as my shadows tore through the cabin. Glass shattered, wood cracked, and somewhere beneath the chaos, I heard Aether calling my name.

I fell onto the bed, my breath coming in ragged gasps, my body drenched in sweat. Aether's hands found my face instantly, his touch anchoring me as tremors wracked through me.

"What happened?" His golden eyes searched mine, filled with concern.

I blinked, fighting back the sob threatening to tear from my throat. The image of Laryk's bloodied sword burned into my mind.

"War," I managed through hoarse lungs.

"We go to war."

THIS HAS BEEN

Duskbound

ESPRITHEAN TRILOGY BOOK TWO

Bree Grenwich & Parker Lennox

GLOSSARY

NOTABLE CHARACTERS:

FIA RIFTBORNE (FEE-ah RIFT-born) - Our protagonist, a duskbound from Sidhe

AETHER (AY-ther) - Second in Command to General Urkin, Leader of the Spectre Unit

LARYK ASHFORD (LAHR-ick ASH-ford) - General of Faction Venom in Sidhe

VEXA (VEX-ah) - Blacksmith turned Umbra soldier, can enchant weapons, member of Spectre Unit

EFFIE (EF-ee) - Noble daughter turned Umbra soldier, teleportation abilities, member of Spectre Unit

RETHLYN (RETH-lin) - Umbra soldier, can manipulate feelings/consciousness, member of Spectre Unit

RAVEN (RAY-ven) - Communications runner turned Umbra Soldier, can create bonds with mirrors that allow communication through them, member of the Archivist Unit

LAEL (LAY-el) - Orphan from Croyg, Strykka contestant, necromancer, member of Spectre Unit

MIRA (MEER-ah) - Strykka contestant turned Umbra Soldier, nightmare illusionist, member of Spectre Unit

THERON (THAIR-on) - Strykka contestant turned Umbra Soldier, fragment illusionist, member of Spectre Unit

LORD SOLEIL (so-LAY) - Noble House in Sidhe, Osta's employer, leader of Sidhe resistance

OSTA RIFTBORNE (OS-tah RIFT-born) - Fia's oldest friend from Sidhe

MALADEA THISTON (mal-AY-de-ah THIS-ton) - Known as Ma, Fia's friend and former employer from Sidhe

VALKAN SYRNDORE (vahl-KAHN SER-en-dor) - Lord of Draxon, leader of the Damphyre, shape-shifter

KRAYKEN VINDSKALD (KRAY-ken VIND-skald) - Traveling bard & author of a historical memoir detailing his life before the crusades

UMBRA GENERALS:

GENERAL URKIN (UR-kin) - Leader of the Umbra combat forces

GENERAL TALIORA (tal-ee-OR-ah) - Leader of the Medic's Unit

GENERAL TALON (TAL-on) - Leader of the Archival Unit

GENERAL KARIS (KAIR-is) - Leader of the Scout's Regiment

UMBRATHIA NOBLE HOUSES:

HOUSE VALTÝR (VAHL-teer) - The royal family of Umbrathia

- Queen Andrid Valtýr (AN-drid) - Current queen, descended into madness
- Prince Andrial Valtýr (AN-dree-al) - The lost prince
- Vilda Valtýr (VIL-da) - The queen's sister

HOUSE SKALDVINDR (SKALD-vin-dr) - Noble family connected to royalty through marriage

HOUSE EIRFALK (AIR-falk) - Noble House, Effie's family

HOUSE GALDRYNNE (GAHL-drin) - Noble House

HOUSE BREIDFJORD (BRAID-fyord) - Noble House

HOUSE BALDURSON (BAHL-dur-son) - Noble House

HOUSE SVEINSON (SVAIN-son) - Noble House

HOUSE VALLGRYM (VAHL-grim) - Noble House

HOUSE ELDGARDR (ELD-gard-r) - Noble House

HOUSE ALFARSON (AL-far-son) - Noble House

RACES/TITLES:

KALFAR (KAHL-far) - The dark elves that live in Umbrathia

AOSSÍ (EE-shee) - The race of elves that live on the Isle of Sídhe and Riftdremar

DAMPHYRE (DAM-feer) - Kalfar who feed on blood/essence from other Kalfar

DUSKBOUND (DUSK-bound) - True shadow-wielders, traditionally only in royal bloodline

RIFTBORNE (RIFT-born) - Children who were saved from the destruction of their homeland, Riftdremar, and brought to the Isle of Sihde. Before they were granted citizenship, these refugees were branded with a symbol of unity on their left wrist and hand. Most were raised in group homes throughout the Isle and were expected to assimilate into Sídhe culture and society.

LOCATIONS:

UMBRATHIA (um-BRAY-thee-ah) - The dying realm of the Kalfar

SÍDHE (SHEE) - The Isle of Sídhe is a thriving kingdom in which all Aossí now reside

RAVENFELL (RAY-ven-fell) - Capital of Umbrathia

RIFTDREMAR (RIFT-dreh-mar) - An Island to the east of the Isle of Sídhe. Riftdremar was destroyed after an uprising against Sídhe's colonial effort to mine and steal arcanite stores, and expand their influence on Riftdremar's culture, economy, and resources.

DRAXON (DRAX-on) - Southeastern territory of Umbrathia, ruled by Valkan

STRAVENE (stra-VEEN) - Neutral territory between Ravenfell and Draxon

CROYG (KROY-g) - Once the largest farming region of Umbrathia, now dead from the drought

VARDRUUN (var-DROON) - The second largest city in central Umbrathia, taken by the drought

ILSTHYRE (ILS-thire) - Small village to the south of Draxon

THE RIP - Tear between realms

MAGIC/POWERS:

ESSENCE - The living energy that flows through the realms

TETHER - Umbra term for magical abilities

FOCUS - Sidhe term for magical abilities

THE VOID - The darkness in northern Umbrathia that creates void burns

VOID BURNS - Marks that allow vessels to absorb shadows

ORGANIZATIONS:

THE UMBRA - Umbrathia's military force

SPECTRE UNIT - Umbra with shadow-wielding capabilities

THE GUARD - Sidhe's military force

THE COUNCIL - Umbrathia's ruling body

IMPORTANT ITEMS/THINGS:

THE DROUGHT - A magical drought in Umbrathia where essence is being drained

VESSEL - A Kalfar who has entered the void and bears it's marks. Able to absorb and manipulate shadows they are given by a duskbound.

SENTINEL - A member of the Umbra combat unit

ARCANITE (AR-kan-ite) - Crystal that stores essence

THE STRYKKA (STRIE-kah) - A set of trials that allow Kalfar to join higher ranking positions within the Umbra forces

THE CRUSADES - A dark period in Umbrathian history when the royal family systematically hunted down and eliminated other duskbound families to secure their exclusive claim to the throne, ensuring House Valtýr would be the only bloodline with the power to control the void. These purges lasted for centuries, nearly eradicating all duskbound outside the royal line.

VOID-LETTING - The process in which a Duskbound shares their shadow magic with vessels

BLOOD OATHS - Binding magical contracts used by the Guard

BLOODWEEP - A plant used in blood oaths, native to Umbrathia

SIPHON - can control and redirect the flow of essence

CREATURES:

DREAD SIRENS - Wraith-like beings that can speak to the dead

VORDR (VOR-dr) - Horse/Dragon Hybrid that share a connection with those touched by the void

RELIGION

Esprithe (Esp-rith) -The pantheon of deities who are worshiped by those on the Isle of Sídhe

Sibyl (Sib-uhl) - The Esprithe of Foresight

Conleth (Kohn-luth) - The Esprithe of Wisdom

Niamh (Neev) - The Esprithe of Dreams

Ainthe (Ah-N-yuh) - The Esprithe of Memories

Eibhlín (Eve-lin) - The Esprithe of Justice

Fírinne (Fehr-EN-yeh) - The Esprithe of Truth

HISTORICAL RECORD

The Esprithe, Second Edition

In the realm of creation, where the cosmos dance in eternal embrace, there existed six Esprithe, beings of divine essence, each imbued with unique powers and revered by mortals throughout the realms.

In the beginning, there was Sibyl, the Esprithe of Foresight. She gazed into the infinite expanse of time, seeing the threads of destiny woven into the tapestry of existence. With her sight beyond sight, she guided the paths of mortals, offering glimpses of what was to come, and thus, she became revered as the harbinger of fate.

Mortals therefore named the first phase of the year, Sibyl.

Next came Conleth, the Esprithe of Wisdom. From the depths of the cosmos, he gathered knowledge, wisdom, and understanding. With a mind vast as the universe itself, he illuminated the minds of mortals, teaching them the ways of the world and the secrets of the universe, earning adoration as the sage of enlightenment.

Mortals therefore named the second phase of the year, Conleth.

Niamh emerged as the Esprithe of Dreams, drifting through the ethereal realms where reality and imagination intertwine. She whispered to mortals, weaving visions of wonder and enchantment, guiding them through the labyrinth of dreams, and thus, she was revered as the patron of reverie.

Mortals therefore named the third phase of the year, Niamh.

Ainthe, the Esprithe of Memories, arose next, holding within him the echoes of the past. He collected the fragments of time, preserving the memories of ages long gone. With a gentle touch, he reminded mortals of their history, their heritage, and their legacy, earning reverence as the keeper of forgotten knowledge.

Mortals therefore named the fourth phase of the year, Ainthe.

Eibhlín, the Esprithe of Judgement, descended from the heavens with scales in hand. She weighed the deeds of mortals, discerning truth from falsehood, justice from injustice, therefore becoming hailed as the guardian of righteousness.

Mortals therefore named the fifth phase of the year, Eibhlín.

Last to emerge was Fírinne, the Esprithe of Truth, cloaked in the mantle of absolute verity, piercing through lies and deceit. He illuminated the path of righteousness, and thus, he was revered as the embodiment of absolution itself.

Mortals therefore named the sixth phase of the year, Fírinne.

As the ages passed, the Esprithe witnessed the ebb and flow of mortality's journey. They observed the rise and fall of empires, the clash of civilizations, and the scars left by countless wars and conflicts. With each passing moment, the burden of their divine duty weighed heavier upon their shoulders.

Despite their efforts to guide and enlighten, the Esprithe watched in sorrow as Mortals veered further from the path of balance and harmony. Their teachings were twisted, their words manipulated, and their guidance ignored by those consumed by greed, power, and ambition.

The once steadfast faith of mortals began to wane, replaced by doubt and skepticism. Whispers of disbelief echoed through the mortal realms, and the bonds that once united Mortals and Esprithe began to fray.

ACKNOWLEDGMENTS

To our readers who fell in love with Fia in RIFTBORNE and waited patiently (or not so patiently) to see where her journey would lead—thank you. Your enthusiasm, theories, and endless support made writing this sequel both terrifying and wonderful.

To our incredible alpha readers: Lizzy Trauer, Emily Nassar, Ashley Craven, Alyssa Puma, Kalea Jones, and Caitlin Callaghan—thank you for catching our plot holes, asking the hard questions, and being our first line of defense. Your feedback shaped this book in countless ways, and we're forever grateful for your honesty and support.

To our amazing Street Team—you've championed this series from day one, spreading the word about Fia's story with such passion and dedication. Your enthusiasm and creativity continue to blow us away.

To the BookTok and Bookstagram communities—your encouragement, memes, and shared love of morally gray men kept us going through countless revisions. The way you've embraced this world and these characters means everything to us.

To our families, who endured our endless rambling—thank you for nodding along even when we stopped making sense. Your unwavering support means the world to us.

To our boyfriends, who never complained when we disappeared into Umbrathia for hours at a time—these books wouldn't exist without your support and patience.

And finally, to everyone who picks up this book: thank you for joining us on this journey. Fia's story means everything to us, and we're honored to share it with you.

ABOUT THE AUTHORS

Bree Grenwich and Parker Lennox are two platonic soulmates who have been nearly inseparable since meeting at 19. Their shared love of fantasy, badass heroines, and steamy romances fueled their dream of co-authoring a novel, which they've finally achieved with their debut, *Riftborne*. When they're not conjuring worlds filled with female empowerment and swoon-worthy relationships, they're binge-watching reality TV or obsessing over the last Dungeons and Dragons session.

Bree enjoys spending time with her boyfriend, who she claims is *indeed* a man written by a woman. A true Pisces, Bree finds solace in weekends by the sea or lake, engrossed in a book with music drowning out the world. She also holds a fascination with the paranormal and all things witchy, a love that undeniably creeps into her writing.

Parker, on the other hand, splits her time between the Southern US and the beautiful wine-country of Bordeaux, France, where she visits her boyfriend (living proof that romance novels can mirror reality!). An artist at heart, Parker expresses her creativity through graphic design, photography, and delectable culinary adventures, always with a sourdough starter bubbling away in the background.

Together, they weave addictive Romantasy novels for the New Adult audience.

www.grenwichlennox.com

Parker's IG: @ParkerLennoxAuthor
Bree's IG: @BreeGrenwichAuthor

ALSO BY GRENWICH & LENNOX

Riftborne
GRENWICH & LENNOX

THE ART OF UNMAKING
PARKER LENNOX

Printed in Great Britain
by Amazon